MR. MANIAC

MR. MANIAC

JOHAN FUNDIN

Matador
9 Priory Business Park,
Wistow Road, Kibworth Beauchamp,
Leicester. LE8 0RX
troubador.co.uk/matador
@matadorbooks

ISBN 978-1-78803-532-3

British Library Cataloguing in Publication Data
A catalogue record for this book is available from the British Library

Printed and bound in the UK
by TJ International, Padstow, Cornwall
Typeset in 11.5pt Adobe Garamond Pro
by Troubador Publishing Ltd, Leicester, UK
Cover illustration by FrinaArt (www.frinaart.com)

Matador is an imprint of Troubador Publishing Ltd

MIX
Paper from responsible sources
FSC® C013056

To a good friend and her spoilt cat Tilly

The knife flashes in the glow of a streetlamp and swishes through the darkness.

She screams.

Terror burns her nerves. The wind whips her face. Tears dim her vision.

The cloudburst splatters and she loses a high-heeled shoe. The handbag with crushed contents spins out of her fist, spilling cosmetics in a wide and fragrant arc.

She glances over her shoulder, sees nothing but trees and shrubs and high-rise buildings, knows nothing beyond the boiling pain. He's panting just behind her but he's invisible in a maze of swirling shadows.

The knife chases her again. It stings and bites.

Her skirt hem bursts at the back. She slips on the wet lawn, slides, falls, crawls to her feet, reaches the sidewalk, turns left, up the hill. The raven-black heaven descends over the cityscape, erasing the full moon.

The darkness sweeps and blocks.

The knife tears and cuts.

Cars, buses and trams are rushing through the curtains of rain, both up and down the road. Nobody takes note of the maniac. She tries to scream again. Only a beep dribbles out between her teeth. A coppery taste fills her mouth. In the terror-night-blackness, the flowing blood is just as dark as the downpour.

The vicious words that resound in her head belong to her so-called boyfriend. The actual voice is the exception. The voice, the muffled whisper, is unknown.

The night begins to rotate like a carousel. Fast, faster. The asphalt beneath her feet wriggles and vibrates and wiggles. The minutes meander away with a serpent's deceiving suddenness. Memories diverge. Moments hybridise.

She shivers.

Teeth chatter.

The city spins and topples.

The kerb mangles her cheek. Red saliva spurts from the corner of her mouth. The claws of eternity snatch the girl from the world's edge. She closes her eyes and dives. And swims through the light towards The Other Side.

1

The next murder plan took shape. But a noise from somewhere in the house had begun to encroach on his psychological space. The clamour diluted his concentration, a little at a time, until the situation became unbearable.

What on earth was going on?

Some kind of switch in his head flicked. *The phone. At this hour?* A sparkle of hope flew through Kenneth Sorin's heart. He took the call. "Alison?"

"Definitely not."

"So it's you."

"Alison probably wasn't your type, Ken. Forget the girl. After all, her parents didn't like you."

"I loved her, Uncle Ash. I still do. She's the only girl I've ever loved." He needed a brief moment to clear his throat. "Inspector Ash Sorin, of all people, what do you want? It's the middle of the night. I'm busy, working." He shot an eye at the ruthless wall clock. Seven minutes past midnight.

Three manuscript pages in thirteen minutes. Thirteen was not the most excellent number but those three pages satisfied him.

"Uncle Ash, let me guess. It's about the serial killer, isn't it? I've already told you the following. We all have priorities and, from now on, I want to focus on my writing career a hundred percent. Do you understand that?"

"I thought you used to disconnect the damn phone cord and turn off the damn mobile before you kick-started the damn typewriter."

"Typewriters aren't kick-started."

"Whatever."

Although he used computers, like most modern fiction writers, he preferred to write his first drafts on the old electric machine.

"Listen, Ken. On my kitchen table is a stack of photos of slaughtered girls. I can tell you now, boy, that these pictures do my stomach ulcer no good."

"You have my sympathies."

"I want to chat about the details, Ken, but not on the phone. I'd appreciate seeing you in my house tomorrow morning."

The workroom door to the corridor was ajar. Kenneth heard a sound from downstairs. "This conversation must end now. I promised Linda the 'night's special'."

"Linda? And you say I interrupted your writing? Nice try. I dare not ask what the 'night's special' is."

"I was talking about my cat."

"Of course you were. Tomorrow at nine?"

"I think you mean today. It's past midnight."

"Not too early for a Thursday morning."

"Let me sleep on it. I'll call you back, I promise."

Uncle Ash chuckled. "Good night, sleep tight, don't let the bedbugs bite."

Kenneth went down to the kitchen, wondering what the miaowing Linda wanted for a speciality. A bowl of corn and salmon pâté satisfied her. "Enjoy your meal, Linda. Don't worry about the bill. Dinner's on the house."

He returned to the first floor, turned off the typewriter and swallowed two headache relief pills. On the way to the bedroom at the end of the corridor, he discovered that he was trudging on Linda's elongated shadow. The blue-black spot under his feet floated across the carpet like a puddle of swift-flowing oil. Linda frequently gave the impression of being in many probability-oriented places simultaneously, as if she were a cat at the quantum level, a cat with the ability to disappear and reappear somewhere else at the same time, like a subatomic particle. Her omnipresence and independence appealed to him endlessly. Without a doubt, Linda was the world's best housemate.

▪

If someone, or something, was sneaking about in the street right now, potential footsteps would be inaudible in the screaming wind. Something that should not move at all at this pitch-dark hour could be down there right now.

Possibly in the house. No, he decided. A cat's senses were superior to those of humans. Since Linda was calm, there was nothing to worry about.

The hammering wind gusts against the house gave the window panes the voices of a hundred rattlesnakes. The roof was squeaking like a ship at sea. Against all odds he drifted towards unconsciousness. The very last thing he registered before the nightmares seized him was the voice of a female student who had been interviewed on the TV news:

"Nothing is worse than trying to sleep at night or being home alone in the dark. The mutilator and killer could be anywhere. He could be out there right now. Or here. Right here, inside, with us. He could be one of us here tonight."

2

The following morning, Kenneth admitted that until now he had not known what Linda seemed to have understood long ago—that he was being absorbed into the most terrifying mystery the city had ever seen. He did not dismiss the fear that he could read in her eyes, as the cat's premonitions had the quality of a sixth sense or even a seventh.

Lousy sleep quality the night before and a fresh headache at dawn made him reject his intention of taking the car. He chose the northbound tram. He got off at the stop Prince View / Line B and walked the remaining distance.

The morning demonstrated a sun-free sky in a monotonous grey. A typical Blackfield day, in other words. Rain spattered his face. Kenneth tightened his scarf and pulled up his collar against the unfriendly December wind. He arrived at Uncle Ash's house nineteen seconds before nine o'clock.

"Sit down in the living room, boy. I'm preparing steaming hot coffee and enough to fill a washtub."

Uncle Ash had not shaved yet. In contrast to the eggshell-white balding head, his face had the same texture as the outer husk of a coconut. The few hairs on both sides of his head were splayed like a cat's whiskers and had greyed three shades since the week before. A burning cigarette was wedged between two nicotine-yellow fingers.

Kenneth hung his coat in the hall and went to the living room. The air both smelled and tasted of tobacco. The coffee table was stained with cigarette ash. The cups on the tablecloth contained the remains of stale coffee that had turned into a thick substance reminiscent of potting soil. In one of the cups there was also a used tea bag and a cigarette butt. A coffee-stained two-week-old issue of the local newspaper *Blackfield Telegraph* served as a coaster for the overfilled ashtray. A second ashtray rested on a windowsill and a third sat in a bookshelf.

Magazines and yellowing newspapers lay heaped on chairs and scattered on the floor. Three bookshelves contained archives of cases that Uncle Ash had been working on during the past quarter century. Was Chief Inspector Frank aware of the files that Uncle Ash stored at home? Or the Chief Inspector's own superiors, for that matter—did they know about Ash Sorin's special archives?

He navigated across the floor, or tried to. The living room was a chaotic miniature world. A mountain of reports from the forensic laboratory. An ocean of full-frame digital photographic prints depicting slashed female students. A jungle of close-ups of empty eye sockets. A maze of records and interrogation protocols.

Madness, Kenneth thought. He felt the cold fist of terror clutch his heart.

Uncle Ash appeared. He splashed coffee into two cups and added generous amounts of sugar and milk to his own mug. Kenneth, who took his coffee black, stared into his steaming beverage. He had read somewhere that bubbles on the surface of black coffee meant that you would get married within a year. He wasn't certain of where that superstition originated, if indeed it could be called a superstition. Anyway, he detected no bubbles and had no idea what the odds might be. Was it a fifty-fifty situation?

"What do you know about the case so far, Ken?"

"I read the newspapers and watch TV."

"Then you don't know that much." Uncle Ash lit a new cigarette. "Kelly Graham, from Coventry, the first girl of four. Murdered on September the twenty-fifth. Twenty years old. Her body found on Hucklow Way, near the junction with Bowfield Street. Forensics fixed time of death at eleven p.m. to midnight. Miss Graham visited some nightclub around Black Square. Afterwards, she wanted to get home on foot. She must have made the fateful decision just before the cloudburst that terrible night. The killer might have waited for the girl somewhere or followed her from anywhere between Colvin Street and Hucklow Way."

Kenneth drank the low-budget coffee. The taste made him grimace. "Boyfriend?"

"A certain Karl Peters. The guy's relationship with Miss Graham was apparently stormy as hell, though he has an alibi for the time of the murder."

Kenneth nodded. "What can you say about the tenants of the residence hall in question?"

"We have heard from every person at Farnwood Hall. No one there could have done it. Moreover, no one at Farnwood has a plausible motive."

"Please continue. If my memory serves me right, Miss Lucy Knowles was number two."

"Has your memory ever betrayed you, Ken? The second lady, Lucy Knowles, nineteen years old. Stabbed to death on October the sixteenth, around ten thirty. The cadaver was found in Broomton, right in the heart of the student district. A pensioner couple in a car discovered the corpse. The half-senile old man and the equally half-senile old woman found the murdered girl when they turned into Tankerville Road a few minutes after half past ten, and only forty yards from their own house. Neither the old man nor the old woman can remember seeing the girl before, but why would they, regardless of their senility? Broomton is brimming with students."

"Our killer is lucky," Kenneth said. "In ninety-nine cases out of a hundred or, rather, in nine hundred and ninety-nine cases out of a thousand, in such a lively district as Broomton, a murderer wouldn't get away unnoticed."

"You said it, boy. The maniac is more than a maniac. He's a lucky bastard, too." Uncle Ash's teeth were as yellow as the sweetcorn that Kenneth had served Linda the night before. "Miss Knowles's left eye was cut out, of course."

"Same ritual as in the case of the first victim?"

"Yes. Like a symbolic message."

"And more than twice," Kenneth murmured.

"Miss Knowles grew up in Portsmouth. Her parents are divorced. We've been able to talk to her mother and sisters but we have not yet got hold of the father."

"What do you know about the father?"

"Major Robert G. Knowles, the British Army, a decorated Afghanistan combat veteran. The army, as well as a private healthcare facility, confirmed that Robert Knowles suffered from war-related anxiety disorders. On top of that, he went through that divorce seven months ago. He suffered a mental breakdown and was then admitted for psychiatric treatment. Four months after the divorce, Knowles was discharged from the hospital. Since then, however, no one has seen the man and no one knows where he is. The rest of the family lives by the south coast. Only Lucy sought a new life here in the north."

"A youth's longing for fascinating adventures." Kenneth thought of his own past, first as a student, then as a chemical physics research scientist. It felt like yesterday. Or a thousand years ago.

"Miss Knowles was indeed an adventurous girl," Uncle Ash said. "Not for a second did she consider enrolling at a local university. She chose Blackfield after being persuaded by a cousin who had studied biochemistry here."

Terrific persuader, Kenneth thought. "Have you talked to the cousin at all?" He coughed secondhand tobacco smoke and loosened his tie knot.

"Of course. But the chap no longer lives in town. After graduating, he landed a job at a company in Newcastle. Don't worry about him, Ken. The only thing that might defile his conscience is an unpaid speeding ticket. He's a victim of circumstance, just like the rest of the immediate family. No family member is suspected of murder."

"And the next girl? The papers don't write much about number three either. You and Mr. Frank are minimising the flow of information to the media."

"Killers read newspapers. And they watch the damn TV. Of course we must filter our material."

"The third victim's left eye was cut out."

"A question or a statement, Ken?" Uncle Ash paused, giving his nephew a peculiar stare. "The third girl is so far the only foreign victim. A Swede. Twenty-year-old Rebecka Månsson was murdered in the city centre's Carriage Lane the evening before Halloween. She'd been out with three friends, two boys and a girl, mixed nationalities, at a pub near Castle Market.

"A lecturer who got on a tram near City Hall a few minutes past eight claimed that he recognised the four students on board. He said they got off at Castle Square. A waiter at the pub said the quartet left at nine forty, so they couldn't have stayed longer than, say, an hour and twenty-five minutes or something like that.

"A quarrel about cheating in exams erupted and the four split. Miss Månsson left alone. It's still unknown why she decided to walk the deserted Carriage Lane westwards, via Elm Street and Bardwell Street. Whether she wanted to take a taxi, a bus or a tram home, or anywhere, the nearby High Street should have been the natural choice."

"Miss Månsson could have met someone on the street outside the pub," Kenneth said. "Someone gave her a reason to take an unplanned way as she was leaving the area around Castle Market. For example, a friend."

His uncle scowled. "Or, for example, the killer."

"Or friend and killer—one and the same. Our man may have been a visitor to the pub. He could even be a regular. As Miss Månsson leaves the pub, he follows her, awaiting the optimal moment to perform the deed. What did forensics say about the time of death?"

"The lab confirmed what we already knew. The last time anyone saw Miss Månsson alive was at nine forty when the waiter noticed the lady leaving. A city council representative walking his dog in Carriage Lane discovered the corpse at ten twenty-five."

"A reliable city council representative?"

"Aren't they all?"

"Family? Relationships? Leisure activities?"

"We've checked everything, Ken, and we haven't discovered anything suspicious anywhere. Rebecka Månsson came from a Swedish settlement called Kungsör. Just don't ask me how to pronounce the name of that exotic place."

"What do you know about Kungsör?"

"Not one iota. How could I know such a place? Kungsör sounds like the name of a mountain on the planet Mercury. Do you know the village?"

"It's not a village; it's a town. Kungsör is located by a lake called Mälaren, Sweden's third largest lake, somewhere in the middle of the country. The Renaissance Swedish kings and queens used the town as a recreation centre. And the late comedy film actor Thor Modéen was from there."

Uncle Ash gaped. "How did you know all that?"

Kenneth shrugged. "I read a lot. Continue."

"Miss Månsson was single, whatever that means in this day and age. Besides spending time with her friends, Rebecka's main recreational activity was singing. As soon as she had settled into university life in Blackfield, she became a member of a choir. But as I just said, there are no known circumstances in Miss Månsson's life that are of interest to the investigation. So far."

An intricate set of murders, Kenneth thought. Enough background material for a new horror suspense novel. He was here to listen, and listen only. But was Uncle Ash hiding something? He, Kenneth, had not promised to assist in any way in the hunt for the killer (*not yet, you mean?* an inner voice said from an obscure corner of his brain). He did not intend to make any promises either. If he had now decided to start writing fiction full time, it was a decision that both Uncle Ash and Mr. Frank should accept instead of trying to make him change his mind. After all, he was a civilian.

"Tell me about the next," Kenneth said.

"Gemma Quigley, the next girl, slashed to death on November the twentieth. She was twenty-one. Originally from Norwich. She faced death sometime between eight forty-five and nine forty-five p.m. This is another Broomton murder. Her body was found on Canongate Street, only a few blocks from one of the previous murder scenes in Tankerville Road. Miss Quigley and her boyfriend, a certain Dean O'Connor, had seen a play at the Andromeda Theatre downtown.

"Straight after the show, the couple took a taxi to Farnwood Road in Broomton. They did not live together. The guy said that his girlfriend would buy a bag of crisps in one of the shops on Farnwood and then go straight home to her student accommodation. O'Connor continued alone to his own home on Wickham Street."

"You mean the taxi driver and this O'Connor man were the last people to see Miss Quigley alive?"

"The last two people who remember that they saw her alive." Uncle Ash threw the cigarette stub in the mug with the used tea bag. "We have tried to trace the corner shop where the girl went, tried to find out if any oddball followed her from there, but she paid in cash and must have thrown away the receipt, if she ever got one. And not a soul remembers her. Can you believe it, lad? Farnwood Road is bustling with activity and brimming with people that time of day."

Kenneth nodded. "Too busy for a murderer."

"The victims didn't know each other and didn't have any common leisure activities. Miss Quigley liked to swim and to play badminton. She enjoyed a healthy lifestyle. In addition, she was a bookworm. A collector of books and magazines about nutrition and health."

"Her fresh lifestyle should be an eye-opener to you."

"You're full of crap, lad." Uncle Ash lit another cigarette.

Kenneth grinned. "I suppose you think that the investigators have analysed every detail."

"Definitely."

"Not really."

Uncle Ash glowered. "What do you mean by that, Ken?"

"The perfect murder doesn't exist. The apparently absent correlation between the victims is an illusion. Aside from the perpetrator's approach, there is at least one common denominator that interrelates the victims. Once you find the key to that denominator, you find the killer." Kenneth paused. "All of them were students. On what courses were they registered?"

"Chemistry, law, geography and Asian literature, respectively."

"What technical details have your people, or Mr. Frank's people, made public?"

"The murder method has been presented in the media but the public doesn't know what kind of sharp weapon, or knife, we are interested in. The eye element is known to the public, though not that it consistently concerns the left eye."

Kenneth swallowed the last sip of the terrible coffee.

What do you know about the case so far, Ken?

I read the newspapers and watch TV.

It had been a while since he'd read about the serial killer in the newspapers. Why did he lie to his uncle? He didn't know.

"Thank you very much for the update, Uncle Ash. And for the delicious coffee."

"You want a refill?"

"No, thanks."

His uncle took a second cup, a full one. "You have done it before and you can do it again, Ken. As external, of course. Flexible rules. Total cover-up."

"Besides that?"

"In about fifteen minutes I'm going down to headquarters. An urgent meeting with Frank."

"Has there ever been a non-urgent meeting with Mr. Frank?"

"Can I give you a ride into town?"

"Thanks but no thanks. I'll take the tram." *Nice try, Uncle, but I don't want to see Mr. Frank.*

"As you wish. You can at least think about it. I could use an unconventional genius."

Kenneth rose and moved towards the hallway. "Good luck in the hunt for the killer."

"I'll talk to you later, boy."

"No doubt."

3

The mental pictures exploded into six common denominators. As the southbound tram was passing through Blackfield Central Station, he could think of eight. In Blackfield there were more than forty thousand students, representing more than one hundred countries across the world. Three dead girls were British. One was Swedish. No forensic evidence. Four clean, expertly executed murders. Arbitrary killings? A madman who murders female students for pleasure only? The buzzing network of ideas worsened his headache. It began to seem as if he had been involved on a personal level since the very beginning.

4

His wife would be away until late. How late? She didn't know, though this particular uncertainty only made the adventure even more exciting.

She was strolling along Ellesmere Street in the direction of Endsleigh Park. The sun stung her eyes. In the sparkling light, she lost her perception of colours. The day consisted of silver silhouettes, which shifted and pushed their way through the afternoon traffic.

She stopped. There was the house, across the street. Annabelle munched the last salt-and-vinegar crisp, fished up a paper napkin from her handbag and wiped crumbs of crisps from the corners of her mouth. She patted carefully with the napkin to preserve the lipstick's perfection.

She crossed the street and slid in an almost trance-like state towards the house. The roar from the traffic fell away. The city stood still. The pulsing thunder in her ears arrived from her heart.

The door opened before her finger touched the bell. She giggled. "Hi." With the tip of her tongue she tried to dislodge a crisp crumb that was stuck between two teeth. The crumb didn't come loose.

"Hello, sweetie. Your eyes and the glowing sun, the crucial elements of a lovely day just begun."

"Do you really mean that?" She nearly laughed out loud. "You're not a pretentious poet, are you?"

"Of course I mean it." He welcomed her into the hall. "Is the lady searching for anything special today?"

"You know it." Of course you know it, she thought. *Wow, how handsome he is.* The handbag slipped out of her hand.

He pulled her to him. "Let me taste your lips, Annabelle."

His kiss almost knocked her breath away. When his tongue pressed in between Annabelle's lips, she sucked it deeper into her mouth. The foreign body part, slippery as a fish with a taste of mint, examined her oral cavity with a brute playfulness. Heat spread through her body with the relentlessness of a fever. She desired him more than any man or boyfriend of her past. He was a gentleman who made most of her former boyfriends look like idiots. Not only did he satisfy her most erotic dreams but he also took her out to the cinemas, the theatres, art exhibitions, elegant cafés and posh restaurants.

They had even spent a romantic weekend in London after he had informed his wife that he was going to work away in the capital. They checked in as father and daughter (he dismissed her thrilling idea to check in as husband and wife) at Brown's Hotel in Mayfair, the most delightful and grandiose hotel that Annabelle had ever seen. She was told that Franklin D. Roosevelt and his wife Eleanor had stayed at the hotel during their honeymoon back in 1905. What a contrast to the B & B in Stockport where she, as a twelve-year-old on a school trip, had spent two nights and—

The pressure from his nice lips on her mouth disappeared all of a sudden. "You didn't call me this morning," she whispered. "I missed your call. Do you still love me?"

"You know I love you, Annabelle."

"How much?" Her fingers started to explore

his crotch. She felt how he was growing hard. "Show me how much you love me."

He took her arm and led her upstairs towards the bedroom.

■

Naked, she walked around the bedroom, gathering her underwear that was scattered all over the floor. "What's wrong? You look exhausted." She tittered but her words had been shrouded in uncertainty. "We've been together for less than an hour and you're already tired? It's so unlike you." In a mirror, she noted a crease in her powder-white make-up.

"I have a lot of work to do," he said from the bed. "I hope you understand what it means to work seventy hours a week, excluding preparations."

"What preparations, huh? Preparations such as getting cosy in bed with me?"

"I'm serious, Annabelle."

"Me too. Very serious. I know how much you enjoy our secret moments but I'm looking for a steady relationship." She stepped into her knickers and hooked her bra.

"Listen, can't we preserve the situation as it is a little while longer? Secret, discreet?"

"No, not at all. I'm worthy of respect. I refuse to act like a fill-in for your wife." She sat down on the edge of the bed and slipped into her tights, one leg at a time. Her make-up was starting to feel like a mask of plaster. She was not accustomed to turning the corners of her mouth downwards. She regarded him out of the corner of her eye.

"I'll call you," he said.

"When?" She buttoned her blouse and stepped into her skirt. "When will you call me?"

"Soon. I promise."

"You'd better or I'll tell your wife about us."

"No you won't."

"Trust me, I will." She rose with a start from the edge of the bed. "Damn it, where're my shoes?"

She paced around with a higher speed than before. She spotted one of the high-heels, not in the bedroom but in the corridor outside. The other shoe was balancing on the top step of the stairs between the upper and lower floor. With shoes on her feet, she returned to the bedroom.

"Listen," he said, still from the bed. "Both my family and my business are very important to me. Do you really think that you and I could have a future together?"

"Divorce your wife and marry me. Easy-peasy."

"Try to be reasonable, darling. Things are not so simple. To rearrange life like that… Firstly, what would people say? I cannot afford a scandal. Imagine the gossip-paper headlines: 'Middle-aged professional falls for first-year student'."

"Don't you think it's a little late to ask me to be reasonable?" Her already raised voice turned into a shout. "I want a straight answer on how it's going to be with us and I want to know soon or I'll tell your wife and all my friends about us. Goodbye!" She left the bedroom, hurried down the stairs, grabbed her jacket and handbag, and disappeared from the house.

▪

I'm only imagining it, Annabelle thought. *I'm only imagining that I'm being followed.* Her gaze swept through the bus, both ways from where she was sitting next to a window. She even checked the reflections in the window—dancing mirror images which startled her each time the cramped vehicle made a turn. Passengers minded their own business. Silence prevailed like in a late-night cemetery.

She did not have far to walk from the bus stop at Holyhead Avenue. Like a delayed omen, a wind rushed through the darkness in the same moment that evil struck. The subtle shades of night mixed with the crackling colours of terror as the knife came flying like a bolt from a clear and starlit sky.

5

Friday morning, December the fifth.

He took the cod fillet from the freezer and put it on Linda's plate. Since she loved her fish raw but not icy, he placed the cod in the microwave to defrost it.

Kenneth served himself organic yogurt, muesli, cinnamon, ginger, one decilitre of fresh blueberries, a chopped apple, a lemon, seven walnut halves, one tablespoon of raisins, three tablespoons of extra virgin olive oil, half a pint of freshly squeezed grapefruit juice and nettle tea. Separately, he would take one tablespoon of omega-3 rich fish oil. He believed that the vitamin and antioxidant-charged breakfast speciality—one of twenty-three special variants—would provide enough typewriter-fuel until noon.

He sat down at the table, with the four-legged lady *on* the table, oblivious to what was going to shake up his life.

▪

The phone by the kitchen counter killed the silence.

"Who do you think the caller is, Linda?"

Linda looked up from her plate but said nothing. She resumed eating her cod fillet.

"Are you expecting any phone calls, Linda?"

Linda still said nothing.

He jumped up and grabbed the handset. "Good morning, Uncle Ash. I felt certain that you said you hadn't talked to Mr. Frank. And I thought you said you'd give me time to think about it."

"How did you know it was me calling?"

"Who else would it be?"

"A fifth girl murdered, Ken. Last night."

"I know."

"How can you know that?"

"I mean, I suspected it."

"We need to talk."

"Where are you now?"

"How fast can you get to headquarters, Ken?"

6

Blackfield Police Service (BPS) had a more or less secret division unofficially named SCDX. He did not know what SCDX stood for. Nobody knew. Officially, the local SCDX was only one of many units in the spiderweb of sections within BPS. SCDX operated like an international octopus. Its flexible tentacles stretched and pulled across the planet. Kenneth knew nothing more than that Mr. Frank was running the local SCDX division and that Uncle Ash was involved somehow. He, Kenneth, neither wanted nor needed to know more. He was here neither unofficially nor officially. He didn't exist here.

Uncle Ash was behind his desk. "Have a seat."

Kenneth found an armchair.

"Ash believes that his nephew has registered

something significant which we haven't yet." Mr. Frank's smooth-shaven cheeks were reminiscent of an infant's buttocks. The man's black hair showed a mirror-like finish as if he dyed it with shoe polish. His hairdo's straight edges suggested that he used a ruler when he combed it.

Mr. Frank's one-liner had carried the tone of a statement, not a question. Kenneth waited.

"He must fill out a special form at the HR department," Mr. Frank continued. "When he gets there, he asks for a Miss Russell. Understood?"

Kenneth nodded, but only to satisfy Mr. Frank. He turned to his uncle again. "During yesterday's summary you mentioned the dates of the first four murders. When you phoned this morning, you said that a fifth girl had been murdered last night. How do you interpret the fact that each of the five murders took place on a Thursday?"

"We're still working on it."

"And the girls' surnames?" Kenneth said. "The students are murdered in alphabetical order. I'm convinced that the victim from yesterday evening had a surname that begins with a letter after Q in the alphabet. A Miss R or a Miss S?"

"Miss S," Mr. Frank said. "Annabelle Stanfield."

"Thursday and the alphabetical order are of course only two of many factors," Kenneth said.

"You really mean that there are more patterns?" Uncle Ash defied the smoking ban and lit a cigarette. "How many?"

"Several."

His uncle frowned. "And?"

"Don't leave us hanging," Mr. Frank said.

"Tell me everything that happened in Creake last night," Kenneth said.

"How do you know that the fifth murder took place in the district of Creake?" his uncle asked. "I said nothing about Creake when I called."

"I heard it on my phone's radio on the way here." It seemed reasonable, he decided. That he didn't remember having listened to the radio must be the headache's fault.

Mr. Frank rose. "I'm in a hurry, Ash. Need to be somewhere else very soon. I shall catch up with you later. And regarding Kenneth, I expect him to stay focused. The young man is free to play psychological games with the killer if he wishes but he must refrain from playing games with me. The young man will keep me updated on his progress."

▪

"Annabelle Stanfield was stabbed to death sometime between four p.m. and five p.m.," Uncle Ash said. "She was nineteen."

"Unbelievable that such an exceptional act of violence can occur unnoticed," Kenneth said.

"Incredible."

"Far from impossible though. The perpetrator is uncatchable as long as he follows his system. He's a perfectionist."

"Perfectionist, uh? Like you, then?"

What did Uncle Ash mean?

"Something troubling you, boy?"

There were several things which were troubling Kenneth. "I'll take a lift down to the HR department and get the paperwork done."

"Take it easy down there, Ken."

"What do you mean?"

"When you see her you'll know what I mean."

7

"Dr. Kenneth Sorin?"

The voice had come from somewhere behind him. He turned around. The girl wore a knee-length dress in dark red. Her clear and glowing skin was as perfect as the finest porcelain surface. The medium-length hair was golden white, like the palest streaks of a rainbow. Her eyes were as dark as the beads of the necklace which accented the demure V neckline. She looked like a woman who had not yet experienced a twenty-fifth birthday.

"Dr. Kenneth Sorin? Mr. Sorin? Welcome, we've been expecting you. I'm Jeanne Russell."

He heard his heart accelerate. He found

himself again on the brink of a daydream. "I know who you are, miss."

"Oh?"

"The name tag on your dress is readable."

The woman forced a short laugh. "In a fraction of a second you made your first detection?"

"It wasn't meant to be a detection. Besides, your identity isn't, wasn't, the world's greatest mystery."

Miss Russell scowled. "Follow me, wit-cracker." She started to walk away.

'Wit-cracker'? He had never heard nor seen the word before. He decided to use it in his next book.

▪

They passed through a subterranean utility tunnel, arrived at a windowless office on an underground floor and sat down at a coffee table opposite each other. Kenneth found himself adjusting his tie, even though no adjustment was necessary. The room looked like a storage spot, with cardboard boxes and equipment piled from floor to ceiling. On the table sat a stack of forms, a phone, a computer and a box of coloured pens.

"I've never seen you before," he said. "How long have you been working for Mr. Frank?"

"We have no time for small talk," she said.

"I'll try to keep that in mind."

"Try hard."

"I'll do my very best."

She snatched a form. "Ready for the formalities?"

"Of course; though from a time-saving point of view I do wonder why you haven't saved my data from earlier days."

"Security. K. Sorin data is always temporary."

Whose security? he wondered. Yours or mine?

"When your contract expires, all the data files associated with your person are destroyed. Twelve former contracts mean that the policy was applied twelve times."

Kenneth could hardly believe his ears but Miss Russell actually giggled.

"What kind of backup function do my files provide?"

"It's none of your business."

"I treasure your honesty, Miss Russell. You have no idea how much it pleases me."

She grabbed a pen (orange!) and started to write down his details. For only a moment, as she leaned forward to reach for a paper clip, Kenneth's eyes happened to catch the depth inside her neck-line. The bra was pink. The top sides of her small breasts were pale as fresh snowballs, or at least they appeared to be in the icy glare that sprayed down from the fluorescent tubes in the ceiling.

The girl suddenly looked up from the form. "Born right here in Blackfield. Correct, isn't it?"

Kenneth's eyes turned quickly upward. His eyes met hers. "Yes, that's right, that's right." His voice sounded shaky as if he had uttered the words in a turbulent wind flow.

"I read it on one of your book's dust jackets."

"I suspected that you did."

"Is there anything at all that you have never suspected?"

"I suspect that there may be something."

She sighed with force. "Age?"

"Twenty-eight. At least, the last time I checked." His mind was unsynchronised with the present. Behind his eyes was still an image of Miss Russell's snow-white breasts.

"Birthday?"

"Still March the sixth. I was born at one thirty a.m. I shop weekly on Monday mornings between ten and eleven. I wash my clothes every Sunday. My cat's favourite dish is salmon pâté with sweetcorn but on Tuesdays—and Tuesdays exclusively—she wants bangers and mash. I change my underwear every day, I brush my teeth every morning and evening, and I avoid picking my nose in public."

She glowered. "I know that these forms may be perceived as bureaucratic but it's not me who designs them, okay?"

"What does the acronym SCDX stand for?"

"The topic does not exist, sir."

"Is it true, Miss Russell, that SCDX is more philosophy or consensus than a department or a division? A philosophy, or an abstract network, that transcends national borders?"

"The topic does not exist, sir."

"Is it true that specific factions within SCDX negotiate with industrial spies and international terrorists?"

"The topic does not exist, sir."

The atmosphere became paradoxically more comfortable after the latest exchange of words. The blonde at the opposite side of the table looked cosy. Was Miss Jeanne Russell only acting her routine professionalism, including practised eye contact, or could she be this nice for real?

8

"This is the receipt that we found in the inside pocket of Miss Annabelle Stanfield's jacket," Uncle Ash said. "Not the slightest traces of blood ended up on it. Incredible but true."

WORTHINGTON'S ELEGANCE
ELLESMERE – BLACKFIELD

100% CUSTOMER SATISFACTION GUARANTEE:
PLEASE CONTACT CUSTOMER SERVICES
FOR TERMS AND CONDITIONS.

FREE DELIVERY WITHIN THE UK AND FOR
ORDERS WITH A COMBINED VALUE OF AT LEAST
£400 WHEN YOU SHOP ONLINE:

WWW.WORTHINGTONS-ELEGANCE-
DELUXE.CO.UK
BLOUSE, DIOR – NEW COLLECTION: £599.00
DISCOUNT £-149.75
SUM GBP £449.25

DATE: 27/11 18:19
YOUR ACCOUNT WILL BE DEBITED
AS STATED BELOW.
CARD OWNER'S PIN CODE VERIFIED.
DEBIT CARD
– – –
ACCOUNT NUMBER **** **** **** 9316

CREDIT/DEBIT CARD £449.25

– – –

A WORTHINGTON'S ELEGANCE CARD WOULD
HAVE EARNED YOU 1158 POINTS TODAY FOR
PURCHASES OF ITEMS WITH A COMBINED
VALUE OF: £449.25

Kenneth produced a small case from his jacket pocket and chose the middle-sized tweezer. With the carefulness of a philatelist, he lifted the receipt.

"The receipt won't bite," Uncle Ash said.

"This is a matter of principle," Kenneth said. "I don't want to risk leaving my DNA on it."

Using the hypersensitive technique LCN

(Low Copy Number), a state-of-the-art DNA-sequencing technology, it was possible to detect and analyse vanishingly small traces of deoxyribonucleic acid (DNA) from, for example, drops of perspiration, saliva, hand or lip prints, or any other skin contact. To generate a genetic profile, five to ten body cells were enough starting material, corresponding to a millionth of the size of a grain of table salt.

"Anxious to leave fingerprints, Ken?" Uncle Ash grunted. "If I suspected that my nephew was the killer, he wouldn't be sitting in that chair now."

"Worthington's Elegance," Kenneth murmured to himself. "In the district of Ellesmere."

"Do you know the store?"

"Only by name. Alison was a customer."

"How many clues do you see on the receipt?"

"Two. Maybe three or four, depending on how you want to count. There are correlated clues to consider."

"Could you be more specific?"

"Two clues reveal the same direct information and are therefore maximally correlated. They also point at indirect information about two persons' psychological dimensions. The two individuals I'm referring to are, of course, the seller and the buyer."

"What kind of clues, Ken?"

9

She had toyed with the idea of bashing his head in with a frying pan. She would use the cast-iron pan which he had bought for her fiftieth birthday. Any household article could serve as a murder weapon. You only had to explore your imagination.

However, she realised that a quick death would spare him pain and suffering. It would be more pleasant to see the bastard disintegrate as slowly as possible, locked up in a room without food, without water. To die of starvation was supposed to be very painful. She would throw away the key to the locked room, pretending it were lost. An attractive plan, assuming that she could work out a beautiful alibi.

Would the storeroom do?

The storeroom here at Worthington's Elegance?

Amy Worthington was convinced that her husband didn't know that she knew what he was doing. Philip had to pay for his behaviour. Philip entertained a too unhealthy imagination: that the world revolved around him. One day, in the near future, it would be payback time.

How could this Phil be the same man she once fell in love with? How could this Phil be the same man who used to make love to her every night? How could this Phil be the same man who had the habit of giving her a bouquet of red roses every Valentine's Day? How could this Phil be the same man who had the habit of surprising her with trips to the world's Capitals of Culture?

She had asked herself these questions countless times in the last fifteen years, despite the crystal-clear answers: he could not be. Philip Worthington today was not the man she once knew and loved. Someone had to finish his unacceptable way of life for him—or finish him off altogether.

Now she heard Philip's voice, inside her. His words were like poison to her brain: "*The company has top priority, Amy. Try to memorise that. The company means everything. For the company's sake, and nonetheless for the sake of our customers, it's critical to preserve a facade of happiness, health and honesty. Think you can handle that, Amy?*"

Now it was evening, soon to be closing time. Amy surveyed the ground floor main department. The wallpaper's peony-red hue sizzled with the same intensity as the anger behind her frontal bone. She inhaled the scent of the hundreds of flowers in rainbow colours that hung in garlands and loops from the corners of the ceiling. A scent, barely perceptible but undeniable. If a genuine rainbow had a smell, she speculated, it might be similar to this mesmerising blend.

From a commercial point of view, Worthington's Elegance had a spectacular impact on the customers' bank account balances. It must be the flowers. The flowers' magical scent led customers to overspend. Why would anyone suspect magic? To live beyond their means was the modern-day consumer's main trait. The credit card circus was God's most appreciated gift to man.

From the ceiling hung a crystal chandelier they had bought during their honeymoon in Rimini just over thirty years ago. Did she care about it now? No, she didn't. It had lost its sentimental value. The crystal chandelier belonged to a bygone time.

The three-storey shop would soon be empty of people. From the far end of the ground floor she perceived the checkout operators serving the day's last customers. Where was Phil? With Worthington's Elegance's extensive team of assistants and checkout operators, Amy's absence for an hour wouldn't be noted. After her errands around town, she could have returned to the store through the main entrance or through the back door or through the door to the loading dock. Irrespective of the way, it was uncertain that Phil had observed her return. What if he hadn't?

Amy surveyed the long aisle in which she stood. No one was there. She could hear the murmur of voices float past the checkout counters and fade away. The final customers paid and left. The electric main entrance doors, which swished back and forth between their closed and open positions, filtered the street-traffic cacophony. Her watch showed five fifty-seven p.m. Three minutes to closing time.

Although she was one of the managers and married to the official owner, she felt like an eavesdropping stranger as she stood behind the rows of clothes on hangers. That was when she got the idea and there was no time to reflect on whether the idea was any good.

She took off her heeled shoes. With a shoe in each hand, she sneaked off in the direction of the information desk. Amy moved without a sound, like an angel. She could no longer distinguish the cash operators' voices nor the slightest mumble from the customer service area. Not quite six o'clock. Had Philip sent the staff home early? Had the very last customer left now, and the sales assistants?

The rows of packed clothing racks were as dense as the walls of a trench. She was The Invisible Woman. Within a collection of purple coats, she found a wedge-shaped gap between two coats. A lookout point, just about large enough to provide a view of the customer service desk and the main entrance. And there he was, at his mahogany desk, at the edge of Amy's limited field of vision.

Phil was leafing through some ring binder and appeared lost in thought. A pile of correspondence sat on the desk mat. Without raising his eyes from the ring binder, he picked up the letters one by one and slit them open with a knife. A knife that was considerably larger than one which the job demanded.

Although Amy had been prepared for the worst, she almost screamed when she had her suspicions confirmed. The sound of tripping high-heeled shoes came from the main entrance.

10

"A number of interesting details you say," Uncle Ash said. "I can see only one."

'You find the most interesting element on the seventeenth line," Kenneth said, "if you consider blank lines, too."

His uncle's nicotine-yellow forefinger wandered down the strip of paper. "The time of the purchase? I knew you would comment on that."

"Six nineteen, November the twenty-seventh."

"A legal transaction, Ken."

"Though unusual. Retail trade after six p.m. is rare, with the exception of certain supermarkets and malls. There are many shops that close even earlier, at five thirty."

"And you think you need to inform me? You weren't even born when I learned how this country functioned. Besides, it does happen that stores temporarily change their opening hours."

"Worthington's Elegance is no exception to the rule of thumb. Closing time at six. Opening hours nine-thirty to six, Monday to Saturday. Closed on Sunday."

"I know that! But for someone who claimed not to know the store, you seem mysteriously well-informed."

"Alison must have told me in passing the store's opening hours. I happened to remember them."

"No doubt. You just happened to remember."

"Annabelle Stanfield got special treatment."

"At least it looks like that, Ken."

"I'm confident that the chain store's prominent owner, Mr. Worthington, knew Miss Stanfield well. They might even have been lovers. I'm not saying they were definitely lovers. Neither do I rule out the possibility."

"I knew you'd say that."

"I knew you'd say that you knew I'd say that."

Uncle Ash showed his dandelion-yellow teeth. "Continue."

"Another detail on line seventeen intrigues me."

"The actual date?"

"Thus the receipt is from last Thursday. If Thursday was their regular weekday to socialise, did they then meet yesterday, the same day she was murdered?"

"I understand what it is you want to say,

Ken, but I think your reasoning is lacking substance."

"I haven't finished yet."

"I'm certain you haven't."

"Line fourteen."

"A discount of one hundred and forty-nine pounds and seventy-five pence. So what?"

"Twenty-five percent is an exceedingly generous discount for a designer blouse from a brand-new collection. Why would a luxury fashion store, in the run-up to Christmas, sell their brand-new winter collections at January sales prices? Easy. Because this man, Philip Worthington, gave Miss Stanfield special treatment. The attention-grabbing discount strengthens the argument regarding the time of the transaction: six nineteen."

"But there's still no evidence that Worthington is murdering female students." Uncle Ash grinned. "However, if he gave this Annabelle Stanfield a special treatment in his store, he might have given her a special treatment in bed as well."

"If we consider the lines thirteen and fourteen simultaneously, we can deduce Miss Stanfield's and Mr. Worthington's psychological dimensions."

"Okay. The actual garment in question. The brand-new posh Dior blouse, for five hundred and ninety-nine pounds before the nice discount. Holy crap. My car cost about the same."

A shiver ran through Kenneth. And a metallic voice, an unknown voice, sang out from a corridor in the basement of his mind: line 13. The third time since last Thursday night that that nasty number had turned up.

"Psychological dimensions? Will you elaborate on that?"

The shiver vanished. The voice in his head, too.

"The dimensions of a human being," Kenneth said, "can be described as the physiological, the sociological and the psychological dimension. The third of these dimensions, the one we are interested in for the moment, is the product of the first two. Is it clear so far?"

"Crystal."

"In the psychological dimension we discover patterns of longing and guilt, mental complexes, phobias, fears, manias, fantasies and inhibitions. The psychological dimension includes details such as habits, special abilities, intelligence, predisposition, sensitivity, talent and irritability. Thus, based on the combined information from the lines thirteen and fourteen, and then by applying the aforementioned classification of human dimensions, I think that Miss Stanfield was a spoiled lady. My conviction in that respect leads us to the bank card number—with the twelve initial digits blocked out—on line twenty-three. I presume that someone has already checked the debit card details. I suppose that Miss Stanfield could not finance a six-hundred-pound blouse with her student loan, with or without a discount. The bank card doesn't belong to the typical student and Worthington's Elegance isn't the typical student shopping paradise. Someone, an adult member of the family, lent Annabelle the payment card. Am I right?"

It felt like a fifty-fifty situation. Alternatively, a parent could have made an electronic transaction from one of their bank accounts to Annabelle's own to subsidise the daughter's lifestyle.

"Spot on, Ken. The card belongs to Mrs. Abigail Stanfield, the victim's mother. That piece of info reached me while you were at the HR department, flirting with Miss Russell."

Kenneth ignored the comment. "When are you going to hear the mother? And the rest of the family?"

"Two from my team, Tina Tanner and Stevie Morrison, are right now with the Stanfields, down in Selmore Village. I expect to be hearing from them very soon now."

"I see. Annabelle was a local Blackfield girl."

"In that sense she's unique among the five victims, Ken. And although her parents live in town, she had a home of her own in a residence hall just north of the university campus."

"There are people who value privacy. I don't live at your place, not without reason."

His uncle glowered. "You had something useful to say regarding this Philip Worthington?"

"Again I want to refer to the lines thirteen and fourteen. I bet that Mr. Worthington is a man who values customer relations, in particular, relations to regulars. Especially relations to female customers."

"If he had a pleasant time with Miss Stanfield, he might have had a pleasant time with the other ladies, too."

"He's the top manager of a successful business and can therefore afford to give specific customers overly generous discounts. It wouldn't surprise me if the company is the most important thing in his life, even more important than his marriage."

"How did you know he's married? *I* knew that, through the investigation. But how did you know already?"

"Perhaps I knew even before you knew, Uncle. There was a biographical article about Worthington in a magazine a few months ago."

"Bravo, Ken. Have you finished?"

"Only for the moment."

"So that's it?"

"What more do you want me to say?"

"Do you believe everything you just said?"

"I believe in the matching jigsaw pieces of the Worthington-Stanfield corner of the puzzle. These two characters knew each other well. You asked me what I saw in this receipt and I have responded. You must agree that the slightest detail in an individual's behaviour can reveal information about that individual's psychological dimension."

"I must agree with nothing, boy."

"I rephrase: you must agree that Worthington's Elegance should be included in the investigation."

"I agree with that."

"When?"

"As soon as I've seen Tina and Stevie's report."

"Call me at home, Uncle, if there's something important." Kenneth got up, took his overcoat and moved towards the door.

"What are you going to do, Ken?"

"Write on my new horror suspense novel. And ask Linda what she thinks of this puzzle murder mystery that has gripped our city."

11

"Do you really think it's a good idea to meet like this, Phil? What if someone becomes suspicious?"

Phil? Not Mr. Worthington. Not sir. Not even Philip. But *Phil?* Amy's heart sank, though not to the bottom. Revenge was the driving force that made her heart hover at an average depth in the blackest of abysses. Through the gap between two coats on the clothing rack, she could see how her husband looked up from the ring binder.

"Hi, Suzanne." He rose and embraced his visitor.

Suzanne?

"Have you ever done it in an escalator?" Philip asked.

"Don't talk like that."

"Sorry. Just kidding."

Suzanne giggled. "No wife about, I hope."

"Amy? No, it's six o'clock. My wife and all the other staff have finished. The bitch is out, doing her Friday shopping. I expect her to come home with something delicious tonight, such as grilled turkey with potatoes, garlic yogurt and a bottle of Château Margaux."

Arsehole thinks I'm still out.

The corners of Suzanne's mouth dropped. "It sounds like you're looking forward to a romantic dinner with your wife."

"Romantic? Only officially, sweetie."

I'll get you for this, Phil, you official idiot.

"I spotted the newspaper ads for Worthington's Elegance's winter collections. I'm interested in the coats, and it would be nice to have some expert advice. My grandmum says I can choose whatever I want."

"It would be my pleasure to show you our new range." He placed an arm around the girl's waist. "Among our latest additions, a new collection of charming purple coats was delivered the other day. Shall we take a look at them?"

They're coming this way!

This wasn't the right moment to confront them, she decided, but even if it had been the right time, she wanted to find out more. Find out what?

She had no simple answer to that question.

She moved as fast as she could—tiptoeing, still with only stockings on her feet—halfway back through aisle number four to an intersection with another aisle, hurried around the corner, slipped, almost lost her balance, and slowed down. At the same instant, she discovered that she was holding her breath as she tiptoed into aisle number five, and didn't breathe until she could hear the murmurs from the other side of the row of clothing racks.

Amy began to breathe again and gritted her teeth when she heard the sound of her own breathing. In the stillness, she was convinced that her breathing sounded like a howling wind.

She listened. The murmur in aisle four turned into an audible conversation.

"I'd hate to be dependent on my grandmum's credit card for the rest of my youth."

I bet you would, Amy thought. *I could end your dependency on anything and everything right now.*

"Don't worry about that," Philip said. "A beauty like you shouldn't have to worry about anything."

With the exception of having to worry about me, Amy thought, on the verge of whispering it.

"A beauty like you shouldn't even have to work."

Suzanne tittered. "Don't be ridiculous. What would you think of me if I wanted to live on my grandmum's money for the rest of my life, huh?"

Your life could be shortened substantially, girl.

"I want a permanent and well-paid job. I'd love to start in a position somewhere up the ladder."

"Now? You're twenty, Suzanne. You have your whole life ahead of you."

"I want a top job soon. Not now but very soon. I could imagine starting as some kind of division manager."

Philip chuckled. "Where?"

"Why not here? I'll graduate from university this summer, with good grades. I could already give you a list of referees."

"Now wait a minute, dear Suzanne. Hold it right there. Let's talk about that at a later date. Have you even taken a certain Mrs. Worthington into account?"

"This summer there won't be a Mrs. Worthington any longer."

Amy clenched her teeth.

"You must be joking, Suzanne."

"Okay, maybe there'll be a Mrs. Worthington this summer. But her first name won't be Amy. It'll be Suzanne, right?"

"Have you lost your mind? How dare you talk like that, here and now."

"Mrs. Suzanne Worthington." Suzanne laughed. "How do you think it sounds?"

Mrs. Suzanne Worthington... Over my dead body.

"Let's deal with things in order," he said.

You're right, Phil. An order is essential. The first thing I have to do includes you.

"Okay, Phil." The girl's giggle petered out.

"What do you think of the coats?"

"Oh, they're wonderful. I also love that one, the emerald one, and that steel-grey one."

"But you're hooked on the purple one, aren't you? As I predicted, sweetie. Purple is your colour."

You spoilt girl.

"They're beautiful, all of them, but yes, I've decided on the purple one." Suzanne paused. "It's expensive."

"With the price comes quality. It's a top brand and you get what you pay for but don't worry, I'll give you a generous discount. Twenty-five percent."

"Oh, thank you very much! Even if it's my grandmum who's paying. Why are you so nice to me?"

"We want to express how much we value our regular customers, and you are a regular customer, even if it is your kind grandmother who pays for everything you buy."

"You value your regular customers, huh? I want to see some evidence of how much you value *me*."

"The key to a successful business is to put the customer at the centre, including the idiots. Ninety percent of customers are idiots. Now, a thoroughly nice person like me is nice to everyone but you must believe me when I say that you're the only customer I've ever…"

"I believe you. I want to because I love you."

Amy realised what they did next. The sounds from Philip and the young woman's activities were unmistakable. Amy couldn't believe her ears. They did it! They did it on the floor in aisle number four.

▪

Amy stroked a hand over her cheeks and discovered streaks of tears. In addition, her stomach ached.

Then, footsteps. Philip's leaden tread. Suzanne's feather-light stride. Receding steps. The man and his mistress, moving towards the checkout area.

How long had she been standing in wait in this maze of clothing racks? Amy dared to look at her watch: six fifty-two. Almost an hour. The tears on her cheeks had dried. She listened again but there was no sound to hear. Not even from the ghosts in her brain. A closed-for-holiday crematorium could not have been quieter.

A variety of options hastened through her mind. Without allowing herself to think about her next action, she moved through aisle number five, turned the corner and tiptoed towards the checkout area. Amy stepped into her shoes. "You're right about that." She fixed her eyes on the girl's neck. "It isn't fun."

Phil and the girl spun around. Suzanne recoiled and uttered a cry. Phil's jaw opened, closed, opened, like the mouth of a fish on dry land.

"*What isn't fun?!*" the girl squeaked.

"You know what I mean, young lady. 'Have you ever done it in an escalator?' My husband's sick humour. Or rather my husband's sick seriousness. His question was sincere."

"Amy? What are you doing here at this time of day? And what on earth are you talking about?"

"Flirting with customers again?" Amy's words turned into slivers of ice in her throat. Reality caught up with her. It rolled in on her with the force of a tidal wave. The time she had spent in the aisles between the rows of clothing racks—the time of artificial security—was a million years ago.

"The Wheelers' daughter is paying the store a visit again. Our customer Mrs. Araminta Wheeler's granddaughter."

"How kind of you to suggest how a daughter relates to a granddaughter. Did you look it up in a dictionary?"

Phil sighed. "Could you refrain from using that tone in the presence of customers?"

"I'm going now," Suzanne said.
"No you don't," Amy said.
"Wait a minute," Philip said.
"Shut up, Phil," Amy said.
"I'm in a hurry," Suzanne said.

Amy realised that the girl had already paid for the coat. Philip had put the item in a carrier bag. Suzanne grabbed the bag, dashed towards the main exit and left. Amy's razor-sharp gaze was tracking Suzanne beyond the window mannequins towards Ellesmere Avenue, until she was out of sight in the evening traffic.

12

"Have you slept with her?"

"Not at all. Miss Wheeler spends considerable sums of money and is therefore the kind of regular customer who we care about here and want to keep. What attitude do you expect me to show towards people who come here to part with their money? What do you think, Amy? Should I be nice to the ugly ones and unpleasant to the beautiful ones? Like some perverse sort of compensation."

"Aha, you admit that she's beautiful? And who are those customers whom you classify as ugly? What a discriminating attitude! You're a disgrace to the company, Phil. A dishonour to the profession."

"I never give certain customers special

treatment. I haven't done it before and will never do it in the future."

Not done it before? That was a lie, and Phil knew that she knew it was a lie. "Aha, now you're talking about special treatment. Do you have a sexual relationship with this Miss Wheeler? Look me in the eyes. Do you?"

"Stop it now. This discussion leads nowhere. The company's popularity and reputation mean everything. You're a shareholder. The firm's success implies a financial success for you, too."

"Is she good in bed?"

"I can't believe my ears. How can you ask such an indecent question?"

"Does she have fine breasts?"

"Drop it, Amy."

"You're old enough to be her father."

"I told you to drop the subject."

"Does she want to give birth to your children?"

"Amy, you're upset and tired."

"*You're* the one who's tired! You're tired of me and you're longing for a younger woman. I'm right. Right? Answer me!" She screamed now. "I'm still your wife and I'm entitled to an honest response from you, you coward."

"That's enough. Calm down."

"I am calm! You've had sex with that girl, and only God knows how many other young women you've had sex with. Now, if you don't change your attitude towards the female customers, I will do something about it."

"Do what?"

"Something."

"Have you met your new psychologist?"

"It's none of your business."

"None of my business? My wife doesn't concern me? It sounds like you need extra therapy sessions."

"You will regret that you said that."

Philip said nothing more. Lucky for him. He just stared. Perhaps he wondered how safe it was to share a home with a mental health patient. If she wanted to, she could remove him from the business sector forever, here and now. She could pick up the letter opener that was lying there on the desk and stick it in his heart or neck.

But, of course, it would look like murder.

13

The electric typewriter was just a mental thing. Some people would claim it was about superstition. A few years ago, his first computer crashed. With no money for a new computer, he wrote, on the electric machine, the final version of Blue Moon Psycho. The book sold and became a resounding success on both sides of the Atlantic. In this high-tech age, he had become a debuting novelist with a manuscript typewritten on an ancient device.

Today, now, unpleasant memories were

trying to block his way forward. They made him feel like a painter who was painting himself into one corner after another. But his persistent writing drove him around and out of the trouble. Around and out and away. The characters—not the author—dictated the story's destination and decided the journey's development. He didn't know how the novel would end. It wasn't his task to know. It was the story characters' job to push the book forward. Stephen King and Dean Koontz were right. Outlines were a waste of time. The characters mould events. Events irradiate the characters.

He rolled a new sheet of paper into the clattering machine. When the sense of not being alone in the workroom overwhelmed him, he had written another five pages of the first draft, line spacing 1.5. It meant he had already exceeded his daily goal.

The awareness of being watched continued to trouble him. Now he could no longer ignore the discomfort. All he had to do to gain clarity was to turn his head and look over his shoulder. No one was there. He glanced through the wide-open doorway to the corridor. Nothing was there except a dead silent gloom. When he turned his head forward again, the thing's reflection crept into the edge of his visual field. The mirror image bounced away from the computer screen to the left and transformed into a furry shadow. The agile animation gave him no time to scream.

"Linda!" He breathed a sigh of relief. "Linda, even though you are my best friend, you have no right to sneak up on me like that."

Linda miaowed.

For a crazy moment, he wondered if Linda was checking his consumption of paracetamol, ordinary painkillers, which, like aspirin, were sold without a prescription at any supermarket. Must he explain to the cat what it took to erase a headache? He almost whispered that he hadn't had a painkiller since the night before, which was true.

People with no common language were in need of translation in order to communicate. The verbal barrier between man and cat was no obstacle. The psychology behind the phenomenon interested him. Cats must be smarter than people. Cats seemed to understand human actions and to foresee human intentions, while humans, the self-appointed rulers of the planet, were often incapable of comprehending their own species.

The phone rattled.

The signals were as painful as gnats.

▪

He fumbled with the phone. "Hello?"

"Are you awake?" Uncle Ash's voice. "You sound dispirited."

"I may sound like someone who has a lot to do."

"I've seen, heard, Tina and Stevie's report. Worthington knew Annabelle Stanfield well."

"What a surprise."

"Miss Stanfield's principal leisure activity was shopping and she liked to discuss everything she purchased at her favourite stores, which included Worthington's Elegance."

"She liked to discuss purchases with whom?"

"With her female friends. This took place not only in the student quarter. When she had friends over at the parental home, it happened that they discussed Philip Worthington's retail chain. Small talk which the parents overheard. Among these friends it was just Annabelle who was a customer at Worthington's. The girlfriends were, are, possible future customers."

"When are you going to see Mr. Worthington?"

"Not until the Christmas week."

"You must be joking."

"Nothing to joke about, I'm afraid. The man is on a business trip abroad."

"It means you have already spoken to his wife."

"Morrison and I visited the store this morning."

"This morning? You mean it's Saturday?"

"Don't say you didn't know."

"I wasn't certain. It could still have been Friday. I'm working at the typewriter."

"If you look out a window, you'll see that the sun is up."

“There’s a black cloud above my house right now. Besides, it’s the darkest season of the year.”

His uncle went silent. Then: “Mrs. Worthington said that her husband travelled to Amsterdam today. Airline confirms this piece of information. Return ticket booked for the twenty-third of December.”

“Brilliant.”

“Although Worthington isn’t our killer, he could be one of the last people to have seen Annabelle alive. I had to work hard for the information the wife eventually surrendered. She said that I upset her, that I interfered with her personal preparations.”

“What kind of preparations?”

“Mental. She’s seeing a shrink. And you?”

“I need a psychologist?”

“I mean, how’s it going regarding your theoretical involvement in the case?”

“I want to solve the mystery of the cut-out eye. At present, I don’t know how.”

“Any plans for the weekend? Jeanne Russell is single, in case you didn’t know.”

“Wit-cracker.”

▪

One second passed before the phone rang again.

He snatched up the receiver. “Dear Uncle, what is it now?”

“Kenneth Sorin, I suppose. But not any

Kenneth Sorin. I'm referring to, of course, the analyst and novelist with a Ph.D. in chemical physics."

An unknown voice, an old woman's voice.

"Yes, Kenneth Sorin speaking."

"Your uncle hung up, at last. Good. Good."

A growing number of questions exploded in his brain. "How did you know my uncle just called? Who are you?" He shot a glance at the caller ID box: a local phone number.

"It matters little who I am. What matters is what I know."

"As the lady pleases. What is it you know, apart from my unlisted phone number?"

"Your number exists at SCDX, and in your head, which means that it's accessible, somehow. Not bad for a ninety-seven-year-old crone, is it?"

"What do you know about SCDX?"

"Nothing. No one knows anything about SCDX. What I know is your mind. Follow your intuition, young man. Follow your intuition." The woman coughed and spat throughout her speech.

"How can I help, madam? What do you want?"

"You should never let your emotions influence decisions regarding others. You must consider your attitude to make sure that you have no preconceptions. Do you understand?"

"I make an effort."

She coughed, spat, croaked. "It's vital that

you pay attention to what I'm communicating before it's too late."

"Too late for what?"

"Too late to live. Too late to die. Nothing can bring back the dead girls but I'm counting on you to find the truth. The most horrific truth."

"Thank you for your encouraging words."

"You can't afford sarcasm, young man."

"Fascinating hypothesis."

"You have to consider each situation as well as your own mindset, young man. A fragment of a rediscovered piece of writing meant to touch your emotions will reveal your secret admirer." More coughing, spitting, croaking.

"Secret admirer? Who?"

"It's predestined that you have to make your own journey of discovery, Mr. Sorin. I can't mention who it is, only where you can look. In... You..." A fit of coughing stopped her voice.

"Where do you want me to look, madam? What should I look for?"

The phone line's background crackle peaked at the same moment as the woman regained her voice. "In you, Mr. Sorin. The key to your problem is in you. Find the key, find your killer."

"In me? What's that supposed to mean?"

"You're facing the darkest case of your career, young man. Your thirteenth case is unlike anything you've ever encountered before."

"Your name? I'd like to know your name."

"Because it's you, Mr. Sorin, and you only, you can call me Christine. Forces from a world you don't know have brought the blackest horror."

"That sounds exciting."

"You're a superb chess player. And Suzanne?"

The nausea grew. "What do you know about Suzanne?" Suzanne Wright, a fictional chess player.

"Preserve our conversation, young man."

"I asked you a question, madam: what do you know about Suzanne?"

"Preserve. Forces fly. Black horror."

"Wait!"

Too late. The line was dead. Phantom ants were crawling on the skin between his shoulder blades.

The sheet in the typewriter, a page numbered thirteen, which he had just begun to write:

CHECKMATE, MISS WRIGHT
(working title; v. #1)
– 13 –

The difference between playing to stay in form and playing to stay alive became clear to Suzanne that scorching day in July.

When the horror slipped into her reality, she discovered that life became as unstable as the weather on a bare mountain. Her existence transformed into a nightmare in time and space.

The footsteps outside the bathroom door approached and

14

Leighton Fenwick looked twelve years younger than his mid-forties. The thick hair yellow-blonde like ripe wheat. The gaze from behind the crocodile-green-rimmed spectacles demonstrated an almost extraterrestrial calm. The suit thundercloud-grey, two shades duskier than the boring wallpaper. The beige tie reminiscent of a strip of cardboard tape.

The man sat behind a black lacquered desk that looked like a coffin. From a box on the desk mat, he lifted a toothpick, bent it between his thumb and forefinger, let it spring, without pause or stop, as if Fenwick—despite his job or because of it—was doing some sort of self-regulated psychotherapy. He looked up from the toothpick. "There are a number of advanced methods to attack the mental problems, Mrs. Worthington. Psychotherapy calls for a sizable effort from the client—you, in other words. No universal programme exists and it isn't unusual for psychologists to use their own individual approaches. I don't care about the procedures your previous therapists may have applied. I have my own agenda. Do you follow?"

Amy fidgeted in the visitor's chair. "Will you be able to help me, Doctor?"

"If I didn't believe so, a conversation like this would be a waste of time. Since the programme frequently involves discussions about more or less terrible or frightening aspects of your life, you will perhaps experience uncomfortable and sometimes unwieldy mood swings, for example, helplessness, frustration, anger, loneliness or liability. However, it has been demonstrated that therapy has positive effects on patients who undergo it, for instance, improved relationships and reduced anxiety."

Improved relationships? As if she would rather have an improved relationship with Phil than to see him meet the most horrendous death.

"I'll lead you through all sorts of phases. It's my profession to know people. I can smell a problem from a thousand miles away and that's all I need to make an initial characterisation of the problem in question. What we want to work on together is to gain insights into patterns of emotions, thoughts and behaviours related to your trauma. Later, you'll be able to use those insights when you implement positive changes in your life."

"It sounds good, Doctor." What Amy wondered was whether she would get some new insight into how she could best eliminate her husband, and how she would apply the new skills when she effected the refreshing plan.

"What you should do, Mrs. Worthington, during my customised guidance and monitoring, is deal with three principal groups of symptoms of post-traumatic stress disorder, PTSD. Personally, I refer to those principal groups as SNSQ orbitals. SNSQ stands for Synapse Neuron Signal Quench. I have my own terminology which I developed, and I apply it within my projects at the forefront of research, which I run together with a multinational team of scientists."

"Really."

"SNSQ relates to the following. In the brain, there exist junctions called synapses, which allow chemical and electrical signals to pass between the neurons, or nerve cells. Orbitals are quantum states describing the electron clouds in atoms and molecules, such as the nervous system's signal substances. An SNSQ extinguishes unwanted signals. The first SNSQ orbital, my SNSQ1, involves recollection of the traumatic event. People who suffer from PTSD often have recurring nightmares about the trauma and might also, when awake, experience hallucinations, which are both painful and confusing.

"My SNSQ2 concerns the symptoms that occur when the mind tries to cope with the trauma. These symptoms are well known as avoidance symptoms, when the patient often experiences indifference to or estrangement from others.

"My SNSQ3 is associated with hyperarousal, including sleep disorders, such as insomnia. Other common symptoms that are sorted under orbital 3 are irritation and anger."

Anger is not seldom a legitimate reaction, Amy thought. "Doctor, what makes you think you can succeed where my previous psychologists failed?"

"Don't worry too much." Fenwick stirred the air with five splayed fingers. "Of course, you have hard work ahead of you but you are cared for with great attention. My nearest colleagues and I work at the scientific frontier regarding new developments in clinical psychology, projects which also involve an international team of psychiatrists and other sorts of scientists. We have already achieved a number of intriguing results. I want to expose you to the new psychotherapy system which I'm in the process of developing in coordination with various divisions of outstanding professionals. I want to use you in my pioneering quasi-psychodynamic experiments. But, of course, not without your consent."

"Do whatever you want, Doctor. If you need to use me as a guinea pig in order to publish a new research paper, go ahead. I have nothing to lose."

"You have everything to *gain*, Mrs. Worthington. Positive thinking is everything."

The toothpick between Fenwick's thumb and index finger burst. In the stillness of the office, it sounded like a shot from a cap gun. Amy jumped.

She had no idea what she wanted to reveal to this man. Did she want to mention how much she would appreciate seeing her husband die? Or how much she enjoyed that certain young women in the city were dead and buried? All the pain, anxiety, fear, terror and despair that could be traced to the abyss of her soul had been kept at bay. Emotions locked up like predators in a cage. Now someone or something had searched through the keyring and found the key that opened the cage. The predators were no longer detained.

For many years, more years than she wanted to count, she suffered from what the self-proclaimed experts called chronic PTSD. Jade was seven when a drug-influenced driver killed her at a pedestrian crossing. Two months later, Amy had a miscarriage. Dead twins. A baby boy. A baby girl. How fast one could lose three children.

"I miss Jade so much. Phil? Talk to me."

"I don't want to talk about Jade anymore."

"Why not?"

"Enough is enough. Now it's time to look forward."

"Doctor?"

"I'm still here, Mrs. Worthington."

Fenwick's eye contact, steady as a cobra's,

made Amy feel like a quirky subject behind a glass wall.

The man reached for a new toothpick.

"Doctor, do you follow the serial killer case?"

"Of course I do. Like every other citizen, I guess. Why do you ask?"

"Two of the victims were regular customers at Worthington's Elegance's flagship store and my husband had a sexual relationship with at least one of them, maybe both."

She knew that the police saw a link between the victim Annabelle Stanfield and the store. She was less certain whether the investigators knew that at least one more victim had been a customer. A lady whose name Amy had managed to repress. The name had been buried with the corpse. Amy almost giggled. And then there was Suzanne Wheeler, but that girl was still alive.

"Your husband knew the three other victims?"

"I don't know. I have no recollection of those customers but my husband could have met them anywhere, anytime, outside working hours."

"Marriage counselling isn't my department and never will be. Concerning relationship therapists, marriage counsellors, soothsayers and wizards, I suggest that you look in the *Yellow Pages*. However, what I do want to know is whether you fear for your husband's relationships with these women or for the possibility that your husband may be the killer."

What if it was me who murdered these women, Dr. Fenwick? What if it was me?

She said nothing. Fenwick smiled, as if he was testing her, as if he already knew what he wanted to know. When the communication deadlock was over, it was Fenwick who spoke first. "How do you cope with your husband's infidelity?"

"I've found an effective way."

"Do you want to talk about it?"

She remained silent.

"How do you feel about the fact that at least one of your husband's mistresses has been murdered?"

"I couldn't be happier." She thought her words sounded like fragments from a killer's confession.

"You are cryptic while honest. Compelling."

"Will you inform the police about our conversation today? You think I'm a murderess?"

"I have a code of ethics. However, it's important that you are aware of the limits of confidentiality."

"You still haven't answered my question."

"Do I need to, Mrs. Worthington?"

"No." She tore her gaze away from his magnetised stare. "If I were the killer, you would have a professional reason to break confidentiality."

"I mean that I'm authorised to break it if I

suspected that you were the killer. I didn't say I would use my authority in that respect in this case."

"You wouldn't?"

"I didn't say that either."

"What are you talking about?"

"You are my patient. Or client, if you prefer that word. If you are the killer, and I manage to convert you through my unique programme, I would make an impression on the scientific community."

"Is it more important to you to impress your colleagues than to solve my problems?"

"Not at all, Mrs. Worthington. What I mean is that if we assume that you are a murderess, and I manage to transform your mind via my unconventional quasi-biodynamic therapy programme, the impression on the science world would pave the way for even more groundbreaking research. What if psychopathic serial killers could be cured?"

Amy faked a smile. "I think I understand the significance of what you're saying," she lied. What were they really discussing? Whether Amy was the killer or not? Whether Dr. Fenwick's code of ethics was waterproof or not? "The police came to see me on Saturday."

"Why?" Fenwick showed no surprise.

"Well, actually, it wasn't me they wanted to see."

"They wanted to exchange a few words with your husband." Between his thumb and forefinger, the second toothpick snapped with the same loud bang as the first. Amy jumped again.

"Just formalities, they said," Amy said. "Anyway, I felt embarrassed by their unexpected visit to the store. They were CID detectives."

"Or SCDX detectives."

"What is SCDX?"

"Officially, SCDX is a division at the local CID, Blackfield's Criminal Investigation Department."

"Officially?"

"Please continue. The visitors at the store?" The psychologist reached for a third toothpick.

"They were two," she said. "A loutish, cigarette-smoking, shabbily clothed inspector and one of his men. What if they decide to get me? How on earth would your therapy programme be effective to me if I have to worry about those pesky investigators?"

"Don't worry about them, Mrs. Worthington. I'll tell you when to worry and what to worry about."

15

He sat in the kitchen, studying the photograph. The background in the photo consisted of a wooden wall plastered with movie posters. In the foreground was a Swedish girl. The same night the picture was taken, the lady would be murdered and the corpse would be mutilated, robbed of its left eye.

The camera has captured a relaxed atmosphere. The girl puts her hand on Kenneth's shoulder. The horror writer tries to look composed.

Rebecka was no fictional lady from the author's fantasy. She had been a real girl with a radiating charm, one of thousands of international students in Blackfield. By sheer coincidence, he had met the Nordic beauty.

The place is the lobby of the cinema complex Twilight Art House on Westminster Road. The time is about eight p.m. Twilight Art House has two screens (A & B), with more or less simultaneous showing times. Kenneth has just seen a horror splatter film (Screen A). Rebecka Månsson and her company, a handful of giggly girls, have seen a romantic heart-warming comedy (Screen B). The boy is recognised—part and parcel of being a famed cult horror author. They spend a few minutes together, the writer and his female fans. One of Miss Månsson's girlfriends takes two pictures with Miss Månsson's camera, the Japanese Tomy Xiao camera, which prints pictures instantly. Kenneth signs a copy for Miss Månsson and is offered the other to keep. Without hesitation, he accepts the photograph. How could he resist?

His uncle knew nothing about this. The timeframe for Uncle Ash's knowledge about the night before Halloween would start less than ten minutes later. His uncle had said that a lecturer who got on a tram near City Hall a few minutes past eight claimed that he recognised the four students on board and that they got off at Castle Square. That sounded right. Kenneth had realised it the moment his uncle had mentioned the tram witness. It takes less than ten minutes to walk from Twilight Art House to City Hall.

Why had he not mentioned to his uncle that he had met Rebecka Månsson, by chance, on the night of the murder? Because he had judged that it wasn't relevant. There were a lot of things that Uncle Ash didn't need to know.

What happened to Rebecka Månsson's signed photograph, Kenneth? Shouldn't the crime scene technicians have found the Tomy Xiao camera as well as the photo? Shouldn't a leech like your uncle Ash then know that you socialised with Miss Månsson as late as only a few hours before she was stabbed to death, perhaps even as late as one hour and forty minutes before?

And one more thing, dude: do you have an alibi for the remainder of that night?

▪

It took him fifteen minutes to drive to Burnhall Valley, one of Blackfield's western districts. The wind and the blazing rays of the sun turned the drizzle into dancing pearls. He glanced at himself in the rear-view mirror. He began to look like he felt. The breakup with Alison Mitchell, the dream girl, had corroded his view of life. The thin lines around his eyes were not as insignificant as they should have been in the face of a twenty-eight-year-old.

Did he get too little sleep? Did he invest too much of himself in his fiction? Now, what was it he remembered about his mirrored appearance? What did he remember beyond the worlds he created in his writing room?

Chris (Christine?) Henderson's address was in a street in the heart of the quiet neighbourhood. He stopped outside a sky-blue house and turned off the car engine. Of course, the house number was thirteen. He adjusted his tie knot and pulled with a trembling hand the key from the ignition.

▪

The front door was equipped with a door knocker in cast iron. He knocked. The door swung open and an aroma-rich cloud hit him in the face. The smoke-filled hall smelled like a fish-and-chip shop. Was the kitchen on fire?

The woman in the doorway was in her mid-thirties. The hairstyle was tight and tuned like a dandy brush, front teeth like a beaver's, tattooed upper arms, clown-red lips. She wore an apron and held a spatula high in one hand.

Kenneth coughed. "Good day, madam."

"What do you want? I'm terribly busy."

"My name is Kenneth Sorin."

"But why are you here? Your point, huh?"

"I got a phone call last Saturday. Via the caller ID, I traced it to this address. Chris Henderson or Christine Henderson. That's right, isn't it?"

"Why would I call you, huh?"

"There must be some misunderstanding here. It was a very old lady who called. She said she was ninety-seven years old."

"I am Mrs. Chris Henderson."

"Is Chris, to you, a short form of Christine?"

"No. My given name is Chris. What possessed you to come here and disturb me, huh?"

"I don't want to ruin your dinner, madam, but it's important to clarify this situation. How would you explain that a certain Christine called me from this house the day before yesterday?"

"Nobody phoned from this house last weekend, Mr. Risson. Nobody at all. We've been away."

"My name is still Sorin. You do see my predicament, don't you? If no one phoned from here last weekend at all, how do we explain that the phone company registered a call from here, timed at eleven twenty-two a.m., on Saturday, December the sixth?" He looked at his wristwatch. "Forty-nine hours and seven minutes ago, Mrs. Henderson."

"That's not my problem. Could you please leave before I call the police?"

Kenneth almost chuckled. "You've never heard of my uncle? If you called the police, we would find ourselves in a pretty amusing situation."

"Amusing? You have a bad taste in humour, Mr. Snirro." Mrs. Henderson took a step backward, into the hall. "You scare me."

Sometimes I scare myself, Kenneth thought. "It wasn't my intention to frighten you. I just need to sort out the predicament." He pulled out his wallet from his coat's inside pocket, took out a tear-off notepad piece of paper, held it up. "Mrs. Henderson, could you please confirm that the phone number on this sheet of paper is associated with your address."

Mrs. Henderson snatched the sheet from him. Her facial features emptied of human expression. "If this is some sort of joke, Mr. Innsor, I'm afraid I don't get it. Should be fun, huh?"

His world now looked fuzzier than he was prepared to admit. "It's not your number?"

"I haven't the faintest idea what you're talking about. What's the meaning of a blank piece of paper?"

He grabbed the sheet from the lady's fingers. In that instant, a wind cruised through the garden, a wind which drove away the sparrows and finches that were not dark enough to match the sombre shades of the afternoon. He stared at the sheet of paper. He couldn't believe what he saw, or rather what he failed to see. Mrs. Henderson was right. The piece of paper was blank.

A voice in his head contaminated his brain. He trawled his senses for answers but found none. He was convinced that he had stumbled into an impossible hallucination. He had written down Christine's phone number with a functioning ballpoint pen. He couldn't have imagined the call. Caller ID displays don't lie. Neither do phone companies.

"Christine is actually my grandmother's name," Mrs. Henderson said. "Christine Corbett."

Why didn't you mention that earlier? Kenneth thought but didn't say. "Aha. I see. Mrs. Christine Corbett. There's the explanation. It must have been your grandmother Christine who called me without your knowledge. The lady was here indeed, perhaps watering flowers on her own initiative. Not bad, considering her age. Your grandmother let herself in with the private key you had lent her, correct? You had earlier informed her about the code to the burglar alarm system."

"The explanation of what?" Mrs. Henderson's voice was drier than papyrus. "My grandmother has been dead and buried for ten years."

16

From his position in the hall, he could hear the sound from the TV in the living room. Dr. Fenwick called out: "Hello, Rachel."

The response came back: "Hi, Dad."

Her voice. So soft. So wonderful. So Amelia…

It wasn't only about the voice. Fifty percent of her genetic composition she had of course inherited from her deceased mother. Rachel *was* Amelia, in a sense. Chromosome expression mirrored biological truth. In his twenty-one-year-old daughter Rachel, Dr. Leighton Fenwick noted the DNA inheritance he wanted to see. Amelia's hot curves, Amelia's sea-green eyes, Amelia's powder-white hair, the outline of Amelia's breasts beneath the fabric of a bathrobe or a nightgown.

He found her stretched out on the sofa. She knew that he was observing her, studying her. He could study his daughter for hours on end. He now thought of his favourite fantasy—to oversee the cloning of several copies of Rachel. He would get one Rachel for each night of the week—six clones plus the original. The seven identical ladies would realise his most extravagant desires. Money, and his contacts in biotechnology and related fields, would fulfill his ultimate dream.

His thoughts dispelled. He was back in real time and space. Rachel wore her peony red bathrobe. His eyes removed the bathrobe. He saw her naked.

He put down his briefcase, loosened his tie and walked into the living room. "You smell wonderful. What shampoo is that?"

"The same as always." Her hair was still damp. With her fingers, she wiped away a drop of water which rolled down the back of one thigh. Leighton Fenwick would have enjoyed capturing that rolling drop with his tongue.

His eyes terminated the trick. Rachel was still in her bathrobe. But her legs were indeed naked. The fabric had slid up against her delicious buttocks.

"I guess you've already had dinner," he said. "I know it's late."

"Mmm." Her eyes were glued to the TV screen.

"Any leftovers?"

"There's grilled chicken with chips and coleslaw in the fridge."

"That's terrific." He began to move towards the kitchen. "Do you want something, sweetie pie?"

"An orange soft drink."

Ten minutes later he returned with microwaved food, a can of light beer, a glass of orange soft drink. Rachel scooted over so he could sit on the sofa. He sat as close to her as possible and felt her body heat. A tingling sensation fluttered like butterfly wings in the pit of his stomach.

She looked at him. "How was your day?"

"Every day's the same, sweetie pie."

"Every day since Mum died, you mean?"

"You know I want you to refrain from talking about your mother."

"Sorry. But sometimes I can't help it."

"I love you, Rachel. You're all I have."

"You have your psycho clinic, too."

"Psych clinic, sweetie pie. Not psycho clinic."

"Whatever."

"You're staying home tonight?"

"Something you wanted to talk about, Dad?"

"Only a routine matter."

Rachel's pretty mouth narrowed. "You're not going away to a conference again, are you?"

"I am, but not too soon. I've been invited to give a talk at a conference in Bristol."

"When?"

"Not until February." He looked for her smile to return. "Hey, sweetie pie." He touched her cheek. "It won't be the first time I'm away for work, right?"

"I'll be fine. No problem." The smile was back on her lips. "Though sometimes I sense loneliness, in particular, at night. Whenever you're away, the nights appear longer and darker than normal."

"How long and how dark is a 'normal night' on a planet with an inclined axis of rotation? You're not a child anymore, Rachel. You're a woman. Young indeed, but an adult."

"I just said I'll be fine." She kissed him on

the mouth. "I suppose I should be proud of you. Not every girl has a dad who's a famous psychologist." Her breath smelled of orange soft drink. "When you're away in February, I'll be at the cinema with Liz every night."

"With Liz?"

"Mmm. She's my best friend. Why do you ask?"

"Oh, nothing." The taste of her kiss lingered on his mouth.

"Was there anything else you wanted to talk about now?"

"Christmas. Just another routine matter. Same procedure as last year?"

"You're right, Dad." She hugged him. "The same procedure as every year."

"There's something else, too."

"I know. Isn't there always something else?"

He wondered if she was referring to his rock-hard erection. "I'm worried about what's happening in our city, Rachel."

She put a hand on his thigh. "Who's the killer?"

"Is it that obvious what I'm thinking about?"

"Mmm."

"How would I know?"

"You're Leighton Fenwick, the great shrink."

"Don't use the slang word 'shrink'."

"Sorry."

"I'm worried, Rachel."

"Why?"

"Isn't that natural? Worried like any parent

of a daughter registered at a university where female students are murdered left and right. Did you know those girls? I mean, do you know who they were?"

"No. None of them." Rachel squeezed his hand. Then she rose from the sofa and moved to the fruit bowl that sat atop the piano.

How would he be able to live if he lost her? No, losing Rachel was unthinkable. Would not happen. Not even in a nightmare.

She grabbed an apple from the fruit bowl. "I can take care of myself, Dad." She nibbled at the fruit.

"I know you can, sweetie pie. You're a Fenwick. But that's not the point."

"So, what's the point?" She joined him again on the sofa, eating the apple.

He turned towards her. "Maybe you take care of yourself too well sometimes."

"I'm not seeing other boys."

"I know. I'm not worried."

"That's good, Dad. There's no reason to worry." A peppy giggle flew from her lips.

"I'm going to bed now. Are you coming?"

"After the TV show."

"Don't stay up too long."

"I won't. Another twenty minutes."

"Could you wear your bluebell-blue nightgown tonight, sweetie pie?"

"Which one? I have two bluebell-blue ones."

He pondered for a moment. "The one I bought for your twenty-first birthday."

"If that's what you want."

"The nightgown is sexy. You look nice in it." He rose and turned away. "I love you, Rachel."

"I love you too, Dad. Do you want me to wear something else as well?"

He considered her question. Something about his deceased wife's red high-heeled shoes spurred his creativity and imagination, then he rejected the idea. "Only the nightgown and nothing additional, sweetie pie. Nothing additional at all."

■

Leighton Fenwick went upstairs to their bedroom. Before he undressed, he was going to make a few preparations for Christmas. Even though his Rachel was no longer a child, they still kept the tradition of Christmas stockings. But then the Fenwick family wasn't conventional. As a cutting-edge scientist, Dr. Fenwick dismissed the conventional, that is, the unimaginative. He embraced the unconventional, that is, the innovatory.

In their shared bedroom, he walked over to her chest of drawers and pulled out the top drawer. He picked out a pair of stockings. They felt smooth and soft between his eager fingers. His nostrils captured the stockings' discreet scent of perfume. The heat in his groin returned. He then selected another pair of stockings—a brighter shade—and sniffed at them, too. The sensational scent of perfume, the same as earlier, invaded him again.

He pushed in the top drawer and pulled out the middle one. Here she kept her bras and knickers. His fingers wandered across the neatly folded bras. He chose a purple-and-white one. Then he focused his attention on the stacks of knickers. He picked up two pairs of knickers, mint-green and lemon-yellow respectively. He recognised them. For one thing, he had played with them before. Moreover, he had seen Rachel take them off or put them on in the bathroom. A grin tugged at his lips. He pushed in the drawer and went downstairs to the kitchen.

From his briefcase, he took out the wrapped Christmas presents. A bezel-set diamond bracelet. Emerald earrings with silver spikes. A gold necklace with a ruby stone. A bottle of luxury perfume. The wrapping papers glittered like veils of stars under the kitchen lighting. He placed the presents in the stockings, a single gift in each of the four stockings.

He pulled out a box of chocolate truffles from the freezer. The truffles were now deep-frozen, hard as rocks, hard as his penis. But after some time at room temperature, in his daughter's knickers, the truffles would adopt a soft and sticky texture.

The stickier the chocolate truffles, the tastier.

17

She stops and looks over her shoulder, squinting through the swirls of wintry showers. No one there.

She continues towards the bus stop just ahead, her hair billowing in the wind. The short skirt that protrudes beneath the jacket is flapping like a mini-sail. The snow-spattered rain shines like sprays of mercury under the alleyway lighting. She could do without the sound of her high-heeled shoes clicking against the pavement. The more she thinks about it, the scarier it sounds, step by step.

Certain now that someone is somewhere behind her, she stops again. “Hello?” She waits. “Is anyone there?” No answer. The night in the street belongs to the whirlwind and the vortex of sleet.

Then, rejoicings in the distance. People leaving a pub or a restaurant. Their laughter is softening, drowning, dying in the snow-mixed shadows.

On the concrete-and-glass horizon towers the landmark Millennium Arts Centre (MAC). Soon she will reach a tram stop.

Nimbler steps. High-heels clicking. She crosses Crowhill Gate, hurrying past the famous museum.

A silhouette detaches itself from the darkness. She shrieks. The metal blade is scratching, slashing, ripping her up. Blood is flying. The cry is spurting.

18

The chessboard rotated through the dream like a flying saucer. In its centre point loomed the ringing phone. The cut-up fictitious character lay on one of the chessboard's edges. She was naked. Suzanne's face was as expressionless as blank paper. Blood streamed from a punctured breast. Yellowish puss was dripping from the empty eye socket.

Mr. Frank's head popped out of the telephone handset. "Doesn't he see how it all fits together? If he doesn't see, he risks becoming a case for SCDX."

Kenneth's eyelids fluttered and the bedroom gained incomprehensible dimensions. He floated in space, fumbled for the ringing phone, got hold of it. "Yes?"

"It's me."

No, it isn't Jeanne Russell. No such luck.

He blinked. "Dear Uncle Ash... do you have any idea what time it is?"

"How fast can you get out of bed, boy? There's something I want to show you."

He groaned. "Your Christmas mood is unbeatable. Why didn't you become a priest?"

"Step out onto the street and do it now. I'll pick you up in my car in less than five minutes."

■

The corpse looked like a horror film special effect on the concrete in front of the Millennium Arts Centre. Gusts of wind attacked the ground and the surrounding architecture. The whirlwinds along the road stirred up dead maple leaves and threw them through the morning air.

"I thought I was external," Kenneth said, "that I wasn't allowed to be here."

"You're external indeed," his uncle said. "You're not allowed to be here. In effect, you're not here."

"I don't understand."

"You don't exist, Ken. Figuratively speaking, you're as fictional as the characters you write about in your horror novels. We have resources to cover up your person. Furthermore, we have resources to keep anything a secret or to silence anybody."

We? Kenneth wondered. SCDX? Blackfield is a sovereign police state? "Do we know who she is, or was?" He squinted against the sun. The morning sunshine was marginally warmer than moonlight.

"The student ID card says Suzanne Wheeler."

You're a superb chess player. And Suzanne?

What do you know about Suzanne?

Preserve our conversation, young man.

"Wheeler... The sixth victim." Kenneth stared at nothing. "You're certain about the surname?"

Uncle Ash frowned. "What a strange question."

"I apologise. Strange question indeed."

"Are you all right, Ken?"

"The alphabet theory is still valid."

"As if that would cheer me up."

"Another local Blackfield girl."

"How did you know that? *I* knew, but how can you know already?"

"I didn't know. I guessed. A lot of students go home to family and friends for Christmas. Suzanne Wheeler was obviously still here, so I guessed she was a local girl."

"I see. You guessed."

"Surveillance photographs?"

"None."

"Why no photos at all? Surveillance cameras sit everywhere in the city. At least three camera eyes are scanning this particular part of Crowhill Gate and the main entrance to MAC."

"We don't know." Uncle Ash lit a cigarette. "The situation here is the same as those in connection with the previous murders. Not a single surveillance camera has recorded anything that we could use."

Unless SCDX covered it up, Kenneth thought.

"Kenneth Sorin looks sick. How is he today? Did he get any sleep at all last night?" Mr. Frank's boisterous voice was unmistakable.

"Merry Christmas to you too, Mr. Frank."

The chief inspector wore a black raincoat and held a folded umbrella. "No one has seen anything and no one has heard anything, as if the citizens suffered collective blindness and deafness. Crowhill Gate is one of the major thoroughfares, for Christ's sake. Someone must have noticed something."

"Could the cadaver have been dumped here?" Uncle Ash asked.

Mr. Frank shook his head. "Nothing is pointing in that direction, Ash. The murder was committed right outside the gallery entrance hall, where the corpse is now."

A crime scene technician shouted: "There's an object in the victim's hand!"

Mr. Frank didn't move. Uncle Ash hurried over to the corpse and crouched beside it.

"What is it, Ash?" Mr. Frank called.

"A tie clip, sir."

▪

"Irish make," Uncle Ash said, "fourteen carat gold, with an engraving: P.W."

"Philip Worthington?" Mr. Frank said.

"It wouldn't surprise me in the least," Kenneth said, "if Miss Wheeler was, like Miss Stanfield, a regular customer at Worthington's Elegance."

"The company's billing history is going to give us the answer to that in zero time," Mr. Frank said.

"He attacks Miss Wheeler," Uncle Ash said, puffing on his cigarette. "In the fight for her life, the girl yanks at the man's clothes. At some point during the scuffle, the tie clip ends up in her fist. The circumstances couldn't have looked worse for Worthington had he lost a business card at the murder scene."

"Assuming that the tie clip is his," Kenneth said.

"If it belongs to Worthington," Mr. Frank said, "it won't be difficult to prove it."

SCDX has resources to prove anything, Kenneth thought. SCDX has resources to determine what will happen and what won't happen.

"What's on your mind, Ken?" said Uncle Ash.

"Philip Worthington's business trip to Amsterdam can't save his alibi," Kenneth said. "The return flight's arrival time was just over sixty hours ago."

"Plenty of time to get back to the city," Mr. Frank said, "and kill the girl."

"A theoretical possibility," Kenneth said.

Uncle Ash seemed to study his nephew. Why?

Initials were tumbling about in Kenneth's mind like lottery tickets in a raffle wheel. But not P.W.

Not at all P.W.

19

He considered hanging his daughter's underwear on the Christmas tree, like some exciting Christmas decorations. But of course he rejected the idea. Only a perverted man would do such a thing.

Dr. Fenwick fished out a sticky chocolate truffle from the mint-green knickers. He went out into the hall, munching on the truffle. "Come here, Rachel."

"What is it, Dad? I'm busy, reading."

"Please, sweetie pie. Come over here. To the hall mirror. Look in the mirror."

From a tight angle, he observed how she got up from the sofa in the living room. She stuck her bare feet into a pair of slippers. Silent as a fairy, she appeared in the hall. He inhaled a pinch of Rachel's perfume, which gave the chocolate that was melting on his tongue an exotic touch.

She placed her soft hand on his shoulder. "What is it, Dad? What is it with the mirror?"

His lower lip trembled. He tried to hide it.

The world was a mystery. He was the renowned Leighton Fenwick, a man with complete control of and insight into the human psyche, but his own daughter Rachel made him weak at the knees. This fact, he argued, that his own offspring marked the only exception to his total control, was the very reason he felt so strongly about her. "Look in the mirror I said, sweetie pie."

"Okay. I'm looking. So, what?"

"What do you see, sweetie pie?"

"What do you think? I see you, me, the hallway runner, outdoor clothing on its hangers, shoes and boots, the three chests of drawers and the Miró paintings on the opposite wall."

"Focus on yourself."

"Me?"

"Yes, that's right." He didn't want to confuse her. "What do you see, Rachel?"

"I see a slightly overweight girl in a T-shirt, jeans and slippers."

"Not at all." He placed an arm around her waist. "You see an exceptional lady in every way—and perhaps more than you will ever realise."

She rolled her eyes. "Dad, what on earth are you talking about?"

"The positive pole of stubbornness is determination. Determined people are smart, but don't get too smart. Think hard before making important decisions."

She sighed. "Do you now have second thoughts about my choice of university courses? Good gravy, Mr. Expert Psychologist is examining my 'stubborn' mind." She drew aside half a metre.

His fingers slid over his daughter's satin ribbon waistband. In a gentle manner, he pulled her to him again. She didn't resist. He kissed her forehead. "There, there, don't worry, sweetie pie. Your choice of courses is superb and the way you look after your studies should serve as an example to be imitated. As far as I know—and I know a thing or two about what happens in the academic world—you're the top scorer in every exam."

"Not every."

He showed his patriarchal smile. "Close to."

"Now, how do you know that? Have you been checking up on me?"

"It would be easy for me to do that, Rachel, but I don't have to. Academic colleagues often mention what a talented daughter I have."

"Oh. So, what is it, then?"

"I'm worried about you, Rachel. Strange events characterise our city. Horrifying events. Murders."

"I know." She turned away from the mirror, kicked off her slippers, put on a pair of socks and stepped into a pair of running shoes.

"Where are you going, sweetie pie?"

"The library."

"Which one?"

"City Library."

"The City Library has reduced opening hours during the Christmas week."

"I know that, Dad." She donned a jacket.

"Lunch at home or are you going out?"

"I'm going out for lunch. If you don't mind."

"What time?"

"Twelve o'clock."

"With whom?"

"Liz."

"Which restaurant?"

"We haven't decided yet. We'll just take a quick meal somewhere and talk about what film to see at the cinema tomorrow night."

"I understand." He pondered. "How are you getting to the city centre, sweetie pie?"

"Tram."

"If you want money for a taxi, just tell me."

"I know."

"Do you want me to drive you?"

"Thanks for the offer but it isn't necessary."

"As you wish." He paused again. "Take care of yourself, Rachel. I love you so much."

"I love you too, Dad."

She gave him an affectionate deep kiss and left the house. Leighton Fenwick stood in the doorway, watching the sunlight envelope his daughter.

Then she was gone.

20

He knew he wasn't crazy. Or at least he thought he knew. Christine, dead or alive, proved that the case was extraordinary. His conscience asserted that the case would be solved, that it was only a matter of time. The only thing he was pleased with at present was his work on the new novel. The text was rolling out of his mind and down on paper with the natural flow of a waterfall. He was tempted to fictionalise

Christine Corbett and introduce her into the book as a new character. Could he do it?

■

When he left the SCDX department, a new head-ache began to torture him. The painkillers were at home in the bathroom cabinet. The lift's descent to the ground floor took a thousand years.

He was passing through the lobby on his way out of the complex when a voice called his name. His thoughts were dispelled like fog in a breeze.

"Dr. Sorin."

He stopped and turned around.

Like a chessboard queen she moved diagonally across the black-and-white-checkered lobby floor.

"Good afternoon, Miss Russell."

"I'm on my way out, too." She stroked away a strand of blonde hair from her cheek. "How about a drink in town?"

"Do I look like I need one?"

"Absolutely."

"I haven't had my most phenomenal day."

"I was joking. Now, are we going?"

Jeanne Russell looked like a movie star dressed for her grand entrance via the red carpet. Today she wore an elegant gown, violet-green as a swallow's wing, and a graphite-grey coat. The dark necklace was the same as before, that is, before his dream about her last night, a dream in which she wore a different necklace altogether, a necklace with ivory-white and burgundy-red pearls. How strange.

You should head home and write on your new book, a voice in his head stated. *You shouldn't hang out with Mr. Frank's secretary*. What he said was: "I guess I could do with a drink, Miss Russell."

"Marvellous."

"On one condition."

"What's that?"

"That you right now stop calling me Mr. or Dr. Sorin. My name is Kenneth."

"Okay. On one condition."

"What's that?"

She smiled. "That you right now stop calling me Miss Russell. My name is Jeanne. Have we reached a new agreement?"

"I suppose so. Despite lack of formal contract."

"Let's go then."

"Any particular place?"

"How about Trix Bar?"

Theoretically, he was in a hurry to get home to his workroom. Practically, in Jeanne's company, he was in no hurry at all.

■

The daylight trickled out of the street outside the café-restaurant windows. December darkness ruled again. Trix Bar was getting packed out. How many SCDX agents were circulating in the crowd?

"What's bothering you, Kenneth?"

He tried to think. "Who's asking? The private individual Jeanne? Or the SCDX secretary Jeanne?"

"Don't use that word."

"What word?"

"You know what I mean. I'm a CID secretary."

"You know more than you let me believe. You are shrewd but want to appear as the employee who is moderately interested in subjects beyond a formal job description."

"What an analysis."

"Lots of unofficial information passes your way."

"Arduous to be Inspector Sorin's nephew, uh?"

Her one-liner sounded like a reproach, as if he were living an arduous double life, using his kinship position as a cover for his compulsive analyses of young women.

"Have you ever considered getting married?"

That was no SCDX question. "Almost twice."

"Almost? Twice?" She giggled.

"Anyhow, I have proposed twice." He omitted the detail that it had been to the same girl on both occasions. "The first time was laughable. I was ten and so was she, a girl at the same school." One second-long memory flashback depicted a ten-year-old Alison Mitchell with crimson-red bows in her pigtails. "The second time was based on serious consideration." The image of a twenty-five-year-old Alison re-emerged in his mind's eye.

"You want to talk about it, Kenneth?"

"Rather not."

"Sorry."

"And you?"

Jeanne sipped her drink. "Divorced. Once."

"I see."

"He was a writer. And a psychopath."

"You're implying a connection?"

"Perhaps I have my reasons."

"Writers spend most of their waking hours all alone in a room. This self-imposed isolation is part and parcel of the job. It's required that we are crazy."

"Fascinating."

"Have you read anything by me?"

"Only *The Blood-Red Shadow*."

The book she mentioned was his second-best selling so far. An international bestseller, translated into three dozen languages.

"What did you think of it?" he asked.

"Not a favourite. If you don't mind me saying so."

"I don't mind at all, Jeanne. You're entitled to an opinion. To me, your negative reaction to the book is better than indifference. The writer's job is to arouse emotions. The stronger the emotions the better. And it would be boring if all readers felt the same about a particular book. Oscar Wilde said that when the critics disagree, the artist is in accord with himself."

She raised the corners of her mouth.

He wanted to trust her. He wished she was here as a private individual. He wished she could keep a secret. Her beauty manipulated his will. He decided to test her. "Uncle Ash and Mr. Frank are interested in certain initials associated with the sixth murder scene: P.W."

"And you aren't interested?"

"For me, right now, it's about S.W."

"Why?"

"Because of Christine, the very old woman who called me about three weeks ago. Except Christine died ten years ago. I got that piece of information from the granddaughter. Thereafter I verified the fact, checking the death certificate and the place of the grave."

She offered a sugar-sweet smile. "Are you living in a fantasy world, Kenneth?"

"We're all living in a fantasy world. The balance between fiction and reality has shifted in the last decades. The functions of reality and fiction have more and more been reversed. Our everyday lives are pervaded by countless fictions: advertisement; politics as a branch of advertisement; filtered news reporting; overhyped consumer goods; cyberspace; TV as a substitute for real experience. We're all living in a huge novel, a fantasy without an end."

Jeanne's smile faded a notch. "It sounds like the real Kenneth has inspired the fictitious character Kenneth from a novel. Or vice versa."

He ignored her salty comment. "Christine said I must look inside my own person to find the key to the mystery. And she was aware of the new book I'm writing, including the characters' names."

"Now you're joking."

"Unfortunately not. Christine was familiar with my interest in chess. In my new horror thriller, a female student and chess player is murdered. The character's name is Suzanne Wright."

"This lady Christine knew that?"

"Right. And thereafter the Blackfield student Suzanne Wheeler was murdered. Do you see what's bothering me?"

Jeanne nodded. "Suzanne Wright and Suzanne Wheeler have the name initials, S.W., in common."

"And they have the same given name, spelt the same way, with a zed as the third letter."

"Couldn't all this be coincidence?"

"Let's be careful, now. There are a number of unanswered questions here and it's important we distinguish them. I agree that a fictional character and a real murder victim can have identical given names and personal initials by sheer coincidence. I also agree that a fictitious death can reflect a real death by sheer coincidence. However, none of those potential coincidences is relevant."

"Oh."

"That someone who's dead and buried for ten years called me three weeks ago is also beside the point. What's essential here is what she said."

"The ghost? The phantom? The witch?"

"Whatever she is, or was, or represented, she didn't lie. That's what's important. She showed her knowledge-oriented power by retelling details of my new novel, details that no one but I, the author, can possibly know at present. Story elements and plot developments that are still unknown to my agent and to my publishers in London and New York."

"Can you prove that it was something other than a bizarre dream?"

"The evidence disappeared."

"Stolen?" The sound of SCDX was back in her voice.

"Evaporated, disintegrated, eliminated. The call is no longer registered at the phone company. My note with the phone number has faded, as if I had used invisible ink. I don't expect you to believe a word of this. The only thing I ask of you is to listen."

"I'm listening."

"Good. I mean, thank you. I needed to talk to someone."

"It seems you have confidence in me, Kenneth."

In Miss Russell's company, time was as volatile as ether.

Her smartphone beeped. "Excuse me."

"No problem."

She checked the SMS then returned the phone to her handbag. "Unfortunately, I have to go now, Kenneth. It's getting late."

The right time to report to the SCDX boss? The text message was from Mr. Frank, wasn't it? Have I become a case for SCDX? Who are you, Jeanne Russell? "It was fun while it lasted," he said. "Time for me to go, too. I have some writing to do."

They left Trix Bar.

"Let me make it up to you, Jeanne."

She raised her eyebrows. "What do you mean?"

"You said you found no pleasure in reading my book, *The Blood-Red Shadow*. Let me make it up to you by offering you dinner sometime."

Something reflected in the girl's eyes. Perhaps nothing but streetlights. "It isn't impossible. If you don't have another book to recommend."

"One of mine?"

"You decide. I look forward to the surprise."

"Either a book or dinner? Or both?"

A smile wiggled the corners of her mouth. "Are all your novels set in Blackfield?"

"So far. But I have plans to write books that are set in new environments."

"If Blackfield is the city of dark secrets, it may be partly your fault."

He buttoned his raincoat. "Which way are you going? How are you getting home?"

"Bus from Colvin Street."

"I take a tram from Black Square."

"Good night, Kenneth."

"Good night, Jeanne."

He fantasised that he kissed her.

He stood still on the pavement, watching her until she was out of sight, absorbed by the night.

21

Uncle Ash flicked cigarette ash in the direction of an empty Coca-Cola can that was taped onto one side of the gearbox. Most of the ash landed on the car mat. The battered Audi jumped a red light and kept whizzing. "Listen, Ken. I've done some digging in Worthington's history and found a pretty juicy story that had been buried in it."

"Go ahead."

"Worthington's Elegance has been in business for decades," Uncle Ash said through a cloud of blue smoke. "The owners, Philip and Amy Worthington, have six branches spread across the country. Each branch manager is a Worthington. The immense Blackfield store is the company's flagship, opened thirty years ago. But the firm's history is much older than that. Philip Worthington, technically the sole owner, inherited the company from his father, Clive Worthington, nearly twenty-five years ago, and four months before Philip's thirty-first birthday.

"Clive Worthington's death was premature. The circumstances were mysterious, to say the least, but a crime—a murder—could never be proven. As the new owner, Philip immediately altered the company's structure, including its workforce, and changed its name from 'Drake and Worthington's Fashion' to the egocentric 'Worthington's Elegance'. Thus, he disrespectfully rejected the name Alexander Drake, his father's closest colleague for forty-two years and the son of Edgar Drake, the founder of the original company a hundred years ago. What do you think?"

"I think that this Mr. Philip Worthington might have been born without a conscience."

Uncle Ash nodded. "Like a murderer."

"Anything more about the story?"

"Indeed. I dug very deep. If it wasn't for Clive Worthington's and Alexander Drake's phenomenal reputation in their line of work, Philip would have had to push even harder to reach his current level."

"You mean Philip Worthington is overrated?"

"No. Not overrated. But his father's millions, and his father's professional network, made Philip's own success possible."

"What happened to Alexander Drake's estate?"

"Drake was childless and married to the job. His will stated that his fifty percent of the company stay with the company he lived for. The man died from a stroke twenty-eight years ago."

"So Clive Worthington got everything."

"At least he got it all in control. Until his own passing only three years later."

Kenneth reflected on the story. "Take a rich man, a rich wife and throw in a mistress with dubious intentions. What do you get?"

"A destructive drama triangle."

■

Uncle Ash parked his old beat-up car in the wrong direction and with two wheels on the pavement. He opened the glovebox and took out a used, outdated parking coupon from a stack of old speeding tickets, as well as old parking coupons. Beside the stack lay a loaded pistol. To keep the gun in the car's glovebox was hardly legal, Kenneth guessed. Unless SCDX was the law. Uncle Ash placed the ancient coupon on the dashboard. He grinned. "In this neighbourhood, the parking enforcement officers aren't too zealous."

"Aren't you here on business?"

"Yeah, but I don't want it to appear that way."

"Don't you lock the car doors?"

"In this swanky district, nobody would

think of stealing my car. Now, let's walk up to the house."

▪

Philip Worthington. In his mid-fifties. Square face. Triangular nose. Bull neck. The liquorice-black hair was slicked-back like the hair on a film gangster's head. A salesman's grin pulled at his lips. He wore a dusk-dark suit, a rosé-coloured tie, gold-plated cufflinks and black shoes that shone with the same intensity as the paintwork of the Mercedes in the driveway.

Mr. Worthington and Uncle Ash were sitting in armchairs. Kenneth stayed in a silent background, standing, and already fascinated by the titles in Mr. Worthington's bookcases. Nobody paid attention to Kenneth and he liked that. Here he found himself in an excellent position to keep an eye on the two older gentlemen.

"How did your father really die, on that night twenty-five years ago?" Uncle Ash asked. "Rumour has it that circumstances were mysterious. Nothing suspicious was proven. Though, back then, forensic science was less developed than today."

"I warn you, Inspector. Stick to the subject."

"I try." Uncle Ash paused. "How come?"

"How come what?"

"That you had expected a visit from the police one of these days. It was the first thing you said to me."

"What game are you playing, Inspector?"

"No game at all. I asked a question. It's part and parcel of the job. To ask questions and to listen to responses. To begin with. Sometimes you have to fire one or another bullet, too. At Blackfield CID I'm internally known as the best shooter. I constantly win shooting competitions with firearms category pistols. Though, on the job, I don't shoot too many people dead. It happens only sometimes."

"Congratulations, Inspector. Your boss must be proud of you. But you haven't come here to shoot me. You want me to confess to murder."

"Not if you don't want to. A forced confession is useless to me."

"You've been snooping around while I was on a business trip abroad. My wife told me. That's why I believed that the police would show up on my doorstep, sooner or later. It isn't official, yet not top secret, that the young woman who was murdered on the evening of Christmas Day was my mistress. When I read about Suzanne's death in the papers, I realised I would be involved in the investigation."

"There's another thing as well."

"What could that be, Inspector?"

"A piece of evidence linking you to the scene of the murder of Suzanne Wheeler."

"I don't understand what you're talking about."

"The tie clip that you've been missing since the evening of Christmas Day."

"What tie clip?"

"P.W. Your initials, sir."

Mr. Worthington laughed. "My dear Inspector Sorin. There must be millions of people in the world who have the initials P.W."

"But only one person could have left a certain fingerprint on that tie clip. You see, we found two prints. One belongs to the victim while the other is unknown. If the second could be identified as yours, we wouldn't even need the engraved initials."

In the background, Kenneth smiled.

Mr. Worthington's face paled. "Fingerprint…"

"And now we just need your cooperation."

"Hmm…"

"An innocent man wouldn't hesitate."

Mr. Worthington glanced at the closed office door. "I'm prepared to cooperate, Inspector. If you intend to check my fingerprints, I can tell you right away. The tie clip you mention is mine."

22

The girl strangled her tormentor and cut off his head with a metal wire.

Elizabeth screamed.

"Don't be so sensitive," Rachel whispered.

"Huh? It's really scary."

Elizabeth's cell phone beeped.

A voice from behind: "*Turn that fucking mobile off, you idiot.*"

Elizabeth squinted. The darkness of the cinema denied her the possibility of discerning the man who had yelled at her. All she saw were silhouettes. She opened her handbag. It contained a hundred items. The phone kept beeping in the gloom, just when the Japanese horror film *Audition* reached its violent and gory climax.

"*Turn that fucking phone off, you numbskull! Do it right fucking now!*"

She found the phone in a corner at the bottom of the handbag, beneath a notepad and a hairspray bottle. With a fingernail, she knocked on the OFF button. Then the cinema screen went black. The end credits began to roll.

"Gruesome movie, wasn't it?" Elizabeth stroked Rachel's cheek.

"The ending was gory and nasty, Liz. Otherwise, the film wasn't particularly frightening. I liked the film's first half better than the second. The first half was romantic and fun."

"The first half was great."

"She was snazzy, wasn't she?"

"Snazzy as a geisha. Her white dress made me think of your favourite nightgown, Rach."

"Dad prefers my bluebell-blue one."

Elizabeth tittered. "Which one?"

"The one he bought for my last birthday. And he likes watching me put it on." Rachel rolled her eyes.

Elizabeth giggled again. "You're so funny, Rach. You're so funny. What a dirty little joke!"

"Dad also likes watching me touch myself."

Elizabeth howled with laughter.

The audience rose and disappeared towards the exit. Queues formed on the stairs of the central aisle. Liz Peckerton and Rach Fenwick were still in their seats, nibbling the remains of the popcorn, sipping the last drops of Coke and listening to the soundtrack that played throughout the end credits.

"I wonder why Asian films shown here seldom have English-language closing credits," Rachel said. "What a long stream of unintelligible symbols. Now I have to learn Japanese."

"What would be the point of translating the end credits of exotic films?" Elizabeth snatched a brush from her handbag and dragged it through her long wavy locks of hair. "Not many cinemagoers care one bit about closing credits. Look around you. There's nobody here but us."

"End credits don't exist without a reason, Liz. They're meant to be read. The film experience isn't complete until the last frame has passed through the projector's image window. Leaving the cinema before the projector dies and the lighting returns is like leaving a seminar five minutes before the end and thus missing the speaker's special thanks to everyone who helped and contributed in connection with the presented work. It's rude, Liz."

"Oh, I've never thought of that. The soundtrack is cool though."

"Yeah, if the soundtrack is cool during the end credits, it's worth staying here until the very end anyway." Rachel kissed Elizabeth on the lips.

"Hi, girls. Ready to get cosy in bed, uh?"

The guy stood in the row just behind them. His breath smelled of booze. By all means, this wasn't the guy who had shouted at Liz. This guy's voice was different to that of the hot-tempered moron.

"Get fucked, arsewipe," Rachel said.

The stranger smiled. "I get fucked every night, sweetheart."

Elizabeth said nothing. She wrinkled her nose.

"Dear ladies, my name is Benjamin. Benjamin Smith. You can call me Ben, as my friends do, since you and I are going to be very intimate friends." The guy stared at Rach, grinning like a vulture. "I can give you a thing that your girlfriend can't."

Elizabeth pulled at Rachel's arm. "Let's go."

"Yup, that's right, let's go." The stranger's gaze was on Rachel again. "You heard that, cutie? The girl with the carrot-coloured hair is already horny. I am your property, ladies. Handsome me. It must be your lucky day. Let's do it in the toilets."

Rachel sighed. "Yes, Liz, it's about time to go."

The stranger laughed. "Wait a minute,

hotties. You don't know what you're missing out on."

"Trust us, we know," Rachel called.

Elizabeth snorted. "Carrot-coloured? My hair is actually ruby-red!"

23

"How was your relationship with Miss Wheeler?" Uncle Ash picked a cigarette from a pocket of his scruffy corduroy jacket.

"I loved her." Mr. Worthington puffed. "Could you refrain from smoking in my house, Inspector?"

Uncle Ash put the cigarette in his mouth and took out his lighter. "Your conscience okayed the relationship, right?"

"It was an intimate relationship between two adults. It's no crime to love someone who is half as old as I am."

"Would your wife agree with that?" Uncle Ash flicked the lighter.

"The cigarette, Inspector! And leave my wife out of this conversation."

Uncle Ash smiled and put the lighter back in his jacket pocket. He kept the unlit cigarette between his teeth. "With how many female customers do you have an awesome relationship?"

"What sort of question is that? I have a professional relationship with *all* my customers.

My job is to sell clothes to people who—unlike you, Inspector—don't want to look trampish."

"Do you mean I'm unfashionable?"

"Bottom line: I'm a professional salesman and therefore I can't afford to be impolite to customers."

"Limitless politeness towards the pretty ones, no doubt."

"You don't give up, do you? You keep perverting my words to make them fit into one of your corrupt structures of evidence."

"Do you feel under pressure already? That was bad. For you, that is. This is only the beginning of my agenda."

"Did you say you were leaving?"

"Not yet. Tell me about the tie clip."

Worthington puffed. "I loved Suzanne. And she loved me. In late November, we started talking about Christmas gifts. I planned to give her a dress from my own store and Suzanne wanted to buy me something that was engraved with my initials. She had a few suggestions. A watch. Cufflinks. A pen. A tie-pin. I liked the last idea best of all. You see, I already have two watches, three ballpoint pens and four pairs of cufflinks engraved with my initials. Suzanne wondered whether it mattered if I knew in advance what I would get. I replied that it didn't."

"How did your fingerprint end up on it?"

"We were together when she chose my gift in a city centre store. I must have picked it up. Yes, I remember now. I held it, but only for a second."

"It only takes a fraction of a second—a contact—to leave a print. When did you exchange the gifts?"

"Nice try, Inspector!" Worthington glowered. "We never made it. We wanted to meet as soon as I could get away from the bone-crushing boredom at the in-laws."

"Had you and Miss Wheeler planned to meet on Boxing Day?"

"As soon as we could find the time to be alone together. It would have been on Boxing Day but I had to change it to the twenty-seventh. Too late I tried to contact Suzanne regarding the change. She never knew." Worthington's eyes clouded. "Fate guaranteed that we would never meet again."

"How can you be in two places at once? How much did you pay your in-laws to back your alibi?"

Worthington raised an index finger. "I'm going to file a complaint with BPS about your behaviour."

Uncle Ash smiled. "I'll make sure you get the right complaints form. Now, the girl squeezed your tie clip at the same moment she was stabbed to death. How would you explain that?"

"I have no idea."

"Give it a shot."

Worthington appeared to hesitate. "When the maniac attacked her, she might have had her hand in a jacket pocket, where the tie clip already was."

"Why would she have the tie clip in her pocket?"

"As I've said, the original idea was to meet the following day to exchange Christmas gifts."

"If it was a gift, why wasn't it wrapped?"

Worthington shrugged. "Maybe she wanted to wrap it herself the following morning."

"The store offered no gift-wrapping service?"

"How would I know?"

"You were there. Or at least you said you were."

"I don't know whether the gift store provided a wrapping service. Go find out yourself."

"Are you lying, Worthington?"

"It's beneath my dignity to answer that question."

"Suppose you and Miss Wheeler, in actual fact, had exchanged gifts, not before the twenty-third, the date of your return flight's arrival, but before late evening on the twenty-fifth. Suppose she happened to pull that tie clip from your tie during the scuffle that occurred when you assaulted her."

"Not true! I loved Suzanne."

"We have only your word."

"I'm a man of my word."

"That's what we're checking."

"Do what you have to do, Inspector, but keep me out of it. Go pester someone else."

"Annabelle. You socialised with her, too?"

"I've had no relationship with an Annabelle."

"You mean professional or sexual? I didn't ask whether you were fucking her, did I?"

"There you go again, Inspector."

"The cut-out eye? Any comment?"

"No comment."

"How strange that young female customers in your clothing store get stabbed to death after dark."

"At Worthington's Elegance, we're conducting a popular and successful business. I'm sincere when I say that I cannot see how it's my fault that some customers have been murdered. People don't have only one store or just one office to visit regularly. Have you checked other shop managers as well? And the staff at the city's banks and post offices?"

"There're no stores or banks or post offices that serve their customers after closing time. No clothes shops that offer exaggerated discounts on brand-new collections in December. Apart from yours."

"Can you find your way out, Inspector? I've seen enough of your face for one day. Besides, I'm busy."

"I'm busy, too. Busy hunting a girl killer."

"Good luck. Bye."

"I want to talk to your wife again."

"Is it necessary? My wife is a fragile person."

"I talk to anyone I want."

"If you're planning to bother my wife again, a Leighton Fenwick wants to have a word with you."

"Who's Leighton Fenwick?"

"My wife's psychologist."

"*That* Fenwick?" Kenneth asked.

Uncle Ash turned his head. "You said something, my boy?"

"The boy did say something," Worthington said. "Or rather, the young man. And, yes, we're talking about *that* Fenwick. Who are you?"

"I didn't get the opportunity to introduce myself earlier. I'm Kenneth Sorin. The inspector's special associate." *No point in mentioning Mr. Frank.*

"Special associate?" The clothing shop manager frowned. "What's so special? Aren't you with CID?"

"Not really. Or not exactly. Rather, an external analyst. Amateur detective, if you prefer that word. Or speculative theorist. Or investigative writer. But the simple truth is more complicated than that."

Worthington looked puzzled. "Another Sorin?"

"The man you're talking to is my uncle."

Worthington's eyes darkened and swept back to Uncle Ash. "You brought a civilian? What do your regulations say about that, huh?"

"Which regulations?" Uncle Ash asked. "Official ones or my own?"

Worthington, still frowning, glanced at Kenneth again. "How old did you say you were?"

"I didn't," Kenneth said.

"Give me Leighton Fenwick's contact details," Uncle Ash said. "I'm sure you don't mind."

Worthington tore a sheet from a notepad and wrote something in a hurry. He handed the note to Uncle Ash. "Now goodbye, Inspector. Your illegally parked car—if 'car' is the right word—ruins the view from my office windows."

"See you again next week, Worthington."

"I doubt that very much, Inspector."

"And take it easy on New Year's Eve."

▪

"It worked," Kenneth said.

Uncle Ash lit a cigarette. "What?"

"How you tricked Worthington into believing his fingerprint was on the tie clip."

His uncle grinned and started the car engine. The vehicle jumped down and away from the edge of the pavement. "You're fascinated by Mrs. Worthington's psychologist? Why?"

"Leighton Fenwick is a world authority. He has a background in clinical psychology and is inspired by natural science, psychiatry and social psychology in his research and development. He is best known for his pioneering and successful therapy methods. Fenwick is exciting, eccentric and has an influence on several intellectual circles."

"It must cost a fortune to consult such a star."

"The Worthingtons can afford him. When are you going to see Fenwick?"

24

"Yes, Miss Russell." Mr. Frank took the call on the first ring. "Where're you calling from?"

"From home."

"Is the KS mission in phase?"

"In phase, sir. I've done what you asked."

"I didn't ask you, Miss Russell. I gave you an order."

"That's what I meant, sir."

"I know that that's what you meant. And?"

"I suspect that KS is insane, sir."

"How sick?"

"Sick enough to retain his qualification for the SCDX list, sir. KS is living in a fantasy. To say that KS is influenced by his fiction is an understatement. KS is communicating with dead grannies. KS knows that deceased old ladies are spying on his novel manuscript and his thoughts. KS means that he had proof of this. Unsurprisingly, the evidence has since disappeared. To KS, life is a novel without an end. KS is like some fictional character's alter ego."

"Any particular fictitious character in mind?"

"The prime candidate is the main character in KS's new upcoming horror suspense novel, a writer who is slashing young female students to death."

"The character's name?"

"I don't know yet, sir."

"It's time to deepen your KS mission."

"Does that mean I'm going to seduce him, sir?"

"It means what you want it to mean. You are our best local and international secret agent, Miss Russell. You know what it takes to achieve a result."

"I suspect that KS is getting fond of me, sir."

"Excellent. It facilitates your mission."

"And if the mission becomes dangerous?"

"A dangerously beautiful woman like you is very used to dangers, Miss Russell."

"How does Inspector Sorin see the new phase?"

"The kinship in question doesn't compromise Inspector Sorin's job as a SCDX detective."

"What's next, sir?"

"You wait for new instructions."

"Understood, sir. Deadline for the written report?"

"To be announced shortly."

"Sir?"

"Yes, Miss Russell."

"Will the new mission be within the law?"

"SCDX *is* the law. There isn't a single politician in Blackfield not owned by SCDX. At present, there are SCDX representatives positioned in a dozen of the world's most significant governments and crime-fighting organisations. In addition, concepts of law become superfluous in the future. Instead, we will speak of 'world order'. A world order where

SCDX is one principal conductor. The goal is to wipe out the human genetic weaknesses. A planet without crime needs no laws. Understood, Miss Russell?"

"I understand, sir."

"More questions?"

"May I give in to my curiosity, sir?"

"By all means, Miss Russell."

"How does nobody know what the acronym SCDX stands for? I, an international SCDX agent, do not know what SCDX means. Is it myth or truth that SCDX doesn't mean anything?"

"Good night, Miss Russell. And good luck."

"Thank you, sir. Good night."

25

Unshaven, uncombed and dressed in a bright pink T-shirt, Leighton Fenwick looked more like a comedian than the scientist he had been on the front cover of the latest issue of Nature.

"Inspector Sorin, a pleasure to see you."

"No kidding? You're the first person this week who's said it's a pleasure to see me."

"I'm always serious, Inspector."

"You know who I am, Dr. Fenwick?"

"Is it possible to not know who you are, Inspector? You're the SCDX manager's right hand. I saw you on TV the other day. You're chasing the serial killer. I can see that you have brought your clever nephew. I do apologise for the T-shirt, gentlemen. Today is laundry day. Since I had no clean shirts, my daughter lent me one of her T-shirts. She's a grown-up woman. The T-shirt fits, as you see."

"It isn't illegal to wear a pink T-shirt," Uncle Ash said. "Not yet; not even in Blackfield."

"I'm pleased that you regard the situation from that point of view, Inspector. As an explorer of the ravines of the human psyche, I don't much value appearance. The mind is more important than how we dress. Now, gentlemen, since you're treading in my doorway, I guess you want to come in. Whatever you came here for, please be quick."

The trio moved through the house. The building was as large as a mansion. The hall was as large as a three-car garage. The living room was as large as a coffee shop or a dining hall. The furniture looked like art deco. Fenwick confirmed Kenneth's guess. White art deco in an all-white room. The inside of an igloo could not have been whiter.

They sat down at a marble dining table in the centre of the room.

"Pretty cool house," Uncle Ash said.

"Thank you, Inspector. How can I help you?"

"I'm aware of the confidentiality and code of ethics that come with your profession. But I need info."

"Under the present circumstances, I'm

obligated to talk to you, Inspector. Let's get to the point."

From the corner of his eye, Kenneth glimpsed a girl dressed in the lush colours of tropical fruits. He turned towards her. What a contrast her outfit was to the surrounding whiteness of the room.

"Here she comes." Fenwick's face brightened. "My lovely daughter. My treasure."

The girl had pale cheeks, sea-green eyes, and hair and teeth as white as snow. Her right thumb was playing with a cigarette lighter's striker wheel. She fixed her gaze on Kenneth. "You're Kenneth Sorin. The writer of twisted horror novels."

"I guess I am, among other things. Everybody has multiple personalities—at least three. We're one person at work, another person in private, and a third person when we appear in polite society."

She grimaced. "But you don't have to be sick to write sick horror stories, do you?"

"If I were a sicko, my answer could be a lie."

She laughed. "I haven't read you. I just know who you are. I've seen your books at Waterstones and WHSmith. I shall try to check out your books at some point. That is, after the next ice age, when I get some spare time."

"I hope I won't disappoint you."

"I hope so, too. I'm Rachel Fenwick."

She held out her hand. He took it.

"Nice to meet you, Miss Fenwick."

"I have to go now."

"To a library?" Dr. Fenwick asked.

"That's right, Dad." The girl disappeared. The sound of a slamming front door followed.

Fenwick's face lost its luster. "Where were we, gentlemen? Could you please hurry up? I need to check the washing machine and get out of this T-shirt as soon as possible."

"I know that you're an influential professional," Uncle Ash said. "I also know you're working on pioneering projects in collaboration with various kinds of psychologists, psychiatrists and scientists. Tell me about the projects."

"I'm sorry, Inspector. Scientists don't discuss professional commercial secrets with outsiders. We can talk about everything between heaven and hell, provided that we leave out the part of my research not yet published. We could debate my published books and articles on therapy and distorted brain function, if you wish, but not my work in progress."

"Are all your patients used in the experiments?"

"No."

"You mean there's a selection criterion?"

"Yes."

"How are the patients selected?"

"I can't answer that question today."

"Is Mrs. Amy Worthington a selected patient?"

"I can't answer that question today."

"How many selected patients in total?"

"No answer. Selection is work in progress."

"Have selected patients had special requests?"

"Some of the selected patients, sometimes. But my work is never compromised."

"What do you think of the following? A: When Mr. Philip Worthington's erotic adventures with the ladies go wrong, he kills them off, one by one. They had threatened to cause a scandal and might also have threatened him with blackmail.

"Or scenario B: Mrs. Amy Worthington, your patient, discovers her husband's infidelity and she retaliates by taking the ladies out of the equation, trying to frame her husband for the murders."

"Far-fetched." Fenwick yawned. "At least, your scenario B. If Mrs. Worthington were a murderess, I would know."

"How would you know?"

"A liar doesn't escape me."

"What if you knew she was a murderess, and you lied to me by saying she wasn't?"

"The odds that my patient is a murderess is one in a million. But I'll tell you something, Inspector. Mrs. Worthington did insinuate her concerns about a possible link between the murders and the chain store Worthington's Elegance."

"When?"

"About three weeks ago."

"In what context?"

"In connection with a therapy session at my city centre office. It was obvious she wondered whether her husband could be the killer."

Uncle Ash nodded. "Philip Worthington's own situation isn't enviable."

"I can imagine that. I just wish I could be of more help. I'll think of something."

"No worries." Uncle Ash handed over a business card. "Please keep in touch, Doc."

Fenwick nodded. "If something new shows up."

"You have dozens of framed photographs on the walls, Dr. Fenwick," Kenneth said. "Your daughter is in all of them, isn't she?"

"Rachel is in half of the photographs." Fenwick paused and sadness clouded his face. "My late wife Amelia is in the other fifty percent of the photos. Amelia at Rachel's current age, or thereabouts."

"Remarkable. The daughter and the mother. To an outsider, these women could be identical twins."

Fenwick nodded. "Indeed."

Uncle Ash rose. "Thank you for your time, Doc."

"No problem."

"And Happy New Year."

"Hardly, in this decadent time and age, Inspector. The odds are again one in a million."

26

Kenneth started the computer, opened a file and sent the three unedited paragraphs to the laser printer:

Blood flowed all the way to the horizon.

The horizon was equal to the brow of the hill.

The eye was separated from the girl's skull.

The steep street, Herbertville Crescent, didn't affect the organ's position. The female eye sat fixed in the dried blood, throwing its dead gaze in the direction of the morning sun.

The eyeshadow was as discreet as twilight.

Friday, January the ninth.

A new day for the residents of Blackfield.

Except for Gloria Wright. The pretty student from Lubbock, Texas, USA was number seven.

27

The girl he was having sex with was a hybrid of Alison Mitchell and Jeanne Russell. The hybrid girl then changed to Jeanne-Rebecka Månsson. Then to Rebecka-Alison. Back to Alison-Jeanne. And so on. Soon the Swedish girl disappeared. Rebecka was replaced by the American girl Gloria Wright. New female hybrids arose. Then the Texas girl vanished, too. Alison and Jeanne remained. He felt awake. Awake in a non-dream.

Did it matter which girl he had on his mind during the sexual intercourse? Did the difference between physical and psychological sex matter?

The bedroom was strange. The dream, the non-dream, timeless. A streetlamp threw a silver light. A new voice asked questions. The words came floating from the outside of the bedroom door. *Red roses*. The white wallpaper featured a pattern of red roses.

Rain began to patter against the window panes and in the same moment the timelessness ended. It was Thursday evening. Again. Another student girl at the local university would disappear forever.

She on top. Rhythmic movements. Close, tight. Fluttering locks of her hair brushed against his face. The pink hard nipples of her breasts seemed to be glowing in the streetlight that radiated through the windows. They came together, the Alison-Jeanne lady and he. The wet sensation spread between the sheets, sharper and clearer than any hallucination, as if the dream or non-dream was more real than reality, some revitalising hyper-actuality. The frisky hybrid girl whimpered, then whispered: "The phone is ringing."

■

He woke up on the floor of his bedroom. *The phone is ringing.*

His head was aching and the phone was blaring.

He fumbled for the device, snatched at its cord and saw the telephone crash to the floor.

He grabbed the handset. "Uh, hello?"

"Have you noticed, discovered, the clue in your bed, Mr. Sorin?" Christine Corbett hung up.

He couldn't believe what he saw in his bed.

Flowers.

At least not a naked and dead girl.

Pink and white flowers, scattered on the pillow and the disordered bed linen.

28

Stockholm, Sweden.

Jeanne Russell crosses Vasagatan. A snowy wind is biting her earlobes. Her boot heels slide in the slush ice. She shivers inside her winter coat. The meeting with Jonasson begins in twelve minutes. The chemical company CentraKem AB's head office is located opposite Central Station.

She steps into the lobby and advances to the security checkpoint. "I have a meeting with Chief Executive Officer Jonasson at two p.m."

"Scheduled by whom?"

"The CEO's secretary."

"And who are you?"

"Betsy Breckenridge. Miss Breckenridge. Legal representative at NebuloxVent Limited, London."

"Identification?"

She pushes an ID card through the slot beneath the safety glass. The bearded security guard picks up a phone. The conversation takes ages. Then he returns the ID card along with a temporary badge.

"Miss Breckenridge. Welcome to Stockholm and CentraKem AB. Nineteenth floor. The left corridor. Office 19100. The lifts are at the far back of the lobby. Attach the name tag to the front of your outermost clothing and keep the tag visible all of the time. Someone will accompany you to the right floor. Just wait for that person at the lifts."

Her badge reads: Visitor: Miss B. Breckenridge

She smiles at the guard, attaches the tag to her coat and moves through the lobby towards the set of lifts. She's waiting. A slim uniformed woman turns up. The two ladies share an elevator with a handful of people. The uniformed lady doesn't talk. She's busy chewing gum. They reach the nineteenth floor. Jeanne is left alone in the corridor right outside the CEO's office. She waits until the uniformed woman is out of sight. Then she rings the doorbell.

■

Emil Jonasson. One of Northern Europe's richest and most powerful businessmen. Sixty-three years old. Dark sparkling eyes like black pearls. Circular glasses. Sombre suit and sky-blue tie. The tycoon poses behind his desk. Jeanne sits in the visitor's chair. She's holding her mini-suitcase on her lap.

"Have you visited a CentraKem branch before, Miss Breckenridge?"

Jeanne smiles. "This is the first time, sir."

"I had expected someone a bit older."

"I'm experienced, sir."

"I'm sure you are, miss."

Emil Jonasson licks his lips and steals a glance at her crossed nylon-stocking-clad legs. Her short skirt must have made an impression.

"The new Prix-Q building opens in London next week, sir. Nearly three weeks earlier than planned." Prix-Q, a Swedish international subsidiary chemical company owned by CentraKem AB.

"That is good news."

"Have you decided whether you want to move CentraKem's head office to an alpha world city, sir? London? New York? Paris? Tokyo?"

"The headquarters stay in Stockholm, miss."

"I understand, sir."

"And the documents from NebuloxVent? You brought them today?"

"Of course, sir. International business law is my field of expertise."

"Shall we take a look at them? Before we go out and have a nice time on the town together?"

Jeanne smiles, opens her bag and pulls out the gun. She squeezes the trigger, one, two, three times. The sound suppressor transforms the bangs to whizzes. CEO Emil Jonasson is sent flying backwards in the wheel-mounted swivel chair. Blood splatters across wallpaper and desktop.

■

It was a year ago. The first time she had silenced someone on behalf of SCDX. Opinion-former Emil Jonasson had been a threat to SCDX, which meant a threat to the new world order. A threat to overall welfare and overall harmony.

Since the Jonasson mission, she had taken care of another five difficult people. The job was well paid and came without the risk of a bad conscience. SCDX morale substituted conscience. With the new world order, consciences would be obsolete. In a society without crime, neither laws nor consciences were needed.

Jeanne had breakfast at the kitchen counter. Tea, half a grapefruit and an oatmeal cookie with cottage cheese. She was on her way out when her eyes landed on the parcel. It lay on the doormat below the mail slot. The packaging wasn't marked with the sender's details. How odd.

She opened the parcel. It contained a book.

A novel.

The Dream Killers by Kenneth Sorin.

29

Linda hissed at the flowers and wrinkled her nose. She jumped down from the bed and rushed like a rocket out of the bedroom, down to the ground floor.

Linda was his reliable witness. Cats didn't lie, unlike people. Besides, he couldn't believe he had gone crazy overnight. Too many peculiarities had taken place. Too many to explain away.

There seemed to be two sorts of flowers, both similar and different. Seven pink ones and six white ones. Perhaps they belonged to the same species, despite their difference in colour. The plants were complete with petals, stems and bracteoles.

He surprised himself by saying aloud: "Duality. Two girls in one. Two sets of flowers."

He went downstairs to the kitchen, opened the cleaning cupboard, took out a sweeping brush and a dustpan, and returned upstairs. He brushed the flowers out of the bed, continued to the upstairs storeroom, threw the plants in a transparent plastic bag, sealed the bag with tape and a firm knot, and placed the bag in the corner behind the storeroom's door.

He still couldn't name the flowers but now he knew he had seen this species before. Not long ago.

In a certain Chris Henderson's garden.

He swallowed two paracetamol tablets, took a refreshing shower and got dressed.

▪

Someone rang the doorbell.

He was satisfied with his insurance and utility companies, that is, to the extent a consumer could be satisfied these days. He was happy with his home appliances. And he was already donating to four different charities. He hoped that it wasn't another salesman on the doorstep. It wasn't.

"May I come in?" Jeanne Russell smiled.

"Is that a straight yes-no question?"

"I wanted to thank you for the book."

The blonde was gorgeous in a blue-grey cotton dress, dark tights and black winter boots. Her hair was backcombed and adorned with a black diadem.

How could he resist her? "You're just in time for tuna sandwiches with mayonnaise and salad. There are enough sandwiches for all three of us."

"All three of us? Who else is here?"

"Linda."

"Who is Linda?"

"My four-footed bewhiskered housemate."

Jeanne giggled.

"Please come in, Jeanne."

"I feel that you have something new to tell me, Kenneth. Something new about the murders."

▪

They sat in the living room. The furniture consisted of a sofa, a table for four (or for five, if Linda was counted, and of course she was), three armchairs, and bookcases filled with several hundred or a thousand volumes and paperbacks. The books were organised into two types of alphabetical order: with respect to the author names and to the titles. He had recently reorganised all of his books—both fiction and non-fiction—from chronological to alphabetical order.

Two boxes in each bookcase held DVD and BD collections. All films contained frequent elements of graphic violence, gruesome murders, sexual torture and effective splatters of bloodshed.

The paintings in his living room brought life and depth to the checkered wallpaper, a wallpaper whose pattern reminded him of a chessboard. He imagined that the beautiful women in the paintings were chess pieces that had sprung to life.

Like a chessboard queen, Miss Russell moved diagonally across the checkered lobby floor.

Linda sat on the table, munching a sandwich.

Jeanne sipped apple juice. “How can you let the cat sit on the table?”

“Why not? Cats have better table manners than a lot of people.”

“That thing you wanted to tell me about; was it about a new clue?”

“It has been there all the time, only overlooked. Let’s consider the days of the seven murders.”

“They are Thursdays. We know that.”

“But there’s another dimension. There are three weeks between September the twenty-fifth and October the sixteenth. Two weeks between October the sixteenth and October the thirtieth. Three weeks between October the thirtieth and November the twentieth. Two weeks between November the twentieth and December the fourth. Three weeks between December the fourth and December the twenty-fifth. And two weeks between December the twenty-fifth and January the eighth.”

Jeanne chewed on her tuna sandwich. “When did you think that this pattern could be important?”

“The same day that SCDX engaged me.”

“You mean CID.”

“Yeah, that’s correct. The murder of Annabelle Stanfield the night before updated the sequence to 3-2-3-2. The previous Gemma Quigley murder involved a 3-2-3 series, too short a sequence to arouse suspicions of any new pattern in addition to the weekday in common. The 3-2-3 could have been nothing more than an arbitrary arrangement of two 3s and one 2. But 3-2-3-2 spurred me on to think in new pathways."

"Can this really be important?"

"We'll see."

Jeanne looked thoughtful. "If this sequence is significant, a family that has a daughter enrolled at the University of Blackfield will be struck by grief on January the twenty-ninth. Kenneth? What does this 3-2 periodicity mean?"

He didn't have to think about it. The absurdities had already sparkled in his brain. "Duality."

"Duality?"

"Or dual, if you prefer the adjective."

"Prefer?"

"Dichotomy. Ambiguous. Double. Ambivalence. Split. Doublet."

Jeanne's eyes narrowed. "Double as in a double life or a double-cross? Two persons in one. A crazy killer and simultaneously a social human being."

He nodded. "Something along those lines." But on his mind were the dual or hybrid girls with whom he had had sex in the dream or non-dream.

"Have you mentioned this to Mr. Frank?"

"Not yet. Not to my uncle, either."

"Why not?"

"There's a lot going on. I want a complete idea before I talk to anyone about this."

"You're talking to me."

"With you it's different." He didn't know why he'd expressed himself that way. The words had slipped out of his mouth. It wasn't easy to stay crystal clear when you had a super-hot girl before your eyes.

He swallowed a sip of apple juice. "The offender is in total control. He directs circumstances. The dates of the killings are decided months in advance. When he took Kelly Graham's life, he already knew that Lucy Knowles had to die precisely three weeks later. That Rebecka Månsson had to die the night before Halloween, no other Thursday. And so on."

"Kenneth?"

"Yes?"

"Something you know that Mr. Frank doesn't?"

"What would that be?"

"I feel that you're hiding something."

He chuckled. "Theories are being formed. Too early to talk about them now, Jeanne."

She nodded. "Thank you for the meal, Kenneth. It was delicious. And thank you again for the book. I have to go now. I must get back to headquarters."

"Can we meet again? I mean, just you and me."

"Why?"

"I want… I just want to see you again."

"When?"

"Anytime. Soon."

"Not impossible."

Her sweet smile made his heart accelerate.

▪

He was about to open the door to the storeroom when he spotted her. Linda stood at an angle to the storeroom door, her back arched, the fur standing out on her back and tail. The posture of a defensive cat. Linda hissed, fixing the door. He studied the animal. The dilated pupils, the flattened ears, the retracted whiskers. There was something else, too. Something he couldn't identify or even guess. In the body language of cats, scientists had found at least twenty-five different signals used in at least sixteen different combinations. Experts said that a number of subtleties in cats were invisible to humans.

In spite of Linda's disapproval, he stepped into the storeroom. He lit the ceiling lamp and snatched the plastic bag in the corner behind the door.

The bizarreness struck him.

He dropped the bag.

Linda miaowed a high-pitched miaow.

Dizziness penetrated his forehead.

Linda hissed.

The empty plastic bag was still sealed. Both the knot and the tape were intact.

How had the flowers disappeared?

30

The electric typewriter's empty display stared at him like a robot's eye. Sometimes he suspected that the machine had its own life and its own soul. The mocking device was an artificial thinker.

He stared at the wordless sheet. Listened to his heart thumping. Downed his fifth cup of coffee. Then it happened. His fingers began tapping keys.

Today he had to push himself towards his target of fifteen hundred words. Letter by letter. Word by word. Paragraph by paragraph. Today, Kenneth was a slave, imprisoned in a vacuum-silent darkness inside his own skull. He wondered if Linda would do a better job with the novel manuscript. The goal seemed light years away.

It took forever, or thereabouts, but he reached the fifteen-hundred-word mark and began to feel better. He remained seated, moulded into the chair like a tin figure. His fingers flew over the keyboard. The book's characters relieved him from the burden of transferring the story from thought to paper.

Adrenaline was dumped in his bloodstream and a familiar taste settled in his mouth. The taste of paracetamol. The painkiller box was there, opened.

■

The pages were bleeding. The splattering blood was as red as a Yorkshire sunset in July. Gorgeous girls were slashed to death, left and right. At some point, he considered incorporating a variant of the murder pattern 3-2-3-2-3-2, and discovered, to his surprise, that he had already flavoured the novel with that clue. When had he done that? Before or after Gloria Wright? Before or after Rebecka Månsson? Or even earlier? He had begun his writing session at eight p.m. The time was now seven thirty-two a.m. He found it hard to accept that he had spent the whole night in the workroom.

He glanced at the stack of sheets, counted the pages and shook his head in disbelief.

Seventy-three pages of a rough first draft.

Seventy-three pages in a single all-nighter.

Kenneth grinned.

Linda yelled at him from the upstairs hallway, scratching at the door to the workroom. Peculiar that the door was closed. He was careful to keep the house's doors wide open. Not exactly all the doors but nearly all. Like every indoor cat, Linda despised shut doors. The house was an indoor cat's territory. The discovery of the shut workroom door confused him. Had he spent the entire night here, without remembering what he had done? He didn't even remember writing, although the stack of evidence was there, right there, on the desk. He detached himself from the chair. "I'm coming, Linda. I know it's time for breakfast.

You wouldn't mind putting on a pot of coffee, would you? Black, no sugar."

He switched off the typewriter and went downstairs to the kitchen. Linda was already there.

"Listen, Linda. Since we don't know with any certainty how Mr. Frank or Uncle Ash would react if they knew what I'm going to do next, let's keep it a secret. A secret between you and me. Agreed?"

Linda miaowed.

31

He removed the foil wrapping paper and held the chocolate bar between two fingers in front of Sadie's glistening lips. He ordered her to suck it. As the previous girls, she obeyed. He informed her to think of oral sex while sucking the chocolate bar.

The previous seven ladies had been blind alleys. Gemma. Lucy. Suzanne. Kelly. Rebecka. Gloria. Annabelle. Sadie would last longer. Sadie would last all the way; that is, until he was finished with her.

The girl was a property. He owned Sadie. The tingling sensation that wandered through his body made his penis stiffen. When Sadie was finished with her initial task, he sank his teeth into a two-third piece of the chocolate bar. He chewed and smacked his lips and swallowed.

He placed the remaining third of the bar on the girl's tongue.

In the freezer sat a chocolate bunny. It was now waiting to be freed from its prison of ice. First, he would study how a naked Sadie played with the chocolate bunny. Thereafter, he would join the thrilling game himself.

Now he hugged her from behind, experiencing her heartbeat. His hands slid in beneath her blouse and continued across her shoulder blades. He wondered if she noticed how his blood rushed. He wished she could. Sadie took off her blouse. He unhooked the bra. Sadie's pretty breasts danced out into the light. The episode had the quality of a forbidden pleasure spiked with both seriousness and thrills. It was like opening a Christmas present before Christmas.

He glanced at the wall clock.

The time was as young and innocent as Sadie.

The time was Sadie.

Sadie was the time.

The new adventure started.

32

He wanted to avoid the HQ switchboard and called instead Jeanne's official mobile number.

"Yes?"

"Hi, Jeanne. It's me." He heard the background rumble of city traffic.

"Hi, Kenneth."

"Did I catch you at a good time?"

"I'm out, shopping away my lunch break."

"Could we meet at dinner time?"

"Have you discovered a new clue that you want to tell me about?"

"Must it always be about a clue?"

"Well, you're Kenneth Sorin, after all."

"Now, suppose I'd like to have dinner with you because… because it's you."

"I can't believe it." She giggled. "Utter scam."

"Okay, then." He felt some sort of defeat. "It's not exactly new. It has been around for a while."

"But a clue nevertheless. I was right."

"I don't have to insinuate female intuition. You can read my mind."

"How many people have you informed about the new clue?"

"No one. Not even my uncle."

"Go ahead then and tell me all about it."

"Not on the phone. What about the dinner?"

"I'd love to. A pub on Westminster Road?"

"Too indiscreet. I don't want to risk bumping into your boss. Before I talk to Mr. Frank and, or, my uncle, I want to know how the subject looks in the light of female intuition."

"Why don't you consult your friend Christine?"

"Very funny. What I intend to tell you later

does involve Christine, one way or another. But I want to talk to a living woman, not a living dead one."

"So, where do you suggest we meet for dinner?"

"How about my place?"

"Your place again? How mysterious."

"Half past seven? And that you stay a bit longer than last time? If you don't mind."

"Okay. If I dare."

"I hope you like sandwiches with mild cheddar cheese and cranberry chutney."

"Sandwiches again?"

"You're insinuating?"

"A tad repetitive."

"Fillings, spreads and toppings can be varied in countless combinations. No risk of repetitiveness."

"How lucky we must be."

"There'll be hash browns, too."

▪

Eight minutes to eight and still no Jeanne in sight. Where was she? If she had had to change her plans she would have informed him. Did she have second thoughts about dinner with him? No, of course not. Something unexpected must have—

The doorbell shrilled.

▪

Here she came. At last she was here.

He marvelled at her beauty. The crimson lips. The perfectly shaped eyebrows. The enigmatic gaze, which transported his thoughts and fantasies. The long and wavy hair of a fairytale princess: blonde, voluminous curls. And a necklace with ivory-white and burgundy-red pearls.

The necklace.

The necklace from one of his dreams about her, the night before they had gone out together for a drink at Trix Bar.

"Welcome," he heard himself say.

"Please excuse me for being so late. The boss phoned me after I had finished for the day."

Waiting is a bitter tonic but it boosts appetite, he almost said. He gave her a hand with her coat. "What did Mr. Frank want?"

"He asked about you."

"Me?" Alarming that Mr. Frank had contacted his secretary in her spare time to inquire about him, Kenneth. What was going on?

"He wondered how you were doing and what you thought about the serial killer case."

"Why would Mr. Frank ask you about me? A bit strange, isn't it?"

"Strange indeed. How would you explain it?"

"Someone within Mr. Frank's team might have spotted us together in town, the afternoon we went to Trix Bar." *Unless you're involved, Jeanne.*

"Does it matter?"

"Possibly not. Probably not, I mean. What did you tell your boss?"

"I told him I had no clue what you were doing and that was the truth. Though when he asked if you had disclosed any of your fascinating ideas to me, I answered no, and that was a lie."

"What do people at headquarters say about me these days?"

"Is there anything special to say?"

"Jeanne?"

"Nothing. I don't understand what you mean."

He was thinking, under a crushing silence. "I'm sorry, Jeanne. Please forgive me for having put you in a situation where you had to lie to Mr. Frank."

"I'm all right."

"You're sure?"

"Yeah. But how are *you*? You look burned out."

He didn't respond. He had hoped he didn't look like he felt.

▪

They sat in the living room, eating sandwiches with cheese and cranberry chutney, and hash browns with ketchup. On the table was a cardboard box with ice-cold apple juice.

"Would you like something stronger than apple juice, Jeanne?"

"Apple juice is fine. Delicious."

Linda ignored Kenneth's question. She was busy drinking her lactose-free milk.

He beamed, or thought he did. (The mirror on the wall across from him showed a sickly grin.)

He thought they were on the same wavelength, all three of them. After the meal, Linda lay purring on the sofa.

Jeanne patted the cat. "She's very beautiful. Her shiny coat appears blue-grey with a pinkish glow. What breed is she?"

"British lilac."

"Tell me about her."

"What would you like to know?"

"Anything."

"Her serenity appeals to me. Her intelligence and at the same time her phlegmatic nature make her solid and reliable company. And, like all cats, she's both independent and freedom-loving."

"What's special about cats? Why do they attract you?"

"Cats are—like women—full of mystery."

Jeanne giggled. "Okay, I see."

"Cats are among the most intriguing and most mysterious of creatures. With a behaviour pattern developed and honed over millions of years, it's remarkable that the cat has become man's main companion without having compromised its natural instincts. We have modified and corrected the dog for it to meet human requirements. The dog varies in size, shape, behaviour and temperament. With the cat, it's different. During the thousands of years that cat and man have lived side by side, the cat has remained essentially unchanged. Researchers have manipulated the genes that determine the cat's coat length and colour but all breeds have approximately the same size and demonstrate basically the same behaviour."

"Like all women demonstrate basically the same behaviour?"

"A legitimate question, Catwoman."

Jeanne tittered. "I bet that Linda loves you."

"I love her, too. She's my best friend."

"How old is she?"

"Three. She's a lady in her prime. Born with a predator instinct."

"I do understand you're fascinated by predator instincts. I saw it for the first time in your book—"

"—which you didn't like—"

"—*The Blood-Red Shadow*."

"With no freaky monsters or psycho killers or sexual predators, I wouldn't have a writing career."

"Must you write in the horror genre?"

"The writer doesn't choose the subject. It's the other way around. The subject chooses the writer."

"Serious?"

"Serious."

"Uh… Can't wait to read *The Dream Killers*…"

■

Jeanne could be useful to him, one way or another, in the near future. He looked forward to talking to her about it one day. Not today, but soon.

"Jeanne?"

"Yes?"

"I had such a strange dream the other night."

"No wonder you have strange dreams. You are, after all, the guy who wrote *The Dream Killers.*"

"I surprised you, or shocked you, the other day when I mentioned earlier oddities. I assume you're better prepared this time."

"I thought you said on the phone you wanted to talk about a new clue."

"It's the dream that is the clue."

"How weird. Go ahead, then."

"For some time, I've been suffering from a headache which comes and goes and varies in its strength. In its mildest form, it's barely noticeable. In its worst form, it's reminiscent of a feeling of severe sleep deprivation. I can't explain why the painkillers don't work. The headache is at its worst whenever Christine is in contact via some mental telephone line, or just after she has finished a contact."

"I haven't the faintest idea what you're talking about, Kenneth."

"Neither have I." He hesitated. "The following

question is going to sound a little peculiar. Please don't misunderstand. I'm going to ask the question in the spirit of a mystery solver."

Jeanne smiled. "Ask the question."

Now or never. "Could you please describe the wallpaper in your bedroom?"

"Huh?"

"As I said, the question would seem a bit odd."

"A bit?"

"She's involved."

"She?"

"Christine from the other side of the grave."

"The wallpaper in my bedroom… The horror novelist is interested in my bedroom… I wonder what the next question will be."

"Please."

"White… White with red roses."

"Red roses on a white background. How remarkable. That's the wallpaper from the dream."

"I definitely won't ask whether I figured in that dream of yours, Kenneth."

"Good."

"What are you trying to tell me? And what has my bedroom got to do with anything?"

Without mentioning any erotic details, he told her about the dream's meanings, how one could interpret the dream images in the context of his duality theory. He mentioned the strange flowers' appearance and subsequent disappearance, and he talked about Linda's reactions. He also showed Jeanne around the house, including the first-floor storeroom.

▪

"What if you were hallucinating the whole thing." Her eyes were dead serious.

"If I did, how would you explain the presence of the sealed carrier bag?"

"It was empty."

"So?"

"There was nothing in the bag in the first place."

"You mean I must have sealed an empty bag?"

"That's right."

"Thank you. Now I feel much better."

She sighed. "I want to believe you, Kenneth."

"Believe me only if you mean it."

"Can you let me try?"

"If you think it's worth the effort. Meanwhile, I have lots of work to do."

"Are you angry?"

"No, no, definitely not."

He saw his half-eaten sandwich and reached for it. "I'd better finish this one before Linda steals it."

He wasn't speedy enough. Linda appeared from nowhere. The cat jumped onto the table and landed with a front paw on the sandwich. The cranberry chutney splattered across the tablecloth.

"No, no, no! That's *my* sandwich, Linda. Look what you've done."

Jeanne laughed—a strained laugh.

Calm down now. It's only chutney. Chutney can splatter just like blood. The red, sticky stains on the cloth disappear in the washing machine.

Disappear as effectively as dream flowers.

"You saw that with your own eyes, Jeanne. Not even the cat is normal anymore."

Jeanne faked a smile. "She may have had a bout of your corrupt view of the world."

33

The clocks were ticking fast in Jeanne Russell's company. Too fast, as if accelerating. Four hours felt like twenty minutes. Now she was gone.

With a sip of apple juice, he washed down the last bite of his last sandwich, the section that was marked with Linda's paw print and therefore, not unlikely, a trace of her DNA.

"Juice is good for health, Linda. Provided that it contains one hundred percent fruit. No additives at all and nothing removed. Squeezed fruit, plain and simple." The cat was out of sight. He was talking to the shadows in the living room. "Juice contains lots of antioxidants. You should try it." He lowered the glass to the table, listening to the silence.

A defective silence.

He perceived a humming noise. From beneath the top of his skull. Flashbacks, he decided. The foggy flashbacks were buzzing like wasps. In his mind's eye, he saw how he was shadowing Rebecka Månsson the night of her murder. It was a memory. But not just any memory. The distinction between different types of memory was indispensable. The memory in question derived from a nightmare, not from something he had actually experienced.

He knew how he could murder them.

The wasps in his head.

To murder it. The noise.

Or the buzzing headache.

He went upstairs, went to the bathroom.

He avoided meeting the eyes of the figure who stared back at him from the mirror of the bathroom cabinet. He swung open the mirrored cabinet door and found the jar of painkillers.

▪

He wondered if Linda had analysed her dreams recently. Cats slept an average of fifteen hours a day, twice as much as most other mammals. Because cats were prominent sleepers, scientists had used them in many studies of sleep. It had been discovered that the cat brain in sleep state displayed an electric activity which resembled that of the human brain in sleep state, including the alternating shallow and deep sleep patterns. Like people, cats demonstrated the sleep stage REM (Rapid Eye Movement). During REM sleep, the lightest of the five sleep phases, the brain's neuron activity was similar to that during waking hours. Most people remembered dreams that occurred during REM sleep. If cats dreamt like us, Kenneth speculated, Linda was possibly just as susceptible to messengers in her dreams as he was in his.

He switched off the light in the bathroom and stepped out into the corridor. The stillness which drowned the interior of the house was quieter than a photograph. All the colours of the dark had crept out of the walls. He stood motionless, breathing the shadow-saturated air, thinking of the new novel.

Thinking of Jeanne.

Fantasising about Jeanne.

He wanted to sleep, but needed to work.

Or you need to sleep, but want to work, an inner voice suggested. The corridor seemed duskier than nightmare gloom. He lacked a cat's nocturnal vision and relied on his feet to steer him towards the workroom.

34

Chief Inspector Thomas Frank's wife Edith served the British classic toad-in-the-hole, the crispy, bowl-shaped Yorkshire pudding filled with juicy sausages, and served with onion gravy and vegetables.

Thomas and Edith shared a bottle of red wine. Their two teenage daughters had lemonade.

Jessica was sixteen and Sarah fourteen. Tom Frank mulled over the unfathomably hard work of raising teenage daughters. He knew how to deal with murderesses and female criminal crackpots but the unpaid work as a father of teenage girls had exceeded his wildest anticipations.

"Mum, Dad, I'm going out." Jessica slammed her empty glass onto the table and jumped out of her chair. Jess Frank, a tornado with freckles and long reddish-blonde hair.

"Going out where, Jess?" Thomas asked.

"Me too," Sarah murmured, her mouth full of sausage. Onion gravy trickled from a corner of her mouth. Sarah Frank, a thunderstorm with a pale face and jet-black hair.

"You haven't finished your meal, Sarah," Edith said. "Don't be fussy."

"Must hurry, Mum, or I'll be late." Sarah wiped her mouth and pushed her chair out from the table.

"Late for what?" he asked.

"No dessert, girls?" Edith asked.

"No time for dessert," Jessica said.

"That's right," Sarah said. "No time at all."

"You carry your ID cards at all times?" he asked. "Especially when you're out on the town?"

"Only our fake ID cards," Jessica said.

"That's right," Sarah said, giggling. "Our fakes."

Thomas decided not to tackle those

comments. A chief inspector's daughters did not carry false ID cards, not even in Blackfield. His daughters must have cracked a joke, and a bad one at that.

"What are your plans?" Edith asked.

"Cinema with Becky and Sharon," Sarah said. "An early screening and, before you ask, the answer is no; the film does not have a fifteen or an eighteen rating."

"The kids are going to watch *Saw 3D*," Jessica said, and grinned. "The age rating is—"

"Shut up, Jess," Sarah said, twitching one of her sister's long locks of hair.

"Ouch," Jessica cried. "Stop it, you muppet!"

"Mum, Dad," Sarah yelled, "Jess called me a muppet! A muppet!"

"Calm down, both of you," he shouted.

"What is *Saw 3D*?" Edith asked.

Thomas wanted to know, too.

"A teen romantic comedy," Sarah said, avoiding her mother's eyes.

"Really?" Edith said. "What a strange title for a teen romantic comedy."

"Not stranger than *Twilight*," Sarah said.

"And in 3D?" Edith said, frowning.

Sarah nodded.

"So, what about you, Jess?" Thomas said.

"What?" Jessica said. "*What?*"

"I asked you where you're going. And I'm still waiting for an answer."

"Why?" Jessica glared. "I'm sixteen!"

"Sixteen is a vulnerable age," Thomas said.

"But for fuck's sake—"

"And don't use the four-letter f-word."

"I'm sixteen; practically an adult."

"Not adult enough to vote."

"Adult enough to have a beer in a pub."

"Only if accompanied by a proper adult."

"Adult enough to get married."

"Not without parental consent."

"Adult enough to get pregnant."

"Don't even think about it."

"You don't see me as a mature girl?"

"You are, Jess. You certainly are. But adulthood begins at eighteen."

"To say that adulthood automatically begins at eighteen is idiotic, Dad, because we all know forty-year-olds who are totally immature."

Thomas sighed. Whenever Jess was hell-bent on having the last word, there was little he could do.

Sarah tittered. "She's going to meet Harold."

"None of your business, Sarah," Jessica hissed.

Thomas had already understood that Jess was going to meet her boyfriend tonight. Harold Baker had no criminal record anywhere on the planet. He was not suspected of any crime; not suspected of sheltering a criminal; not suspected of sheltering a suspected criminal. The boy had never been caught shoplifting, littering, or cheating at school. Harold had never had any malignant diseases. His DNA featured no serious mutations. The youth had never expressed himself politically, though both parents were on the electoral register. In public elections, Harold's parents voted the correct way.

Thomas Frank had checked everything that it was possible to check. Thomas Frank had even checked everything that it was impossible to check. Moreover, SCDX was scanning the boyfriend's family tree and nearest relatives, spanning five generations. Harold Baker appeared clean enough to be Jessica Frank's boyfriend, at least until further notice.

"There are a lot of dodgy people, Jess," he said. "Blackfield is no paradise. Your mother and I want you and Sarah to be cautious when you are out and away from the house. You understand that?"

Jessica frowned. "The girl killer? The guy who gouges out an eye on each of his victims?"

"Yes. The girl killer is a case in point."

"If the fucker tries something with me, I'll give him a hard kick in the balls. Trust me."

He sighed again. When Jessica was talking like that, he wished that her younger sister was out of earshot. Most of all, he didn't want Jess to use such language at all in any company, with or without Sarah's presence, but he had resigned himself to the fact that it was hopeless trying to do something about it.

The daughters snatched their jackets from the clothing rack in the hallway and dashed out, slamming the front door.

"And don't slam the door," he called. "And don't stay out later than…" *Not later than what?* he wondered. *What was reasonable?*

"Relax a bit, Tom," Edith said from the kitchen counter. "They've already gone and can't hear you."

He turned to look at Edith, the woman he had known for more than a quarter of a century. "Am I too conservative, Edith? Overprotective?" Before Edith could answer, he continued: "No, I don't think so. I know this city and its underworld better than most. Besides, it's a school day tomorrow."

Edith returned to the table with dessert: vanilla ice cream and steaming hot blueberry muffins. "I know you, Tom. It isn't our daughters who bother you the most nowadays. There's something else, or someone else. What's troubling you?"

He looked up from his ice cream and muffin and fixed his wife's deep-blue eyes. "It's a detective."

"How? Who?"

"Morrison."

"Steve? What about him?"

"He has appeared a little strange lately."

Edith chuckled. "Steve has always appeared a bit strange. Pat should know. She has been married to the man for twelve years. It wouldn't surprise me at all if it was because of Steve's oddity that Pat fell in love with him. Who, if not Steve Morrison, would get the idea to dress up as an Easter chicken at last year's BPS fancy dress ball?"

"Okay, but—"

"A chocolate-munching Easter chicken."

"Edith, I'm thinking of actions or behaviour in certain situations. Morrison is hiding something."

His wife leaned towards him and put a hand on his arm. "Talk to me, Tom. What is it about Steve?"

"Could you promise me something, Edith?"

"What?"

"Don't tell Pat anything of what I've said. Don't tell anyone."

"But what have you actually said? A girl killer is terrorising the city and you're worried about Steve's peculiarity? You don't mean…" She went silent.

"Morrison is hiding something, Edith. And I'm determined to find out what it is."

35

He was having a nightmare in a nightmare.

The gravity of a black hole in the universe of dreams twitched his body and sent him tumbling, back to his worst day at school. That day had been a living nightmare and now he dreamt the evil dream again. Mrs. Davenport had been nastier than usual that day in April, nineteen years ago. The ten-year-old Kenneth was a prisoner in Mrs. Davenport's classroom, the school's torture chamber. He wished he were outside, in the light, sharing the freedom of the birds. He wished he could fly, though he was ensnared in the dark, on the inside, the room where the dragon lady could swallow him alive.

The world outside the classroom windows was stained in orange and achromatic greyscale shades. And then, birds. Countless sparrows swept through the playground, which was sprinkled with sparkling colours of fire. An apricot-coloured light shot across the sky, and the rain fell. The combination of drizzle and crackling colours gave the school playground a fluorescent quality.

"What do you brats want to be when you grow up?" Mrs. Davenport's gaze was as biting cold as a hailstorm. "What does a bunch of brats like you want to be when you grow up, huh?"

Shadows filled the classroom now, although the sunshine radiated in through all the windows, as if the darkness deleted the sunlight rather than being diluted by it.

"What do you brats really want to be?" Mrs. Davenport wore a raven-black costume. She started swinging her pointing stick like a cutting weapon. Her hair was flying around her head and the floor was swaying, as if she were a pirate on a ship's deck in a hurricane at sea.

"What do you brats want to be? What exactly? Be serious. Don't you dare waste my time, or your own. Answer my question with unshakable honesty, or I'll rip you up like fish." The teacher's pointing stick transformed into an actual sabre, with which she continued to cleave the air.

Mrs. Davenport's booming anger reverberated down the corridors of Kenneth's mind. And from the corner of his eye he noticed the pretty giggling girl with purple ribbons in her hazel-brown pigtails.

Alison Mitchell.

"What do you want to be when you grow up, Alison?" Mrs. Davenport asked.

"I want to be a nurse, Mrs. Davenport."

Alison's great grandmum had been a nurse. Her grandmum was a nurse. Her mum was a nurse.

Mrs. Davenport patted Alison on her head and straightened the ribbons in the girl's pigtails. "Well responded, Alison. An excellent career choice."

The girl's sniggering increased in strength and reached grotesque proportions. This wasn't the real Alison but a freak with overwrought emotions. The creature was just as sweet as the actual Alison but it wasn't Alison—couldn't be.

"We need nurses today, tomorrow and forever," Mrs. Davenport told the class. "Everybody will die but most people die too slowly. That's the reason a healthcare business is so terribly expensive to run." Mrs. Davenport fired off her pirate's grin. Her face had the colour of garden cress. She glanced down at Alison.

"You shouldn't exaggerate your eyeshadow, my dear child."

"My sister says that boys like it when girls wear eyeshadow," Alison said, rolling her eyes.

"Your sister Beatrice is seventeen."

"I'm almost—"

"Alison, you're ten."

Kenneth agreed it was a splendid career choice. Whatever you thought of Mrs. Davenport, she was fair in her judgement of Alison's future ambition. Only it felt so predictable. Who couldn't guess that Alison wanted to be a nurse? But what we think we know as ten-year-olds isn't necessarily true. Against all expectations, Alison never fulfilled her ambition to be a nurse. She became a florist. A superb florist.

Mrs. Davenport turned her attention to the big Peter Cullen. "What do you want to be, Peter?"

"I want to be a plumber, Mrs. Davenport."

The smirk was back on the dragon lady's face. "How would a fat fuck like you become a qualified plumber? Peter, have you not considered the many cramped and confined spaces where plumbers have to work, huh? Your arse is wider than a maintenance hole cover." Mrs. Davenport's hand then changed in shape and structure. Her hand became a separate organism. A living, twisting crab. The crustacean grabbed Peter's neck. Pinched, scratched and cracked. Blood sprinkled. The boy screamed.

"Plumbers will always be in high demand," Mrs. Davenport continued. "Wherever people live, work and travel, there is water, and hence a continuous need for qualified plumbers." Her grip—the crab's grip—on Peter's neck seemed to harden. She stared into the boy's tear-filled eyes. "Listen, Peter. I don't want to see you pick your nose ever again. I don't want to see you pick your bum ever again. Got it?"

"Don't pick your arse before you pick your nose," Alfie Donner said, and laughed.

Mrs. Davenport glowered at Alfie. "*Close your mouth, frog face! Or I'll shut you up forever!*"

Alfie went silent, the grin on his lips gone.

Peter now looked like he was trying to breathe and scream and answer Mrs. Davenport's question at the same time. The colour in the boy's face changed from pig-pink to purple to ice-blue.

"If you were aware of basic etiquette, Peter, you would blow your nose using a sheet of tissue paper," Mrs. Davenport said. "How had you planned to get rid of that sticky snot blob, huh? Wipe it off on your trousers? Now, run out to the toilets and wash your hands with soap. You have thirty seconds."

The crab let go of Peter's neck. The crustacean transformed into Mrs. Davenport's hand. In the crazy teacher's fist, a stopwatch materialised from nowhere. "The seconds are ticking, Peter. Why are you still here? Run! Twenty-five seconds remain of your initial thirty. You don't want to know what I'll do with you if you're late."

Peter coughed, gasping for air, drooling on his shirt. He managed to rise from his chair, with an effort, trembling like a crunchy autumn leaf. Then he stumbled out of the classroom and down the corridor, towards the toilets.

Mrs. Davenport laughed.

Although the fumes of the nightmare poisoned Kenneth, he could perceive the characteristic falsity of the real Mrs. Davenport. As a teacher, the woman did precisely what was expected from her according to the curriculum but only because it was her job. She never showed any interest in her pupils, never cared whether the kids were learning or not. Her only interest was her monthly pay cheque.

Kenneth was convinced Mrs. Davenport hated children, though the children's parents admired the woman for the discipline she instilled in her classes. The parents were obviously unaware of her tyranny. Why didn't Mum or Dad or anyone else outside the school system know what was going on? Why didn't the other teachers at the school know? Because the kids, Kenneth included, were too frightened to tell.

"What about you, Erica?" Mrs. Davenport said. "What do you want to be when you grow up?" She expressed a smile, as if she cared what Erica wanted to be when she grew up.

The normally rational Erica Appleyard believed she knew how to circumvent the teacher's affronts. She got the idea she had outwitted Mrs. Davenport—her biggest mistake in her ten-year life.

"I want to be a schoolteacher just like you, Mrs. Davenport," Erica said. "You're the best teacher I've ever had."

Mrs. Davenport clamped Erica's nose between two fingers on the hand that no longer was a hand but once again a twisting crab. The teacher flicked her wrist forty-five degrees clockwise, with ease, as if she were turning a key in a padlock. The sound that occurred when Erica's nose broke reminded Kenneth of the sound of a walnut that gets crushed in a nutcracker. The girl's scream escalated through the classroom and the blood flowed.

"Listen carefully, Erica," Mrs. Davenport said, grinning. "If you ever try to ingratiate yourself with me again, I will force you to drink your own piss with your lunch sandwich."

"Your piss, Erica," Alison said, giggling loudly. "Your piss!"

Mrs. Davenport shot a look at Alison but left the snickering girl unpunished.

Erica held her bleeding nose, weeping and still screaming. Blood trickled between her fingers.

"Erica," Mrs. Davenport said, "when your mum and the school doctor wonder what happened to your nose, you'll tell them you had an accident in the school gym." She laughed. "Everything sorted."

Warren Aylesworth wanted to be a construction manager. Aabirah Bhatti wanted to be a zoologist. Teresa Nettlefold wanted to be a film star. Philippa O'Malley wanted to be prime minister and a new Iron Lady. Birger Jarl, the Swedish immigrant boy in the class, wanted to be a footballer in the Premier League, just like his dad, top scorer Henrik 'Henke' Jarl. Mrs. Davenport thrashed the aspirations of all the kids with scathing criticism and bitter sarcasm. It was the 'failure' of either ambition or person, or both. More kids—girls as well as boys—experienced a physical pain the teacher delivered through her pointing stick, her crab-imitating hand or her hand-imitating crab.

"What about you, Kenneth?" Mrs. Davenport said. "What do you want to be when you grow up?"

"Me?" Sweat dribbled down Kenneth's back.

"Yes, you." She grinned a dragon's grin.

Please don't hit me, Mrs. Davenport. Please don't hit me, please don't hit me, please don't hit me. "I want to be a writer, Mrs. Davenport."

All the kids roared with laughter. He didn't care the least bit about the troublemakers' laughter. What did hurt was that Alison laughed, too.

Mrs. Davenport didn't laugh at all. She stared at him with an angry expression on her face, as though he had somehow wronged her and offended her.

"I'm actually a writer already," he continued. "I've written stories since I was six."

More laughter.

Now he was almost sure Mrs. Davenport would stab one of her claw-like fingernails into his eye. It didn't happen. She said: "Dear Kenneth, writing can be your hobby at best but I asked what you wanted to do with your life. A serious profession in mind?"

"But I want to be—"

"Yes, I heard! A writer."

More laughter from the class. Alison looked like she was laughing her head off. If it was possible to laugh so hard your head came off, he speculated, then Alison Mitchell was at high risk.

"Who do you think you are, brat?" Mrs. Davenport asked. "The new William Golding?"

The eternal laughter made the horror funhouse sway and shift. The school was a madhouse.

"But can't I—"

"What, Kenneth?! What?!"

"—live my dream, Mrs. Davenport. Can't I live my dream?"

"You can dream, Kenneth, of course you can, but don't throw away your life."

From that moment, he hated her more than he had ever believed he could despise a human being. Assuming that Mrs. Davenport counted as a human being. Mrs. Davenport whipped him in his face with her pointing stick until the blood was flowing from his cheek. The crimson body fluid splashed across his table: *plop, plop, plop, plop, plop*…

Alison glanced at him, smiled her sugar-sweet smile and whispered, "Don't you get it, Kenneth?" She fiddled with her pigtail bows. "Don't you get it? Call me sometime."

▪

Call me sometime.

He found he was sitting on the edge of the bed, staring. Staring at nothing. From an oceanic trench, he heard a girl whisper.

Don't you get it, Kenneth?

Darkness was pulsing before his eyes. He rose, moved in the direction of a polygon with four sides, a rectangle too large to be a window or a painting.

It must be the bedroom door.

Don't you get it?

It happened when he arrived at the door. The object he tripped on was a hairy ball under his foot.

Call me sometime.

The hairy ball sprang to life, growled and hissed.

"Uh, sorry, Linda. Are you okay?"

Linda expressed no more complaints, at least no urgent ones. The door was ajar, just enough for a cat to pass. Linda strolled out of the bedroom and disappeared. The dimness of the bedroom had the same shade as the air in the corridor right outside. Although it was the middle of the night, he wanted to have a shower. His sleeplessness was gone. The nightmare had left him soaking in sweat.

Something had awakened him. What? Who?

If he couldn't sleep when he ought to, he could always use his sleeplessness for a creative purpose. After all, he had a book to write. He fumbled for the doorknob, stepped out into the corridor and went to the bathroom. He groped for the light switch, moving towards the shower cubicle. The light stung his eyes like the acrid fumes of chopped onions.

Something crunched underfoot.

He turned his gaze downwards.

Flowers.

Pink and white flowers, scattered all over the bathroom floor.

36

She looked forward to being a widow. With Philip out of the way, she calculated, no more student girls would be marked for death. Amy Worthington was waiting, listening. She wanted silence in the house before she sneaked up the stairs and ended her husband's breathing for good.

She got a new insight. Marriage was hypocrisy.

If it was meant that people would live as married couples or even as live-in lovers, there would be no such thing as infidelity. Soaring divorce rates and the frequent cheating on wives and husbands and live-in lovers proved that marriage and monogamy were inappropriate living arrangements.

Philip was sleeping. Thus she wouldn't have to waste any last words on him. Instead, she could instantly focus on her life-improving proactivity.

"Okay, Phil," she whispered. "Till death do us part. It'll be as you said that time in church."

Till death do us part.

The moment had come. The metallic aftertaste in her mouth grew. The ecstasy of fury tasted much better than any of Dr. Fenwick's prescriptions.

She was freezing where she stood in the chilly kitchen at midnight. Goosebumps dotted her arms and shoulders. Amy shuddered, her eyes fixed on the woman reflected in the window above the sink. When the night was moonless, when the kitchen ceiling lights were on, the window above the sink could deliver better or worse surprises. The nipples of her breasts were as hard as the goosebumps on her arms and she wondered why. Then she realised it was the pleasant smoothness of her nightdress which titillated her nipples and thighs. Not much but enough. Was she—for some reason—sexually aroused? Yes, somehow, she admitted. Amy was also able to track the source of her emotion: she had the power to end Phil's existence. A moral feeling.

Amy unbuttoned her nightgown and looked at the half-naked woman in the window's reflection. She stroked her breasts, squeezed them and pinched the nipples. "Tits are firmer than ever," she said. "Not bad for a fifty-three-year-old bitch. Better to be a proud bitch than a condescending arsehole. Boobs still untouched by Philip's patronising vocabulary. Verbally immune boobs." She chuckled, licking her lips. "Phil has cracked his last joke."

She lifted the cast-iron pan, and puffed. The pan was so heavy she had to use both hands. Phil's skull would crack as easily as an eggshell. Perfect.

She tried to swing the kitchen utensil, clutching the handle with both fists. Amy pretended she was a tennis player at Wimbledon, practising a backhand. A two-handed backhand. Just like the legendary Jimmy Connors and Björn Borg in their time. Did Connors or Borg ever practise with a frying pan? She fought a sudden urge to giggle.

A sensation struck her—here and now. She was no longer alone. Phil was also there. He stood in the doorway to the kitchen.

"Phil? How dare you sneak up on me like that in the middle of the night?"

Philip said nothing.

"What the hell are you looking at, Phil?"

Philip still said nothing. Her husband was as quiet and immobile as a mummy. How long had he been there? Had he heard her talk to herself? Heard her plans?

"Say something, Phil. Why are you just standing there? Why don't you say something?"

The picture of Philip tattooed her retinas. The image then faded like a dying TV signal. Electronic snow spattered her visual field. Her husband was gone. He had never been there. How lucky she was. Amy walked out of the kitchen carrying the heavy frying pan and tiptoed up the stairs.

37

Stockholm, Sweden.
CentraKem AB, Vasagatan.

The alarm goes off. Already?

Jeanne clenches her teeth and makes fists and stifles a swear word. She's alone in the lift. A display above the lift doors shows the floor numbers: 18; 17; 16… Three seconds between the displays. One minute to the ground floor is an optimistic guess. She tears off the black wig, rips off the white winter coat, takes good care of the badge labelled 'Miss B. Breckenridge', kicks off her boots, opens the mini-suitcase, puts on the black winter jacket, zips up the jacket, steps into running shoes, adjusts her skirt, unscrews the gun silencer and puts the gun in her jacket pocket.

The lift car vibrates, leaps, stops, leaps again, stops again. The display is flashing '13'. She presses the control panel button which operates the door mechanism. Nothing happens. She pushes at the doors, tries to pry them apart using her fingers, breaks a fingernail, grimaces, attacks the doors again, wrests, achieves a gap and peeks out.

The car is stuck between 14 and 13. No lift shaft doors within reach of the lift car doors.

The light goes out. Darkness encloses her. She's listening. Waiting. Thinking.

Thinking about today's achievement. She has freed the world from Emil Jonasson's influence. She has a reason to be proud of herself. Mr. Frank and the rest of the SCDX top brass have a reason to give her another attractive pay rise. With Mr. Jonasson's early retirement, the planet has advanced another step towards total harmony.

The emergency lighting comes on. The soundlessness stays. The lift car is still hanging between floors 14 and 13.

She examines the confined space of the car—walls, floor, ceiling, doors, control panel. The four metal perimeter strips of the ceiling are screwed.

She puts the mini-suitcase on end, steps up and inspects the ceiling's four aluminium strips. Eight screws. The screw-head pattern looks like a six-pointed star. The screw-head make is Torx and the screw material is galvanised steel. Through internal training at SCDX, she has learnt a few things about construction materials.

She wonders how long it would take to defeat eight Torx screws without a screwdriver. Time she doesn't have. She has to get out *now.* She digs deep in the mini-suitcase and snatches a floral washbag. The imagined sound of ticking seconds is blaring in her ears. For want of a better alternative, she attacks the Torx screws with a nail file. Jeanne hisses and puffs. The nail file breaks. She swears.

She stands still, listening.

Rustle and crackle in the distance.

38

He continued to visit the scenes of the murders in chronological order: Hucklow Way, Tankerville Road, Carriage Lane, Canongate Street, Creakemoor, Crowhill Gate and Herbertville Crescent. He used his car, as the killing scenes were spread across four different districts—Broomton, Creake, Ellesmere and the city centre. One afternoon, he took bus No. 49 to Creake. Annabelle Stanfield's reflection hung like a horror painting in the window at which he sat. The girl's face froze in the middle of a scream. The blood was flowing like liquid watercolour from the empty eye socket.

Who killed us, Kenneth? Who killed us?

The seven female voices clung to the air around him. Seven simultaneous whispers, like a choir of phantom voices addressing him, and him only. The whispering chorus of death wasn't his only concern. He felt watched, followed.

If someone was shadowing him, he speculated, the most likely candidate must be the killer. Unless Mr. Frank and Uncle Ash were double-dealing men.

▪

He stepped into a coffee shop in Broomton—a few blocks from Farnwood Road—and found a free corner table. The place was full, or nearly so. How long had he been wandering about on the latest Death Tour? To be honest, he didn't know. The perception of time was infected. The virus was called déjà vu. New experience was mistaken for old. Besides, the present didn't exist. The present was an illusion. The flow of time consisted of only two fields: the past and the future, separated by an infinitely thin line, a demarcation line which was moving forward continuously through eternity.

Déjà vu. *Has to be. The cognitive phenomenon that explains your false but nonetheless eerie sense of having recognised the murder scenes when you visited them for the first time. As if you'd been there before, Kenneth. As if you'd been there before...*

He unbuttoned his raincoat and turned off

his phone. The warmth in the café soothed him and made him forget the cold rain outside. For the first time in hours, hours he had experienced as days, he began to remember how it was to be relaxed.

He closed his eyes and heard his own voice in his head express a sentence he couldn't decipher. His eyelids fluttered, opened. He saw a waitress nodding to him. The girl scribbled something on a notepad. A moment later, a tall glass landed on the table before him. The best cappuccino in town. He lifted the glass and sipped. The sparkle inside him returned.

Customers arrived and customers left. Kenneth envisioned a scene. Suppose the murderer was here right now. Suppose the killer was sitting here right now, drinking a cappuccino, just like him, Kenneth. The maniac could be the man over there, the guy in the ill-fitting suit. Or the sporty guy over there, the gent in the tracksuit. Or over there, the tattooed construction worker. Or the musician right there, the violinist, whose violin case was leaning against a wall. It certainly looked like a violin case but could very well contain a range of stabbing weapons and a variety of torture devices.

Kenneth took a tablet PC from his pocket, clicked up a street map of Blackfield and opened the word processing software. A street map resembled a chessboard in the sense that it was structured as a two-dimensional coordinate system, with letters in alphabetical order along one axis and numbers in numerical order along the other.

The murders in the city centre had taken place in Carriage Lane, Crowhill Gate and Hucklow Way, respectively. He read the city map's check pattern and then keyed the three coordinate pairs into the newly created document. The Herbertville Crescent killing represented an odd case from a geographical point of view. He wrote down its coordinate pair separately. The deaths in the districts of Broomton and Creake made up the third category: Canongate Street, Tankerville Road and the Creakemoor-Roderick Avenue intersection. He knocked out the final coordinate pairs.

He pondered the text, the complete picture:

City: N14, P15, P16

Herbert Ville Crescent: J17

Broomton & Creake: J15, G15, J15

He looked up from the tablet. An idea crackled in his brain. The thought grew into a realisation. He saw it in the distance. The puzzle piece appeared, straight out of the fog.

39

In the dreamscape, he was trapped like a budgie in a cage. He was ten years old again and at dinner at his grandmum's house, a dinner event derived from reality, except that the dream version, a nightmare version, ended worse than in the actual version.

The nightmare version ended in pure terror.

He glimpsed her in the dream. He could hear her voice as well. This had happened before, more than once. It worried him that it kept returning. His thoughts about Alison showed up at random times. In the classroom or in the schoolyard or at home. Anywhere. He wanted to talk to a doctor about it. No, not wanted, but ought to. Doctors were good at figuring out what was wrong with people.

An inner voice said: *Alison is pretty. Too pretty to ignore. Too bad she doesn't like chess. But that can change, Kenneth. Teach her the game. Get her interested in chess and her giggles will disappear.*

Grandmum returned from the kitchen with her homemade chocolate fruitcake. It seemed to weigh ten kilograms. Kenneth and his little brother Simon reached for the cake straight away and quickly, as if it were a competition, and, well, perhaps it was.

"Whoa, take it easy, boys," Mum said. "There's cake enough for everyone."

Eve and Bernie repeated from within the parrot cage: "*Take it easy, boys, there's cake enough for everyone!*"

Mum raised a warning finger at her sons but Grandmum laughed. Tracy, Grandmum's poodle, barked. The TV was rumbling in the background.

Dad was silent, his nose buried in a newspaper.

In a month, Mum and Dad would divorce in order to go their separate ways to live in different worlds. How many worlds were there? An infinite number of parallel worlds, if you believed what scientists said on TV and in newspapers. Every time a quantum event took place, a new world, a new universe, split off from the old. 'Every time' meant 'all the time' since quantum events occurred continuously.

In his leisure, ten-year-old Kenneth was reading quantum mechanics, nanotechnology, psychology, cosmology and evolutionary biology. Since he was seven, he followed scientific publications and read pop-science books by the intellectual giants.

(*Who killed us, Kenneth?*)

After finishing dessert, Kenneth and Simon moved to Grandmum's kitchen. Here, at the kitchen table, they were alone. They had smuggled in a bag of popcorn. Kenneth had prepared his mini-lesson. He had brought his chess set, which Mum and Dad had given him for his fourth birthday.

(*Who killed us, Kenneth?*)

Kenneth would be playing as White, and Simon, consequently, as Black. "The board consists of sixty-four squares organised 8 × 8," Kenneth said. "In algebraic notation, the board is divided in files and ranks. The files are the eight verticals labelled from 'a' to 'h'. The ranks are the eight horizontals labelled from '1' to '8'. Thus you can identify each square by a unique combination of file and rank, Simon. The first four files from White's left, a-d, are collectively known as queenside, and the remaining files, e-h, are collectively known as kingside."

"No shit," Simon said.

"Shut up and listen. Now, for example, the start position of the black bishop on queenside—that's your bishop to your right—has the coordinate pair c8. You understand?"

"I understand," Simon said. His eyes flickered across the board. "Any idiot could understand this."

"Right, Simon. Any idiot. By the way, there's a rule about starting positions that is easy to remember: white queen on white square; black queen on black square."

The Queen is a fashionable lady. She likes her dress to match her shoes…

"Any fool can remember that too! Can we start playing now? Kenneth?"

The dream changed. At the opposite side of the chessboard was no longer his little brother. Instead, pretty Alison Mitchell was sitting there. Her giggles echoed in Grandmum's kitchen. Her snickers made the china, glass and silverware clink and rattle and slam in cupboards and drawers. A poltergeist was sweeping straight through the kitchen.

The blood-red pointed bows in the girl's pigtails looked like the horns on the devil's daughter's head. "Will you teach me how to play, Kenneth?"

Her grimace made him think of Mrs. Davenport. He trembled.

"I'll teach the boy how to play!" Her laugh turned giddier, if possible. "You want to peek under my skirt?" The girl laughed so hard that tears were rolling, tears tinted by raven-black eyeshadow. The dark drops were tumbling down her cheeks and blouse, spattering her skirt, dripping to the floor. Streaks of tears spread like cobwebs on the kitchen floor. She hissed and screamed like a girl possessed by the Prince of Darkness. "*Don't you be so fucking fussy! Hrgrgrgrgrz! Hrgrgrgrzz! Hrgrgrgrzzzz…*" Her voice malfunctioned before it died completely, like the cracked voice of a battery powered doll with a broken voice chip. Then the girl's head exploded in a cloud of blood.

From somewhere he perceived his own screams and his own sobbing. Both time and space changed. It was only the start of another beginning, another horror, and a parallel discovery.

▪

He found himself standing on a chessboard, which was larger than Grandmum's garden. And there they were, right in front of him: Lucy, Rebecka, Annabelle, Kelly, Gemma, Gloria and Suzanne. Not their bodies, only their heads. They shouted at him.

"Who murdered us, Kenneth?"

"Suppose it was you, Kenneth?"

The ladies belonged to the army of black chess pieces. The rook from the a8-corner had Rebecka's head. One of the bishops had Annabelle's head. The queen's head belonged to Lucy. Kelly's head had been screwed onto the b8-knight's neck. Gemma's, Suzanne's and Gloria's severed heads were worn by the second black rook, the second black knight and the second black bishop, respectively.

Suppose it was you, Kenneth?

The Lucy-queen-hybrid said: "Where's my eye? Where is it? I miss my eye."

Dead girls don't talk.

A worm squirmed in Lucy's empty eye socket. Three beetles scampered out of the corner of her mouth. The beetles then struggled in the dirt and the smeared lipstick on her dead and mottled face.

Kenneth screamed.

The Rebecka-rook hybrid bellowed. "You mean you haven't figured out who the killer is?" Lumps of coagulated blood dangled in her twisted hair. She laughed a humourless laugh, shaking her head from side to side. The clusters of blood clots rattled like castanets from an unspeakable underworld.

A bishop rushed forward, grinning like a witch. Its head belonged to Annabelle. The left eye was missing. The remaining eye was as dark and wrinkled as a prune. Tears were spilling from the gaping hole in the skull. "What if it was you?"

His stomach made a double somersault. Some sort of sickness was bubbling in every cell of his body. He wanted to vomit. He heard his own mind. Your fate wasn't my fault, Annabelle. What could I have done?

The Annabelle-bishop hybrid roared like some aggressive predator. The chessboard was shaking. He lost his balance and staggered. Cracks in the checkered floor were spreading in all directions. He was in an earthquake.

Annabelle hissed. "We will punish you."

▪

"Here, Kenneth!"

The voice came from everywhere.

"Here I am!"

He spun around.

"Here!" She waved. Alison looked like she had just stepped out of a photograph from her twentieth birthday. She wore a short dove-grey dress and pearl-white running shoes. A wind of dreams was caressing her hazel-brown hair. "How do I look?"

"You look sensational, Alison."

Her hand rested on a chess piece. A waist-high pawn. How strange. How did the pawn get there?

"Catch me if you can, Kenneth!"

"I can't. I'm on the e3-square. I can't catch your pawn with any piece from this position, according to the rules of the game."

Her smile faded. "I didn't ask you to try to catch me like you would a damn chess piece, you idiot! I meant that you could try to win my heart."

"What's the matter, Alison? Why is the tone in your voice so peculiar and arrogant?"

"I wonder if you could win my heart, like before, when we first got together."

"We've never been together. Not yet. Not until seven years from now. I'm still only a kid in Mrs. Davenport's classroom."

"I won't go out with you again, ever. We weren't meant for each other."

"Why are you here? What are you doing here?"

"It's a free country, kid. I go where I want."

"The country might be free but our dreams are private matters."

She sighed. "Don't you get it, Kenneth? Call me sometime."

"I'll do that. I promise."

"I'm leaving now. My new boyfriend is waiting for me. Take care of yourself, kid."

"Who's your new boyfriend?"

"Someone who understands girls."

Alison left, towards a dimming horizon, quicker than the blink of an eye. He was watching her until she became a tiny white star in the far distance.

Then the star went out.

40

He leaned over the bed and kissed her. “Wake up, Jeanne! Wake up!” He perceived her scent of violets and roses, last night’s wonderful perfume.

She blinked, startled. “Uh, what is it, Kenneth?”

“I want to show you something.”

She stared at him. “Why do you have a knife in your hand?”

He followed her gaze. “The knife? I’m about to slice pears in the kitchen.”

“Now? At this hour?”

“What time is it?”

“It’s the middle of the night. Get back to bed.”

“Get up. I must show you something.”

“A new clue?”

“Do you want to put on your robe?”

“Why?”

“Well, you’re naked.”

“The robe?” Jeanne yawned, crawled out of bed and brushed locks of hair away from her face. “Robe? In the middle of the night?” She put on her nightgown.

▪

They sat in front of a computer in his workroom.

“There’s another pattern, Jeanne.”

She was munching on a slice of pear. “Go on.”

"If each letter of the alphabet has a numerical value according to its position, what chronological sequence, expressed in numbers, do we get?"

She rolled her eyes. "Get from *what*?"

"From the murder victims' surnames."

Jeanne yawned. "*You* say it. I'm tired."

"The series G-K-M-Q-S-W-W returns 7, 11, 13, 17, 19, 23, 23."

"So what?"

"They're all prime numbers."

"Oh. Is it important?"

"Furthermore, the series contains every single prime in the interval from 7 through 23."

"I haven't thought about prime numbers since school, if I even did back then, but let me see if I remember the definition of such a number… A prime number is an integer greater than 1 which is evenly divisible only by itself and 1. Right?"

He tried to smile politely. "Unfortunately, that's a somewhat flippant definition. It ignores negative divisors. For example, the prime number 98,473 is evenly divisible by four numbers: 98,473; 1; – 98,473; and – 1. A perfectionist—and mathematicians are perfectionists—would possibly express themselves in the following way: a prime number is a natural number greater than 1 that has exactly two positive divisors: itself and 1."

She looked at him with suspicion. "That

very large number you mentioned, what was it, ninety-eight thousand and something?"

"Not *very* large. It's *relatively* large compared to twenty-nine, but relatively small compared to fifty-eight billion. The number I mentioned, only as an example to clarify a point, was ninety-eight thousand four hundred and seventy-three."

"And you just happened to know it was a prime number, huh?"

"Yeah."

"How does your mind function, Kenneth?"

"I don't know."

"Aha. And what is a natural number?"

"A positive integer or a non-negative integer. Two definitions exist."

"Oh. Okay. But I don't understand why you're talking about this at all. Could you summarise the uses of prime numbers? And put the knife down?"

He nibbled a slice of pear—and put the knife down. "Today, many of the world's secret codes are dependent on a key, which is a very large integer, and the ability to factorise that key into its prime components. Before quantum computers advance from science fiction to real life, security systems controlled by electronic digital computers require increasingly large prime numbers.

"In 1859, the mathematician Bernhard Riemann presented a hypothesis which seemed to explain the spectacular relationship between prime numbers and composite numbers. Unfortunately, Riemann's housemaid burned all his papers after his death in 1866. No one knows if he ever managed to prove his hypothesis."

Jeanne placed a naked foot between his thighs. "The housemaid probably just wanted the house to be clean and tidy. Boys can be terribly careless."

He chuckled. "The Riemann hypothesis remains one of the most significant problems in the world of mathematics. A solution to the Riemann hypothesis would have revolutionary consequences for human existence. Internet commerce and industrial data security would implode. In addition, the Riemann hypothesis unites several different scientific areas, with critical implications for chaos theory, quantum mechanics and the future of computing."

She looked thoughtful. "Bottom line, Kenneth?"

"I believe my latest discovery proves the killer's characteristics. We can dismiss theories about some primitive crackpot who kills young women through arbitrary selection. The person we are hunting is a very organised individual, a well-educated professional who has developed an interest in mathematics, number theory, statistics and related topics."

"Not unlike yourself then."

"Unfunny."

"But W is the last letter of the alphabet with

a position-oriented value which is a prime. X, Y and Z return three composites."

"Studying the twenty-six letters in a restricted alphabetical order would be a mistake, Jeanne."

"Why? How? You've been arguing a point about alphabetical order and now you say the maniac is too smart to operate according to it. What if you made up your mind? I can't wait to return to bed."

He lifted her bare foot and kissed it. "If the killer was following a strict alphabetical order, why didn't he start with B? The first victim, Miss Graham, is linked to the prime number 7. However, there are three primes which are smaller than 7. They are, of course, 2, 3 and 5, associated with B, C and E. Why didn't he commence with B?"

"I don't know."

"I suggest we consider the twenty-six letters as a crypto. In addition to the standard sequence from A through Z, there are twenty-five unconventional ways to write the sequence in increments of 1, if we neglect strict reverse sequences. For example, from B through A, from M through L, or from J through I. I'm confident that in the first instance, or in a first cycle, we can focus on one particular sequence: from G through F in increments of 1." He tapped a key on the computer keyboard. "Look at the screen."

Jeanne looked.

From G through F,
the forward (non-reverse) mode:

G (7), H (8), I (9), J (10), *K (11)*, L (12), *M (13)*, N (14), O (15), P (16), *Q (17)*, R (18), *S (19)*, T (20), U (21), V (22), *W (23)*, X (24), Y (25), Z (26), A (1), B (2), C (3), D (4), E (5), F (6)

"Thus, within the brackets are the position-oriented values," Kenneth said. "Positions related to the murder victims are in italics for the sake of clarity."

Jeanne nodded. Her bare foot touched the front of his pyjama bottoms. "Kelly Graham was the first victim. That's why you start the sequence with G."

"And I have underlined B, C and E, the three remaining letters associated with primes which the killer has not yet used."

"Not yet, uh? You expect more murders?"

He didn't answer.

She took another slice of pear from the saucer and licked pear juice from her fingers. "According to your system, Kenneth, the next victim's surname will begin with B."

"Not necessarily. It *could* be a Miss B the next time, alternatively a third Miss W, after Wheeler and Wright, such as a second Miss Wright, or a Miss Wrigley or a Miss Wyatt or a Miss Wu."

"Miss Wu?"

He smiled. "There are in all likelihood at

least thirty million Chinese women whose name is Wu. One or two could be studying in Blackfield."

Telephone signals shattered the silence in the midnight darkness.

Jeanne let out a short squeal.

Kenneth reached for the phone. "Hello?"

"That was a quick response indeed."

"Good morning, Uncle Ash. I mean—of course—good night." He looked over at Jeanne. The beauty stopped chewing the slice of pear she already had in her mouth. "Why the heck are you calling at this hour?" Nobody called at half past midnight with good news.

"Were you awake, my boy?"

"Yes. I happened to be awake. I'm reading."

"That could be the explanation."

"The explanation of what?"

"You took the call on the first ring."

"What are you driving at?"

"Do you have female company?"

"I'm alone." He glanced at Jeanne again. She sat leaning back in her chair. Mischievous Jeanne! Her outstretched bare foot continued to wander about between his thighs. She knew he knew she wore no knickers under her short nightdress. She also knew he had a nice view right now.

"Ken? You're still there?"

"Still here, Uncle."

"Have you been out tonight?"

"Why?"

"I called earlier but there was no one at home."

"If I'm busy writing, it happens that I ignore a ringing phone."

"So you were at home, after all?"

"Could you get to the point? Why are you calling at half past midnight?"

"There's been another murder, Ken."

"Where? When? Who?"

Have you been out tonight?

"Endsleigh Park. A few hours ago. A Miss Sadie Bentley."

I called earlier but there was no one at home.

Kenneth knocked on the keyboard keys and gestured to Jeanne to read on the computer screen:

New Murder – Endsleigh Park – a few hours ago

– Sadie Bentley

So you were at home, after all?

"Uncle Ash?"

"Yes?"

"You did say 'a few hours ago' and that means Thursday, January the twenty-ninth. Formidable."

41

The corpse lay in the northeast corner of the park. With a cauliflower-coloured complexion and with arms and legs outstretched in odd directions, Sadie Bentley's body looked like a discarded retail display mannequin. The remaining eye in the dead girl's skull presented an emerald-green iris.

Uncle Ash pulled an over-ripe apple from his coat pocket and sank his nicotine-yellow teeth in it. Apple juice dripped from his lower lip.

"How can you eat under these circumstances?" Kenneth said. "Here, in this dreadful place?"

"It was *you* who said I needed more fruits and vegetables, at least five portions of fruit and veg a day. The five-a-day guideline, you know? This apple is my light lunch."

Kenneth shook his head and changed the subject. "The killer can't be bothered to hide the bodies."

"The killer can't be bothered to hide the bodies because he knows we can't track him through the bodies." Uncle Ash walked away, threw the core of the apple in a litter bin and put a cigarette in the corner of his mouth. He started to mingle with the forensic scientists.

Crime scene technicians filtered the whole park. Although Kenneth knew they had to do their work, he considered it a waste of time. They wouldn't find anything. Who had fabricated this thought for him? Christine from beyond the grave?

He wanted to get away from here right now,

out into Ellesmere Street, and flag down a taxi which could drive him home. Yet he lingered in the park. He was here and at the same time he wasn't. SCDX orchestrated the parameters which determined his circumstances. The CID (or the SCDX) technicians lifted samples with tweezers. Scraped beneath the cadaver's fingernails. Photographed, and filmed a video which Uncle Ash would use in connection with his next briefing at headquarters.

"You okay?" Uncle Ash's voice, from straight behind Kenneth's back. "No, you're not okay. You're as pale as the cadaver."

Kenneth turned around. "I don't feel very well."

"There may be a good reason."

"What's that supposed to mean?"

"You tell me."

Kenneth hesitated. "It struck me that this Sadie Bentley murder is a carbon copy of a murder in my debut novel."

"I know that, Ken."

"It's eerie. It's crazy."

"I know that too, Ken."

He had modelled a fictional park on Endsleigh Park, while other places described were authentic. Factors surrounding the murder of Sadie Bentley copied the park murder from *Blue Moon Psycho* in every detail—the surroundings, the actual murder scene, the position of the crime scene relative to its surroundings, and the pose of the corpse at the spot of the killing. Arms and legs were spread and bent in ways that gave the corpse a symmetric aesthetic, which from a bird's-eye view was reminiscent of a galaxy with four spiral arms.

Had Uncle Ash noticed all this?

"The victim from your book, Ken? The dead girl in the park? What was her name again?"

Kenneth knew that his uncle knew. What was he driving at? "Sabine Braun. A German-American computer engineer at Jacobi RoboTronics."

"And she had the same initials as Sadie Bentley. Intriguing, Ken, isn't it?"

Kenneth looked around. "We finished here?"

"Jacobi RoboTronics. That's a local company?"

"Not quite. Sheffield."

"I see. Still Yorkshire though. Fictitious?"

"I asked: are we finished here?"

His uncle's gaze swept across the park. Then he moved. "Come on, Ken. I'll drive you home."

They walked towards the southern gate and the car park facing Ellesmere Street. The shy sun had already dropped below the concrete horizon of the cityscape. The December darkness was back again.

Eight girls murdered. Eight mutilated corpses. Never before had Kenneth been involved in a case with such high stakes.

Involved?

He didn't like that word for now. He didn't like that word at all.

"Ken?"

"Hmm."

"Do you like *Blue Moon Psycho*?"

"A debut book always has a special place in a writer's heart."

"*Blue Moon Psycho* is too bizarre—too fucked up—to appeal to readers outside your die-hard fan club, Ken, though I want to praise you for another novel. *The Dream Killers* is the best book you've written. It's really cool. A work you can be proud of. Do you think you will ever write a better book than *The Dream Killers*?"

"I believe I can. Every novelist must believe he can outdo himself. Or his creative drive would die."

He sank into the front passenger seat. But his thoughts were still in the park. The headlights cut through the swirling drizzle. His uncle steered the beat-up Audi into the street and squeezed it into the Endsleigh Square roundabout. Soon they were in Endsleigh Road, heading east towards the city.

"I'll tell you something, Ken." Uncle Ash kept his eyes on the road. The rain clattered against the windscreen. "Something I couldn't say in the park."

Here it comes, he thought. More references to *Blue Moon Psycho*. Another nail in the coffin.

"It's about Stevie."

False alarm. He sighed a silent sigh of relief and then curiosity hit. "Morrison?"

"Yup." His uncle lit a cigarette.

"What is it with Detective Morrison?"

"Recently, he hasn't been himself. I felt it first weeks ago and so did Mr. Frank. Now Frank has told me to keep an eye on Stevie."

42

Stockholm, Sweden.
CentraKem AB, Vasagatan.

Jeanne gets a new idea. She lets go of the broken nail file, digs in the mini-suitcase, rips out the pink handbag, shakes out all the contents and finds the necklace, the necklace adorned with pearls and six-pointed metal stars of various sizes.

One disadvantage with Torx—perhaps its only disadvantage, she thinks—is that the screwdriver must fit the screw head with exactitude. Jeanne tries the various stars in the necklace. The fourth star-size is spot on. She unscrews the aluminium strips, pushes up a ceiling panel and peeks out into the lift shaft.

Semi-darkness. Total silence.

She recognises the lift model and make, with a steel cable and a counterweight. The lift is powered by an electric engine. The wire is secured to a clutch plate on the car roof. The counterweight is currently out of sight but

Jeanne has identified its separate rail system in the up-and-down gloom.

From the mini-suitcase she grabs the umbrella and an extra ammunition magazine. She places the umbrella on the car roof and puts the ammo magazine in her skirt pocket. The mini-suitcase with contents cannot be traced to SCDX. She leaves it.

She climbs up onto the car roof and notices the 14th-floor lift shaft doors. She stands at the edge of an eighty-metre-deep abyss, peering over the edge. The bottom is invisible.

"You'll definitely love Stockholm, Miss Russell," Mr. Frank had said. *"Stockholm is a fantastic city."*

The 14th-floor lift shaft doors are shut. Still, they're within her reach. She grasps the door edges, trying to pry them apart. The doors don't budge a millimetre. She sticks the umbrella's metal tip into the joint between the doors and applies pressure on the pole, twisting, bending and prying.

Her foothold disappears all of a sudden. The umbrella drops from her fists. She's a free-falling girl in the abyssal darkness. She's howling, paddling with her arms and legs. Vertical emptiness swallows her. In the same second, a heavy blow to her elbow. She screams in pain. Something sharp cuts through her jacket sleeve, braking the fall, not much, just a little. Her fingers find something along a seemingly 'upward-speeding' shaft wall or along the 'upward-speeding' counterweight rail system. A cable, a wire or a cord. She clutches at it with both hands.

Her tumble stops with a painful jolt. A pulsating pain in the palm of one hand. Blood trickles down her arm. She's hovering in a crow-black sea.

She grimaces, tearing and pulling the cable with both hands. The extra pistol magazine tumbles out of her skirt pocket and disappears into the gaping blackness. She swears and clenches her teeth and climbs upwards and reaches the lift car roof.

The umbrella survived. It's right there, on the edge of the lift car roof. She's thinking about the ammunition. She has spent three bullets on Emil Jonasson and lost a fully charged gun magazine. Seventeen bullets left. She wipes the bloody palm of her hand on the inside of her skirt, picks up the umbrella and resumes the backbreaking work on the lift shaft doors. A slit appears between the doors. She continues to bend, pry, push and twist, using the damn umbrella. The gap widens.

43

Stephen Morrison made the decision. He would never utter the truth. Not to Patricia or their sons.

Not to anyone.

Truths were suppressible. Destroyable.

Life was built on priorities—the clear message that Father had drummed into his children's heads. Stephen and his sister Chelsea had been exposed to Father's philosophy throughout their childhood in Grimsby. Father was still arguing from his grave.

A job well done brings inner satisfaction. Then, secondly, if absolutely necessary, you could listen to your family's needs and thoughts.

Father's voice, the eternal company, seemed as sombre and haunting as Stephen's own shadow. He hadn't despised Father. He had been scared of him. He learnt his lessons and respected Father's words. Father was the law. Father was the control. From Father to SCDX. Learn to love Father and Mother. Begin to worship SCDX. The human brain wasn't hard-wired for altruism. Turn a despotism to your advantage.

Stephen and Chelsea had believed—beyond a shadow of a doubt—that taking a beating once in a while was part and parcel of a standard upbringing. He wanted to protect Chelsea when Father attacked her with his hard fists. But there was nothing he could do to stop him. Eventually, both Stephen and his sister acquired the ability to live with the pain. The physical, unavoidable, pain.

Mother had her own priorities: firstly, the drugs; secondly, the bingo hall; thirdly, the children. Stephen and Chelsea had never really known Mother. How could you actually know a mother, or any person, who was stoned or high all the time? Mother had never expressed any genuine emotions, had never been clear-headed or sober enough to engage in any important conversations.

Chelsea studied to earn a bachelor's degree in Interior Design at a Yorkshire university, then got a job at a modern art museum in London. After six years at the Lincolnshire police and several glowing testimonials, Stephen requested and was granted a transfer to Blackfield, Yorkshire. He had mentioned family reasons: his wife Patricia had been offered and had accepted a job at a law firm in the 'black city' on the River Claxton.

He became an SCDX detective just like Father. As he later realised, he was an SCDX detective only to satisfy Father. As a youngster, he hadn't dared value his own thoughts about what he wanted to do with his life. With SCDX, you needed no values or opinions of your own. SCDX handled it all.

SCDX was no organisation you could approach through a query letter. You couldn't apply for a job at a company that didn't exist. And once you were in, you couldn't leave, at least not of your own free will. SCDX recruited and dismissed staff, in silence.

Although Stephen and Chelsea were close, visits and telephone calls got sparser. Both blamed it on stressful careers and their own family responsibilities. Stephen and Patricia had two sons. Wayne was eleven and Timothy nine. Chelsea was a mother of four and had a fifth on the way. Her husband loved her. Chelsea's own family was the comfort zone she never had as a child.

Now, right now, he felt Father's psychological presence with a fresh threatening strength. Where was the limit? He didn't remember the last time he had called his sister. Three months ago? Or was it five months ago? About time to call Chelsea. About time to see her again. He decided now that when he got home tonight… if he got home again tonight, alive… he would…

44

He needed to talk to a florist but not just anyone. He would call Alison tomorrow.

Don't you get it, Kenneth? Call me sometime.

He sank down onto the sofa in the living room, still in his outdoor wear—overcoat and boots—sat in the dark, listening to his own breathing, studying the gloomy silhouettes of the furniture.

Maybe the nightmares hadn't been nightmares. What if he had *hallucinated* the scary dreams? Was that possible? Could his dreams be imagined rather than perceived? Did the difference matter?

He lit the lamp on the coffee table. The gleam left behind rugged shadows in every corner of the room. The wind whispered outside the windows. A lime tree in the avenue threw dancing shadows onto the walls of the living room. He resisted an urge to move to the windows and draw the curtains.

Where was Linda?

"Linda!"

No answer. Not the slightest miaowing. All he could hear was the rushing wind in the treetops along the avenue. The least sound from the front door, including sounds inaudible to humans, would attract Linda's attention. With an ability to perceive sound frequencies from about thirty hertz to about sixty-four thousand hertz (ultrasound from twenty thousand hertz and above), the cat had one of the widest ranges of hearing among mammals.

"Where are you, Linda?"

He returned to the hall, hung his coat, took off his boots and stepped into a pair of slippers. Back in the living room, he picked up the Whitley Strieber novel from the coffee table and put it in its proper place under S in one of the bookcases.

He went out to the kitchen and looked in the fridge. On a shelf in the door were two bottles of sparkling water. He took one and returned to the living room. He sipped the water, looking at the bookshelves. He owned books by authors filed under every letter of the alphabet.

From Asimov, Isaac to Zebrowski, George.

From Abe, Kōbō to Zola, Émile.

Via Goldberg, Leonard or Laymon, Richard.

Letters convertible to position-oriented values.

Prime numbers. Composite numbers.

Perfect numbers.

Perfect order in the chaos of life.

He focused his hearing on the house itself, tried to shut out the noise of the wind and passing vehicles in the avenue. The house creaked, squeaked and groaned. Unremarkable sounds but undeniable. The house gave the impression of crumbling under the weight of its Victorian age; it seemed to writhe in pain like a church in a Vincent van Gogh painting.

He returned to the kitchen and inspected the refrigerator—a broccoli-and-cheese pie, beetroot and Linda's special dishes. In a cupboard above the cooker he found a tin of minestrone soup. Fine. No, not fine at all. His gaze had landed on Linda's bowls on top of the chest of drawers in front of a kitchen windowsill. The bowls were full. Someone had been in the house. Someone had been in the house and topped up the bowls. Who? Maybe the person was still here. He looked over his shoulder. There was no one there. Nothing but the four-legged shadows accompanying the kitchen furniture.

Again, he went to the hall, stopped, and peered into the living room. Only the fluttering shadows, tossed through the windows by the lime tree in the avenue. No other movements. *Why did he top up the bowls?*

Maybe Linda had surprised the intruder. Maybe the invader had misjudged the surprise, had seen it as nasty—and had overreacted. Linda wasn't an aggressive guard dog but a harmless cat. Could her piercing eyes in the darkness have unsettled the interloper? What if, during his search of the house, the invader had got annoyed at Linda for some reason and decided to silence her? What if he had killed her and dumped her body into the garbage, either in the kitchen waste basket or in one of the two rubbish bins outside?

The bowls... Why?

Could the invader have committed such an evil act? Of course he could. He had killed eight young women in cold blood so why would he hesitate to eliminate a pet that happened to be in his way?

Kenneth returned to the kitchen and opened the cupboard under the sink. He lifted the lid of the waste basket and reluctance hit him. He forced himself to peek inside. The basket was half full of cardboard packaging and empty tins. No Linda.

He continued to the rear of the kitchen, stopped at the door to the laundry room, and listened. Silence ruled on the other side. He twisted the door handle, swung the door open, crossed the threshold and at that moment he was convinced the intruder would step out of the tall drying cabinet, with a knife in one hand and an axe in the other. It didn't happen.

He opened the drying cabinet and glanced inside. A towel and three shirts. No Linda. He looked inside the washing machine. Empty. No Linda. He moved to the back door of the laundry room, opened it, slipped out into the night and continued around the corner of the house.

Dead leaves swirled through the air like exotic insects. In the dark, he got the idea that the rustling leaves weren't leaves at all but giant beetles that owned the evening air and crawled across the lawn and the stone-tiled garden path.

He took on the green bin first. The instant he lifted the lid, he envisioned Linda with a broken neck, one eyeball gone, her tongue hanging from her mouth like a pink fabric strip. He stared down into the bin, which was now filled with shadows, and the vision of the maimed Linda faded away. She wasn't there. Of course she wasn't. What a stupid idea to kill a cat and throw the body into a litter bin. *Except there was the exclusion method: since she isn't in the green bin, she must be in the black.*

"Shut up," he muttered, and turned to the black bin. He opened the lid and peered down. No Linda there either. The only dead animal he saw was a rat. The red rat eyes glittered in the gloom. Reflected street lighting, he guessed. It was probably some neighbour's anti-social children who had tossed the lifeless rodent into his rubbish bin. He returned to the house through the back door and locked it.

That was when he heard it for the first time. A sound from upstairs, or in the stairs between the ground floor and the first floor, a noise not caused by the pounding wind. This new sound came with an internal quality, for instance, from a creaking floorboard or a stair step. Back in the kitchen he pulled out the drawer holding a knife storage tray, snatched the first thing he got hold of, a fruit knife, and examined it. He concluded it was too small. Too small for what? He had no answer. He put the fruit knife back, picked up the very largest carving knife, pushed in the drawer and listened to the house.

The smallest squeak. From upstairs, no doubt. A brief mechanical noise, not unlike that from a chalk stick used on the blackboard in his workroom. He didn't believe that someone was actually using his blackboard, it just sounded that way. Besides, for the sake of argument, if someone *was* using the blackboard, it wouldn't be possible to hear it from here, downstairs.

Who would search the house? The murderer, of course. The killer was still here, checking Kenneth's secret files and documents on the case.

He tiptoed out into the hall, to the foot of the stairs and stopped. He didn't like what he saw in the hall mirror—a grinning character with a carving knife in his fist. The grin was out of place, let alone the carving knife.

"I won't actually use it," he told the mirror. "The initial idea was self-defence but the trespasser has probably gone now." He laughed a muffled laugh but it came with a false tone that made him fall silent at once. He began to walk up the stairs.

Morrison? Mrs. Worthington?

Mr. Worthington?

He stopped at the first-floor landing, listening. A rattling sound, from the upstairs bathroom. His gaze darted along the corridor. Too gloomy.

He flicked on the ceiling lights.

The noise vanished, replaced by perfect silence. Fear gripped him again. What if the intruder had drowned Linda in the washbasin and cut out one of his dead cat's eyes and flushed it down the toilet? Could any of the previous sounds have come from a whining sewer pipe?

"Shut up," he murmured. "You're paranoid."

The bathroom door was ajar. Bathroom lighting off. He remained in the corridor, unmoving. Time stood paranormally still, as if shock-frozen halfway through a late-night millisecond.

The wind kept battering the house. The corridor lights flickered, died, came back on, flickered.

He noticed a motion ahead.

45

Stockholm, Sweden.
CentraKem AB, Vasagatan.

The lift shaft doors are creeping apart at a snail's pace. Jeanne is panting, moaning. Her hands and jacket sleeves are dirty with dark dust and black oil.

She peers into the 14th floor. If she stands on tiptoes, the floor is level with her waist.

A corridor. Empty, though not silent. At the far end, a T-junction. Several voices to the right and/or to the left beyond the T.

The alarm has stopped blaring. By now, every exit must be closed, locked and guarded, she thinks. CentraKem AB is a huge complex. The hunt for the CEO's killer is on but they can't search everywhere at once. There might be thousands of people in the building. Many departments, a lot of visitors, a vast number of stairs, several lifts and uncountable hiding places. She can't be certain whether a Betsy Breckenridge tops the list of suspects, yet people would arrive here, sooner or later, in a minute or two, hunting her. Any second, the lift car on which she stands could start moving again, up or down. She must get out of the lift shaft *now*.

She can no longer hold the doors apart with her bare hands. She's tiring. The opening is shrinking. She keeps pushing with her elbows and fists. With her mouth, she puts the slim umbrella horizontally into the shrinking gap between the doors. The gap is in this instant less than twenty inches.

The doors stop. The umbrella creaks.

The doors squeak. The umbrella curves.

She heaves herself up and above the edge of the 14th floor before her eyes, throws herself forward through the narrow opening, the umbrella snaps with a bang, the doors rush shut with the speed of lightning and she catches her left foot. She flounders in the air, screams in pain but maintains her forward momentum. She crash-lands (fortunately not on her head) in the 14th-floor corridor and rolls around before reaching a total stop. From the corner of her eye, she sees how the lift shaft doors mash her left shoe.

Jeanne gets up on her feet, limping, grimacing. She surveys the situation, wiping her dirty hands on the inside of her skirt, and discovers a tear in her brand-new stockings.

She moves to the nearby stairway… and stops dead. Emerging voices from below. She can already see moving shadows on the staircase wall. Bad luck.

She turns back and moves through the corridor. Still no people in sight. The activity on the 14th floor might be less than usual, she speculates. Buckets with paint and boxes with paint brushes, rollers, trays and paint pads are stacked along one wall. There are several doors on both sides. The signs on the doors say, in Swedish, Storeroom, Computer Room, Laboratory, Reception, and Men's and Women's Changing Room. She can read the signs. Through the SCDX internal training, she has learnt some Swedish.

She freezes. People are coming. They are about to turn into this very corridor via the T-junction just ahead. She's in the middle of the corridor.

46

It startled him. The sudden movement—out of the bathroom and into the corridor. A four-footed creature. "Linda? It's really you. You're okay?"

Linda miaowed.

Relief washed over him. But the fact remained unchanged: an intruder had been in the house. The proof was Linda's topped-up bowls.

"Do you realise how worried I've been for you, Linda? Do you?"

Linda miaowed.

■

Blackfield's Winter Garden was a natural meeting place in the heart of the city. The glass-enclosed park gave him no direct privacy but he appreciated the shielding atmosphere of a crowded landmark, where he could feel an anonymity he called indirect privacy. Although he wasn't alone, he was alone.

And loneliness triggered memories. He phoned Alison's mobile number. A robotic voice encouraged him to leave a voicemail or to call the floristry shop. The machine gave him the number. He almost left a voicemail, changed his mind and called the shop.

"Kenneth?" Pause. "Is it you?"

"It's me."

"What a surprise."

"Positive or negative?"

"What do you want?"

"Don't worry, Alison. I'm not calling to try to win you back."

"It would be too late anyway."

He tried to read between the lines. He had only dreamt she had mentioned a new boyfriend.

"I'm getting married in a month, Kenneth."

He hadn't expected his heart to sink but it did. "Congratulations, Alison. I'm happy for you. Who's the lucky guy?" Her retort from the dream came back to him: *Someone who understands girls.*

She said: "Someone who understands girls."

"In contrast to me?"

"You were okay, Kenneth. It just wasn't meant to be, you and me."

"Too true."

"What about you? Someone new in your life?"

An image of Jeanne flashed once behind his eyes. “No.” Pause. “I’m calling from the Winter Garden,” he said, as if it mattered.

“We’re busy here. I have no time for chit-chat.”

“I want to talk about a dream.”

“I’m not interested in dreams.”

“It won’t take long. Do you remember a special April the first, in school, about nineteen years ago?”

“How could I ever forget? Mrs. Davenport went berserk. Well, she went berserk most days but the day you mention was the worst of all.”

“I relived the day in a recent nightmare.”

“Was the nightmare a copy of reality?”

“The verbal abuse was spot on and the physical violence was a tad exaggerated, just a tad.”

“Uh, how did you survive?”

“Do you remember what you said to me in the classroom that day?”

“Not a chance.”

“You said, ‘Don’t you get it, Kenneth? Call me sometime.’ ”

“Why is this important?”

“A week later I called you. We became friends. You started to teach me the names and characteristics of flowers. In exchange, I gave you free copies of my collections of short stories.”

“Yeah, I remember those so-called ‘free books’. Handwritten on stapled office paper and—”

"I've discovered a clue in the bad dream where Mrs. Davenport terrorises us on that April day. I extracted the clue by dismissing a false premise: I thought at first you were an out-of-place character."

"What on earth are you talking about?"

"In the classroom from the bad dream you were misplaced, both physically and psychologically. You were yourself and not yourself at once. You were both present and absent. Strange, isn't it?"

"You appear a bit strange yourself, Kenneth, as if you were someone else altogether, both physically and psychologically."

"I'm in no joking mood, Alison."

"Neither am I."

"In my dream the other night, you were Mrs. Davenport's favourite pupil."

"Me?" She laughed a short laugh. There was no humour in it.

"Then I discovered you were not at all out of place. On the contrary, you were the nightmare's most significant character."

"Why?"

"Because of what you whispered, 'Don't you get it, Kenneth? Call me sometime.' In those sentences, there is a hidden meaning, not on that day nearly nineteen years ago, since that was reality, but in the dream, and only because the words returned in the dream. Do you see what I'm talking about now?"

She sighed. "If I did know how to

understand you, Kenneth, perhaps our relationship wouldn't have faded and died. What do you think?"

He ignored her effort to distract him. "My point is that the meaning of what you said in the dream is duplex. I called you later that week nineteen years ago and I'm calling you now because the information I'm convinced you can provide is associated with the current serial killing in our city. Do you see the connection?"

"Absolutely not."

"Never mind. I was hoping you could inform me about a plant."

"What plant?"

"The flowers are white or pink. The bracteoles have a reddish tone and a surface layer of silvery hairs on the underside. The stems are about three inches long." He recalled Mrs. Henderson's garden. "This is an outdoor plant, which blooms in winter. I saw them in a garden recently."

"It sounds like the Christmas rose."

"Uh-huh. What can you say about it?"

"The plant was in your dream too, wasn't it?"

Alison's female intuition had reached out to him from across the city. It had sailed the telecommunication network in zero time and was now tugging at his brain cells.

"Later I could tell you about the background to my problem. Let's focus on the plant for now."

"You need protection against vampires?"

"I didn't request info on garlic, did I?"

She giggled. "Let me guess. You're writing a new horror novel. How surprising."

"Let's stick to the subject. Christmas rose?"

"What do you want to know?"

"Anything. Whatever comes into your mind."

"As you wish. But I don't have much time."

"I'm grateful for any time you can spare."

"The Christmas rose—also called black hellebore—is one of Britain's oldest cultivated plants. The Latin genus name is *Helleborus*. The Christmas rose, or black hellebore, is the oldest garden type of *Helleborus* and it's a magical herb."

Magical? "Why is it called black when the petals are pink or white?"

"Its complete Latin scientific name, *Helleborus niger*, refers to its black roots. The name hellebore derives from two Greek words: *hellin*, to kill, and *bora*, food. It's believed the ancient Greeks rubbed *Helleborus* on their hunting arrows because of the toxic nature of the herb. The accepted theory is that it was the Romans who first introduced the Christmas rose in Britain. For centuries, the plant survived in monastery gardens and eventually found its way into domestic gardens, where it was planted near the house to drive away evil spirits, witches and lightning. Until the 1700s, the herb was considered a cure for madness and was also used to treat sick livestock, in particular, the animals thought to be possessed by witchcraft."

"Thank you, Alison. Evil spirits. Magic. Witches. Madness. I'm on the right track."

"This is a dangerous plant, Kenneth. It must be handled with respect. The Christmas rose is one of the most toxic plants in the buttercup family. If eaten, it burns the mouth. People and animals seldom die of it though."

"Seldom, huh?"

"Could you tell me what this is all about?"

"The spirit of a not too dead woman has given me signals to contact you. It doesn't matter whether you believe me. The Christmas rose is significant. These plants—the pink and white flowers—mean something to the killer. I see pieces of a picture."

"Are you involved in the murder investigation?"

"Me? No. It would be illegal, wouldn't it?"

"You implied that the Christmas rose is linked to the serial killer. What's your agenda?"

"I only speculate a little on my own."

"Oh. You speculate. That sounds safe. That picture you see in your mind's eye. Pieces of a picture. Do you mean an emerging image of the murderer?"

"Yes."

"Who's the murderer, Kenneth?"

47

Stockholm, Sweden.
CentraKem AB, Vasagatan.

Without thinking, Jeanne takes three quick steps to the left, pushes the door to Women's Changing Room and sneaks inside in the nick of time. Men and women pass through the corridor right outside. She stands still, listening. She hears voices beyond the door. Someone says: "—name is Betsy Breckenridge and she speaks a bit of Swedish, with some British accent. Her height is about five feet five inches. Black hair. White coat. She couldn't have left the building. Check the jammed lift."

Jeanne waits until the voices vanish. Then she turns away from the door and continues deeper into the changing room. Three chit-chatting women in white lab coats show up. They're all giggling.

"—hilarious office party but—"

"—could tell he wanted to fuck me—"

"—got completely shitfaced and—"

"—someone should tell the CEO—"

"—his arsehole friend stole my ice cream—"

They ignore Jeanne on their way out. Silence returns. She notices rows of lockers, washbasins and shower cubicles. Next to each washbasin sits a basic first aid kit. She washes her hands and face, uses disinfectant to clean the wound to the palm of her hand and applies a dressing gauze. Finally, she re-makes the quick and easy hair bun.

In a mirror's reflection she discovers a locker whose door is ajar. In the locker she finds a lab coat with the CentraKem AB logo on it. She puts on the coat and buttons it up. The somewhat too large size is compensated by her jacket underneath. The name tag on the front of the coat says: Ingrid Häckner. Jeanne detaches the tag and throws it in a bin.

She leaves the changing room, passes through the T-junction and continues through the 14th floor, meeting more people. She finds another stairwell, disappears downwards through the complex, now running, taking double steps on each flight of stairs. The collision with the security guard is inevitable.

The big man in dark uniform frowns and raises a forefinger. "Watch out, young lady! And don't run on the stairs!"

"I do apologise, sir."

He regards her. "Where's your name badge and your left shoe?"

She utilises the element of surprise and kicks him in the groin. The big man falls, howling. Her next kick hits him on the temple. He passes out. She leaps over him and continues down the staircase.

She meets even more people—CentraKem staff, visitors, security personnel, homicide investigators. Several members of staff wear CentraKem lab coats. No one appears to notice that Jeanne is missing her badge. Everybody has other things to think about. And people are hunting a black-haired girl, not a blonde.

The CentraKem complex has several exits. She avoids the main lobby and the lively Vasagatan. An arrow points her in the direction of an exit towards Bryggargatan, a considerably less lively street. She moves through another corridor, passes a laundry room and meets two cleaners with their trolleys. Out of sight, she dumps the lab coat in a laundry basket. She meets more people. She avoids eye contact but still tries to look like she knows exactly what she's doing. Another lobby, this one smaller than the Vasagatan lobby. Almost out of the building now, unless the doors are locked and already guarded from the outside. Forty feet left.

"Miss Breckenridge?! Stop! Do not move!"

She spins around, jerking the pistol out of her jacket pocket. Her index finger pulls the trigger.

Bullets fly through the vestibule. Bullets shatter, scratch, ricochet and bang. Bullets transform the four policemen to flopping blood-spurting jumping-jack toys. She continues firing shots without counting the number of times she squeezes the trigger. She runs towards the exit. Her shoeless left foot slides. The nylon stocking skids on the parquet floor. The remaining shoe betrays her big time. The shoelace knot comes undone. She trips on the damn shoelace and falls, bumps her knee and drops the gun.

She swears, lying on her stomach. A standstill with twelve feet to go. Pain in her knee. Ache in her bleeding hand. She knows the exit is locked. She stares at the glass doors from a frog's perspective, listening to the noise of her thumping heart.

48

Kenneth had brunch at the Hispanic restaurant El Cocodrilo Rojo on Kingfisher Street. He made the phone call in the middle of his main course.

He waited. Five signals. Six.

"Sorin."

"Uncle Ash, it's me. I thought you were out."

"I *was* out. Until now. I just got home."

"Someone has been in my house."

"Someone? Someone other than Miss Russell?"

"Funny." Did Uncle Ash just crack a joke? Or did he know that his nephew and Jeanne had spent some nights together? "The killer, I guess. The murderer has been in my house."

"Why would the murderer check your house?"

"The killer must know I'm involved in the hunt. My external contract, which doesn't really exist."

"When did the intrusion take place?"

"Yesterday. While we were in Endsleigh Park."

"Why didn't you mention this earlier?"

"I'm busy, in case you didn't know. And I have plenty to consider. The intruder must have left my house in the afternoon, sometime between four twenty and five twenty.

"Why?"

"Linda's bowls with food and water."

"What does the cat have to do with anything?"

"When I got home, around five twenty, Linda's bowls were already filled."

"What if the cat wasn't too hungry yesterday?"

"I know her. She eats every serving. Moreover, I found the food still refrigerated. It must have been served sometime during the hour I just mentioned. The invader knew my cat's habits. The person who filled Linda's food bowl with salmon pâté knew she loves human home-cooked food and rejects tinned cat food. But why on earth would the invader do it? What a risky action, to feed my cat."

"And what a spoilt cat. Salmon pâté, huh?"

"By feeding Linda, the intruder left a deliberate trace. A calculated mark of passage. A mark which he thought he could afford to leave."

49

Stephen Morrison brushed away some cat hairs from his trousers and finished his chocolate bar.

Major Robert Knowles, father of the dead and buried Lucy Knowles, had been located after four months of searching. The man had been tracked to the town of Pineborough, northeast of Blackfield. Stephen summarised—in his mind—the man's life story: decorated army officer; Afghanistan combat veteran; deteriorating mental health; war-related anxiety disorders; divorced since May last year; a mental breakdown; four months at the clinic; 'fully recovered' and discharged on September the twenty-fourth, the day before the murder of Kelly Graham. Then, the disappearance. Now, arrested for anti-social behaviour in Pineborough of all places.

On the same day he had been discharged from Brown's Clinic in Portsmouth, Robert Knowles had withdrawn significant amounts of cash from ATMs using several different credit cards. Then the cash withdrawals stopped abruptly. For four months he had lived on that cash. Why? Perhaps he had spent his nights in cheap B & Bs until the money ran out. Again, why? It was remarkable that the man could have disappeared for four months. Now it was pure luck, Stephen speculated, that Knowles had gambled on using an ATM card in yet another cash machine, this time in Yorkshire. Though he must have known he would be tracked electronically. Did he want to get caught? Or had he become careless due to drug abuse? He had checked into his last B & B under his real name.

Stephen was driving the Mitsubishi police car into Pineborough town centre. He reached for the glovebox and took out another Mars chocolate bar. With the wheel in one hand and the chocolate bar in the other, he tore off the wrapper using his teeth. Now he saw the local police station. He glanced at Tina Tanner. "Would you like a Mars bar, Tina?"

"You're kidding?" Tina grinned. "I brushed my teeth an hour ago! Now let's go get this fucker."

"Robert Knowles?"

Tina rolled her eyes. "No. Michael Myers!"

Stephen ate his chocolate bar. And he thought about his future. If he had one.

▪

The mission was half done when it happened.

Stephen and Tina were on their way back to the CID car with Knowles in handcuffs.

"*Watch out!*" someone shouted—a civilian—in the crowded street.

Knowles had already broken free. Somehow, he had slipped out of the handcuffs as if he were an escape artist. The man rushed down the pavement, crashing into pedestrians and parked cars.

Stephen considered pulling his pistol. Only as a warning. He didn't intend to fire the weapon. Then he dismissed the impulse. Too many people in the street. The Mitsubishi was parked just around the corner in the opposite direction but if he turned back to get the car Knowles would be handed a chance to disappear. Stephen made a split-second decision. He took up the chase on foot. Where the hell was Tina? Somewhere in the chaos behind him on the pavement? Calling for backup?

He chased Major Knowles down a cross street, a pedestrian zone, experiencing how people shouted from a background of backgrounds. The morning light stung his eyes, distorted his vision, diluted the colours and erased contrasts. The asphalt glistened like a sun-spattered slow-moving stream. Knowles had a lead of eighty feet. A shrinking gap.

In an unexpected manner the man then slowed down, stopped, turned around and faced Stephen. The major did what should have been impossible. He took a knife from his trouser pocket, squeezed the blade between thumb and index finger, and threw the knife. Where did he get a knife? Weapons must have been confiscated by the Pineborough police. But then, the major shouldn't have escaped from the handcuffs in the first place. What kind of guy *is* he? Stephen wondered. The knife rotated through the air—a flicker of bright steel—towards Stephen. He estimated it would hit the ground a few feet in front of him. He advanced but he was too quick. The knife sank into his left leg, just below his knee.

He screamed and fell to the street. He fumbled with a fist, grabbed the knife and snatched it out of his leg the instant before the major's body fell on top of him like a heavy rock. He grunted under the weight. Adrenaline boosted his physical strength. He hooked an arm around the major's throat.

Knowles writhed and snarled and pressed his chin against Stephen's forearm and then pushed himself up from the street with one arm. Stephen felt the major's body rise and before it started to slip away he swung a leg over the major's hip. The major knocked away Stephen's hooked arm.

They rolled around and tore at each other and grappled. The knife was back in the major's hand. He made a thrusting motion with the knife at the detective. Stephen caught the blade in the air with a bloody handgrip, then pressed his teeth against the major's head. The major squealed and swung his elbow downwards. It hit Stephen just below the detective's armpit. The major pulled his head away from Stephen's teeth. Stephen grabbed the man's neck again. Major Knowles rammed his elbow into Stephen's side, again and again. Each blow eroded the detective's strength. The major freed the blade from Stephen's grip. He broke free and rolled away.

Stephen lay on his back, gasping for breath.

The major crawled on all fours. The man looked at Stephen, panting for air. "I didn't do it! I didn't kill those women! I didn't do it!"

"I know you didn't," Stephen said.

Robert Knowles raised his head. His eye caught something. Stephen knew what it was. He couldn't have missed it himself. Exhausted, with eyes half-open, he saw how the Mitsubishi police car came flying down the cobblestones with the speed of a cannonball. Tina Tanner was driving like a racing car driver from hell. Through the lowered window on the driver's side, Tina was at once shouting at civilians to get out of the way and pointing her Glock 17 semi-automatic pistol at the major. The Mitsubishi bounced, skidded and wobbled down the cobblestones.

Knowles pointed a gun at Stephen's stomach—the detective's own Walther PPQ 9mm, Stephen's unofficial service pistol. He preferred the Walther to the Glock, just personal preference. He realised he must have dropped the weapon during the fight.

Major Knowles squeezed the trigger.

50

Stockholm, Sweden.
CentraKem AB, Vasagatan/Bryggargatan.

The lobby towards Bryggargatan is quiet. But

that will change any second. Jeanne has mowed down a limited opposition using her unique SCDX semi-auto pistol. Shortly, the lobby will be stormed by armed professionals, from inside the complex and from the street.

She notices the ceiling-mounted cameras. She has been caught on video, undisguised. It doesn't matter anymore. Are there any bullets left in the gun? Is there bulletproof glass in the doors? Jeanne raises the gun and aims. Her hand trembles. Her index finger jerks the trigger. Again. Again. And again. She pumps off the remaining shots. Five ear-splitting bangs. The custom-made ammunition has great firepower. The glass doors explode in a silver-bright shower of splinters. The sudden drop in temperature shocks her body. As if straight from the North Pole, snowflake-filled gusts shoot into the lobby. She clambers to her feet, limping. She walks out onto the pavement and trips on a glass-spattered snowdrift.

■

She runs through the blowing snow. Never before has she seen so much snow in a capital city—or anywhere. Her shoeless foot feels and seems like a block of ice. The relentless gusts whip her legs and skirt. An electronic on-street information screen says the temperature is minus twenty-five degrees Celsius. Minus twenty-five, that's colder than the freezer in her kitchen in her home in cosy England. Have the police sealed off the whole neighbourhood by now? Her mobile phone rings.

"Ari? Is that you, Ari?"

"Where are you, Jeanne?"

Ari Nieminen, a Finland-Swede SCDX representative and Jeanne's closest local contact.

"I got problems, Ari."

"I understood that half an hour ago, gorgeous. How about a Swedish beer at the Nobis Hotel?"

"What I need is a warming cup of tea!" She's panting in the headwind. "Cut the crap and pick me up. I'm somewhere in Bryggargatan." Her numb fingers squeeze the mobile. "Where's the car?"

"I had to circulate due to roadblocks. As we speak, the car is rolling into the intersection with Klara Norra Kyrkogata. Hurry up."

"Should I hurry? Thanks for the advice!"

▪

"You're even prettier without the wig, Jeanne. I must say Mr. Frank does have a great sense of style. By the way, are you a natural blonde?"

She sighs. "Drive the car, Ari."

"Where would the lady like to go?"

"Stockholm Arlanda Airport."

"You have everything you need?"

"Contacts at Arlanda will sort things out."

Ari drives the Volvo S90 northwards

through the Swedish capital. Twisting clouds of crispy snow rattle against the vehicle's bodywork. The cityscape to the west, beyond the Concert Hall, is dominated by the five glimmering skyscrapers between Sergel's Square and Haymarket. He steals another glance at her. "Where's your left shoe?"

She hands over the pistol to her colleague. Ari puts the gun in the glovebox. Everything seems legitimate. If the car is stopped, no SCDX details would be found by Swedish authorities. Moreover, the power of national authorities was temporary. Sweden, the United Kingdom, the United States of America and all other nations are the future provinces of the total police state. The future couldn't look brighter.

51

Philip Worthington's gaze floated. Left, right and ahead. Another five beds. All empty. He was alone. His headache slammed and banged like fireworks. His vision rolled through blood-red veils. His throat was as dry as desert sand. Vapours of disinfectants crept into his nostrils. A silhouette in the doorway proceeded into the room and stopped at his bedside.

"Good afternoon, Mr. Worthington. I'm Lizzie. I'm a nurse. You called. Are you in pain?"

"Amy… my wife… she tried to kill me…

Feels like she succeeded… My head… My head…"

"How are you today, Mr. Worthington?"

"I've never felt better. Next brilliant question?"

"An Inspector Sorin and his handsome nephew are here to see you, sir."

"Great news, Nurse Lizzie. My day couldn't have started in a more excellent way."

He realised he was thinking of Annabelle. He missed Annabelle. Too bad she was gone forever. However, with Annabelle dead and buried, his life had become less complicated. And Sorin couldn't nail him for any of the murders, not even for the murder of Suzanne. Philip grinned. The pestering inspector had no proof.

"Mr. Worthington?"

He had no idea how long he had stayed in the clinic or even *which* clinic. Someone must have told him. He remembered nothing. Anyway, he wasn't sure he wanted to know. The only thing he knew was that he wanted out of here.

He glanced at a bowl of gooey breakfast muesli on the nightstand. Or was it his vomit? His stomach turned around and around and around, like a hamster's exercise wheel. He didn't remember his last meal.

"Mr. Worthington?"

The same voice, the same tone. The same effort to try to get an answer out of him. In the fog of his eyes, Nurse Lizzie's uniform was scarlet-coloured. Only earlier, while she had stood in the doorway, her uniform had been marble-white. He wondered why his vision was messed up in this way. It was a question to ask the medical staff, if he dared. "Will I survive?" he heard himself ask.

Nurse Lizzie placed a glass of water on the nightstand. "Dr. Klammer will answer your clever questions in due course, sir."

"I look forward to the surprise."

"You have lost your memory, sir."

"What a revealing piece of information."

"Memory loss for two days, that is, since you arrived here the day before yesterday in the morning."

"What day is it?"

"You have no recollection of your meeting with Dr. Klammer?"

"Who is he? What meeting?"

"Dr. Klammer, the clinic's top director, is also in charge of the neuro-surgery division. The man is a magnificent brain surgeon."

"Brain surgeon?!"

"Nothing you need to worry about, sir. What Dr. Klammer doesn't know about skull fractures isn't worth knowing."

"Now I feel much more at ease."

"That's what the inspector hopes."

Philip frowned. "To be honest, I don't want to see the inspector today." *Or ever again.*

"Inspector Sorin says it's important, sir."

"It's always important. Ash Sorin wouldn't be here if he didn't think it was important."

"Dr. Klammer is going to see you first, sir. You two are going to have a confidential conversation. Inspector Sorin and his handsome nephew will talk to you afterwards. I shall be at my station in the far wing. Just press the alarm button if you need something. Do not press the button for non-urgent requests. The alarm button must not be abused."

"I ought to remember that, Nurse Lizzie. Now I'm no longer in the grip of a coma."

▪

The ringlets in Dr. Klammer's shoulder-length hair resembled toilet-paper rolls. His whisky-coloured eyes scanned the room. The man's face was a grey maze, marked by decades of work in the borderland between life and death. The black-stained wooden pole which passed for his artificial leg looked like it had come in a self-assembly kit from IKEA.

"You've suffered a depressed skull fracture, sir. The result of a targeted blow to a small area of your head."

I'll get you for this, Amy. Just wait until I get out of here.

"A piece of bone was depressed, that is, shifted inward, creating a risk of increased pressure on the brain. A surgical procedure was required to lift the bone fragment."

"And?"

"Everything considered, you've been lucky. You had a concussion and a couple of days of alternating unconsciousness. The outcome could have been—"

"—far worse," Philip finished.

Klammer nodded. "No brain surgery necessary. You should take painkiller tablets and drink plenty of water. I have treated the skull fracture. Routine operation."

"What happens next, Doctor?"

"I want to keep you here for a series of neuropsychological tests, sir."

"What have you done so far?"

"Medical imaging. MRI and CT."

"Am I supposed to know those acronyms?"

"Magnetic Resonance Imaging and Computed Tomography. The former is based upon the science of Nuclear Magnetic Resonance, NMR. The latter is based upon the science of X-ray spectroscopy. The principle of NMR relies on the magnetic properties of certain atomic nuclei. How certain atomic nuclei have magnetic properties is explained by quantum mechanics."

Philip grimaced. "Sounds like physics to me."

"There's plenty of physics in medicine."

"How long will you keep me here, Doc?"

Klammer didn't answer. He pulled something from a pocket of his coat. A packet of cigarettes? No, a pack of playing cards.

Waddingtons No. 1 playing cards in their classic blue-white box. He took out a card and held it up. "Look at the card."

"Yeah?"

Klammer returned the card to the pack and showed another card. "Look at the card."

"Yeah?"

The man put the card away and showed another. "Look at the card."

"Yeah?"

The whole pack of cards returned to the doctor's white poplin coat pocket. "Do you remember the cards?"

"Is this one of your neuropsychological tests?" Philip grinned a shit-eating grin. "Queen of clubs, seven of diamonds, eight of hearts."

"Good. Both accurate and speedy. And then?"

"And then what?"

"The fourth card?"

"Nice try, Doc. There was no fourth."

Klammer smiled. "Very good."

Philip's eyes wandered about the room again. "This isn't Crow City Hospital or Southern General, is it? I have the feeling I'm at a private clinic." He hadn't forgotten the exchange with Nurse Lizzie but he wanted to hear what the top director himself had to say.

"You know it's a private clinic, sir. Nurse Lizzie told you, didn't she?"

"Though she didn't say why. Why am I here?"

"We responded to a phone call."

"Dr. Klammer?"

"Yes?"

"*How did I get here?!*"

"That, sir, is another mystery."

"What do you mean? Was it Amy? Was it my wife Amy who called an ambulance?"

"*You* called, sir. Strange... You didn't call 999, but a private ambulance service, one of our own independent contractors."

"Me? In my condition? With a bashed-in skull? Impossible, and you know it."

"I'm a doctor, sir, not a detective. I answered your question about the caller."

"Are there any more surprises?"

"A homicide detective and his nephew are here. Exciting, isn't it?"

▪

"I have something to show you, Phil."

Phil? Philip looked up from his bed. "I'm dying of curiosity, Inspector. If Dr. Klammer doesn't kill me first. I know why you're here. You're trying to frame me for the student murders." *Why is the nephew here?*

"A peculiar note arrived in my mailbox down at headquarters. A note in an envelope."

"And you say it has something to do with me?"

The inspector placed a sheet of paper on the bedcover, a few inches south of Philip's chin. Philip grabbed the note, stared at it and grimaced. The message went home with a sting. The note, a single sentence, comprised four words without a full stop or other punctuation at the end:

Phil Worthington did it

"Created using a word processor," the inspector said, "and printed on a laser printer. What's your first impression, Phil?"

"Don't call me Phil."

"Tell me about the note, Phil. First impression." The inspector put a cigarette between his teeth.

"You're not going to light that one, Inspector. Not in here." He tried to read the detective's tactics. Why was Sorin provoking him? And why was the nephew still as quiet as a sculpture? "I have no idea who may have written the note," he lied. "All I can say is that it looks like an evil person's attempt to frame me for murder."

"Sure you have an idea who wrote it, Phil. What is it that stands out about it?"

Philip pretended to take a closer look. "No. I have nothing to add."

"You know who wrote the note. We'll return to that part of the discussion in a bit. Now, let's focus on the salient details of this four-word message. Firstly, we can assume the last word, 'it', refers to the series of murders. It's a reasonable assumption, since the note was addressed to me. Secondly, we have a detail that's conspicuous by its absence."

"What are you talking about?"

"The absence of a punctuation mark after 'it'."

"That's significant?"

"You know it is in this context, Phil. Of course, the absence of a full stop often passes unnoticed in connection with freestanding sentences or isolated sets of words. For instance, newspaper headlines and titles on book covers are written without a full stop at the end. The case of this four-word message, however, is special. Omitting punctuation marks such as full stops is your wife's habit.

"We checked the bookkeeping files your wife is responsible for in her capacity as co-owner and co-manager of Worthington's Elegance. In spite of the carelessness with dropped punctuation marks, your wife's writing is perfectly legible, since she writes the first letter of the first word of each new sentence in upper case according to praxis.

"The third indicium concerns the first word of the note. Phil is a short form for Philip. Among your closest friends, employees and business associates, your wife is the only person who calls you Phil."

"You've checked it?"

"I've checked it."

"What's all this supposed to mean?"

"Dead girls, for example, Suzanne Wheeler, can no longer call anyone Phil."

"Have you finished?"

"Not yet, Phil."

"I don't like that you call me Phil!"

"I know that, Phil." Inspector Sorin grinned. "I wonder why you're protecting your wife."

"I have nothing more to say to you."

"Who do you think cracked your skull?"

"I don't know."

"Could it have been your wife?"

"Leave my wife out of this, Inspector."

"She might have used a frying pan, Phil. What do you think of this Leighton Fenwick, your wife's therapist?"

Philip sighed, staring at the ceiling. "I have no opinion of him."

"What do you think of Dr. Fenwick's therapy programme? Is it effective for your wife?"

"I don't have the required qualifications to have an opinion on the matter." I have no interest either, he almost added.

"I think you do have an opinion on Fenwick." The inspector moved the cigarette from one corner of his mouth to the other. "Have you had a long chat with Klammer today?"

"Why?" Why did this leech Sorin want to talk about Klammer? Had the clinic manager mentioned something which Sorin could use?

"Klammer wasn't thrilled when I barged in here to meet my prime suspect," the inspector said.

"You mean you're jeopardising my recovery by coming here and interfering?"

"I hope not."

"Klammer let you in?" Worthington wanted to scream.

"The man thinks your skull fracture is interesting from a medical point of view. I think your skull fracture is interesting, too. From a law enforcement point of view."

"It's obvious you want to provoke me. Why?"

"Doc says you called an ambulance yourself."

"I know what he says."

"How did you manage to do that?"

"I don't know. Perhaps I could have made the call just before I lost consciousness or in connection with a brief waking moment between two periods of unconsciousness. Despite the blow to my head, I must have managed to use a telephone."

"And must have managed to find the number to a private ambulance firm you didn't even know in the first place, which brought you to a clinic you didn't know existed." The inspector laughed.

Something happened. Philip floated back to the rough beach of memories. "You haven't been honest with me, Inspector."

"What do you mean?"

"I'm no longer your prime suspect. It's just a game you're playing. Listen, there was something a nurse mentioned today. Nurse Lizzie said I've been here a couple of days. Since last Thursday, in other words. Before you got here, I saw on the

TV news that an eighth student was murdered on Thursday evening. Sorry, Inspector, but it looks like I have a foolproof alibi."

"It might look like you have a foolproof alibi for last Thursday but there are eight Thursdays to take into account now. Get well soon, Phil."

52

"A one-in-ten-million chance of that happening," Uncle Ash said. "It wasn't a job which would have required a ballistic vest."

"Still, I shouldn't have allowed the scenario," Morrison said.

"Everything will be all right, Stevie. In addition, we finally nailed the guy."

"I have cancer, sir."

"Huh?" Uncle Ash dropped his unlit cigarette.

"Terminal."

"Certain?" Kenneth asked.

"I mean, I'm dying. The doctor here says I have a maximum of three years left."

"Klammer?" Uncle Ash asked.

Morrison shook his head. "This philanthropic woman, Dr. Kołodziejska, may be under Klammer's overall command but she's the manager of the oncology division."

"How long have you known?" Uncle Ash asked.

"Since November."

"Tell me about the shooting, Stevie."

Morrison collected his thoughts. "The situation was puzzling, sir. Knowles had a knife. I know it's impossible but he had a knife anyway. We fought about the knife. How long, I don't know. Knowles must have grabbed my hidden Walther PPQ. We're talking about a guy who had just escaped from the handcuffs as if they were made of party streamers. Without realising what was happening, I was shot with my own service weapon. Right then I thought of nothing. I didn't care if I died."

"You're strong, Morrison," Kenneth said. "You'll get through this. It's not unheard of that doomed patients defy medical predictions."

"Listen to the boy," Uncle Ash said.

Morrison looked up from his bed, fixing his eyes on Uncle Ash. "This Major Knowles—he has nothing to do with the student murders, right?"

"Right. It has emerged that Robert Knowles has an alibi for the timeframes of three murders."

"Which ones?"

"Månsson, Wheeler and Wright."

"I have no grudge against Robert Knowles. The man is an unstable war veteran. He wasn't in his right mind when he shot me. I want to deal with this as a professional."

"There's also something else you should know, Stevie. Worthington is also here. The floor below."

"Oh? What have I missed?"

"Someone cracked his skull. But he'll survive."

"Any idea who did it?"

Uncle Ash nodded. "The wife failed to take her husband's life, while she supplied him with an alibi for the time of the murder of Sadie Bentley."

"What next, sir?"

"Concerning Worthington, he's protecting his wife for some reason. His actions must be linked to an advantage of his own or to an opportunity to gain an advantage. The man is an incurable egotist. Mr. and Mrs. Worthington don't come across as the happiest of couples. Ken has an idea regarding the wife's psychologist, a Leighton Fenwick."

Morrison looked up at Kenneth. "What idea?"

"Code of ethics and conduct do not apply in murder investigations," Kenneth said, "at least not completely. Principles of confidentiality cannot be used to protect a killer. I think that Fenwick ignores the restrictions. I think he withholds information. It is my belief that the more we get to know Fenwick, the closer we get to solving the mystery." What he thought was something different: *The more I get to know my own person, the closer I get to solving the enigma. Life is the grandest of mystery novels, a character-driven game.*

"Stick to your theories, young man. Moreover, I want to mention—to a cat lover like you—that Pat and I have got a cat."

"Brilliant news, Morrison. Cats are wonderful animals and the perfect pets."

"I can understand what you mean, Kenneth. My sons love it—sorry, *him*—already."

"What breed?"

"A Tiffany. His name is Igor. The only trouble we have with Igor is that he sheds hair. Cat hair ends up on clothes, furniture and floors."

"Many breeds shed fur. It's normal. You should groom your cat daily."

"Thanks for the advice, young man. I'll inform my family."

"I think you have a long life to live, Morrison. A life enriched by Igor."

53

"Divorced. Once."

"I see."

"He was a writer. And a psychopath."

Jeanne could have told Kenneth she had almost been married twice but she hadn't told him that. 'Divorced once' was technically true enough and it was simpler and easier to express than the details of the actual truth. Over the past fifteen months she had cancelled one wedding on the very day of the wedding, only a few minutes before the ceremony in church, and later gradually escaped one actual marriage. How speedily you could dump two guys: one husband-to-be and one actual husband.

"That's cool, Jeannie," her younger sister Rose had joked. "You're the coolest girl in town. Do you have the time to dump another two arseholes before the end of the year, huh?" Rose had laughed like a lunatic, making faces. Except it wasn't fun. Didn't Rose understand that?

By chance, she had met Frederick back home in Sheffield in the summer a year and a half ago, in a late-night bar on Devonshire Street. At first, it didn't appear to be a mistake but soon she realised she had got two new insights for the price of one: first, why 'love at first sight' was terribly overrated and terribly impossible; and second, why that kind of 'love' seldom lasted beyond the superficiality of nightclub society.

How practical it was—or rather, appeared to be. Of all the places in the universe, fate brought them together in Sheffield, where Frederick Beresford happened to attend an architecture conference the very same weekend as Jeanne was back in her hometown to see Mum and Dad. Back then, both Jeanne and Freddy lived and worked in Blackfield. Soon it turned out that Freddy preferred to hang out with his rugby-fanatic pals in pubs on weekend nights and enjoy an occasional after-work beer with architect colleagues on weekday nights. 'Occasional' meant—according to Freddy's own definition—that it never happened more often than three times a week.

Jeanne kept her presence of mind and broke off the engagement in the nick of time, on the very wedding day, in October the same year. If people thought Freddy was furious, they should have seen his mother. Jeanne thought Bertha Beresford would kill her. Bertha had financed a wedding party for five thousand pounds, including a five-course dinner for two hundred guests. But how could the would-be mother-in-law blame Jeanne for the mess?

In the wake of the ordeal with the architect and his overprotective mother, Jeanne assumed she had gained all the experience she needed to avoid falling into a similar trap again. Then, when she met Felix Leerman, a mild-mannered award-winning Belgian writer for an international sports magazine, she was convinced she had met her perfect man—talking of clichés. They got married in May last year. At the time, the wedding day was the greatest day of her life. It was just that Felix's word processor turned out to be his permanently superior priority. And it didn't stop there. Felix Leerman turned out to be crazy but he was an expert at hiding it.

Not all psychopaths were monstrous killers. Her husband's psychopathy revolved around thefts, lies and manipulation without remorse. He stole from his publishing company, his boss, his colleagues, his worldwide network of professional contacts, and even from her. The range of Felix Leerman's thefts was beyond belief. One day he could nick next-to-worthless items such as a pencil or a paper clip or a bag of crisps. Another day he could steal luxury cars or pull off multi-million-dollar bank jobs from international e-payment systems. Felix didn't care about other people, including her. He understood people's emotions at an intellectual level, a knowledge he used to his advantage. He had no conscience and lacked empathy.

It's not easy to spot a psychopath but eventually she did. Her training had paid off. A few months earlier, she had been recruited by SCDX, hand-picked by Mr. Frank himself. Thomas Frank had discovered Jeanne through her then job as a top secretary at one of the major police departments in Britain. Overnight, she had tripled her salary. Her so-called marriage to Felix Leerman collapsed after only three and a half months. The less Kenneth Sorin knew about her, the better, or so she thought.

▪

Jeanne swung out of bed and shivered. Kenneth's bedroom was freezing. She sat on the edge of the bed, raised her nightgown and put on her knickers and socks. She glanced over her shoulder. Kenneth was snoring in the fractured darkness. She was about to stand up when his arm slipped around her waist.

"Where are you going, gorgeous?"

"The bathroom." She stroked his arm.

Kenneth returned to sleep, snoring. She tiptoed out of the bedroom. Halfway along the corridor, she met gleaming cat eyes. “Hi, Linda.”

The nocturnal creature miaowed, sat down and tracked Jeanne with her curious gaze.

Jeanne slipped into the bathroom, locked the door, lowered the toilet lid and sat down. The time was twelve thirty-one a.m. She keyed in a number on her phone. It was still early evening in Denver, Colorado, USA.

■

“It must be urgent, Miss Russell, if you’re calling in the middle of the night.” It sounded as if Mr. Frank was sitting in a restaurant. Background murmurs, soft music, clinking of plates and cutlery.

“I’ve discovered a number of interesting details, sir. The info can’t wait until the written report.”

“Dinner time, Miss Russell, but I’m listening.”

“Kenneth Sorin, sir. Reversing the order of first name and surname gives us Sorin Kenneth. From the word Sorin we can create the anagram Ronis and from the word Kenneth we can create the anagram Nethken. The crazed killer in Sorin’s new horror novel is named Ronis Nethken.”

“Amazing, Miss Russell.”

“Just like Kenneth Sorin, Ronis Nethken has a Ph.D. in chemical physics. Like reality’s killer, Ronis Nethken stabs female students to death with a letter opener. He cuts out the corpses' left eyes. And, of course, the book is set in Blackfield."

"Wonderful, Miss Russell."

"There's more, sir. Dr. Nethken's female victims are named Korinne Greaves, Liu Kitakawa, Rosina Mainbach, Greta Quarico, Annabelle Silva, Suzanne Wright, Vicky Walker and Sara Blomberg. All of the surnames' initials match. The first names' initials match except Vicky. The first names Suzanne and Annabelle are picked from two of reality's murder victims and the fictitious Suzanne shares a surname with reality's Gloria. Suzanne Wright is, just like Kenneth Sorin, a chess player. The fictitious girl Sara Blomberg and reality's girl Rebecka Månsson came from the same place, the town of Kungsör by the lake of Mälaren, somewhere in central Sweden."

"Excellent, Miss Russell. Who inspires whom? Is Sorin a model for Nethken or is Nethken a model for Sorin? Does imagination stimulate reality? Or vice versa?"

"The answers are horrifying, sir. The dates for Ronis Nethken's murder series are September the twenty-fourth, October the fifteenth, October the twenty-ninth, November the nineteenth, December the third, December the twenty-fourth, January the seventh and January the twenty-eighth. Also, the dates coincide with Kenneth Sorin's chapter schedule for his first-draft work at the typewriter."

"You're serious, Miss Russell?"

"Dead serious, sir. Kenneth Sorin wrote each of Ronis Nethken's murder scenes the day before each of reality's murders, respectively."

"How did you find all this information?"

"The horror writer creates a separate file or folder for each novel chapter. He writes first drafts on an electric typewriter and all of the other drafts on a computer. Sheets of paper are lying around in his workroom, on the desk or in unlocked desk drawers. And I must mention a letter, sir."

"What letter?"

"The author has visited the Swedish town of Kungsör. There's a handwritten letter by Kenneth Sorin, signed and dated in Kungsör last year."

"Now, are you saying that Sorin shadowed Miss Månsson all the way from that Swedish town?"

"I think he was curious about Rebecka Månsson and wanted to study the girl's hometown. Rebecka became a model for his fictional Sara Blomberg."

"Good work, Miss Russell."

"Thank you, sir."

"What about his computers?"

"I haven't checked any computers yet."

"Do it."

"Understood, sir."

"Where are you now?"

"The writer's house."

"Hold position until I get home."

"When will you return home, sir, if I may ask?"

"I'm flying to London tonight."

"There's a peculiar theory, too—prime-number mathematics as some pattern in the author's new theory."

54

"I've prepared everything," Rachel said: "pizza, peanuts, crisps, dip sauce, white wine."

Elizabeth kissed Rachel. "Party tonight?"

"You got it! But a party for two only."

"Sure your dad's away?"

"Don't worry. He's at a conference in Bristol."

The girls moved towards the opposite end of the house, a three-storey house that Elizabeth thought should be called a mansion. The building featured two wings and a pavilion for the large kitchen.

"Make yourself at home, Liz. I'll go get a couple of bath towels. Back in a minute."

Elizabeth sneaked into the prodigious bath and shower room. Why am I sneaking? she wondered.

The swimming-pool-equipped room resembled a bathhouse in size. A fog-like darkness from the outside pushed against the windows at the opposite side of the pool. If we bathe naked, she thought, we must draw the curtains, the white plastic curtains with a pretty pattern of turquoise dolphins. *Don't get paranoid now. The window glass is frosted for privacy. Yeah, but if the glass is frosted, why are there curtains here at all?*

This time of year, sunset arrived too soon for comfort. The swimming pool surface—flat and calm as a mirror—glimmered in the cracked moonlight which seeped through the frosted glass patio door.

She placed her toiletry bag on a dressing table and undressed. She shuddered when she got out of her bra and knickers. *What if Rachel's dad saw me right now?* She peered out into the corridor. "Rach? Darling? Could you bring my cigs on your way back, please? They're in my handbag."

The response came from the depth of the house: "Sure. I'll be right back, Liz!"

Rachel turned up with two packets of cigarettes (the girls smoked the same brand, Virginia Slims Menthol), a matchbook and two bath towels.

"What if your dad shows up, Rach?"

"As I've said, he is away. Relax."

"Okay. I guess I'm just a little nervous. It would be truly embarrassing if your dad caught us."

Laughter flew from Rachel's lips. She looked into Liz's eyes while she undressed—blouse, skirt, tights. She stepped out of her cotton floral knickers, undid her bra and let it fall to the floor. "Touch me," she whispered.

Elizabeth's heart fluttered. The tip of her index finger stroked the tiny slit between Rachel's legs. Rach giggled and cupped Liz's right breast carefully in her hand. The moment passed.

The girls lit cigarettes. The flame of their shared match reflected in Rachel's sea-green irises. What a nice evening, Elizabeth thought. A private party and then to bed with the most wonderful girl she had ever loved.

"Bikini or swimsuit, Rach?"

"Neither."

"Me too."

"Since we're naked, Liz, we ought to draw the curtains."

"The window glass is frosted for privacy. Why are there curtains here at all? I love the curtains, they're cute, but I don't see the benefit of hanging them here when the glass is frosted."

"My dad has a camera that sees through frosted glass and even around corners, from one room to another. I discovered that he had photographed me naked in the swimming pool at least twice."

Elizabeth wanted to laugh but couldn't. "You're joking, Rach, aren't you? Tell me you're joking."

"I'm not joking, Liz."

"But… What happened? You confronted him?"

"Nothing else happened. I never let him

know I caught him doing it. At least I haven't yet."

"Why not?"

Rachel shrugged. "I don't know."

"How is such a camera supposed to work, huh?"

"I don't know. I'm not a techno geek. People who know stuff like this say the most exciting thing about the innovation is that the camera uses natural light to take pictures, not lasers or X-rays. Scientists at the Weizmann Institute in Israel invented it. The light is scattered by the frosted glass, creating white noise. The camera takes those specks of noise and enhances them to recreate the original image. The approach is supposed to be simple and relies on an off-the-shelf technology: an old invention called a spatial light modulator—SLM. When light scatters off an object, each portion of that object changes the phase of the light in different ways. An SLM is an array of pixels that changes the phase of the light passing through it, depending on the electricity that flies through each pixel. The scientists used a thing called a genetic optimisation algorithm to adjust each pixel of the SLM until a sharp picture appeared from the white noise. One potential future application is medical imaging using natural light. Cool, uh?"

Elizabeth gaped. "As you said, Rach, you're not a freaking techno geek. Neither am I. How do you know all this stuff you just said?"

"I don't know a crap about it. I only

happened to find a research paper on the subject. I spotted the article on my dad's desk in his workroom, together with a bunch of nude pics of me in the pool."

Elizabeth grimaced. "Wow. What can I say?"

"Let's have a bath now. Okay?"

"Okay. But let's draw the curtains first..."

■

Rach was wiping Elizabeth's back with a bath towel. "You make me jealous, Liz. I wish I had a body like yours."

"Don't be silly, Rach. You're gorgeous."

"My thighs are a bit thick."

"Your thighs are possibly a bit thick but I love them anyway. Look in the mirror! You're beautiful. You're my dream girl. I don't want anyone but you."

"Despite my thick thighs?"

"Despite your thick thighs. Or *because* of your somewhat thick thighs."

They giggled, stepped out of the bathroom and ran naked through the corridors to Rachel's room. They used hairdryers, sprayed deodorant and applied nail polish, lipstick and perfume, as if they were getting ready for a night out on the town. Rachel then went out to the kitchen to fetch two glasses of wine. Since the house was equipped with a multi-room wireless speaker and home audio system, the girls could communicate even when they were in different rooms on different floors in different parts of the building.

"Cherries!" Rachel said from the kitchen. "Dad has left a bowl of cherries in the fridge! Dad knows I love cherries!"

"That's great," Elizabeth said.

Rachel appeared with white wine, cherries and peanuts. Elizabeth sat at the dressing table.

"Yes, yes, yes," Rachel said. "You do look good. 'Magic mirror on the wall, who is the fairest one of all?' Have you asked the mirror?" She put the wine glasses and bowls with cherries and peanuts on the bedside table, crawled up onto the bed, grabbed one of the glasses and took a sip.

"At least you got the movie quote right, Rach."

"Of course I did."

"Did you hear something?" Liz asked, without turning around. Rachel was partially visible at the edge of the dressing table mirror.

"What?" Rachel popped a cherry in her mouth.

"I thought I heard something from somewhere in the house, as if someone else was here. Did you turn off the wireless speaker and audio system? Can someone hear what we're saying?"

"Don't get freaky on me, Liz. There're only two people in the house: you and I. The wireless system is still on. If you heard something, it may have been the electric oven in the large kitchen. Sometimes it gives off a sound during the first few minutes of use. A pizza is baking right now. Could you get it when it's ready? In fifteen minutes?"

"I'll get the pizza." Elizabeth put a cigarette between her lips and lit it. A thin darkness fell into the room. Rachel lay on her stomach on top of the bed covers and smoked. Her naked bum was visited by moonlight which seeped in between the blinds. The glow of Rach's cigarette was a distant red star in a twilit sky.

Elizabeth listened to the house again, without knowing what she was listening for or why. After only four puffs, she stubbed out her cig. "Rach?"

"Mmmm."

"Do you think your dad would want to have a nice time with me if he got the chance?"

Rachel propped herself up on one elbow. "What do you mean?" Perhaps she wrinkled her pretty forehead or perhaps not. For the moment, her face was undefined in the unlit room.

"You know what I mean, Rach."

"Trust me. There's only one woman for Dad. And before you ask, the answer is no. It isn't me, in spite of those weird photos I told you about."

"Who is she?"

"She's… She's blonde like me."

"Rach?"

"Mmmm."

"Aren't you scared of the killer who's prowling the city and seemingly everywhere in the city?"

"Of course I'm scared."

"Do you think we're safe tonight?"

"It's Tuesday. The maniac kills only on certain Thursdays, according to newspapers and TV news."

"Yeah, but what if he changed his habits?"

"Don't be pessimistic. Pessimism is unsexy."

"I'm not pessimistic. I'm thoughtful."

Rach blew smoke rings that looked like circular waves of moonlight. "Do you still think you heard someone else in the house?"

"You remember the creep at the cinema?"

"How could I ever forget *that* lunatic?"

"The nasty things he said he wanted to do with us."

"Ben Smith, right?"

Elizabeth grimaced. "Unless the name is false."

"You think he's still out there looking for us?"

Elizabeth thought for a while. "I do worry too much. You're right. I promise to relax."

"Good. Could you get the pizza now, please? I'm hungry. Are you hungry?"

"Yes, I am." Elizabeth moved with light, quick steps to the kitchen. As a guest of the Fenwicks countless times, and as Rachel's closest friend, she knew she could make herself at home. *Oops! Still no clothes on.* She shuddered when she realised she was in Dr. Fenwick's kitchen stark naked.

What if Rachel's dad saw me right now?

She opened the oven door and took out the classic ham and pineapple pizza. From a drawer she got a bread knife and cut the pizza into eight slices. Neither Rachel nor Elizabeth wanted cutlery. They preferred eating pizza with their hands. She caught herself fantasising that if there was a killer in the house tonight, a psychopath who at any time could appear and attack them, the bread knife would come in handy. Could they keep the knife in Rach's room? Under the bed? Elizabeth frowned at her own idea. She shook her head and put the knife in the dishwasher. She returned to Rachel's room and placed the pizza dish on the bedside table.

"Yummy!" Rachel put out her cig.

Elizabeth sipped white wine, put three peanuts into her mouth and crept onto the bed. "Should we turn on the bedside light?"

"No. The light would destroy the moonlight."

On her way back from the kitchen with the pizza, Elizabeth had got the idea she saw a figure in one of the building's wings. She had been certain she noted the silhouette of a man outlined against the geometric-patterned wallpaper. A man had been standing there, motionless, watching her nudity.

The madman who slaughters female students.

But it must have been her imagination that had frightened her. Imagination only.

Or Rachel's dad.

Of course they were alone in the house.

55

Under cover of a lime tree on the avenue, Jeanne observed how Kenneth left his house, got into his black Peugeot 108 and drove out of the neighbourhood towards the city centre. She stepped out of her white Nissan Qashqai, crossed the avenue and sneaked up to the house. With the multi-functional SCDX electric lock-pick gun, it took one second to open the front door and three seconds to circumvent the burglar alarm. In the hallway, she met Linda. "Hi, Linda." Jeanne lifted the cat, kissed her on the nose and lowered her to the floor again. Linda miaowed, yawned and strolled into the living room.

Jeanne went upstairs, to the writer's workroom. A sheet of paper was inserted in the typewriter. The headline read, 'Dr. Nethken's work'. The rest of the sheet was blank.

She walked over to the computer. The screen saver resembled nothing she had ever seen before. The program was running fancifully choreographed murder sequences: sparkling colours, shiny murder weapons and scantily clad ladies. Jeanne tapped the keyboard's space bar. The sick screen saver went out, leaving room for a document. Title: 'Mr. Maniac'.

Mr. Maniac? she wondered. Who's Mr. Maniac?

She read a few pages. The minutes passed. She threw a glance at the digital answering machine on the desk. Her gloved hand hovered over the unit's control panel. Her fingers performed a few taps. A message was played back, *"From Ronis Nethken to Kenneth Sorin. No… From Kenneth Sorin to Ronis Nethken. Puzzle pieces fall into place according to the pattern of the eye."*

Jeanne pushed the stop button and froze. A sound from the ground floor. From the front door. He's coming.

Kenneth was already back.

She surveyed the workroom. She ran everything through her memory, everything she had done and touched since entering the house. Kenneth wouldn't know that someone had circumvented the burglar alarm. She had reset the alarm and—

Footsteps on the stairs towards the first floor.

Jeanne hadn't lit any lamps. From the avenue outside, the house looked exactly as Kenneth had left it. Fortunately, the computer had returned to sleep. The screen saver was back on, running its perverted killing sequences.

She dived down behind the desk. She heard the writer entering the workroom.

"Did you find what you were looking for, Jeanne?"

56

The town of Kungsör by the lake of Mälaren. One June, not long ago, he decided to visit the Swedish resort. He spotted the girl out of the corner of his eye. His rental car seemed to be flying through the midsummer air. Could a day be brighter than this? The traffic rumblings evaporated. He experienced only the sun. And the hitch-hiking girl.

She disappeared beyond the periphery of his visual field. A few minutes later, he slowed down, without thinking. The speed of his Volvo dropped like a stone. The lorry in the rear-view mirror grew. Several horns roared.

Kenneth spun the steering wheel and cut to the left. The rental car wobbled towards the centre line road marking, crossed the line and skidded. The tyres cried out then re-found traction. He pressed the accelerator. One U-turn done, one to go. The hitch-hiking girl was strolling southwest. His rental car was now speeding northeast. He hoped that no other motorist would have time to pick her up.

Then, a gap in the traffic. A gap of hundreds of yards in both directions. Not many hundreds of yards but enough. Perhaps.

What am I doing? he wondered. I'm driving

a car in an unknown country in unknown right-hand lane traffic and I want to pick up this unknown girl?

The wheel spun, the car lurched, tyres squealed and horns bellowed. U-turn number two completed—in a left-hand drive car. Not bad.

His car accelerated again. He was approaching the wandering girl. She was still available to him. What luck! Her blonde hair was in a bun with a red bow. She wore a short skirt, short-sleeved blouse and bright pumps. No tights, as far as he could see. In the heat of this midsummer, her legs were bare. He passed the girl, slowed down and pulled over.

In the rear-view mirror, he saw her first waving then running in his direction. He opened the front passenger-side door.

"*Tack så mycket!*" She jumped into the seat and put on the seat belt. Her smile was as attractive as the midsummer sun. Her handbag sat on her lap.

Although he didn't know the language, he could guess what she had said. She had thanked him.

"You're welcome," he said in English. "Is it okay if we speak English?"

She tittered. Her teeth were pearl-white. Now he saw she wore white earrings. "No problem."

He returned her smile.

"What a reckless U-turn you did. Wow."

"You have to do what life requires."

"Aha."

His rental Volvo was rolling through the exotic landscape. He was on an alien planet where the sun never set.

Why doesn't she say where she wants to go? Where *is* she going?

He loosened his tie knot, cleared his throat and said, "I'm on my way to Kungsör."

"Really? So am I! What a coincidence!"

"Are you from Kungsör?"

"Yes." Pause. "I'm Rebecka."

"A pleasure to meet you, Rebecka. My name is Nethken. No, I mean Kenneth."

A wrinkle appeared on Rebecka's forehead. "Do you often forget your name?"

"Not often. Only when there's a beautiful girl in the passenger seat."

She laughed. "I see."

"I identify myself with characters."

"Characters?"

"Imaginary characters. Nethken is a fictitious serial killer. Dr. Ronis Nethken. He murders young, pretty ladies."

"Oh, you're a writer. So, what are your plans in Kungsör? Research for a book?"

"No research. Only recreation. And inspiration."

"What inspires you in Kungsör?"

A girl named Rebecka, he almost said.

He loosened his tie a little more. "I've read that the town of Kungsör inspired the sixteenth-century king Gustav Vasa to write. Gustav Vasa wrote more than a hundred letters in Kungsör. I want to investigate this further. But it isn't research for a book."

"On the small headland Kungsudden there's a museum about the royal history of Kungsör."

"Interesting. Where do I find Kungsudden?"

"At the northern end of the thoroughfare."

"Thank you, Rebecka."

"You seem to be very warm in that suit."

"Correct. I'm very warm in this suit. I'll change into something more comfortable as soon as I get to the hotel."

"There aren't many hotels in Kungsör. Are you staying at the Kungsringens Gästgiveri?"

"I think so. But I don't know how to pronounce the name, let alone spell it."

"The word *gästgiveri* means guesthouse."

"Thank you. I hope the staff speak English."

"From that guesthouse it isn't far to the town centre."

"Thank you for the information, Rebecka."

"In Kungsör it isn't far to anything."

He glanced at the girl. Tried to guess her age. Seventeen to nineteen years. In other words, seven to nine years younger than him.

She searched for something in her handbag. "I plan to study in the UK next year." She snatched up a brochure. "Look here. I read about all the possible courses at British universities."

"Intriguing. Where do you want to study?"

"Not sure yet. But I do love London.

London offers everything. And in my spare time, I enjoy singing. I hope I'll find a choir to join."

"You haven't considered Blackfield?"

"Blackfield? Where's that?"

"Northern England. Yorkshire."

"Do you know Blackfield well?"

"I'm from there."

"Aha. What's so special about Blackfield, then?"

"Blackfield is the city of dark secrets. Or, as its citizens like to call it, the City of Crows."

"How exciting. But can the university and the city offer what I want?"

"The university is one of England's finest. I'm convinced there are plenty of courses of potential interest to you. Regarding your spare time interest, there are several choirs and orchestras in the city."

"Oh. I see."

The rental car passed a town sign, turned right and continued through an industrial area intersected by the very road to the town centre. A railway ran parallel to the road.

"What's the name of the local football team?"

The girl flashed a smile. "Kungsörs BK."

"Any good?"

"Third division. The KBK football ground is just a stone's throw away." She pointed through the side window. "Just beyond the railway."

He took in the beauty of her dark-blue eyes.

"Where do you live, Rebecka? I mean… Where do you want to get off?"

"I live in Gersillagatan, walking distance from town centre. You could actually drop me off at the intersection between Kungsgatan and Drottninggatan. You're going the other way."

"Am I?"

"The fastest way from here to the guesthouse is to continue straight ahead along Kungsgatan until you reach Kungsringen, a curved road on your left. This so-called guesthouse is located halfway down that road. You can't miss it, Kenneth. It looks like a fairytale castle."

This 'so-called' guesthouse?

"Of course I'll drive you all the way home."

"It isn't necessary, Kenneth."

"To drive you home is the least I can do as a gesture of gratitude for the information and for the exceptionally pleasant company."

She snickered. "If it isn't too much trouble."

"No trouble at all."

▪

The rental car whizzed up Drottninggatan and passed some restaurants, supermarkets and convenience stores. And a statue. He wondered whom the statue represented. Certainly not the medieval king Gustav Vasa, that was clear, but perhaps the town mayor or the local sports director. No, no. Now he knew. The statue represented Thor Modéen, the late actor.

He drove the car past a cinema, a café and a library. He glimpsed a tower of red bricks on the crest of a hill. The tower looked like an antique water tower or observatory.

"Turn right, Kenneth. Then immediately left. At the end of Odengatan, turn left again."

He followed the girl's instructions to the letter then navigated the car along Gersillagatan. "What house number?"

"There." Rebecka pointed.

He pulled over in front of the house. He guessed it was her parents' house. Rebecka was too young to be a house owner.

"Thanks for the ride, Kenneth."

"You're welcome. And thanks to you, too. For the chat and the advice."

She smiled. Her teeth sparkled in the sun. "I'll consider Blackfield. Studies in the City of Crows."

"Do that, Rebecka. And good luck."

She stepped out of the Volvo.

He waited until she had disappeared into the house. Then he glimpsed at the mailbox. The brass nameplate read, 'Familjen Månsson'.

It was easy to guess what the first word meant. It was reminiscent of the English word. The second word must be the family name.

Månsson.

Rebecka Månsson.

Dr. Nethken grinned. He took out his notepad.

▪

The rental Volvo was equipped with GPS. He could have used the vehicle navigation system to find the girl's address, and the guesthouse. But it was more enjoyable to listen to Rebecka. The choice between the girl and the electronics was an easy choice.

Rebecka had been right, of course. The hotel (*the so-called hotel*) looked like a castle right out of a fairytale. Impossible to miss it. Kungsringen was a thoroughfare without buildings, except for the hotel and accompanying conference centre.

The ornate facade was bright-pink with cream-white trim. The pointed pitch-black roof stabbed at the sky like a dark mountain. On the rooftop sat three bright-pink towers in a straight line, the central tower taller than the flanking towers. The windows were triangular and white as sugar cubes. One-way glass? What secret conferences demanded premises with one-way glass in the windows? And in *this* neighbourhood?

He steered the Volvo into the car park, stopped and turned off the car engine.

Silence. A paranormal noiselessness.

He peered out through the side windows. The car park was deserted. Not a soul. Not a car. Not a bird or a cat. A crater on the planet of Mars could not have been quieter. Kenneth pulled the key from the ignition and spotted the object. The rectangle-like thing lay on the passenger-side rubber car mat. The thing turned out to be a booklet or a diary. Lemon-yellow with cat pictures on the covers. No text on the front or back cover. He opened it. On the front free endpaper was a handwritten note which read, '*Rebecka Månssons almanacka*'. In English, this must read, 'Rebecka Månsson's diary'. Easy.

Ronis Nethken grinned but the grin in the rear-view mirror faded. He wasn't Ronis Nethken. His name was Kenneth Sorin. He knew well that he should return to a certain house with the diary now, not later. But he wanted to check in at the hotel, take a shower, change his clothes and eat something. Anyway, in the diary there might be a phone number or an email address as a contact detail. Before he drove back to the house he might be able to inform the girl that her diary was in safe hands.

In safe hands? The grin flashed on his face.

▪

Ronis sat in the restaurant Rundelborg in the town centre. "I'd like a Rundelborg Special pizza with extra peppers and olives, please."

The young waitress nodded, scribbling his order on a pad. She was as pale as a vampire. Her wavy hair was as dark as a solar eclipse. Her painted lips were as red as blood. "Any drink?" She smiled at him.

"Black coffee, please."

The restaurant, or bistro, was named after the seventeenth-century horse-loving queen Kristina's riding track, which she had called Rundelborg. In Kungsör it isn't far to anything, Miss Månsson had said. The medieval riding track still existed, a stone's throw from the royal museum at Kungsudden.

Kenneth took out a notebook, English-language tourism brochures, a pen and Rebecka's diary. Of course he hadn't read the girl's diary. It would be beneath his dignity.

The Special pizza and the black coffee landed on the table. The vampire waitress flashed her teeth. "Enjoy your meal."

He looked up at her, beyond the swell of her breasts, and met her gaze. "Uh, thank you." He took a bite of the pizza and chased it with a sip of coffee. It tasted wonderful. His fingers began to flip through Rebecka's diary. Exciting details and private words. A range of secrets discovered and requisitioned by Dr. Nethken for Dr. Nethken. On page 1 he found a mobile number. He took out his cell phone and called. No answer. What luck! He closed the diary, pushed it aside, opened his notebook to a new page and wrote:

Fictional character: Sara Blomberg.
Murder victim.
Swedish. 17–19 years.
Blonde hair swept up in a pretty bun. Red bow.
Short skirt. Short-sleeved blouse. Bright pumps.

Legs bare in the heat of midsummer.
Pearl-white teeth.
Gersillagatan, Kungsör.

He closed the notebook, ate pizza, looked out the window, sipped coffee and enjoyed the tranquility. He unfolded the tourism brochures, identified the source of the material, opened the notepad again, sought words of his own, simple sentences, and wrote:

King Gustav Vasa (Gustav I of Sweden).
Vasa comes to power in 1523.
Vasa buys the town of Kungsör in 1538.
Vasa stays forty times in Kungsör.
Around the time when Vasa's youngest daughter
Elisabeth is born, he stays here for seven weeks.
Vasa's children love oranges.
The town of Kungsör
inspires Vasa to write letters.
111 of those letters have been preserved.

One hundred and eleven letters? By the king Gustav I of Sweden, written right here, in this dead-end town in the middle of nowhere? Wow. Perhaps he would research a new book after all. Now, what was there to read in those letters? Where were the letters now? He looked forward to visiting the museum and the tourist office—tomorrow. He would ask his questions about King Gustav Vasa's letter writing tomorrow. Today, and tonight, he had other things to do.

Kenneth phoned again. Sara Blomberg's mobile number. Again, no answer. What luck!

He pocketed Rebecka's diary, opened his cell phone's Internet, performed a search and found a local car rental: Bertil Karp's Car & Boat Rental. Street address: Ågatan, Kungsör, down by a small river named Arbogaån. Kenneth already had a rental car but he needed another one. A car which neither Sara nor Rebecka would be able to recognise.

▪

He drove around the streets in car number two, a steel-blue Toyota, the evening rolling through lights and colours. Darkness didn't exist, not even inside his own skull. Thoughts about Rebecka illuminated his time like a thousand suns.

▪

He had nothing to hide. He was here to return a lost diary. Yet he felt like a sneaking spy. An inner voice wondered why someone who had nothing to hide would rent another car. The answer was that he wanted a car with automatic transmission for urban traffic. The rental Volvo from Stockholm Arlanda Airport had manual transmission.

▪

He turned into the street Gersillagatan for only the second time in his life, this time from the opposite direction, via the street Torsgatan. An intentional deception, he thought, and chuckled. The car rolled towards the right house. Kenneth's brain seemed as automatic as the Toyota's gearbox. The midsummer night hypnotised him, turning him into a robot.

In a few domestic gardens and in one public park, he noted leaf-clad poles with large circular wreaths just beneath the top. Children and adults were dancing around the poles, singing songs which to him sounded exotic. People wore colourful floral wreaths on their heads. Participants too tired to dance by now had started to eat and drink.

Ronis Nethken had done his homework. No one did midsummer like the Swedes. This very day, Midsummer Eve (always on a Friday that occurred between June the nineteenth and June the twenty-fifth), was the most important festivity in Sweden (along with Christmas) and a public holiday.

The rental Toyota stopped. The engine died. He got out of the car and moved to the door. Kenneth rang the doorbell. Waited. Rang again. He listened. Nothing. Nobody home. Neither the girl nor the parents. What luck! Now he could keep Sara's diary even longer. Ronis Nethken looked forward to more interesting reading in his hotel room. Hopefully, her diary would feature more juicy details. He rejected the idea of dropping the diary into the mailbox. The diary could be stolen. Instead, he would take good care of it. Rebecka would be grateful.

■

The guesthouse. A bright-pink fairytale castle at the end of the world. He moved through the deserted lobby, the desolate stairway and the sterile corridors, wrapped in quietness. The door to his single room creaked like the lid of a coffin. He stepped into the tomb, flicked on the dim light and sensed the presence of corpses. He checked under the bed and in the wardrobe and in the bathtub. No corpses.

Kenneth sat down at the wooden desk and opened Sara's diary to the current week. Rebecka's handwriting was as soft as cotton. Like cotton pads, her slanted letters were all devoid of sharp edges. Sara's text was a delight to the eye. Dr. Nethken's index finger wandered to the correct date. A single note: *Midsommarfest i Kung Karls Skolas matsal.*

Kenneth or Ronis keyed the text into the tablet PC. A translation app returned the words in English: Midsummer party at King Charles School Dining Room. Had Rebecka and Sara gone to the party together with their parents? Or alone? How long would the house be empty tonight?

■

You could use the telescope for other purposes than studies of the sky. He mounted the equipment. The telescope caught images from Rebecka's bedroom. From one world to another. From Saturn's rings to Sara's eyelashes. It took only a fraction of a second to shift the telescope's angle of incidence. Via the telescopic eye, multiple worlds were in continuous juxtaposition with one another.

▪

Night. Three minutes past two a.m. No one but the girl was at home. She was in bed, sleeping. The floral quilt had slipped downwards. A naked breast gleamed like a crescent moon in the telescopic eye.

Dr. Nethken nodded in an approving manner, demounted the telescope and placed it in the Toyota's boot. He moved through the sleeping neighbourhood, passed through a gate and went across a lawn. Could a night be brighter? He reached Rebecka and Sara's bedroom window. The window was equipped with a latch which allowed the window to be ajar in the midsummer heat. Fortunately, the window was ajar right now, not closed and locked.

He peered inside. The girls' shared bed.

Rebecka. Sara.

Sara. Rebecka.

No.

Månsson. Blomberg.

No, no.

He blinked, blinked, blinked.

One girl in the visual field. Only one.

The house belonged to the Månsson family. The girl in the visual field was Rebecka Månsson.

He took out the diary and checked the owner's name. Right. He was right. The right girl, the right house, the right midsummer night in the pattern of the eye.

An advantage of outward opening windows was that you didn't have to move flower pots from the interior windowsill. He was lucky.

A gloved hand pressed up the latch and swung the window. The hinges stayed dead silent.

Dr. Nethken climbed inside. The girl's bedroom had the scent of summer flowers and perfume.

On a wooden bench stood a doll's house. Bright-pink with cream-white trim. Three towers, pointed roof. A plastic model of the guesthouse back on the Kungsringen street. Ronis Nethken sat in one of the doll's house's single rooms, working on a new novel.

The author stood still in the room, listening to the girl's breathing. He fixed his eyes on her naked breast. The pink nipple was moving gently up and down to the beat of the girl's breathing. Her nipple was a swaying star in the night sky of midsummer. He wondered if she was dreaming. Wondered what she dreamt about. The dreaming dream girl, his reality, now, forever.

57

"You can come out from behind the desk, Jeanne." He walked deeper into the workroom. "What are you doing in my house?"

He noted movement.

Jeanne appeared. She looked at him and sighed. "I came here to get something, Kenneth."

"Get something?" He frowned. "What?"

She pulled out the desk chair, rolled it under the ceiling lamp, took off her shoes, stood on the chair, reached for the lampshade, snatched something, stepped down from the chair and put on her shoes. She held the thing out in the palm of her hand. "This."

He looked. The object was almost invisible. A transparent shard, thin as plastic wrap, small as a ladybird's wing. "Is it what I suspect it is?"

She nodded. "A transmitter/receiver."

"SCDX?"

"Latest nano- and femtotechnology, Mr. Frank says. Non-commercial and impossible to track or disturb. It can zoom in on every single speck of dust in this room, every single pixel on a screen, each letter on a computer screen or printed paper regardless of angle of incidence. It can pick up every sound in the house and the rest of the neighbourhood, including ultrasound. It can record human brain electrical activity and human brain magnetic fields and link those measurements to patterns of thinking. It can filter sound and picture selectively, for example, unwanted background noise or unwanted levels of darkness. The device is at present set to an automatic connection with all of your household electronics, including phones, watches, computers and printers."

"Phenomenal equipment. How could there be any job left over for yourself?"

"Even if the equipment is phenomenal, it can't become a substitute for human activity. Therefore, my employer planted me in your life." She returned the office swivel chair to its proper place. "You're no longer on any list."

"SCDX list? And no longer? Am I supposed to be grateful?"

"You're innocent of the killings, Kenneth. It has turned out that you have alibis for the times of five of the murders. So, it's reasonable to assume you're innocent of all of the murders. You're not a killer. But I'd like you to explain a few things."

"I want explanations, too." He struggled to keep the tone of his voice under control. His heartbeat was slamming in his ears. "I want you to explain a few things."

"Kenneth?"

"Huh?"

"Could you do me two favours, please?"

"Favours? Why? I owe you nothing."

"Please."

He took a deep breath. "What?"

"Firstly, that you lower your voice and secondly, that you brew a pot of tea."

"Tea?" The last thing on his mind. "Tea?"

"Let's go downstairs to the kitchen." Jeanne was moving out of the workroom. "We have a few things to talk about. And yes, let's enjoy a nice pot of tea."

▪

"That PC screen saver is disturbing, Kenneth."

"I know. It's supposed to be disturbing. But it isn't my screen saver. It belongs to Ronis Nethken. I installed it only temporarily—borrowed it from Dr. Nethken—as part of my way of working."

"Your way of working? How do you mean?"

"I identify with my fictional characters. To write characters whom I can believe in myself, I must see the world from their perspective. To identify with a particular character doesn't mean that I see myself as that character. It only means that I'm supporting that character's intentions as long as I'm working on the book in question. That is, getting into a character's head. I'm not writing about myself, Jeanne. My own screen saver is a bit nicer, I believe—jumping, multi-coloured cats."

They sat at the kitchen table, drinking tea and eating scones with butter. Linda sat *on* the table, chewing sweetcorn.

Jeanne raised her teacup and sipped. "Mr. Frank gave the order. I obeyed the order."

He had no appetite but he nibbled on a scone anyway. "How long has this transmitter/receiver been in my study?"

She looked at him from across the table. "Since the night we made love for the first time."

Fortunately, we didn't make love in the workroom, he thought. "How many times have you been in my house uninvited, Jeanne?"

"This is the only time."

The only time? The correct answer must surely be two times? At least twice.

He regarded her eyes. Had her beauty skewed his thoughts? Didn't he know? Or did he not want to know? Couldn't he accept, admit, that he loved Jeanne's mystique, even though she was a spy?

"Are you telling the truth, Jeanne?"

"I'm telling the truth."

He sipped tea. "I find it hard to believe you've been in my house uninvited just once."

"I've been here six times in the past. The times we've been together, including the four times we've made love."

"Why should I trust someone who works for Mr. Frank's organisation?"

"Why is it unreasonable that I've visited your house uninvited just once?"

"The day after the murder of Sadie Bentley, in the late afternoon, an intruder searched the house. And fed Linda. While I was in Endsleigh Park."

"I'm asking you to believe me. It wasn't me."

He thought. Considered her words. He wanted… wanted to believe. He couldn't help but love her.

"Kenneth?"

He met her gaze. Waited.

"It began as a mission, Kenneth. To Mr. Frank, it was a one-hundred-percent mission all the way. To your uncle, it was also a one-hundred-percent mission all the way. Inspector Sorin was worried, of course. He wanted to know, as quickly as possible, whether his nephew was linked to the murders. To me, it became less and less a mission. More and more emotions. The first time we made love, I was unsure of my feelings. Later, I got convinced. Our lovemaking had nothing to do with the mission. I admit that our intimacy facilitated my mission but it was a freestanding and genuine intimacy. I made love because I wanted to. We made love because we both wanted to." She reached out a hand and patted Linda. Linda miaowed.

He pondered. His breaths sounded like sighs. "How many people know that you and I…"

"No one knows with certainty. I never discuss my sex life. But Mr. Frank is suspicious. Inspector Sorin is suspicious. Mr. Frank knows

I've been here at night but he has no knowledge of the details of our relationship."

"That time in the dead of night, when we talked about my prime-number theory? In my workroom."

She smiled. "No one saw or heard how naughty I was. No one saw me wearing a short nightie. I had turned off the transmitter/receiver at the time."

"How?"

She licked scone crumbs from her lips. "There are a few different remote controls. One is sitting in a button on the nightdress I was wearing that night. This is a non-electronic remote control. The button on the nightie releases a substance which affects the air which affects the transmitter/receiver."

"Did you come here today only to retrieve the transmitter/receiver?"

"Right."

"You touched the answering machine and the computer keyboard."

"I apologise. Today's mission was to collect the equipment in the lampshade only. I just happened to be curious about the answering machine and the computer. I couldn't resist the temptation."

"How much do Mr. Frank and my uncle know?"

"Everything you've told me about, including your so-called prime-number theory. Mr. Frank still thinks you're crazy because of your perception that life is a novel but it isn't illegal to be crazy."

"Thanks for that."

"You're welcome."

"How have you determined my alibi?"

"Cameras have caught you in the wrong places at the right times."

Or in the right places at the wrong times, he thought. "Why has it taken so long to gather this information?"

"Uncertainties surrounding the identification of the various individuals who appear in the films. The uncertainties have been eliminated. By the way, the details of the uncertainties are top secret."

"Whose surveillance equipment is this?"

"Top secret. Illegal to discuss."

"SCDX?"

Jeanne took another scone with butter. "How do you explain the dates of Dr. Nethken's murder series? We regarded this as the strongest circumstantial evidence against you. How could a fictional character commit the murders before they took place in reality?"

"The working dates relating to the files you refer to are imaginary. I changed the dates retroactively just because it would then appear as if Dr. Nethken inspired reality. Nethken is living in a genre which doesn't exist. I call the genre fantasy-documentary. Nethken's story is the first fantasy-documentary novel I've written." And the last, he thought.

"What about your visit to the Swedish town of Kungsör? Rebecka Månsson's hometown?"

"It was actually the Swedish sixteenth-century king Gustav Vasa who took me to that town. The king had written more than a hundred letters in that town and I went there with the intention of investigating. I met Rebecka Månsson by chance. She inspired the fictitious character Sara Blomberg."

"Who's Mr. Maniac? The title character."

"Who do you think? Me?"

"You said you didn't write about yourself."

"Right."

"Ronis Nethken is Mr. Maniac, isn't he?"

"If he's guilty."

"Is he?"

"You have to read the book."

Pause. Silence.

"Can you forgive me, Kenneth?"

"For doing your job?"

"Where do we go from here?"

"Is there still a 'we'?"

"I hope so. Let's find out."

He thought for a moment. "There's something I have to admit, Jeanne."

"What?"

"There was a time, not long ago, when I was afraid I might be Ronis Nethken. Afraid that it was I who had murdered those girls. If you and Mr. Frank and Uncle Ash have discovered that I didn't…" He tried to complete the sentence but couldn't.

"We don't have to talk about it now, Kenneth."

They sat in silence, drinking tea and eating scones.

Seldom had silence been more comfortable.

58

The sunlit mist. An airliner in the corner of her eye. The aircraft's jet engines sprayed stripes across the heaven, white strings like a sky monster's legs.

Amy Worthington looked up and let her eyes flow along the concrete horizon of the cityscape. Cries echoed in the passageways. Ghost voices whispered, spoke and guided. The city of the lost souls. Pulsating murmurs, corrosive silences. Shrieking demons.

Demons communicated events characterised by terror, violence and murder. The demons moved along the cobblestone street. They showed her the nearest way through the morning light. She tolerated their style but despised their appearance: half human, half dog. Genetically recombined creatures. Demon voices bounced off the brick walls like alternating roars and sobs. The voices dribbled down the exteriors of buildings and rolled down the street, like rainwater in gutters.

Her amber hair was combed back and gathered in a ponytail. Her salt-white make-up made her look like a phantom. It wasn't Philip's opinion. The idea about her ghostly look was her own. She didn't care. Amy wasn't on her way to a party. It didn't matter how she looked or felt.

59

The girl looked smashing for being dead, Kenneth thought, apart from the missing eye. The corpse still smelled of a perfume, even though it lay in a rainwater puddle. Her red ringlets of hair floated on the puddle like some exotic seaweed. It was too rainy for the birds to sing and too early for the golfers to play. Death reigned in Paradise Park.

■

Kenneth sat in an armchair in Uncle Ash's office. "Elizabeth Peckerton shouldn't have been killed last night. It was Friday."

Uncle Ash scratched his head and lit a cigarette. "Your system has crashed, Ken. Also, you can say goodbye to your so-called duality theory."

"P is the sixteenth letter in the English alphabet. My prime-number system has also crashed."

■

Sunday, February the fifteenth. Kenneth and Uncle Ash sat in Mr. Frank's office.

"What's going on?" Mr. Frank said.

"The maniac got bored with Thursdays," Uncle Ash said. "Maybe. Or he harbours a hidden motive? According to the alternating two- and three-week intervals which my nephew theorised about, Miss Peckerton should have died last Thursday. Why was she eliminated the day after? Did the killer meet an impediment that made him adjust his original plan? Or did he change his agenda to distract us?"

"Elizabeth Peckerton shouldn't have died at all," Kenneth murmured. "She had the wrong name."

"Ash is asking new questions," Mr. Frank said. "I asked what was going on and Ash responded with several new questions."

Kenneth guessed that Mr. Frank was worried. Worried about his teenage daughters. So far, there had been no reason to fear that a Miss Frank risked attracting the madman's interest. F happened to be the sixth letter in the alphabet. The number six was a composite, not a prime. But the discovery of Miss Peckerton's lifeless body in Paradise Park forced everyone to think along new pathways.

The trio left the SCDX manager's office. In the lift to the ground floor, Mr. Frank turned towards Kenneth. "The young man is very quiet today. Has he nothing to say about recent events?"

Kenneth had plenty to say but the only thing he managed to exhale was used air, no fresh words. His mind drifted to the hot nights with Mr. Frank's secretary and spy. The lift appeared more cramped than usual. He wanted out of there, out of Mr. Frank's shadow, out of the lift and out of the building. He had to see Jeanne again. Jeanne's existence in his life carried a deeper meaning.

▪

Monday, February the sixteenth was a key day, he realised later, and in more than one sense. He sat in his uncle's office, in the background, in a position to survey the course of events. Uncle Ash sat at his desk, smoking a cigarette.

The young woman in the visitor's chair unbuttoned her winter coat and loosened her scarf. "Sir, I had to contact you. It was the most rational thing I could think of doing." Miss Karen McNamara was a plump lady with rosy cheeks and pecan-coloured hair. She looked at Uncle Ash with expectancy in her big blue eyes.

"What do you mean, Miss McNamara?"

"I want you to know that I'm innocent. It wasn't I who killed Liz."

"Liz?"

"Elizabeth Peckerton. 'Liz' to her friends."

"I understand. Continue, Miss McNamara."

"Well, this strange and horrible story—that Liz has been murdered—drives me crazy."

It drives us all crazy, Kenneth thought. Unless we already are.

"I became acquainted with both Rachel and Liz at university and—"

"Hey, wait a minute." Uncle Ash raised a hand. "Rachel who?"

"Rachel Fenwick. Rumour has it that her dad is a world-famous psycho-doctor or something. She's Liz's girlfriend. Or, hmm, was… The thing is, I was in love with Liz too but Liz and I slept with each other only once."

"It's all beginning to sound really interesting, Miss McNamara. Please continue."

"As I said, it wasn't I who killed Liz. I loved her and became upset when she said she loved Rachel, not me. Liz said she was ashamed of having cheated on Rachel and that the night we had spent together was a mistake she deeply regretted."

Miss McNamara popped a chewing gum bubble. Then she wiped away a tear which spilled from one eye. "Liz and I didn't choose the same courses but, as you probably know, you meet new people all the time and everywhere on campus—the libraries, the cafeterias, and so on."

Uncle Ash nodded. "Definitely."

"On the other hand, both Rachel and I chose to study for a BA degree in history. We read the basic courses together, the so-called core modules, while we differed on how we specialised in the subjects which interested us the most. Rachel opted for The Making of the 20th Century, and I picked American History: From Settlements to Superpower. Are you interested in the social, political, cultural, economic and diplomatic developments that have shaped our world, Inspector Sorin?"

"Uh… Let's return to something you mentioned a minute ago. You used the word 'acquainted'. Now, there's a difference between being acquainted with someone and knowing someone. You didn't know Rachel particularly well? Not like a friend or even an enemy would know her? And Elizabeth?"

"Okay, I'll explain. I'm well acquainted with Rachel Fenwick, nothing more than that. It turned out we didn't get along very well though. However, Liz and I got really close. See what I mean?"

Miss McNamara put a new piece of chewing gum into her mouth. "Liz said she and I shared an emotional intimacy, and one night we simply ended up in bed together, but later I realised she loved Rachel more than me and I pretended to accept it." She paused and took a deep breath. "Oh yes, Liz and Rachel were deeply in love. What happened between Liz and me that night wasn't planned. It just happened. And it was a secret. It's still a secret. I'm convinced Rachel knows nothing because if she knew she would've confronted me. Rachel has never confronted me on that point."

Kenneth's eyes were glued to Miss

McNamara's myrtle-green scarf. He decided to strangle a pretty girl with her scarf. In his next book, that is. A quote from Edgar Allan Poe surfaced to his mind: 'The death of a beautiful woman is unquestionably the most poetical topic in the world.'

"Tell me about Miss Fenwick," Uncle Ash said.

"Why, Inspector? What can I say about Rachel that she can't tell you herself?"

"I want to hear an outsider's view."

"Okay. Hmm, by all means, Rachel has positive qualities or Liz wouldn't have been with her. It's just that Rachel and I are on different wavelengths, so to speak. She's terribly intuitive and often eager to try to help solve other people's problems, both private concerns and study-related trouble. I know she just means well but it can get tiring."

Miss McNamara paused. "Inspector, there's one thing about Rachel that I really like. Although she's a colourful person who uses swear words now and then, she never flares up. She often seems to look at life and existence with the open and peaceful mind of a philosopher."

Kenneth wondered if Miss McNamara, with her simile, referred to a particular philosopher or a group of philosophers. The inner circle around Socrates in ancient Greece? He didn't bother to ask.

"Is there anything more you can tell me, Miss McNamara?"

"How do I know what's important or not?"

"You don't. Therefore, you can tell me anything that comes to mind and let me decide what's important or what isn't."

She seemed to ponder. Then, "There're these peculiar little things about Rachel, such as her fear of walking under a ladder or opening an umbrella in the house."

"I see. Anything else?"

She bit down on her lip. "Maybe. If you don't mind hearing second-hand information."

"I don't mind at all."

"Okay. I've never slept with Rachel but Liz once said that Rach Fenwick could be extremely romantic and sensual in bed."

"Intriguing indeed." Uncle Ash lit a cigarette.

I'm certain she can, Kenneth thought but didn't say.

"Sometimes, on the university campus, Liz liked to talk about Rachel," Miss McNamara continued. "I wasn't interested in listening, I just pretended to be, to preserve harmony with Liz. According to Liz, Rachel's sexuality was fantasy-driven when supplied with the right mix of fulfilled desires, emotional stimulation and appropriate environment. Rachel idealises her lover and allows her fanciful emotions to cloud her judgement when it comes to erotic attraction. You think I'm crazy to talk about this, don't you, Inspector?"

Uncle Ash grunted something inaudible.

"Anyway, Liz found that Rachel was

intuitive and sympathetic while she risked being deceived by the people who fitted her imagination. Well, *Liz* fitted her imagination and if the deception which Liz was talking about had to do with me and Liz in bed—" Miss McNamara paused, took a pocket mirror from her handbag and checked her lipstick. When she began to speak again, still with her eyes in the mirror, she appeared to be addressing herself. "Now, one side of Rachel's person is amorous, creative, sensitive, optimistic, sexually satisfied, responsive, imaginative and innovative, while her other side is depressed, guilt-ridden and dispirited. She can flip back and forth between her two sides with alarming ease."

Miss McNamara slammed the lid on the pocket mirror and looked up. "May I go now, Inspector?"

"How would you describe Rachel's relationship with her father?"

"She never mentioned her father to me and I have never met him. What I now want to know is whether you believe me when I say I'm innocent. That was the very reason I came here, to sort the matter out. I didn't kill Liz."

"Of course I believe you. Elizabeth Peckerton's murder represents a jigsaw piece in a larger puzzle comprising nine dead girls. We're hunting a serial killer. Anyway, thank you for telling your story."

Yet you don't know everything that's happening, dear Uncle, Kenneth thought.

"Aren't you going to ask me whether I have an alibi, Inspector? I have one."

Uncle Ash tried to smile. The result became a grimace. "All right, miss, I'm listening."

"Liz was killed on Friday night, right, Inspector? I was at a private party in Creake from about seven p.m. to about two forty-five a.m."

"That was a long party. You realise I have the resources to check if the details are true."

"Please, Inspector, do it. Check the details."

"I have more important things to do."

"I believe you, too, Miss McNamara." Kenneth's gaze was no longer on the lady's myrtle-green scarf but in a paperback novel he had fished out of his inside jacket pocket.

She winced and turned her head. "Who're you?"

"Dr. Kenneth Sorin. The inspector's nephew."

"Doctor? You're not a detective?"

"Not really. Or not exactly. Rather, an external analyst. Amateur detective, if you prefer that word. Or speculative theorist. Or investigative writer. But the simple truth is more complicated than that."

"I don't understand what you're talking about."

"What's relevant is what I think of your story."

"So you believe me?"

"You have nothing to fear, Miss McNamara." *At least not until it's time again for the letter M.*

60

Leighton Fenwick pushed the front door open. This time he wore a sunflower-yellow bathrobe. "Inspector Ash Sorin. Dr. Kenneth Sorin. I've been waiting for you. But that doesn't mean I've been longing for your company. Let's get the formalities over with as soon as possible."

"We don't have time for a three-course dinner anyway," Uncle Ash said.

They moved through the house to the all-white living room and sat down. The room now seemed whiter than white, as if some ultra-white glitter was cruising walls and ceiling, a brilliance which chased and erased every shade less pale than diamond. The three men sat in a space devoid of shadows.

On the table between them was a tray with a misty jug, a few glasses and a small bowl filled with ice cubes. Fenwick offered nothing to drink.

"I've just stepped out of the pool," Fenwick said.

"Not quite just now," Uncle Ash said. "Your hair is dry as gunpowder."

"I used an electric hairdryer."

"Hairdryers are noisy. You mean you heard the doorbell anyway?"

"When the front doorbell is ringing, a flash light indicator goes on in... Inspector Sorin, would you be kind enough to get to the point?"

"You look good in a sunflower-yellow

bathrobe, Dr. Fenwick. Much better than in a pink T-shirt."

"Thank you." The man reached for the jug and a glass for himself only, dropped an ice cube into the glass, filled the glass to the brim and sipped. "Ah! Ice-cold raspberry juice is exceptionally refreshing. Now, you're sitting in my house again since recent developments have brought you here. Elizabeth was my daughter's best friend. I'm shocked."

"But not too shocked to enjoy a swim in the pool," Uncle Ash said.

Fenwick glared. "My daughter is inconsolable. She has been crying ever since I phoned to tell her the terrible news."

Uncle Ash raised his eyebrows. "Phoned?"

"My Rachel had looked forward to visiting her grandmother Elise in Carlisle. She travelled up to Cumbria on Thursday morning and returned home yesterday. My phone call ruined the remainder of Rachel's weekend, to say the least."

"When and how did you learn the news?"

"Last Saturday evening. A late newscast on TV."

"When did you call your daughter?"

"Yesterday morning. A horrible phone call to make but I wanted to be certain she knew. Elise, my mother, has no TV."

"Radio?"

"No radio. And before you ask, no Internet. She prefers traditional newspapers and I couldn't know whether Elizabeth's murder would be mentioned in a late Saturday edition anywhere, let alone in a local Carlisle paper."

"Why didn't you phone until yesterday morning if you knew on Saturday night?"

"It was too late at night to call."

"But maybe not too late for a swim in the pool."

"What did you say?"

"How did you spend your own time last Friday, Dr. Fenwick?"

"I gave a talk and presented two posters at a conference in Bristol. This was a five-day meeting, from Monday through Friday."

"What meeting?"

"The 16th International Symposium on Applied Clinical Psychology and Psychiatry."

"How did you travel? By car? By rail? By air?"

"Car. My own."

"We'll check that."

"Please do."

"What time on Friday did the conference end?"

"Not until nine p.m."

"When did you give your talk?"

"My talk, one of the plenary lectures, happened to be the last contribution on the last day. Thus on the very night Elizabeth was murdered. The plenary lectures are usually scheduled for morning sessions but the Bristol meeting organisers wanted certain high-profile talks to take place during the evening sessions.

I started my own talk at eight p.m. and ended around eight forty-five. Inspector, I don't know what time Elizabeth was murdered but not even you could theorise that I drove a car from Bristol to Blackfield late on Friday night to do the macabre deed."

"Driving from Bristol to Blackfield takes a little more than three hours," Kenneth said. He could read disappointment in his uncle's eyes. Kenneth agreed that this new development stung. It didn't matter if Fenwick had beaten the land speed record with a jet car. The man couldn't have been in two cities at the same time.

"Inspector Sorin, I think I deserve an answer to the following question. What time on Friday night was Elizabeth murdered?"

"Sometime between seven fifteen and eight fifteen."

Fenwick grinned. "Dissatisfied, Inspector?"

"Congratulations, Doc. It looks like you have an alibi for the time of the murder of Miss Peckerton."

"I'm glad you realise that." Fenwick's grin was wider than ever. He drank his raspberry juice. His bared teeth were whiter than the living room walls. "You came here thinking I had murdered Elizabeth. But there are no perfect people. I'm convinced that Inspector Sorin is mature enough to admit he had just made a mistake."

"And your two poster presentations?"

"My posters were, like all the others,

mounted for continuous display throughout the five days."

"I want to talk more about your Bristol visit a bit later. Let's now focus on Miss Peckerton."

"Elizabeth, yes, of course."

"You knew her well, didn't you? She was and still is 'Elizabeth' to you, not 'Miss Peckerton'. And the tone of your voice makes me almost imagine you're talking about a family member."

"You're right. I knew Elizabeth well. Almost as if she had been a second daughter. It's no secret and I have nothing to hide. Elizabeth was Rachel's best friend and she visited our home often, more times than I can remember."

I thought you were a man who remembered everything, Kenneth thought.

"I liked Elizabeth," Fenwick continued, "and I'm sorry she's dead."

"Did you know that Miss Peckerton and your daughter were more than just friends?"

"Of course. The girls tried to keep it a secret but neither truths nor lies escape me. I see straight through people. Rachel doesn't know that I know."

"What do you think about your daughter being a lesbian?"

"Is that a relevant question?"

"You have something to hide?"

"Rachel is bisexual."

"How do you know?"

"She has had boyfriends as well as girlfriends in the past."

"What do you think about your daughter being bisexual?"

"I'm indifferent. I don't discriminate against people, neither on the basis of sexual orientation nor any other trait. My own daughter is no exception."

"Were you opposed to Miss Peckerton's sexual relationship with your daughter?"

"Not at all. Elizabeth was twenty-one, the same age as Rachel. At twenty-one, you're old enough to decide how you want to live your life."

"Did you ever sleep with Miss Peckerton?"

"Is it relevant? I could ask you to go to hell with your insolent questions, Inspector Sorin. But I'll do you a favour here and cooperate. The answer is no. I never slept with Elizabeth. Even if I had had the opportunity—and I did say *if*—I would never have done it. Rachel would never have forgiven me."

"Were you lusting after her?"

"No. Elizabeth was an attractive woman but I wasn't lusting after her. Not in the least."

"Is your daughter home?"

"My daughter is in her room. And she's upset, as you'll certainly understand."

"I want to talk to her."

"I said she's upset. You can talk to Rachel but not today. On any other day, but not today."

Uncle Ash seemed to ponder. "Okay, Fenwick. Some other day. In the near future. Let's return to your Bristol visit."

Fenwick said nothing. He looked as

confident as a tennis player leading 6-0, 6-0, 5-0, and 40-0 on his own serve.

"Where were you staying in Bristol?"

"At a hotel in the vicinity of the conference."

"Which hotel?"

"Parlingham."

"I want the contact information for the conference organiser and the hotel."

"No problem, Inspector."

"I also want the contact information for your mother in Carlisle."

"Why?"

"Do you mind?"

"I asked why?"

"So you do mind? You must know I can get your mother's contact info without your cooperation."

Fenwick sighed. "As you wish. I'll give you her address and telephone number. But I warn you, Inspector. Don't push my mother. She's an old woman."

"From where did you call your daughter?"

"From my landline in the kitchen."

"Excellent. There should be a record of that call with your phone company. You wouldn't mind if I checked it out, would you?"

61

Uncle Ash called the University of Bristol from his office and turned on the loudspeaker so

Kenneth could follow the conversation. Uncle Ash wanted to talk to one Professor Wendy Rolstow, the manager of The 16th International Symposium on Applied Clinical Psychology and Psychiatry (ISACPP-xvi). As Mrs. Rolstow was unavailable for the rest of the day, the switchboard operator transferred the call to the conference office. A secretary answered.

The Bristol meeting had covered one thousand and eleven research presentations, comprising ten plenary lectures, five hundred and sixty fifteen-minute talks (spread over four parallel sessions) and four hundred and forty-one posters. Remaining work after the meeting closure date included the production of the updated conference publication in three formats: hardcover book, e-book and CD; the updating of the official ISACPP website; and several other administrative jobs.

"One Leighton Fenwick from Blackfield gave his plenary lecture from eight to eight forty-five on the Friday night, February the thirteenth," the secretary said.

"Are you sure about the time?" Uncle Ash said.

"Of course I'm sure," the secretary snapped.

Uncle Ash called Hotel Parlingham.

"Yes, Leighton Fenwick checked in on Monday morning, February the ninth, and checked out on the Friday of the same week, the thirteenth," the hotel receptionist said. "Besides, Dr. Fenwick is well known at our hotel. He paid the bill by credit card. I can confirm that the credit card details belong to the respected Dr. Leighton Fenwick."

Since the conference had ended at nine on the Friday evening, Fenwick could have chosen to leave his suitcase in the hotel's guarded baggage room to collect later, but in connection with his seven fifty check-out on the Friday morning, he had taken all his baggage with him. There was nothing strange about keeping the suitcase in the car throughout the final day. And other conference delegates had done the same thing. It wasn't uncommon that congress representatives had to hurry on closure day. There were traffic jams to avoid, and flights and trains to catch. Leighton Fenwick's alibi was as waterproof as a Rolex wristwatch.

62

"Have a seat, Mr. Smith," Uncle Ash said.

"Cheers, boss." Benjamin Smith sat down in the visitor's chair. A sly shadow danced across his brow.

"I got this internal message," Uncle Ash said. "You wanted to see me." He leant forward and held out a packet of Benson & Hedges. "Cigarette?"

"Awesome, boss." The guy snatched a cigarette with trembling fingers and threw glances around.

Smith had hesitated, Kenneth noted, as if he had suspected that Uncle Ash would withdraw the offer of a free cigarette. Who was he anyway? Ben Smith looked like he slept in his clothes.

"My office is an exception to the smoking ban." It sounded as if Uncle Ash meant it or believed it. First he lit Smith's cigarette, then his own. "Mr. Smith, what do you have to say? I understand it's about the young woman who was found dead in Paradise Park on Saturday morning."

"Yeah, that's right, boss." Smith's haggard face brightened behind the cloud of smoke. "This babe with the carrot-coloured hair was walking with this guy and—"

"Wait," Uncle Ash said. "Carrot-coloured hair? The woman in question had ruby-red hair."

"If you say so, boss. If the babe was a redhead, she was a redhead. Doesn't matter to me. I saw her. Saw her. What a lovely piece of arse."

"All right, Mr. Smith. You saw her. Let's assume it's true. Now, what did you see, in concrete terms? What happened and where? Tell me everything you know and tell me from the beginning, please."

"Okay, boss." Smith puffed on his free cigarette. "I was sitting on a street bench, knocking back a few beers, when this hottie with carrot-coloured... sorry, ruby-red hair, whose picture is in today's papers, walked along the pavement with this guy."

"Where exactly?"

"Exactly? Outside the cathedral. Well, uh, I met them on High Street, boss. They came walking from the direction of City Hall."

"They were actually out on the town together?"

"Yes, boss. The guy and the babe were out on the town together."

"Did you get the impression they were together as acquaintances or friends or as a couple in love? Did they hold hands?"

Smith was thinking. Then he shook his head. "No, boss. They didn't hold hands."

"How did you perceive their body language?"

Smith seemed thoughtful. "They didn't look like a couple, no, no such thing. They didn't even look at each other when they were talking but…"

"But what?"

"I want to say they were more than friends."

"What makes you say that?"

"Well, as far as I could see they could have been father and daughter. They hugged once."

"You mean the man was much older than the woman?"

"Sure, boss. The guy was old enough to be the girl's dad. I don't mean he *must* have been her dad, just that he was old enough to be."

"An older family member or an old friend? How does that sound, Mr. Smith?"

"Sounds cool as fuck, boss."

"What time was this?"

"Time? I have no idea, boss. But it must have been in the evening because it was as dark as the hole in the Lord Mayor's arse."

Uncle Ash nodded. "Sometime after five or six? If we consider the February darkness."

The night when Elizabeth Peckerton was killed, the sunset occurred at five eleven, Kenneth thought.

"What you say sounds reasonable, boss. The fuckin' yuppies were leaving their city offices so the time must have been five or six. It wouldn't surprise me in the least if the guy we're talking about belongs to the fuckin' Financial District."

"Aha? The man was smart? Suit and tie? Black, polished shoes?"

"Spot on, boss. Just like the yuppie who's sitting there in the corner." Smith pointed at Kenneth with his forefinger. "Who're you? The boss's bodyguard or something, huh?"

"My name is Kenneth Sorin. I'm the inspector's nephew."

"No shit," Smith said.

"Your description of the man you saw in the city centre is too general," Uncle Ash said. "Thousands of office workers dress like that. Could you mention anything else about him? Anything more specific?"

Smith tightened his lips. "I had other things to look at. The sexy redhead stole all my attention."

"Elizabeth Peckerton, I suppose."

"The name tells me nothing but I'm sure it was the same babe who's pictured in today's papers. Did you say her name was Elizabeth?"

"So that's why you remember the man at all. He just happened to be with Miss Peckerton."

"Absolutely, boss. Without the hottie, I wouldn't even have noticed the guy. Thousands of gurus look like that in this fuckin' city. You can't distinguish between them motherfuckers." Smith finished his cigarette. "Can I have another smoke, boss?"

"Keep the packet."

Smith's eyes narrowed. "Seriously?"

"I'm trying to quit."

"Oh, thanks a lot, boss." Smith lit his second free cigarette and pocketed the packet.

"How was the style of talking between the woman and the man you saw on the town? Energetic? Unpleasant? Aggressive? Hostile? Suspicious?"

"They seemed to be having a good time. At least to begin with…" Smith paused.

"Continue, please."

"I was then close enough to hear the tones of their voices. The babe and the yuppie were totally preoccupied with each other. They ignored me and the rest of the world. Their chat was pleasant to start with, as I said, but soon the guy got pissed off."

"Were they still walking along High Street?"

"Sure, boss. In the direction of Castle Square."

"What were they talking about?"

"Sorry, boss. I couldn't hear a fuckin' word, just noticed their emotions. Yeah, exactly. Emotions. That's a fuckin' good word, isn't it? The guy was pissed off at the babe."

"Miss Peckerton's own mood? How was it?"

"She looked comfortable at the beginning. But when the yuppie or guru got pissed off, she seemed scared. Maybe not scared shitless, just a little."

The horror that happened caught Kenneth off guard. Smith's head swung around like a propeller and he stared at Kenneth with sparkling eyes, his gaze a mosaic of firework colours. The hairs on the haggard visitor's head acquired the same texture as reed grass. His entire haircut rose as if charged with static electricity. Kenneth had guessed that Smith was in his late twenties (possibly the same age as Kenneth himself) but right now the visitor looked at least seventy. The words that fell from the young (old?) man's lips were cast out in Christine Corbett's dead voice. Benjamin Smith/Christine Corbett said, "*You realised the importance of the Christmas roses, young man. But it wasn't I who planted them in your dreams.* You *did it. You or Ronis Nethken. You must take responsibility, not only for your actions but also for your dreams. I weaken faster now. Soon I'll disappear forever.*

"*Everything has an end, even bad dreams. I see that you already understand the significance of the ninth murder, how lady number nine fits into the puzzle. Goodbye, Kenneth Sorin. Goodbye forever... forever... forever...*"

Christine's voice vanished.

Benjamin Smith's head was spinning back to its natural position. Kenneth tried to breathe again, his throat sounding rusty. Something stung his eyes like tropical sunlight. Tears wanted to spill like corrosive drops of acid. His headache rushed back with the pitch-dark swiftness of a tiger's shadow.

Uncle Ash turned to Kenneth. "Do you have any quest...? Hey, Ken! Ken? Are you okay?"

"Your nephew looks like he's just seen a fuckin' ghost or something," Smith said.

"I feel fine. Only, my mind was elsewhere for a while." He took the packet of painkillers from his jacket pocket, shook out three tablets and swallowed them dry.

"Headache?" Uncle Ash said.

"Not at all," Kenneth said. "Only the echo of a phantom voice."

Smith and Uncle Ash laughed. Not Kenneth.

"What was it you wanted to ask me?" Kenneth said.

"Do you have any questions for Mr. Smith?"

"Mr. Smith," Kenneth said, "did any item pass between the woman and the man?"

Smith blinked in surprise. "What kind of item?"

"Anything."

"Sorry, pal. Not a damn thing passed

from the man to the woman or the other way around." Smith was thinking. "But wait... The guy did at least seem interested in getting something from the redhead."

"What could it have been?"

"I have no fuckin' idea, pal. Whatever it was, the man got nothing, at least not there and then, as far as I could see, but you never know what might have happened after they disappeared."

"Please continue, Mr. Smith."

"No more 'Mr. Smith', pal. Call me Ben. Okay?"

"Okay," Kenneth said. "Ben."

"Well, the guy was interested in her handbag."

"Or an item in her handbag? Not the handbag itself. How does that sound, Ben?"

"Sounds cool as fuck, pal."

"And she didn't want to give up the item, right?"

"Spot on, pal. The hottie wasn't keen on handing it over. This happened only a minute after they had hugged. The atmosphere turned worse and worse. I thought they would start to fight about the fuckin' handbag, right there on the fuckin' pavement."

"What happened then?" Kenneth asked.

"They disappeared around the corner of a side street. I just can't remember which one." Ben Smith paused. "Now I've told you everything I know."

"Thank you, Mr. Smith," Uncle Ash said.

"Ben," Ben Smith said, and grinned.

"You've been very helpful," Uncle Ash said.

"I hope so, boss. Today's newspaper headlines scared the fuckin' shit out of me."

63

Ten-year-old Kenneth told his younger brother Simon that Granny's gigantic house was a haunted castle and, like all castles, he argued, Granny's was a hangout for ghosts and demons. It was reasonable to assume that phantoms and vampires lived there too. Simon looked terrified but he didn't protest. Little brother must have arrived at the correct conclusion that big brother was always right.

Grandmum's castle and dead Granddad's book collection inspired Kenneth's stories. The collection comprised four large cardboard boxes of horror and mystery paperbacks. Mrs. Davenport was unaware of this collection, of course. In a school world where Mrs. Davenport ruled, you had to have secrets of your own to survive.

Although Mum and Dad had been married for eleven years, the atmosphere between Mum and Dad's mum remained tense. Ten-year-old Kenneth guessed that mothers overprotected their sons, that a mother regarded every other woman of a younger generation as a threat to her son's safety, morale, well-being, career, interests and integrity. He felt that Mum was watching him just as Dad's mum was watching Dad. Was it this scepticism that formed the basis for Anna Sorin's inability or unwillingness to accept her daughter-in-law without reservation? The ten-year-old thought so. No, not only *thought*. He was *convinced*. Every generation of parents underestimated their children's ability to observe adults' problems or the consequences of adults' problems.

(Who murdered us, Kenneth?)

▪

The trouble was, he didn't know what to call the peculiar sensation which formed in the pit of his stomach whenever he thought about Alison. It didn't hurt, it wasn't unpleasant, but it felt strange. It could be a symptom of an incurable disease. How did you talk to a doctor about this? Alison's giggles didn't cease to irritate him. Every time he happened to walk past her in the playground or in the school canteen it felt as if her giggles arrived from inside his own skull. Her sniggers were at their loudest whenever she was in the company of her girlfriends, glancing in his direction.

▪

The chessboard developed a third dimension. It turned into a cube. The cube expanded. He was trapped in a three-dimensional chess game, as big as Granny Anna's house—a chess cube. The inside illumination came from an external source. The alternating white and black squares of the six sides of the cube filtered the incoming light, providing heavy shadows contrasting with dazzling white. He was no longer a ten-year-old boy but a young man. Alison was gone, or the false apparition of her.

He stood on the chessboard's kingside, which now served as a flooring to the chess-cube world. Kenneth turned towards the deserted third row on queenside. He tried to walk but his feet froze on the e3-square. Someone, or something, neighed nearby. He detected movement out of the corner of his eye and spun around. The white knight on the f4-square panted his bad breath in Kenneth's face. Kenneth tried to step aside, without success. He couldn't displace his centre of gravity. In dreams, unknown laws of physics flourished. The air in the chess cube carried the same sinister quality as quicksand. He couldn't move at all.

The white knight's neighing turned into speech. "How's the search for truth going, Ken? Any new clues?" The thing's drooling mouth was a nest of razor-sharp teeth. Its tongue reached out, searching Kenneth's face. The creature's breath smelled like rotten eggs and gave him a bout of nausea.

Kenneth managed to move, dragging his feet along the third rank towards queenside.

He noticed that the creature's red-rimmed eyes continued to sweep in his direction. Then, a whining sound, from the junction between the third rank and the d-file. He looked to his right. Two multi-coloured objects flashed past his head with the speed of cannonballs. The cannonballs were Eve and Bernie, Grandmum Anna's parrots. The birds changed like everything else in this weird place. They appeared as flying tiger babies, roaring and growling during their journey down the d-file airspace, moving in an arc through the space between the pawns on d2 and e2. They landed on the white queen's crown.

The chess cube grew. Or Grandmother's house shrank. The cube was ten times bigger than the house. Then, infinitely big. Its eight corners became invisible to the naked eye. He had walked for ages and still had only passed through two squares. He had started on kingside's e3 and advanced to c3 on queenside. He turned his head to the right and peered up the c-file. The army of black pieces must be somewhere in that direction. Why hadn't White started the game and advanced pieces? The white knight with a nasty attitude on f4 had advanced itself. Who was actually playing? He looked over his shoulder, along the third rank towards kingside. Nothing there. At least nothing in sight.

He turned his gaze forward again and noted that the mirage of a black bishop on c5 wasn't a mirage but a real piece. Now it jerked forward and diagonally to a3 and stayed there, two squares in front of him. Something else also appeared on a3. This thing lumbered back and forth between the a3-bishop and the white a2-pawn. The creation, a live humming contour, expressed a noise so agonising and pervasive that Kenneth thought his eardrums would burst. When he recognised the prowling figure, his fear exploded in psychological pain.

The monster version of Granny's poodle Tracy glowered. "What the heck are you doing here, pal? The game of chess has new SCDX rules."

He tried to say something but his tongue was frozen to the roof of his mouth. The cold was accompanied by a crisscrossing draft that whipped up ripples in the mayonnaise-thick air. The wind arrived from the far edge of kingside. Where he now stood, deep into queenside, the gusts accelerated, transitioning into a storm. This Tracy couldn't be Tracy, like Rebecka couldn't be Sara, like Kenneth couldn't be Nethken.

Tracy who wasn't Tracy snarled at him. "When the game ends, you're checkmate, pal."

"What do you want?" he managed to say. "What do you want from me?"

She turned her back to him and disappeared into the windy darkness.

64

He spotted her on Tuesday afternoon, at the City Library, Crowhill Square. Rachel Fenwick wore a neon-green untucked T-shirt which had on its front the Blackfield University logo, a montage of the University Hall bell tower and a close-up of a flying crow. The posh headphones to the portable music player sat like a headband on her blonde hair. He guessed the girl had turned off the music here in the library environment.

Miss Fenwick examined bookshelves, bending her neck, stretching, standing on tiptoes, shifting her weight from one foot to the other in order to reach the right volumes. Her left-hand fingers twirled a pen. She clasped a paperback book under her arm, Kenneth could see, something about the kingdom of the pharaohs.

"May I help you, Miss Fenwick?"

She spun around on one heel and her balance faltered. "Oh, you scared me."

"I'm sorry, Miss Fenwick. Are you all right?"

"It's okay to call me Rachel." The untucked T-shirt covered her buttocks like a short dress.

"Okay. Rachel." A good start, Kenneth thought. He hadn't expected to be included in the circle who could address Dr. Fenwick's daughter by her first name, not at this early stage.

She flashed the alluring smile he remembered from before. In contrast, her eyes were filled with sadness. One cheek showed the faintest traces of tears, a dry fleck mirroring a recent past, like watermarks on glassware. Her lips trembled. “Sorry…”

“For what?”

“The first time we met, I was too busy to talk. I had to hurry to the library. The second time, I was too upset to talk, as Dad certainly explained. And now… I’m still upset.”

“How about a third attempt, Rachel?”

▪

The City Library was composed of three floors. In the same building, above the library, spread over two floors, was Crowhill Square Museum of Art. They took a lift to the museum cafeteria. In the crowd, they found a vacant corner table for two.

“I can’t promise I won’t start crying again.” She breathed the words in a whisper.

“I don’t blame you for expressing your feelings, Rachel.” He ordered and paid for drinks. Rachel had an orange soft drink, Kenneth had sparkling water. “Do you think it’s true that most students spend one hundred percent of their library time in academic libraries?”

“I would think so, Dr. Sorin.”

“Call me Kenneth.”

“Okay. Kenneth.” The girl looked up from her orange soft drink. “Most students but not all. I spend a hundred percent of my library time in academic libraries and another hundred percent in public libraries such as the City Library. That's two hundred percent in total."

He smiled. "I like your wit. I see its meaning."

"Do you?" A tear slid down from the red rim of one of her eyes.

"Of course. You're talking to a writer. Libraries are my second home."

"Dad taught me to read a lot and widely. Read as much as you can, Dad says, books from all the continents of the world."

"Your dad wants you to live well. Life without books would be poorer and the drive of our development wouldn't even exist."

"Books are vital?"

"Literature is essential to a democratic society."

"What do you want from me, Kenneth?"

"I was hoping to have an informal chat. Let's forget my uncle and Mr. Frank for the time being. You could think of me as an investigative writer. What do you think?"

Rachel sniffled. "I'll try."

"How was your stay in Carlisle?"

"I love my granny, Elise."

"I can understand that. I love my granny too."

"What's her name?"

"Anna."

"I try to see Granny as often as I can but

it isn't easy to travel up to Cumbria at short notice."

"Who suggested your trip?"

"Dad. Why?"

"I'm only curious."

"It wasn't just that Dad *suggested* my trip. He *insisted* I go and see Granny."

"Really?"

"Dad would be away, at a conference, and he didn't want me to be all alone in the big house for several days. Isn't that weird, Kenneth? Sometimes it seems like Dad thinks I'm still twelve. I told him I didn't have time to travel anywhere right now since I'm having a very intense study period and want full access to the various libraries of Blackfield."

"I see."

"Does it matter?"

"When did he persuade you to take the trip?"

"Last Wednesday."

Kenneth nodded. "It wasn't planned."

"What do you mean?"

"If it were planned, he would have talked to you before he left town. Last Wednesday, February the eleventh, your dad was in Bristol. He called you? He persuaded you, by phone, to travel to Carlisle?"

She appeared puzzled. "That's right."

"Were you surprised by the short notice?"

"Not at all. Dad is always like that."

"How?"

"Fast thinker. Effective advisor. Strong decision-maker. And he always puts me first."

"How did he react when you said you didn't have time to travel anywhere?"

"He was cool about it, as expected. He said I would only need a couple of days of reading to catch up on four lost days. He said I was an intelligent girl and that it would be very easy for me to catch up. Now, in hindsight, I think he was right about my trip. Dad is always right. It was nice to see Granny again." She paused, lifted the drinking glass to her pink lips, drank nothing and lowered the glass to the table again. "Dad can be convincing."

I bet he can, Kenneth thought but didn't say. "Let's talk about Elizabeth."

"Liz..." Her voice faded.

"If you don't mind, Rachel. It won't take long."

She sniffled again. "I keep myself busy, studying and watching TV, in order to fight the distressing thoughts about Liz's death." She wiped the corners of her eyes with a paper napkin. Her breath left her in a shaky exhalation. "What do you want to know about Liz?"

"Anything. You decide."

Rachel gathered her thoughts. "Liz and I met through university. We got along very well and eventually we became best friends."

"Was she a local girl?"

Rachel shook her head. "From Hastings."

"When did you last see her?"

"Last week. She came over to our house on the Tuesday afternoon. We had a party, just Liz and I. She stayed overnight and left after breakfast on the Wednesday morning, the day before I travelled up to Carlisle. But…"

"But what?"

"When she arrived at the house on the Tuesday, she was happy and talkative and we had the most wonderful evening. However, on the Wednesday morning, she was almost like a different person."

"How?"

"Worried, I would say. Introverted. Maybe a little scared too."

"Were you alone in the house all night?"

"Yes."

"Just the two of you?"

"Yes."

"Did the doorbell ring?"

"No."

"Any phone? Landline or mobile?"

"No."

"Could someone have left a message on Elizabeth's phone at some point during the night or the following morning, without your knowledge?"

"I suppose it isn't impossible. Who killed Liz?"

"Elizabeth's murder represents a single piece in a jigsaw puzzle comprising nine gruesome killings."

"You're not answering my question, Kenneth. You're avoiding it."

"Did Elizabeth have a landline phone?"

"No, just a cell phone. Why?"

"We have reason to believe that Elizabeth was in contact with someone in the city centre, the night of the murder, only hours before it happened."

"The killer? Liz was seen with someone in town on the Friday night? She was seen with the killer?"

"We have reason to believe what I just said but we can't discuss those reasons whatsoever. Sorry."

"'We'? Who're 'we'?"

"I meant *I* can't discuss it."

"No phone was found on Liz's body, right?"

"Correct."

"I want to tell you something, Kenneth."

"I'm listening."

"Liz always had her mobile, wherever she went and whatever she did. And it was always turned on, even when she was in places where switched-on mobiles were forbidden, for example, in university lecture theatres or at the cinema. If Liz was found murdered without her mobile on her body or in her handbag then there's something more than just the murder itself that's terribly wrong."

"Thank you very much for the information, Rachel." He finished his sparkling water.

"Do you know what I think, Kenneth?" A mist moderated her sea-green eyes.

"Yes, Rachel, I know what you think. You think the killer made Elizabeth's phone disappear."

"That's right. What do *you* think?"

"Thank you very much for the chat, Rachel." He checked his watch. "Now it's time for me to go."

The girl's facial expression revealed that she didn't like that he kept avoiding her questions. "Time for me to go too, Mr. Busy."

They took a lift together down to the ground floor. Outside the complex, in the drizzle, he turned towards the girl. "Take care of yourself, Rachel."

She returned a strained smile and walked away. Rachel Fenwick became a silhouette in the dusk in Crowhill Square. Then she was gone.

He turned around.

The wind made him shiver.

The new night came draped in an eerie blackness, darker than a black hole in space.

65

Kenneth pulled her to him and kissed her. Jeanne's lips were as sweet as strawberries. "Somehow you're part of the equation, the puzzle, I'm about to solve. Both you and I are part of the equation."

She rolled her eyes. "Sometimes I actually think you're not quite sane."

"Let's have breakfast or the coffee will get cold."

Jeanne had prepared a full breakfast (she was as good as Mum) and carried it into his workroom on a tray—bacon, eggs, hash browns, sausage, HP sauce, ketchup, beans in homemade tomato sauce, toast, coffee and apple juice.

"How many days off do you have, Jeanne?"

"Five. My first holiday since last summer." She was still in her blush-and-white dressing gown.

"Any travel plans?"

"No. The guy I've fallen in love with is still in town. He's a workaholic who's currently working unofficially on solving the weirdest serial killer case in the history of Blackfield."

"It sounds alarming."

"Yes, indeed."

"I have a job for you."

"Didn't I just say I was on holiday?"

"A job as my assistant."

She laughed. "How much will you pay me? Mr. Frank thinks I'm a tough negotiator."

"There's no pay but I'd like to take you on a trip abroad when this case is over. You decide the destination."

She placed a hand on his thigh. "To the Swedish west coast?"

"If that's what you want, gorgeous."

"Yes, that's what I want. I love the Swedish west coast. In the summer. That is, when the weather is nice. I've been there twice already."

"Mr. Frank sent you there on jobs?"

"No. They were holidays."

"Mr. Frank sent you there for holidays?"

"Silly you."

They laughed.

"Through my job I've been sent to the Swedish capital once," she said, smiling. "A lovely city. What do you want me to do today?"

"We'll do some research."

"We?"

"You on your own and me on my own. I have an extra laptop with wireless Internet somewhere. I'll start it up for you to use. And *I'm* going to use this old companion." He pointed to a stationary machine.

"What are we going to research? Me on my own and you on your own, whatever that means."

"Everything and anything Leighton Fenwick."

She looked at him. "Although he has an alibi? Why do you think Fenwick is interesting?"

"He combines several fields in his research and several sub-disciplines of various fields, including clinical psychology, social psychology, psychiatry, physical chemistry and neurophysiology."

"And he can beat any lie detector, right?"

"His daughter says his control is impressive."

"In other words, her father rules the house with an iron fist."

"Interesting conclusion but too sensitive to be published in the local press."

"Fenwick's range of interests... Do the different fields complement each other somehow?"

"Certainly. Clinical psychologists often work with psychiatrists and other health professionals at psychiatric hospitals or clinics. However, there's a significant difference between the way they handle patients. Where a psychiatrist uses their knowledge of physiology, a clinical psychologist applies their knowledge of the human psychology to tackle the problem. And physical chemistry lies at the heart of the behaviour of those molecular assemblies that have critical functions in all living organisms."

Jeanne rose and unbuttoned her dressing gown. "I want to have a shower and get dressed. Could you give me half an hour?"

"Since when would half an hour be enough?"

She glared. "You're not even half as funny as you think you are. Now, are there any clean bath towels in the house?"

"There should be towels in the cupboard under the washbasin in the bathroom, right where Mum decided the towels should be kept."

She rolled her eyes. "I look forward to meeting your mum, Kenneth."

▪

The moisture in Jeanne's hair after the shower gave a darker nuance to her marble-blonde curls. She wore a floral blouse, blue jeans and slippers. "Have you had time to find out something new and exciting about Fenwick?" She sat down in front of the laptop. The glow from the computer screen gleamed in her eyes. She wore a soft perfume which turned him on.

He reached out a hand and stroked her neck. "On several reliable and independent websites, I just read that Leighton Fenwick has not only one Ph.D. but two. The first in clinical psychology, the second in mathematics. The title of his first thesis was, 'The Brain's Decision-Making: A Computational Study of Striatal Microcircuit Dynamics'."

"If you think I'm curious to know what that means in plain English, you're dead wrong."

"Then he did a post-doc in his primary area of psychology at an institute in Paris, led by a certain Professor Laurent Decantonneaux. This new project meant three years of full-time work. At the same time, he was working on his second Ph.D. His B.Sc. in mathematics from the University of Blackfield qualified him for postgraduate maths studies in the French capital. He also had superb references."

"What was the title of his second thesis?"

"I don't know. That information wasn't on the websites I visited and I didn't make an extra effort to find it. I thought it could be your task, Jeanne. Try also to find info about

Fenwick's collaboration with this Professor Decantonneaux."

"How do we know what's important?"

"What's important, we decide later."

"Was this Professor Decantonneaux involved in Fenwick's mathematical project?"

"No. The collaboration between Fenwick and Decantonneaux is regarded separately."

"Game on, then." She touched the keyboard.

▪

Jeanne used more than thirty different web search engines, general as well as profession-oriented engines, and she kept varying the search criteria. By lunchtime, she hadn't found anything that related to Fenwick's mathematical work. By the time of the afternoon coffee break, she had found one single mention but it was too general and lacked details. Apart from this meager result, she encountered only one web page that linked Fenwick's research to Laurent Decantonneaux, a link that provided nothing more than the French professor's official contact information.

Jeanne sipped her afternoon coffee. She didn't look disheartened. On the contrary, the adversity made her seem even more resolute. She looked at him. "What do you think it means that it's so difficult, if not impossible, to find something on the young Fenwick's second Ph.D.? Even though the project is more than twenty years old,

I would have thought that something would be picked up by the search engines."

"I could guess. Fenwick's mathematical work is too obscure to figure online. Or the web-based information we're looking for isn't available to the public without special login permits and licences. Regarding scientific and technical journals on the Internet, it isn't unusual for potential users to need to enter into subscription agreements to establish access to records. Or..." His words died in the roar of new thoughts.

Jeanne waved at him. "Hello?"

"... Or if Fenwick is the killer," Kenneth continued, "and if the Parisian project of his youth had a focus that risked attracting the interest of today's homicide investigators one way or another, then he would do his utmost to complicate any research such as we're trying to do right now. City Library has a dozen books by or about Leighton Fenwick. I was recently there, checking. Guess what I found."

"Each book was about some aspect of Fenwick's interdisciplinary research? But not a word about the mathematics project from his time in Paris?"

"Spot on. Though this reasoning is irrelevant if I don't manage to crack Fenwick's alibi wide open."

"How would you be able to unravel a foolproof alibi? No one can be in two places at once."

He didn't answer her. "Keep searching, Jeanne. Try new combinations of search criteria."

"If Leighton Fenwick is determined to keep the details of his mathematical work secret, would this Laurent Decantonneaux have to be in agreement?"

"It's possible but far from certain. Although the two men collaborated on the psychology project, Fenwick could have covered up the second project he was conducting at the same."

He left Jeanne alone with the notebook again and turned back to the stationary computer. Since he knew that administrative post-conference work was still being done in Bristol, he kept visiting the official ISACPP website. The original version of the ISACPP-xvi website, with the reference code 1.0.0, had remained unchanged since last Friday. Not a single update. Until now.

The reference code no longer read 1.0.0, but 1.0.1. When he noted the meaning of the update, he couldn't believe his eyes. "And here it comes." His voice sounded as if it was floating up from the bottom of a deep well.

"What is it?" Jeanne rose. "What has come?"

"The breakthrough." He stared at the computer screen. He was only just aware of Jeanne's hand on his shoulder.

Fenwick had indeed participated in the Bristol meeting from Monday the ninth through Friday the thirteenth of February. He had indeed presented two posters for continuous display throughout the conference week. On Friday evening at eight o'clock he had indeed given a talk about one of his fascinating research projects. The man had indeed been the Friday night superstar during the appreciated Q&A session which had taken place immediately after his high-profile lecture. He had aced his presentation and hadn't let the Q&A take him down.

Only, Leighton Fenwick hadn't been there on the Friday evening. How on earth was that possible? Kenneth thought. The updated information, in all its simplicity, showed him it was possible.

The 16th International Symposium
on
Applied Clinical Psychology and Psychiatry
Bristol, UK, February 9–13

Keynote Speakers:

Almada, S. G. (Detroit, USA)
[Day 2; 20:00]
Andersson, D. (Uppsala, Sweden)
[Day 4; 09:00]
Fenwick, L. W. (Blackfield, UK)
[Day 5; 20:00]
Heidelmann, P. (Mainz, Germany)
[Day 1; 09:00]
Lefèbvre, B. (Longueuil, Canada)
[Day 3; 20:00]

Montelizzino, A. (Turin, Italy)
[Day 2; 09:00]
Ping, X. Z. (Guangzhou, China)
[Day 4; 20:00]
Seneredar, A. Y. (Alexandria, Egypt)
[Day 5; 09:00]
Tsukamito, T. (Sapporo, Japan)
[Day 1; 20:00]
Xabatorono, O. (Jakarta, Indonesia)
[Day 3; 09:00]

1a: S. G. Almada and L. W. Fenwick communicated their respective talks via HD telepresence & video.

"Oops," Jeanne said. "Video conferencing. He *has* been present at two locations at once. Actively and creatively present. That S. G. Almada, too."

"And not just any type of video conferencing," Kenneth said. "Telepresence is the most advanced form of video telephony today."

"Through my work in Mr. Frank's organisation, I've learnt a lot, though not yet everything." Jeanne pressed her soft torso against him. Her pretty lips touched his neck. "Could you explain?"

He looked at her reflection in the PC screen, her attractive smile flashing. "In short, HD telepresence refers to a set of sophisticated technologies that allows users to feel as if they are present, to give the impression of being present, or to produce an effect, via telerobotics, at a location other than their real location. Every participant is shown in their actual dimensions and in high-definition video. The crystal-clear sound is also in HD format. People talk to each other and read one another's body language with the same authentic experience as if everybody were present in the same room."

"Is it that realistic?"

"So realistic that doctors of medicine routinely use telepresence to show the complexity and fine detail of their work to colleagues anywhere on the planet. So realistic that some auction houses apply telepresence to display multi-million-dollar artwork for potential bidders around the world."

He grabbed the computer mouse and clicked his way around the ISACPP-xvi website, away from the keynote speakers and over to the short talks. Among the five hundred and sixty fifteen-minute presentations, fourteen had been communicated using some form of video-conferencing technology.

He navigated to the section that covered the poster presentations. Here he found abstracts and computer graphics of the four hundred and forty-one posters, including Fenwick's two. Every single poster had been on continuous display throughout the conference week, just as Fenwick had said. But no compulsory attendance, Kenneth now saw. At large and extensive conferences with hundreds or thousands of delegates, it wasn't uncommon that the poster discussions took place under less formal circumstances than the Q&As associated with the talks. Fenwick's checkout from the hotel at seven fifty a.m. on the Friday wasn't possible to trivialise any longer. The man could have returned to Blackfield early on the Friday evening, murdered Elizabeth Peckerton after seven p.m., dumped her body in Paradise Park and gone home to his workroom to give his phenomenal plenary lecture at eight p.m. via video telephony, with a murder on his conscience. An incredible feat.

"Kenneth?"

He looked up, confused. "Uh?" While he had been engrossed in the updated website, Jeanne had returned to her chair in front of the HP notebook.

"I've found something."

He turned towards her. "I'm listening."

"There's a short passage here—a statement, only three paragraphs long—by a certain Mrs. Triquet, Professor of Archeology at the University of Maine in Le Mans, France. This small article, in which Fenwick is mentioned, was written more than ten years ago in connection with an international Egyptology congress. The text is a translation from the French original. I quote this woman, Professor Triquet: 'When a young Leighton Fenwick arrived in Paris to pursue post-doctoral research in clinical psychology and social psychology, he also started studying for his second doctorate, this time in mathematics. The title of the second thesis was, *Is God a Mathematician? – Mystery and Applications of Prime Numbers in Modern Society.*

'Fenwick is more than just a brilliant scientist. He's an intricate phenomenon, as if the man were possessed by nature's mysteries. He's an extremely dedicated person who wants answers to everything. It turned out that Fenwick was fanatically driven by his mathematics project and wanted—or even needed—to find solutions to Landau's problems.

'Rumour had it that Fenwick was an extraordinary man, albeit possessed by the peculiarities of prime numbers. During his years in Paris, the man became acquainted with Klemens Osbeck, the famous Swedish-American Professor of Egyptology and one of my closest colleagues.' End of quote." Jeanne smiled. "Fanatically driven? Obsessed by the peculiarities of prime numbers? What do you think?"

He kissed her. "You're wonderful."

She glanced at the laptop screen. "Kenneth?"

"Yes?"

"What are Landau's problems?"

"In the 1912 Fifth Congress of Mathematicians in Cambridge, the German mathematician Edmund Landau presented four basic problems surrounding prime numbers.

They are: Goldbach's conjecture—every even integer larger than 2 can be expressed as the sum of two primes; Twin prime conjecture—there's an infinite number of primes p such that $p+2$ is prime; Legendre's conjecture—there's always at least one prime between two consecutive perfect squares; and the fourth conjecture—there's an infinite number of primes p such that $p-1$ is a perfect square."

"Aha. I should have realised that right away."

"And Landau's problems are still unsolved," Kenneth said. "None of the four conjectures have yet formally been proven or disproven."

Jeanne smiled. "But Fenwick is a very dedicated person who wants answers to everything."

"Seems too fantastic even for an obsession."

Jeanne looked thoughtful. "A psychologist with a burning interest in mathematics? How do you think that sounds?"

"Nothing strange. On the contrary, it's common for successful scientists to have many interests and multi-disciplinary backgrounds. The superstars of science are often also interested in subjects outside of science or technology, for example, music, art, philosophy or literature. They pick up inspiration from every conceivable direction and from all sorts of people."

She looked deep into his eyes. "Fenwick's alibi for the Friday is a bogus alibi and his fascination with prime numbers matches your prime-number theory. You were right. A lot of people sneered at your theories but you were right all along."

"Don't underestimate your own effort, Jeanne. Perhaps it was meant to be you who found that passage in cyberspace. If that's true, I was also right about you being part of the equation, or the puzzle." He thought that what he said was close enough to the truth. At the same time, he sensed that Jeanne's influence on his life was even more integrated. "Listen, this breakthrough should be enough to get a search warrant for the Fenwick residence. Also, it's time to engage a prosecutor, hopefully Dee Barmby."

"I haven't heard of her. Who is she?"

"Uncle Ash's favourite prosecutor. Mrs. Barmby has never lost a case."

"What about me? You said I was part of your so-called equation or puzzle."

"Didn't I explain just now?"

She sighed. "Yeah, but I can feel that you think I also have another meaning, like a symbolic value of something. There are a lot of symbols in equations, aren't there?"

"You have a cat's intuition, Jeanne. You and Linda will have plenty to discuss."

"You know what I find a bit freaky?"

"What's that?"

"That Fenwick is profoundly fascinated by prime numbers, and so are you."

66

The text message: NEED 2 C U ASAP. – LIZ.

The final SMS from her cell phone had been sent at six twenty-two p.m. on Wednesday, February the eleventh.

"The recipient's number belongs to our dear friend Leighton Fenwick," Uncle Ash said.

"How did the phone turn up?" Kenneth asked.

"A golfer on his way to the club in Paradise Park found it," Mr. Frank said, "half a mile from the scene of the killing."

The warming sunlight penetrated Mr. Frank's office. The time of spring was arriving outside the windows. Spring came even to Blackfield, the city of darkness and the residence of demons.

"Now, how would you gentlemen explain that?" Kenneth asked. "The distance between the mobile and the murder scene."

"We don't need to explain it," Uncle Ash said.

"It was Elizabeth Peckerton's phone," Mr. Frank said; "that's the important thing."

"With an SMS to a certain Dr. Fenwick in the outbox," Uncle Ash said. "The last text message she would ever send."

"The text message is clear and straightforward, isn't it?" Mr. Frank said. "'Need to see you as soon as possible – Elizabeth.' It's pointing in the same direction as Kenneth's prime-number theory, with Fenwick as the common denominator."

"It's just that Miss Peckerton is the exception which doesn't fit any theory," Uncle Ash said.

"Unless she represents some kind of exception that proves the rule," Mr. Frank said, "and therefore fits into the picture. How would Ash summarise the latest development?"

"Elizabeth Peckerton, who knows that Fenwick is in Bristol the week in question," Uncle Ash said, "texts him on the Wednesday night and says she needs to see him as soon as possible. The phone number to Fenwick's work mobile is publicly accessible. Alarmed, he agrees to see the girl. For some reason, she suspects that he's the killer but she makes a promise there and then to forget about it—her idea that Dr. Fenwick is the murderer is probably silly anyway, she begins to think—and never ever bring up the subject again. Elizabeth is a good friend of the family and also has a secret sexual relationship with the man's daughter. Elizabeth doesn't want to jeopardise that. However, Fenwick takes no chances and decides to silence the girl for good.

"Mobile calls between them are registered at first. Since Fenwick is aware that his smartphone can be located via GPS coordinates, he avoids using it in Blackfield on the night of the murder. Things are urgent. He fixes the time and place of their meeting in the city centre. But there's no time to plan a murder and he's in the middle of a conference in Bristol. He therefore decides to gamble. If he chooses the Friday night, which is only two nights away, he can accomplish his missions in two cities apparently at the same time: give a high-profile lecture at the Bristol meeting and kill Elizabeth Peckerton in a park in Blackfield."

"He turned his predicament into an advantage," Kenneth said. "He used his complicated situation in his construction of an alibi."

"It's this meeting between Fenwick and Miss Peckerton in the city centre that is observed by Benjamin Smith," Uncle Ash said.

"Why didn't the conference office mention that some of the lectures were delivered via some form of video telephony?" Mr. Frank asked.

"It simply wasn't brought up," Uncle Ash said. "We didn't ask specifically about it and Bristol couldn't guess that such a detail might be important."

"Find Fenwick's telepresence equipment, Ash."

"Yes, sir."

"If Leighton Fenwick were innocent, he would have mentioned the technical details surrounding his oral presentation," Mr. Frank said.

"To omit facts is a sophisticated way of lying," Kenneth said, and nodded.

"Funny that *he* would say that," Mr. Frank said, looking at Kenneth. "To stretch the truth—isn't that what writers do for a living?"

67

"Begin with the workroom and don't mess around," Uncle Ash said.

The team of detectives, and one Kenneth Sorin, moved through the vast residence to a workroom that was as large as a seminar room. One entire wall was occupied by a single high-definition monitor. Spread over the remaining walls were a dozen HD displays of varying sizes, and built-in control panels. In a corner stood a holography machine. In another corner was a beverage machine that offered both chilled and hot drinks. In another part of the room bookcases stretched towards the ceiling. Rows of lamps threw automatically adapted lighting.

On a triangular laboratory desk were several computers, projectors, HD webcams, ultra-wide-angle point-and-shoot cameras, remote controls, a touchscreen interface and many other IT accessories. Opposite the desk was a graphite-grey sofa of modern minimalist design. Across the tiled floor coiled various types of cables and wires. The patterns in the tile floor appeared to have been inspired by Benoit Mandelbrot's fractal geometry of nature. The lab-like workroom reminded Kenneth of the control room of an alien spaceship from a science-fiction film he had seen as a teenager.

"All sorts of high-tech gadgets," Uncle Ash said.

"One complete integration of communication," Kenneth murmured. "Internet, IP telephony, visual communication, such as an HD telepresence set-up which is much more elaborate than Fenwick needs."

"What the heck is that?" Uncle Ash pointed a finger at the lasers and related optical instruments.

"A state-of-the-art holography device," Kenneth murmured. "So advanced that it almost belongs to the realm of science fiction."

"What the hell does he use it for?"

"To generate 3D virtual images of his therapy victims," Kenneth tried to joke. "In HD format."

Uncle Ash took a closer look at one of the PC machines. "It takes a username and a password to get in." He moved towards the spot where Fenwick had been standing for several minutes, seemingly in his own world. "Give me the username and the password for the computers, Doc."

A mischievous grin tugged at Fenwick's lips. "If I refuse, Inspector, will you shoot me? I do refuse."

Detectives searched the room. Stacks of papers accumulated across the floor as they rummaged through the immense desk. They dismantled the bookshelves, flipped through hundreds of volumes and checked the vertical cavities of the book spines. They found forty-three receipts used as bookmarks. Forty-three was a prime number, Kenneth noted. Was this just a coincidence? Specifically, 43 was a twin prime. Two prime numbers were twin primes if the difference between them was 2. The number 43 was part of the sixth twin prime pair (41; 43).

"Look here," Uncle Ash said. "Fenwick has one of your sick horror novels. Your debut book."

Kenneth looked. "Indeed. A copy of *Blue Moon Psycho*. That day in Endsleigh Park, I felt that Sadie Bentley's murder had been a carbon copy of the park murder in my debut book. Here's the inspiration for the eighth murder. But this copy has not been handled well. The title page is missing."

Detectives knocked on the walls, checked the window blinds, scrutinised the curtain poles and tracks, examined the overhead lighting and looked behind paintings and mirrors. No clue to the computer username or password anywhere.

"Sir, isn't Dr. Fenwick too smart to write down the username and password?" asked a detective. "Or even leave behind clues which point in the direction of sensitive data?"

"Since we don't know how this place is organised in detail, we must believe that some kind of clues exist," Uncle Ash said. "Maybe he updates the systems now and then with a new username and a new password. Therefore, we must keep looking."

"I can break into every computer anywhere," a technician said, frowning, "or almost anywhere, but these machines are impossible to hack into."

"Uncle Ash, if you were a killer, and you knew your computer contained incriminating evidence, where would you hide the information that revealed how to access the files?"

"I have no time for guessing games, Ken."

"If, for whatever reason, you were unwilling to destroy the information, you would hide it in one of the least likely places to hide something."

Uncle Ash shot him a hard look. "I'm not in the mood to decipher your mind, Ken."

"One of the four radiators in the room is turned off. Why, in the middle of winter?"

"It's warm enough with three radiators on."

"That's the point."

Uncle Ash grunted something and then turned towards two male detectives. "Disassemble the cold radiator."

The two detectives obeyed Uncle Ash's order. They found a note on a card inside the core of the radiator and a rolled-up printout of women's names.

"How many names?" Kenneth asked.

"No less than eighty-three ladies on the list," Uncle Ash said.

"Eighty-three, another prime number," Kenneth said.

"Am I supposed to get excited?" Uncle Ash said.

"83 is the ninth Sophie Germain prime."

"What's that?"

"A prime number *p* where also $2p+1$ is prime. $2\times83+1$ is 167, which is a prime number, so 83 is by definition a Sophie Germain prime. The prime type got its name from the French scientist Sophie Germain, who used these primes in her investigation of Fermat's Last Theorem."

"And you just happened to know that?"

"What can you say about the ladies' surnames?"

"The list begins with Gault, Karlsson, Keeley, McKenna, Quinney, Smyth, Suzuki, Weber, Wu, Bruce… and so on… all fit into—"

"—my prime-number theory," Kenneth finished. "I knew it."

"I knew you would say you knew it."

The note, no bigger than a postage stamp, was taped to the back of an expired discount card from Blackfield Public Transport:

l7w5fu49#k28eHdl&0he8¤k9g6C7
ap4Ri39gr¤pSn593?g9sbl&8me0sr

"We're back in the game," Uncle Ash said. "I'm going to test those sequences. The first one might be a temporary username and the second one might be a temporary password. Or vice versa."

"Give it a shot," Kenneth said.

With gloves on his hands, Uncle Ash went over to one of the PCs and keyed in the two sequences. "Bingo, ladies and gentlemen. We're in."

The PC's hard disk drives contained hundreds of folders and thousands of subfolders with scientific documentation: published articles, Fenwick's own research papers and those of others; Fenwick's yet unpublished papers in various stages of editing; unpublished articles by others to be reviewed by Fenwick; statistical data; reference lists; upcoming conferences; review articles; and electronic subscriptions to all sorts of scientific journals, etcetera.

"Fenwick's deceased wife," Uncle Ash said; "her name was Amelia." He clicked on the folder called Amelia. It contained hundreds of files, the latest accessed one being a calculation file. He clicked on it.

Amelia_InMemoryForever.tecxxz
[Technite3000]

Project Qz81H
Subject – Prognosis

7: Kelly Graham:
e4c5c3d5exd5Qxd5d4Nf6Nf

11: Lucy Knowles:
3Bg4Be2e6h3Bh5O-ONc6
13: Rebecka Månsson:
Be3cxd4cxd4Bb4a3Ba5Nc3
17: Gemma Quigley:
Qd6Nb5Qe7Ne5Bxe2Qxe2
19: Annabelle Stanfield:
O-ORac1Rac8Bg5Bb6Bxf
23: Suzanne Wheeler:
6gxf6Nc4Rfd8Nxb6axb6R
23: Gloria Wright:
fd1f5Qe3Qf6d5Rxd5Rxd5exd5b
2: Sadie Bentley:
3Kh8Qxb6Rg8Qc5d4Nd6f4Nxb
?

Page 1 – Sec 1 – 1/1

Kenneth nodded, satisfied with his prediction. "The first eight girls with the accompanying primes. And some kind of coding system." He paused. "I don't recognise this type of calculation file. I guess that this software is used exclusively by Fenwick's professional network. But I have cracked the coding system."

"What?" Uncle Ash looked at him with suspicion. "What did you just say you'd done?"

"The code language Prognosis. I can read it."

"Tell me you're joking."

"Not at all."

"How the hell can you read those sequences?"

"The flow of characters are chess notations."

"Chess notations?"

"Algebraic chess notations; although the proper spacing is missing. But then this isn't a normal game of chess. Moreover, the move numbers and periods are omitted and some notations have been split between consecutive lines. However, it's clear where the eccentric Fenwick took inspiration."

"You saw this straight away?"

"Yeah."

"Continue, Ken."

"Fenwick's code system, in this case, for this particular calculation file, is based on one of the most publicised chess games of all time: the first game in an epic six-game match played in February 1996 between the then reigning world champion Garry Kasparov and the IBM supercomputer Deep Blue. The hyped match took place in Philadelphia, Pennsylvania, USA. The supercomputer won this first game but the subsequent five games resulted in three wins for Kasparov and two draws. Every win is one point, a draw is half a point for both players, and a loss is zero points. Thus, Kasparov won the match 4–2."

"You don't mean you know the whole six-game match by heart, move for move?"

"I know countless chess games by heart, move for move. Famous games played between today's or yesterday's top players, including games between top computers and human top players. But to know the moves by heart isn't the most important thing. The essential thing is to understand the consequences associated with each move. It's the ability to reason that separates man from machine."

"Continue."

"The IBM supercomputer Deep Blue—the most powerful chess computer of its time—was playing as White in the first game. Kasparov, consequently, was Black. The opening, the first four moves, can be discerned in the sequence in Fenwick's data which is associated with Miss Graham, with the exception of the final two characters, Nf: e4c5c3d5exd5Qxd5d4Nf6.

"This means: White moves pawn to e4-square; Black moves pawn to c5; White moves pawn to c3; Black moves pawn to d5; White's pawn captures Black's pawn on d5; Black's queen captures White's pawn on d5; White moves pawn to d4; Black moves knight to f6. The final two characters in the Kelly Graham sequence, Nf, are part of a split notation. 'Nf' is related to the '3', the first character in the Lucy Knowles sequence. Hence, the complete notation is Nf3, which means White moves knight to f3, the supercomputer's fifth move.

"And so on, through all the sequences. The last three characters in the Sadie Bentley code, Nxb, are part of a split notation in the game's twenty-ninth move."

"How do you interpret all this, Ken?"

"Fenwick regarded the women as chess

pieces in psychological games of chess, a vision he combined with his fascination with advancing technology and man-against-machine situations. I'm convinced the PC data files contain more compelling information, such as a link between prognosis and diagnosis."

"It sounds as if you're talking about *your own* fascination with advancing technology." Uncle Ash fixed his eyes on the computer screen again. "There are several links to strange document files, created by some word processing software that's unknown to me."

"Miss Peckerton isn't here," Kenneth said.

"True. The letter P isn't associated with a prime, so the Peckerton girl isn't here. Or Fenwick hasn't yet had the time or even the motivation to update the file. After all, the ninth murder was carried out in a hurry."

"There's a question mark at the bottom."

"There would be more killings, which explains the question mark."

"The last time he downloaded the file he didn't know who would be the next victim. I wonder how long in advance he chose his subjects for Project Qz81H."

"Project Qz81H—whatever that means—has just been shut down, boy, and for good. When we're done here, I shall talk to Frank, ask him to have a word with Prosecutor Dee Barmby."

In accordance with Kenneth's suspicions, more data files were found with codes based on algebraic notations of several other well-known chess games, plus coded links between prognosis and diagnosis. What they found under a floorboard in Fenwick's living room was as thrilling as the Amelia PC files. A cardboard box of ladies' wigs. Genuine and all identical, wigs made of powder-white, curly human hair. Their style was a spot-on match to Amelia and Rachel's hairstyle in the dozens of photographs on the living room walls. The number of wigs turned out to be nineteen.

"How odd," Uncle Ash said. "Nineteen. Why would he order nineteen copies of a certain wig instead of rounding up to twenty in a first batch? After all, as the list in the radiator suggests, he had planned dozens of murders."

"Because nineteen is a prime," Kenneth said. "Twenty is a composite."

The wigs were numbered 2, 3, 5, 7, 11, 13, 17, 19, 23, 23, 29, 31, 37, 41, 43, 47, 53, 59 and 61.

"There are two twenty-threes," Uncle Ash said.

"Must be Misses Wheeler and Wright," Kenneth said.

Technicians checked the wigs using magnifying equipment.

"In some of the wigs there are foreign human hairs," Uncle Ash said later, "a few hairs which are different from the sugar-white in colour and length. Meringue-coloured inside number thirteen, black inside number two, hazel inside number nineteen. Some wigs have lipstick stains."

In Fenwick's bedroom there was a chest of drawers with used lingerie, chocolates and several chocolate boxes of different varieties. Knickers and bras filled with pralines. All the drawers had been locked but it was an easy job for the technicians to open them. "What a sicko!" a female detective cried.

"What a neat art collection," Uncle Ash said. "Perfect for the Museum of Modern Art. We nailed him, ladies and gentlemen. We nailed him."

68

Before it happened, no one had suspected it. The reason the psychologist could gain a head start through the southeastern district of Rockthorpe, Kenneth guessed later, was that his Alfa Romeo had been parked in the direction opposite to that of both the labelled and unlabelled CID cars. In addition, his car key had already been sitting in the ignition switch of the Alfa Romeo.

"It can't be true," Tina Tanner cried. "He's trying to get away." Tina and her colleague Muhammad Nausherwani got into a CID car and disappeared down the street after the Alfa Romeo in a cloud of dust.

"Damn!" Uncle Ash lit a cigarette and spat out a cloud of smoke through his Audi's side window. "And why are *you* sitting in my car?" He glared. "This is an emergency situation."

"You could pretend I'm a crime reporter who needs field research for a new documentary article," Kenneth said.

"You're shitting me?"

"I don't think so, Uncle."

Before Kenneth knew it, the chase had started. Although he hadn't planned to be there, and right now, he had already fastened the seat belt. There was no time to get out.

Uncle Ash stomped on the accelerator and the Audi swung around 180 degrees, coughed and hacked and groaned and leapt, then shot off down the hill. Tina and Muhammad's vehicle was already a vanishing dot in the distance.

▪

The Alfa Romeo flew down the hill, slammed into parked cars, smashed fences, mowed down bus shelters, ruined lawns and plowed through several flowerbeds. Screaming pedestrians tossed themselves out of the way. Cars, double-decker buses and trams honked and slammed on the brakes or swerved. Fenwick's car mashed another flowerbed and bounced and spun like a pinball machine ball between the street lighting poles on a steep slope.

Kenneth and his uncle saw nothing of this, of course. Although the initial downward slope had granted Uncle Ash's car extra acceleration, they had fallen behind. Muhammad Nausherwani in the CID car informed the two Sorins about the chase via the high-tech Airwave system.

Tina sat behind the wheel of the CID vehicle. Muhammad operated the communication equipment and weaponry.

Muhammad: "Fenwick has gone mad."

Tina: "High time to puncture the rear tyres."

Uncle Ash: "Hold on, guys. No shooting yet."

Muhammad: "Waiting for the go-ahead, sir."

Welcome to Blackfield, Kenneth had the time to think. *No total order without SCDX.*

Fenwick's car skidded and wriggled between a roadway and a pavement. People threw themselves out of the way, yelling. Dogs barked. Cats hissed. Vehicles honked. A truck slammed into a car that rammed a van that struck another car, and so on. The chain-reaction crash was inevitable. Tina was spinning the steering wheel like a lottery wheel, back and forth. The CID car zigzagged through the chaos and noise. Fenwick's car thrashed a hedge.

Muhammad: "Sir?"

Tina: "Ash?"

Uncle Ash: "Take him down, guys."

Muhammad lowered a power window, took aim at the Alfa Romeo's rear tyres with an unofficial SCDX automatic pistol and squeezed off four shots. The gun was a high-velocity firearm with the same destructive power as an assault rifle. Both rear tyres collapsed, chunks and crumbs of rubber spraying into the air. Fenwick's car jerked, swayed, rumbled and struck more lampposts and parked vehicles, but it didn't stop.

Tina: "Give me one!"

Kenneth knew Tina had addressed Muhammad. Her colleague gave her a weapon. Kenneth saw Tina pointing the handgun through the side window, saw how Tina transformed from a mere driver to a pistol-shooting driver—one hand operating the gun and the other on the steering wheel. The CID car swayed. The Alfa Romeo lurched. Tina pulled the trigger and kept blasting away. Bullets slammed into the Alfa Romeo's rear with a rattling noise and the right rear-view mirror shattered.

The chase continued across Rockthorpe Bridge, a grand bascule bridge across the River Claxton. The bridge was one of the main traffic links between the districts of Rockthorpe and Burnhall Valley.

Tina: "Bridge's opening!"

Kenneth's gaze swung between windscreen and side window. On the horizon, he saw the bascule bridge begin to rise. A cargo vessel was advancing through the rippling grey-black water.

Muhammad: "We'll make it."

Uncle Ash: "Quicker than piss through a fox?"

Tina: "We're trying, Ash!"

The road traffic warning systems were already on, flashing light and an audible alert. An automatic boom barrier moved downwards. The Alfa Romeo crashed through the crossing barrier, followed by the CID car and Uncle Ash's Audi. The vehicles flew through the air gap in the bridge. Muhammad took aim with a gun again and fired another four shots. The Alfa Romeo dived through the air. The bullets from the SCDX weapon hit high instead of low. The rear window exploded. The Alfa Romeo crash-landed on the tarmac on the opposite side of the river, slid, jerked and lurched. The CID vehicle and the Audi completed the airborne journey and crash-landed in the district of Burnhall Valley only seconds behind Fenwick's car. The Audi shook as if gripped by a car-crusher machine. Kenneth tried in vain to hold on to something. Despite the seatbelt, he hit his head on the ceiling and his knees on the dashboard.

The impact demolished the CID car's windshield. Tina let go of the steering wheel, squeezed her gun with both hands, aimed straight across the dashboard and fired shot, after shot, after shot. Metallic clatter stabbed the air. Shrieking bullets destroyed the boot and the rear bumper of Fenwick's car. Tina swore into the Airwave radio system.

This isn't happening, Kenneth thought.

The slowing and dying Alfa Romeo rammed a classic red cast-iron mailbox in Burnhall Avenue, spun around in a full circle, bounced across a traffic island and crashed through a shop window, spraying glass splinters at screaming customers.

Uncle Ash's Audi (or what was left of it) stopped with a spluttering noise behind two CID cars and an unmarked CID (SCDX?) vehicle in Burnhall Square. Kenneth and his uncle stepped out and joined Tina and Muhammad on the pavement. Fenwick crawled out of his wrecked and smouldering car. He no longer looked like Fenwick. Kenneth guessed that the man could pass for one of his own patients who was now showing the darker alter ego of their dissociative identity disorder. The streaks of blood and oil-black dust on his cheeks looked like an Indian's war paint. In the sunlight, the crisscross-cracked right lens of his glasses became a mouse-grey glass collage. His lips seemed like synthetic rubber, shaping a soundless 'O'—an expression of unspeakable anguish?

Blood dribbled from a cut on the man's forehead, down onto the ruined shirt. The silence of his O-shaped mouth then gave way to a cackle. "They were subjects! Subjects! Nothing but subjects! For the sake of humanity!"

"For the sake of humanity you're under arrest, fuckface," Tina said. She grabbed the doctor's jacket collar and pulled him to his feet.

Then she turned towards Uncle Ash. "You need a new car, Ashley. Your current one is a *dud*. Do you understand what I'm saying?" Tina

Tanner was a freckled brunette with lead-grey eyes. The dusk-dark birthmark that extended from one eyebrow to her cheekbone looked like a permanent black eye.

Uncle Ash puffed on a cigarette. "Are you trying to tell me, darling, that you will consider giving me a new car for my birthday?"

"In your sick dreams, Ashley." In spite of the hard words, Tina's voice was as soft and as sweet as a ripe mango.

Several years ago, Uncle Ash had saved Tina's life in connection with an undercover operation. In a crackdown on one of Blackfield's many drugs and guns gangs, something went wrong. Tina and the drug lord Emilio Cabrera fired their weapons at the same time. The bullet from Tina's pistol missed marginally. Cabrera's bullet pierced through Tina, a hair's breadth from the aorta. The drug baron had no time to pump off another shot. Uncle Ash made the difference between the mission's overall success and failure. A special relationship had developed between Uncle Ash and Tina since that dramatic night. Kenneth just didn't know how special.

69

Mrs. Barmby was a burly woman with a low centre of gravity—late fifties, iron-grey hair, a face which seemed hewn from oak, a nose the same shape as an avocado. Her gaze belonged to a predator who had got wind of a new quarry.

They were sitting in a cafeteria on Colvin Street. Kenneth, Uncle Ash and the star prosecutor.

"The forensic evidence is overwhelming," Uncle Ash said, "but witnesses are scarce here. Peculiar, isn't it? Sure, we have Benjamin Smith's story, but otherwise, there's nothing. Will the lack of decent witnesses be a problem for you, Dee?"

Mrs. Barmby laughed. "Too many cooks spoil the broth, Ash."

"What will happen next in our own bureaucratic stew?" Uncle Ash drank his caffè latte.

"Well, the prison psychiatrist who's preparing the forensic report needs a copy of my case file. Hence, the defendant—Leighton Fenwick, in other words—will be subjected to a psychiatric examination."

"The psych expert himself wouldn't be able to manipulate such an assessment, would he, Dee?"

Mrs. Barmby didn't answer. She sipped her iced tea. "Fenwick's data files. The data printout, hidden inside a radiator. The ladies' wigs. The lingerie. The forensic evidence, found in a number of those wigs and underwear. The small dots of Miss Peckerton's blood on one of Fenwick's overcoats. The omission of essential facts concerning the Bristol congress. The complete lack of alibis. And the mathematical patterns—a perversely baroque pleasure. But you wouldn't expect a mad professor to act with what a normal person referred to as common sense."

"It depends on how you define normality, Mrs. Barmby." Kenneth lifted his glass of lemonade. "Human nature is complex."

Mrs. Barmby laughed. "Are you trying to tell me, young Mr. Analyst, that Fenwick is sane?"

"I mean that the line between genius and insanity is unclear. You could be a fabulous organiser, a brilliant technician, a dazzling communicator, whilst being driven to acts of destruction and terror through your visions and beliefs."

"Tell me, young man, how could the young women join Dr. Fenwick's perverted sex games and experiments with chocolates, wigs and underwear?"

"Obedience to authority."

"Really? What if you elaborated on that, huh?"

"To understand the unconventional Leighton Fenwick and his influence on these women, we need to know the man's history. Fenwick has many interests, including a social-psychological interest. Social psychology is the scientific study of how people think, act and feel in the context of society. Three significant social psychologists stand out amongst Fenwick's books and collections of articles on the subject. Solomon Asch, Philip Zimbardo and Stanley Milgram. Asch was a specialist in the study of peer pressure, conformity and impression formation. Zimbardo studied how situational forces and group dynamics could interact to produce monsters of decent men and women. Asch's student Milgram was the creator of—among many experiments—the Milgram experiment on obedience to authority, a series of famous experiments conducted at Yale University in the USA in 1961–62, and he was the designer of the well-known theory of six degrees of separation. Stanley Milgram was one of the most innovative scientists of the twentieth century.

"Milgram's obedience experiments confirmed that good-hearted people would blindly obey orders to inflict pain on innocent individuals. The results showed that moral beliefs were significantly more flexible than previously thought. The controversial obedience experiments have been discussed in the most diverse areas, for example, political science, economics, medicine, law, education, philosophy, art, sociology and military.

"From how ordinary individuals can commit the most atrocious crimes if placed under the influence of a malevolent authority, Dr. Fenwick could have extracted the obedience concept and used it in a different context. Such a context, in Fenwick's own interest, and with Fenwick himself in the role of the authoritative character, could have been to see his subjects submit to an absurd kind of erotic slavery."

"But the girls' psychological self-defence?" Mrs. Barmby said.

"They were in love, Mrs. Barmby. No matter how intelligent they were, they were all in love with Dr. Fenwick. Love became their Achilles' heel." He paused. "Love, the most powerful of emotions, has a treacherous effect on common sense."

"That was what I told my ex-husband before I kicked him out," Mrs. Barmby said.

Kenneth took a swallow of lemonade. "There's more to say about this story, Mrs. Barmby."

"I bet a month's salary that you're about to tell me, young man. For the record, I have an obscenely high monthly salary." Mrs. Barmby laughed.

"These intelligent ladies were more than just manipulated mistresses," Kenneth said. "Fenwick also used them as subjects within the framework of a project that focused on groundbreaking therapy."

"Why? The girls were not mentally unstable."

"They didn't need to be, Mrs. Barmby. Fenwick was a part-time professor at Blackfield University, and a national as well as an international academic guest lecturer.

Thus he came into contact with women all the time in academic environments. Even if he was operating on his own, he might have given the impression of having a whole team of collaborators and a larger base of subjects than he actually had. Experimentalists in social psychology are experts in designing virtual conditions or virtual situations, in meticulous detail."

"Outrageous, young man," Mrs. Barmby said. This time she didn't laugh. "Truly *outrageous*."

"Fenwick's actions or my ideas?"

"Both."

"You look tired and worn out, Ken." Uncle Ash slurped his coffee like a camel. "Why don't you send yourself home now and get some rest. It's over."

"Not quite over," Kenneth said.

"It is for you. The authorities will handle the rest."

"*Thank* you, young man," Mrs. Barmby said, looking at Kenneth, waving him 'goodbye' or 'get lost'. "*Thank* you for *everything*."

70

Selection of newspaper headlines:

February the twenty-third:
Renowned psychologist turned serial killer

February the twenty-fourth:
Team Frank & Sorin sinks 'prime-number killer'

February the twenty-fifth:
'Prime-number theory' captures monster

February the twenty-sixth:
How famous scientist murdered female students

■

He had finished writing the novel. He had revised it, again and again, and sent a polished version of the manuscript to his publishers in London and New York. Since the repugnant case of the prime-number killer was behind him now, he began to concentrate on his next book. Thoughts of Jeanne, however, surfaced to his mind, beautiful thoughts which interfered with his concentration on the new writing project.

How long had he known her? Since December only? He felt as if he had known this wonderful girl for a hundred years. The bachelor Kenneth thought he was old enough to get married. He also believed Mum would agree. Mum wouldn't be able not to like such a pretty girl as Jeanne. He was convinced. He wanted to marry Jeanne Russell and he wanted to do it soon. And somewhere within him a voice whispered that she was sharing his desire.

■

Uncle Ash was as busy with work as usual. He was changing, too. He smoked less and less every day. The workaholic had even thought about going to the gym. Tina Tanner was persuading him.

▪

Retail king Philip Worthington wasn't sure what was worse: seeing his photo in the local papers for the wrong reason (after all, the law had found him innocent) or hearing sarcastic voices behind his back whenever he was outdoors. Nevertheless, one thing was certain. He had to leave this terrible city. To some people, especially in this neighbourhood, he was no better than the real killer.

With a B.Sc. in economics and an M.Sc. in computer science from Blackfield Business School on his CV, and rigorous professional experience, he would always find various ways to make a living. Also, he had experience from two service and manufacturing companies with roles in design, production management, information systems and project management. He didn't have to stay in the county, or even in the country. He was employable anywhere.

Did he suffer from paranoid delusions? No, he decided. Moreover, people were wrong about him. Suzanne Wheeler had been the only customer he had slept with. He had been in love with Suzanne and she had been in love with him, and there had been nothing wrong with that. Their love had been mutual.

It was a miracle he had somehow made that phone call to Klammer's clinic back in January. A miracle, with or without a cracked skull. What else could it be called? And because of the crime he had suffered prior to the miracle, the yellow-teethed Inspector Sorin had arrested Amy. Perhaps there was a God after all, somewhere. A God of Justice.

▪

It was proven that Amy Worthington had cracked her husband's head with a cast-iron pan. Hence she was facing an attempted murder charge. But that didn't mean Mrs. Worthington had *admitted* to anything. True, she had admitted that she'd struck her husband on his head but stressed that she had done so without the intention of killing him. She was also facing a charge of criminal obstruction through the false clue she had planted in Uncle Ash's mailbox at headquarters.

The Worthingtons' marriage was over for good, to no one's surprise. In a way, Mrs. Worthington ended up as both a winner and a loser. After all, she had reached half of her goals. Although she had failed to murder her husband and was now facing criminal charges (her super-rich lawyer had a good chance of seeing those charges waived, due to his client's mental condition), she was leaving her marriage a wealthier woman than when she had entered it.

Mr. Worthington had neither the time nor the patience for litigation. He sought no revenge. The man had begun to accept that his wife's actions were rooted in her mental disease. He seemed to pretend to forgive his future ex-wife. The only thing he expressed an interest in was the divorce.

▪

Leighton Fenwick didn't talk much. He had nothing revolutionary to say, he said, and added that both the evidence and his actions spoke for themselves. "Charles Darwin said that a scientific man ought to have no wishes, no affections—a mere heart of stone," Fenwick said, with dry eyes focused on nothing. Then, after an eerie pause, "I have nothing to add, ladies and gentlemen."

▪

Press conference. Filtered and angled, of course, by SCDX.

"Understanding Leighton Fenwick is a complex, challenging process," Mr. Frank said. "Imprisoned serial killers are studied by forensic psychiatrists and psychologists for years. I don't anticipate that Dr. Fenwick will deliver answers today. But some day…

providing Dr. Fenwick is aware of why he committed these heinous crimes."

The trial would be a formality. The authorities would be playing to the gallery. Dee Barmby would thrash her opposition and walk away with another solid win, another solid paycheck and refreshed laughter in her throat.

Kenneth felt that something was unfinished. A loose end disturbed his sleep at night. He knew he wanted to meet Professor Klemens Osbeck in Paris. Osbeck—Fenwick's Parisian friend—was himself an interesting subject. Not until the middle of March would Kenneth realise he wanted to see Professor Osbeck for a reason he had never dared fantasise about.

71

On Wednesday, March the eighteenth, a week before Fenwick's trial, Kenneth visited his uncle down at headquarters. He sat down at the coffee table in the corner. "How's it going, Uncle?"

Uncle Ash sat behind his desk, flipping through ring binders. "If you're wondering whether Fenwick has started to talk, the answer is still no."

Kenneth nodded. "What's this?" He pointed at a number of objects that lay scattered in front of him on the coffee table.

"Just some of Fenwick's personal items that

are important to him. He requested to have them sent to him in custody. Request granted. The stuff was picked up at his house, checked and approved."

Two issues of a scientific journal; a novel; three textbooks; a photo album; a pack of playing cards; a chess set.

"May I take a closer look at the items?"

"Be my guest."

"Has it ever happened that a detained person or an inmate has cut their wrists with a playing card?"

"You want me to remove the ace of spades?"

Kenneth shook his head. "No. A pack of fifty-one cards is useless, or strongly limits the number of games you can play."

"For better or worse." Uncle Ash paused. "There are a couple of jokers in the pack too. Jokers are tricky bastards, aren't they, Ken?"

Kenneth didn't answer. He lifted the bible-thick photo album and began leafing through it, more or less at random. "Family pics," he murmured. "Nice wedding photos… honeymoon… barbecue party… Christmas celebration… sun and beach holidays… A young couple in these photographs, Leighton and his wife Amelia. And—this is fascinating—you have to read the captions to—"

"I know," Uncle Ash interrupted. "To be able to distinguish between the wife then and the daughter now. Amelia at twenty-one and

Rachel at twenty-one, so much alike."

Kenneth looked at the dates. "The pics I'm looking at right now are from a time before Rachel was born."

"There's a tragic chapter in the family's history."

"How did Mrs. Fenwick die?"

"She died in childbirth, when Rachel was born."

"How horrible." Kenneth turned the pages and arrived at the photo album's next section. "Now we are at pictures of the newborn… a pretty baby."

"Indeed."

The caption to the first Rachel photo said:

'1A: My beautiful daughter Rachel Amelia, born at midnight, March the sixth. She has her mother's sea-green eyes and you can already see she has inherited her mother's sharp mind. Rachel cried a lot during her first day on earth. From her second day, her screams and weeping became sparse. My clever baby realised that nothing was solved by screaming.'

He stared at the caption, wishing he had read it wrong. But he hadn't read it wrong. The words were the same, remained organised in the same order, continued to form the same sentences. No escape routes existed. No excuses. No way to dodge the truth. The caption left him suspended in a vacuum.

"Are you all right, Ken? Do you feel sick?"

Kenneth raised his gaze from the photo

album. "'Logic will get you from A to B. Imagination will take you everywhere.'"

His uncle frowned. "Huh?"

"Albert Einstein said that."

When a physicist talked like that, the words bore an additional effect. We expected scientists to be all for logic but here was a famous one cheering on limitless imagination. Fantasy was more flexible, and therefore more useful, than logic.

Kenneth experienced an acute shortage of time.

'From A to B' wasn't the right way to think.

He found that he had left the coffee table.

'From A straight to X' was the correct way. X, the common symbol of the unknown everywhere.

He was no longer in Uncle Ash's office. He had a vague idea that his uncle was calling him from somewhere but there was no time to reflect on it. Kenneth was already halfway down the corridor in the direction of the stairs.

72

He called Jeanne, telling her he had to give their dinner a miss, a dinner for two which would have started in less than two hours at her place. The strength of her yelling forced him to keep the phone at a distance of six inches from his ear. "I'll make it up to you in due course, sweetheart. I promise."

Promises were so easy to make, weren't they? He hung up. There was no time to explain the new situation. He had already scheduled explanations and apologies for later.

▪

He found Professor Osbeck's contact information on the website of the Paris-based research institute. Kenneth emailed:

KSorin99 to KOsbeck.Prof1Z
16:23 (UTC + 0); March 18

Dear Professor Osbeck,

My name is Kenneth Sorin and I'm an investigative writer based in the UK. I presume you have learnt from news reports that one of your old colleagues and friends, Dr. Fenwick, is charged with the murder of a number of female students in northern England. A few details about these awful crimes keep me awake at night. I would appreciate meeting with you in Paris to discuss these issues as soon as possible. I'm sure you realise the urgency of the matter. I look forward to hearing from you. By the way, the police inspector who was in charge of the investigation is my uncle. Thus, I have a solid relationship with local authorities here and I know how to preserve confidentiality.

Sincerely,

Kenneth Sorin
Investigative writer

Blackfield, UK

His thoughts wandered to the switchboard of the Parisian institute. He lifted the telephone and rang. No answer. Too late to call the switchboard at this hour, he decided. Then he dialled the direct number to Osbeck's office. No answer there either. Did he want to call the professor at home? Did he want to find out the man's home phone number? Kenneth rejected the idea. He guessed that his already slim chance of meeting with the professor would decrease further if he came across as intrusive.

He went downstairs to the kitchen and had an evening meal with Linda. Did the kitchen's wall clock need a new battery? The time crawled forward with the speed of a turtle.

He checked and re-checked the inbox of his email account. Nothing. He sent a new email, this time to the Paris university's personnel department. He called Uncle Ash and said he would explain everything later. Right now, the subject was too hot to be discussed, maybe even too hot to be handled in complete silence. He was only going to check a few things out, he said—without a word about his French plans—and hung up.

Then he went to bed. Before he turned off the bedside lamp, he read up on Klemens Osbeck:

Born in Västerås, Sweden. Fatherless at the age of three months. He grew up in Atlanta, Georgia, USA, where his Swedish mother moved after being offered a better position with her employer. The mother had been a prominent surface and colloid chemist at the multinational Georgia-Pacific, one of the world's largest paper manufacturers.

Klemens Osbeck obtained a Ph.D. in archeology from a Georgia university, then moved from one research group to the next in a handful of states: Wyoming, Minnesota, Idaho, Vermont and Pennsylvania. He had a reputation for being difficult. Even though he was well known for his phenomenal ability to locate archaeological remains, he was criticised for his frequent use of unscientific methods. Although Osbeck was successful, the scientific establishment kept questioning the way in which he reached his successes. At one point, in Vermont, he was asked to leave his research team. Osbeck was accused of mixing established science with witchcraft, voodoo, numerology and other pseudosciences.

Through his contacts, Osbeck found a research environment that was liberal enough to tolerate his peculiar style. After five great years in Pittsburgh, Osbeck left for Europe and Paris, where he had lived and worked for over two decades.

▪

Christine Corbett had meant what she'd said when she spoke to him through Benjamin Smith's body. Since then, Kenneth was on his own. He knew why. He didn't need Christine any longer. The phantom had opened the back door of his mind, stepped out and shut the door behind her.

Had she locked that door in his head?

Locked it with a key from the outside?

He wondered if the old and not too dead lady was still sneaking around somewhere outside his body. He listened for her lifeless footsteps but heard nothing. Christine, the phantom, was gone, like his headaches. His eyelids became heavier. He floated downwards and away.

He slept. The night was devoid of dreams.

73

He woke up when the light of dawn spilled through a gap between the curtains and stroked his face. His thoughts floated away to the City of Light and the diverse blend of French memories. Linda miaowed somewhere in the house. High time for breakfast. Twenty-two minutes later, he phoned the Parisian university's human resources department.

He listened to the repeating ringtone—and kept listening. The line buzzed and crackled. A message machine kicked in and trumpeted a dozen dialing options. Then music started to play in the handset, classical music from the early 1700s. The composer was Élisabeth Jacquet de La Guerre, one of the few well-known female composers of her time. Kenneth looked at his watch. The music played on. Nothing else happened and he hung up, waited, and called the same number again. The line crackled a few times before it died. Was March the nineteenth a French public holiday? He checked his European calendar. No, it seemed to be a normal Thursday in France.

He dialed a third time. The line was no longer dead. At least the grating ringtones were back on. He checked his watch. Eleven minutes past eight. Eleven minutes past nine in Paris. It was too early for lunch in the French capital but not too early, or too late, for a coffee break. He counted the ringtones. Midway through the seventeenth tone, somebody on the other end bothered to answer.

"*J'écoute !*" A young woman's voice.

"*Bonjour, mademoiselle.*" Kenneth spoke fluent French. He introduced himself and continued, "Did you by any chance receive my email of last night?"

"No email, mister. The technician responsible for email is not here. On holiday. Back on Monday next…" Her voice faded. Whispers and laughter. An eternity later, she returned to the phone. "Hello? Still there, mister?"

"Still here," he said through clenched teeth.

"Sorry, mister. We seem to have received no email but…"

"Doesn't matter at all. I would like to know how I can contact a Professor Klemens Osbeck, Research Director at the Institute of Egyptology."

He could hear the clicking of a cigarette lighter at the other end of the wire, a sound he had learnt to identify through countless phone conversations with Uncle Ash. In the background, murmurs and loud discussions mixed with chants and laughter. Some sport event—probably a football or a rugby game—was on TV. The atmosphere of this academic HR department recalled the buzz of a sports bar. The lady who had answered his call yawned into the phone. Kenneth hid his irritation. The last thing he wanted was to antagonise the receptionist. This was arguably the most important phone call he had ever made. He needed her cooperation.

"Professor Osbeck doesn't work here anymore, mister," she said. "Professor retired last October."

"The department's website said no such thing."

"What a shame, mister."

"Is it possible to contact Professor Osbeck on professional terms at all? It's very important."

"Hmm… to disturb the professor?"

"I would be very grateful. Now, this matter is about one of the professor's old acquaintances, a Dr. Leighton Fenwick. That should be enough to attract the professor's interest."

"Sorry?"

"Fenwick."

"*Comment ça s'écrit, monsieur ?*"

"The spelling is F-e-n-w-i-c-k." He heard how her pen was leaping across a sheet of paper.

"*Bien*. Okay. Finished."

His life experience had taught him that there's often a difference between what people say they're going to do and what they actually do. "May I have Professor Osbeck's mobile number, please?"

"Absolutely not."

"Why not?"

"Simple. The professor has no mobile phone."

"What bad luck."

"Not bad luck. The professor plans and controls his lifestyle. Bad luck is something quite different. Bad luck is something you cannot control. Chance determines bad luck, mister."

"Thank you for the enlightenment."

Someone scored in the football game and from the celebrations which rumbled through the phone, he knew it was the right team that had scored. The singing and the exclamations exploded into his ear, reminding him of the buzz of the Champs-Élysées on a July the fourteenth. More Parisian memories came back to him, such as the noise from the loud parties at his neighbours' flat in the multi-storey building in Boulevard des Gobelins in the thirteenth arrondissement; the magnificent view of the Eiffel Tower he had had from his balcony on the fourth floor; and the pretty red-haired girl (whose name he never knew) who had worked as a counter service assistant at a local boulangerie.

"What was your name again, mister?" the lady on the other end of the line asked.

"The name is still Kenneth Sorin." He noted an edge in his voice and regretted it at once.

"If you give me your contact information, I will contact the professor. All right, mister? Of course I guarantee nothing. Professor Osbeck might not be at home. You see, the professor likes fishing."

"I'm confident it'll be all right, mademoiselle. Please contact Professor Osbeck on my behalf."

"*D'accord*. Okay."

He provided his contact information.

"Thank you very much, mademoiselle. I look forward to hearing from you again, soon."

"But I guarantee nothing."

"Right. That's what you just said, wasn't it?"

Someone scored in the game on TV. And, again, it was the right team which had scored. Chanting and exclamations followed. The receptionist hung up.

▪

A new email in the inbox:

> KOsbeck.Prof1Z to KSorin99
>
> 10:57 (UTC + 1); March 19
>
> Mr. Sorin (or Dr. Sorin; a few years ago, I came across one of your papers in the field of condensed matter physics),
>
> Leighton Fenwick was a scientist for both the present and the future. What we have witnessed is a tragedy. A sad mystery. I have much to do even as a retired old man; I'm busy into the foreseeable future, so I have no time to meet with you and I don't see how I could be of any help in your so-called investigation. And on top of that, you say nothing specific about what you

want to talk to me about. But I'm not an unreasonable man. I'll give you a chance to express your points, provided that you're not wasting my time.

The matter is urgent, you say. How soon can you be in Paris? I'm going on a fishing holiday for one week, from tomorrow night. If you can get here tomorrow morning or early afternoon, I'll be able to welcome you. Could you please confirm whether you'll have the opportunity to meet me tomorrow, Friday, at the bar of La Coupole, Boulevard du Montparnasse?

Yours sincerely

Klemens Osbeck, Professor Emeritus
Egyptology/Archeology
Ancient Number Theory/Numerology
Rue du Cherche-Midi, Paris, 14th district.

"Tomorrow?" He stared at Osbeck's email. To get an opportunity to meet with the professor as soon as tomorrow sounded too good to be true.

He knew La Coupole very well. One of the most famous restaurants in Paris and the world. One of Kenneth's own favourite restaurants in the French capital. He had eaten there many times. Grandiose interior, superb meals, excellent service.

He turned towards Linda. She was resting on top of the laser printer. “Linda, I will travel to Paris. And you know what? I travel tomorrow morning!” He patted her. “This is important business but I won’t be gone for longer than a day. I’ll ask some neighbours to keep an eye on you. Mr. and Mrs. Anguiano, okay? The Spaniards have looked after you before and you do like them, don’t you? If you behave yourself, you’ll probably have some of Mrs. Anguiano’s yummy paella again.”

Linda miaowed. Then she jumped down from the laser printer and scurried out of the workroom.

Travel tickets.

Tickets, tickets, tickets.

Flight or rail?

Rail, he decided.

The high-speed Eurostar through the Channel Tunnel was convenient, reliable and time-efficient. The Eurostar took you directly from city centre to city centre, London-Paris. In the fast web browser, he navigated to the Eurostar site and found that if he took the five twenty-seven a.m. train to London St. Pancras, he would have time to board a Eurostar service and arrive at Gare du Nord International in Paris at eleven forty-seven local time.

He had another email exchange with Professor Osbeck to arrange the details. They decided to meet at the bar of La Coupole the following day at one p.m. There would be plenty of time to get to the district of Montparnasse. Or so he thought.

74

The five twenty-seven train from Blackfield Central Station to London St. Pancras on Friday morning, an Intercity service, was cancelled because of some technical problem. The next departure for London would take place at five twenty-nine, on a route that included two changes, with an estimated arrival time in the capital of eight twenty-nine. He had no time to wait for the next Intercity service. He boarded the five twenty-nine train.

He wondered if he would still manage to catch the eight thirty-two Eurostar connection in London. Seemed tight indeed. At seven fifty-five a.m. UK time, he decided to contact the mobile-phone-less professor. Easier said than done. He called the same personnel department as the day before but received an engaged tone. He waited for five minutes then dialled again. Still a busy signal. He waited another five minutes and tried again. Someone responded. The phone connection was fine but there were screaming and crying babies on the train. How did you quiet a screaming baby?

"No problem, mister." An unmistakable

voice, the same lady as yesterday. "I'll call the professor at home and inform him of the new situation and then I'll call you back."

"Thank you, mademoiselle."

"But I guarantee nothing, mister."

"Sounds familiar."

He considered contacting the Paris restaurant and asking the staff to forward a message to Professor Osbeck. He should have done it earlier, he thought. Right now, there was no time. The train rolled into London St. Pancras. Six minutes late. What he had suspected would happen had happened.

▪

Another Eurostar service, the one minute past nine, departed while he was queuing for a new ticket. Tickets for the next train were sold out. He had saved the phone number of the restaurant La Coupole in the smartphone's memory. He telephoned. An engaged tone shot back into his ear. He navigated to the restaurant's website and found the link to the email contact. He sent a concise message.

He could no longer deny the feeling of time pressure. But then, something happened. A pinch of renewed hope. There was a cancellation of a ticket in connection with a sold-out ten twenty-four departure.

He paid, grabbed the ticket, passed through the passport control and the security control, boarded the Eurostar train, crossed the English Channel and arrived at Paris Gare du Nord International at one forty-seven local time, two hours later than planned and already forty-seven minutes late for the important meeting with Professor Osbeck. He hoped that Osbeck was a magnanimous character.

75

He hurried through the giant railway station in the direction of a local commuter train.

With forty-four platforms and handling more than two hundred million passengers a year, Paris Gare du Nord was the busiest railway station in Europe. The station serviced destinations in northern France and several major international cities such as Brussels, Amsterdam, Cologne, Essen and London. The large complex was well connected to the Paris Metro transit system and the Réseau Express Régional (RER) railway system and several bus routes. Kenneth tried to increase the pace of his footsteps. It didn't work. It was like trying to walk with a brisk pace in a nightmare. The harder you tried, the slower you advanced.

He passed cafés and restaurants and sandwich bars, experienced the mingling smells of coffee and beer and croissants and raisin bread. He saw old men with ice-chilled pastis in their glasses. Young ladies sipped café noisette or white wine. Children slurped lemonade or gobbled ice cream. Stressed businessmen and equally stressed businesswomen had croque-monsieur for a snack on the go. And he saw tourists, countless tourists, from every corner of the world. On certain occasions, the act of travel was as beautiful as the destinations themselves. Paris Gare du Nord, one of the most iconic stations in the world, made that happen, providing you weren't occupied by thoughts about frenzied killers.

He bought a T+ ticket and rushed towards the platform that serviced the southbound RER line B, the route that would take him almost to the heart of the Montparnasse district. The RER train arrived at the platform. Kenneth squeezed aboard in a sea of people. No sooner had the doors closed than the train resumed its southbound journey through an underground tunnel darkness. At the RER-Metro station Denfert-Rochereau on the Left Bank, he would switch to Metro line 4. Then, from Vavín, two Metro stops from Denfert-Rochereau on the westbound line, he would walk to the restaurant.

Only his planned route didn't happen. The RER train was taken out of service even before crossing the River Seine, at Châtelet-Les Halles.

What bad luck.

Bad luck is something you cannot control.

Chance determines bad luck, mister.

Passengers pushed their way out of the cars and spilled onto the platform. Kenneth's small suitcase slipped out of his hand. A legion of feet kicked the suitcase here and there. It disappeared behind a forest of legs. People pushed into him like runaway cattle. A series of shoulder tackles caused him to spin full circle. He crouched on the concrete floor, looking for the suitcase. Worried, yes. The suitcase must not be lost. His baggage contained his private notes and data files concerning the prime-number murders, all the important material he had brought for the meeting with Professor Osbeck. The suitcase also contained a change of underwear and a toiletry bag but those items were trivial, of course, and easy to replace. The documents, however, were priceless. Certainly there were digital backups, but at home. He must find the suitcase.

It would have been convenient to access all of these files via his smartphone and a cloud account instead of carrying a suitcase with hard copies but he had avoided cloud computing this time. He didn't want to store any prime-number killer data on the cloud. Not without Mr. Frank's permission. Besides, he wasn't sure he wanted to store his files on a cloud account which SCDX had access to. And he couldn't use his own cloud account. For all he knew, there existed cybersecurity firms with links to SCDX. He couldn't trust the security level of any of his own Internet-based activities any longer.

Something soft and sticky landed on his head. At the same time, he heard the voice of a giggling child. Kenneth dared not raise his gaze. He ran five fingers through his hair, scooping up what looked like a caramel pudding, or what was left of it. The rich custard dribbled down his earlobe and cheek.

"*Monsieur ! Monsieur ! Monsieur !*"

With his ear that wasn't clogged with caramel and custard, he could hear a woman somewhere in the crowd, a woman who was trying to get a man's attention. He ignored her shouts and continued to look for his baggage, crouching on the platform floor.

"*Monsieur !*"

He felt a tap on his shoulder, and looked up.

"*Votre valise, monsieur !*" A lady, mid-sixties, in a wine-red dress and a black hat, smiled at him. The heavy eyeliner, the garish lipstick and her lacquered complexion competed for primary attention. If she tried to smile even wider, Kenneth caught himself speculating, her make-up would crack.

The lady held out a suitcase. "Yours, mister."

He rose from his crouched position. "*Merci beaucoup, madame.*" He let out a sigh of relief. "Thank you very much, madam. You have saved my day." He wondered if there was anything left of the day to save.

"No problem, mister!" The woman handed over the baggage. She also gave him a paper towel so he could wipe the caramel and custard from his hair and ear and cheek. He started to feel a bit better, or imagined he did. The lady hurried towards one of the escalators and disappeared in the crowd.

He asked around, in French, regarding what was going on, and got a plethora of explanations: some technical hassle; an accident; a case of illness aboard the RER train; a strike; Line B was no longer in operation today, or not until 18:00 or 19:00, or whatever.

The cluster of travellers in front of the nearest RATP information desk looked and sounded like a mob. Loudspeakers sprang to life and spilled out a message he couldn't perceive. The chaos grew. And the temperature rose, not a little but a lot. Châtelet-Les Halles, the largest underground station in the world, began to feel like the largest sun-flooded greenhouse on the planet. A teenage girl staggered like a zombie towards a tiled wall, leaned forward and vomited into a litter bin. A dark, middle-aged man in exotic clothes swore in an incomprehensible language. A bearded man who looked a hundred years old mumbled something about a bomb threat.

A bomb threat? Was that what the loudspeakers had trumpeted? Was there any truth to this or had it just been the bearded man's own wild guess?

Kenneth didn't know and didn't care. He didn't care about another forthcoming rapid transit train either. All he knew was he had to get out of this subterranean gateway before he suffocated.

He clenched his fists and gritted his teeth

and moved towards an escalator among the increasing aggregation of people.

▪

He found himself in the deafening traffic on Rue de Rivoli. The sky was a steel-blue shell, the sun a dazzling silver disc. Taxis whizzed by him with their orange roof lights on. An orange light meant that a cab was occupied.

When he crossed Boulevard de Sébastopol, his gaze landed on Hôtel de Ville, the magnificent city hall. Kenneth remembered it best for its role in the French Revolution. King Louis XVI of France had been received here by the Parisian Municipality in 1789. Three years later, revolutionary politicians Marat, Robespierre and Danton established Hôtel de Ville as their government headquarters.

He saw a taxi with its white roof sign '*Taxi Parisien*' lit. He waved. The driver veered towards the kerb and stopped dead, the taxi's tyres squeaking.

Kenneth sank into the back seat. It began to look like he was going to make it. "La Coupole, please."

▪

It took an effort to glance at his wristwatch. Already half past two. He was one hour and thirty minutes late—so far. In his mind's eye,

Kenneth saw Mrs. Davenport, the monster teacher from his childhood, bashing one of her laws into his head, her law about the importance of being on time.

Somehow, the taxi driver managed to perform a U-turn through the dense Rue de Rivoli traffic. The large Saint Bernard dog in the front passenger seat barked and growled and snarled at everything that moved outside the windows.

"Nice dog," Kenneth said, and hoped. The dog in front wore a seat belt. For whose safety? The dog's own or the passengers'?

"Thank you, mister," the driver said. He was bald, thin and spoke with a foreign accent. His olive-black eyes were caught in a web of wrinkles. Between his fleshy lips dangled a lit cigarette. He appeared southern European or Middle-East Asian. Kenneth's gaze returned to the furry creature.

"This is Lucifer," the driver said, patting the dog's back. "He keeps an eye on my lunch box."

"How kind of him," Kenneth said, not knowing what else to say. He loved dogs but he wasn't in the mood for small talk.

The power window on the driver's side was wide open. The draft of wind subdued Kenneth's voice.

The driver chuckled. "In Paris on a business trip, mister?"

"Yeah… a business trip."

"A long stay?"

Kenneth shook his head. "Not too long."

"In Paris, no stay is too long." He examined his passenger in the rear-view mirror. "American?"

"British."

"London?"

"Blackfield."

"Aha. The City of Crows."

"And the city of dark secrets."

"What did you say, mister?"

"Nothing."

"Yorkshire!" The driver chuckled, drumming his fingers on the steering wheel. "I have a brother in Huddersfield."

"Congratulations."

"A pleasure to meet you, mister." The driver flicked cigarette ash towards the draft by the open window. "Lucifer, say hello to the gentleman."

Lucifer turned his large head, glowered at the passenger in the back seat and bared his teeth. A growl trickled out between his jaws.

The driver laughed. Not Kenneth. Lucifer was the largest dog he had ever seen.

The driver zigzagged between cars and buses. Unafraid of the steady stream of oncoming vehicles, he attacked the next intersection, swung around in a quarter circle, without slowing down and pressed the accelerator to the floor, steering into Boulevard St. Michel. The taxi was rushing forward and up the hill like a crazy dinosaur.

The driver chuckled. "You're in a hurry, aren't you, mister?"

"I guess I am," Kenneth admitted.

"Don't look afraid, mister. Lucifer doesn't like passengers who look afraid."

"Got it."

"If you're scared, mister, Lucifer won't like you, and if he doesn't like you, he might bite you."

"You're an excellent driver."

"Excellent?!" The driver chuckled. "Remember that when you sign for the tip."

Lucifer barked. And smirked.

This isn't happening, Kenneth thought. Dogs don't smirk. *Except this one does.*

The driver continued to speed along Boulevard St. Michel southwards. Kenneth looked out the side window and caught glimpses of the territory in the heart of the Latin Quarter, his home district during his three years in the French capital. To the left, at the far end of Rue Soufflot, he glimpsed the Panthéon, the massive neoclassical structure, one of the most impressive architectural works of its time. Several celebrities had their final resting place in its crypt: politicians, statesmen, scientists and writers, such as Voltaire, Rousseau, Victor Hugo, Émile Zola, Pierre and Marie Curie. To the right, the Luxembourg Palace appeared, and the Luxembourg Gardens, the quintessential Paris park.

Paris seemed familiar and at the same

time it didn't. A mystery was hanging in the air, affecting the cityscape, as if the case of the prime-number murderer had followed him here, all the way from northern England. But that was precisely what had happened, wasn't it? Or else he wouldn't be here. The mystery brought a strange dimension to the City of Light, as if Christine's spirit and Fenwick's madness continued to distort Kenneth's existence.

He thought about the people and a cat back home. Jeanne. Linda. Uncle Ash. Mr. Frank. Mum. No one knew where he was. No one except Linda.

Much was at stake. He felt as if his whole future depended on the outcome of this afternoon.

76

During the decades that had passed since its opening in 1927, La Coupole, the largest restaurant in Paris, had turned into a global concept, with a continuously growing list of visiting celebrities from the worlds of politics, art, literature, sport, cinema, theatre and fashion. Kenneth was shown to the busy bar area. He looked around, absorbing the colourful atmosphere. The white-and-black-uniformed waiters were hurrying back and forth through the bar, balancing fully loaded drinks trays on their fingers. The wide mix of voices in a confined space recalled the buzz of a crowded bus terminal.

A customer who sat at the bar's counter slid off his seat and turned around. The corpulent man, overshadowed by the tall bar stool, had a large cup of coffee in his fist. Cheeks like a bulldog and dotted with liver spots. Yellow hair like spun gold. An invisible neck. The man wore his head directly on his shoulders.

Their eyes met. Kenneth nodded.

A grin spread across the old man's face, from one corner of his mouth to the other. He put down his coffee cup and moved across the floor.

"My fourth cup of coffee was getting cold."

Kenneth shook the man's hand, a small white fist that felt like a deep-frozen haddock fillet. "I'm terribly sorry for the delay, Professor Osbeck. And grateful for your patience."

"Perhaps I'm patient, Mr. Sorin," the professor said, "but I expect you to make up for the hassle."

"A reasonable request, Professor."

The old man's eyes gleamed like platinum coins in an abyss of knowledge.

Kenneth added, "And it'll be good. My story will make up for the hassle."

"Your story—will it be good enough to make me postpone my fishing trip to the countryside?"

"I promise."

"Well, we'll see."

"You knew I would be late, didn't you? It's

one of the reasons you're still here, waiting for me."

"Earlier today, I was out on my daily walk in the Luxembourg Gardens, to exercise my heart, and at one point I called, from a pay phone—yes, you can still find those—the personnel department at my old research institute, about my pension money. I was informed of your delay, indeed. And now, Mr. Sorin, follow me." Osbeck rotated a half-turn and started to walk away.

"Where are we going, Professor?"

"To the restaurant."

▪

Klemens Osbeck was possibly a local celebrity, a character whose very presence contributed to the venue's immortal cultural heritage. The restaurant's more than 6,450 square feet had a capacity of four hundred and fifty people. The downstairs private dance hall's more than 2,400 square feet had a capacity of one hundred and eighty guests for a seated meal or three hundred and fifty guests for a cocktail party. The multifaceted street-level brasserie was almost full. Given La Coupole's popularity, queues for table space were not uncommon.

The professor doubled his order: two starters and two main courses. From the starters menu, he chose avocado with crab millefeuille, and prawns with mango chutney. For his main courses, he ordered fish meunière and sweetbreads with truffle juice, and macaroni gratin. Kenneth had smoked salmon with blini and spicy whipped cream for his starter, and the restaurant's world-famous lamb curry for his main course.

"So, Mr. Sorin, what's your story?"

"It's a long story, Professor. Long and intense. I'll compress it as best I can."

"I'm a good listener."

"'Logic will get you from A to B. Imagination will take you everywhere.'"

"Einstein." Osbeck sipped a deep-red Bordeaux. "Tell me your story, young man. I'm all ears. By the way, it wasn't only Einstein who realised the limitations of logic. The history of the world is full of scientists who defied logic and predominant conventions on their way to great discoveries."

Kenneth told his story from beginning to end, a summary which took about two hours. He talked about each of the murders. The receipt in Annabelle Stanfield's jacket pocket. How the investigation had involved retail manager Philip Worthington. How the focus later shifted to research psychologist Leighton Fenwick. He talked about his nightmares. The intruder who had searched his house and filled up Linda's food and water bowls. The spirit of the dead woman Christine Corbett. He talked about his duality theory and his prime-number theory.

The overwhelming evidence against

Fenwick: the man's false alibi; the early check-out from the hotel in Bristol; the lie by omission; project Qz81H; the data files; the scientist's second doctorate, in mathematics; his obsession with prime numbers; the chest of drawers filled with chocolate boxes and ladies' underwear; the wig collection; hairs found in several wigs and then identified; the nineteen wigs numbered using primes only, from 2 to 61; the list of at least eighty-three future victims kept inside a radiator; the copy of Kenneth's novel *Blue Moon Psycho* found in one of Fenwick's bookcases; how the murder of Sadie Bentley in Endsleigh Park had been almost identical to the murder in Kenneth's book; Elizabeth Peckerton's last text message; the microscopic dots of Miss Peckerton's blood found on one of Fenwick's coats; and the intense discussion in the city centre witnessed by Benjamin Smith.

"—and that brings me to the end of my story, Professor. My story in broad outline. Thank you for your attention."

Osbeck remained quiet for almost half a minute before he spoke. "But now you're sitting here."

Daylight outside the windows began to disappear. The boulevard with the growing shadows and the constant flow of honking vehicles would soon belong to dusk. The pavements were overcrowded by a world in miniature. Two police cars with their flashing rooftop lights and ear-splitting sirens got stuck in the traffic jam. Parisian rush-hour—a time of heart-stopping moments and agitated emotions.

"Yes, Professor. Now I'm sitting here."

"Why?"

"What does Christine Corbett mean to you?"

"The dead woman in your story? Why?"

"I simply got the impression that her name was familiar to you."

The professor scratched his thin golden hair. "I dream about her. The phantom lady, as you call her, visits the corridors of my dreams."

"Did you ever meet Christine Corbett?"

"I *knew* her. Knew her very well."

"Please continue."

"Christine was an Egyptologist. We met through our profession, many years ago. I have colleagues from around the world." To emphasise this, Osbeck drew a broad ellipsoid in the air with a fork. "A few years before Christine died, we decided we would write a non-fiction book together. It was her idea, an idea which I instantly loved. But the book was never completed. It would have been the product of a collaboration. When Christine passed away before the first draft was done, I decided to abandon the project. I didn't want to continue it on my own."

"I understand, Professor. Please tell me more about the dream."

"It's the same recurring dream. A very old and decaying Christine says she's dead and that there's a young man who's doing a private investigation of a murder mystery, a young man who sooner or later will want to meet with me." The professor lifted a fork loaded with macaroni gratin to his mouth. "The young man must be you, Mr. Sorin. Why do you think her words are cryptic? Why doesn't she say your name in my dreams and why doesn't she say what it's all about?"

"Because her powers were limited to begin with and then continued to decline until her definitive disappearance… or final death… as if no one and nothing lasted forever, not even on The Other Side. Christine spoke to me like she did to you. Her tone was as cryptic as that of a prophetess. I was left on my own trying to detect the meaning of her words."

"And did you succeed in detecting the meaning of what she said?"

"The answer to that question is related to the fact that I'm here. I'll return to that in a moment. How did you meet Fenwick?"

"We met by chance at a congress in Tunis many years ago. At that time, Leighton was still young and relatively unknown. He had just completed his doctorate in clinical psychology. His wild interest in mathematics drove him to yet another Ph.D."

"Within the framework of prime numbers."

"Right. And there was something special about his attitude that fascinated me, for two reasons."

"How do you mean?"

"Firstly, his interest in prime numbers stretched to levels deeper than mathematics itself. He wanted 'in under the surface' of these numbers, as he liked to say, always searching subtexts and fresh potential applications. Since prime numbers are the atoms of mathematics and thereby nature's most important numbers, there must be a natural link between prime-number mathematics and the biochemistry of our central nervous systems, he reasoned, as the functions of the mind are basically directed by electrochemical reactions."

"And secondly?"

"The second reason was connected to my own profession. Egyptology has a relation to numerology which has a relation to mathematics. Of course, today, numerology isn't considered real mathematics but is seen as pseudoscience. I only mean that both maths and numerology deal with numbers."

"Why is it so difficult to find any literature on Fenwick's mathematical work?"

"I don't know."

"Fenwick was probably aware that his profound interest in prime numbers could be linked to his controversial experiments. Somehow, someone has made his mathematical work unavailable both to the authorities and to the public."

"Possible," the professor said. "Either Leighton himself or an accessory who knew how to make all sorts of records disappear."

"I can imagine a third possibility, Professor. Even if Fenwick completed a second doctorate, in mathematics this time, he may have refrained from publishing material associated with primes."

"Leighton's mathematics project was indeed surrounded by rigorous secrecy."

"How do you know, Professor? How could you know anything about that?"

Osbeck shrugged. "Academic rumours."

"A dear colleague of mine did find an obscure notation on the Internet," Kenneth said, thinking that the professor didn't need to know that Jeanne wasn't exactly a colleague.

Osbeck nodded. "Françoise in Le Mans was also a good friend of mine."

"She mentioned you in that passage. That was how I learnt that you knew Fenwick."

"If Leighton had been aware of that seemingly insignificant notation in cyberspace, he would have made an effort to make it vanish." The professor paused in the middle of a bite of sweetbreads with truffle juice. "Leighton… Nine women killed, with an additional eighty-three lined up. Perhaps it was just the beginning."

"I have wondered why he did it, Professor."

"Why Leighton murdered the girls with whom he socialised?"

"Why he failed to eliminate the evidence that made it look like he murdered the girls with whom he socialised."

"I don't understand. What do you mean?"

"I mean that Leighton Fenwick didn't murder his mistresses, the women who also represented his research subjects for his project Qz81H."

"He didn't kill them?"

"No, he didn't. Fenwick is not, and never was, the prime-number killer."

77

"Where did I put the necklace?" Jeanne trotted back and forth between the flat's different rooms, slamming drawers and wardrobe doors. "Where's the necklace? Where?"

With sixty-nine necklaces in her collection, she suffered no shortage of necklaces. Sixty-eight were in their right places. But she was now searching for the sixty-ninth and therefore wanted to find the sixty-ninth. A matter of principle. Today she wanted to wear the necklace with ivory-white and burgundy-red pearls, no other necklace.

She stopped mid-pace in the hall and clenched her fists, thinking. When was the last time I used the necklace? *Ivory-white. Burgundy-red. Pearls.*

"Yes, yes." She remembered now, smiling. The last time they had had sex in his bedroom, she had worn the necklace with ivory-white and burgundy-red pearls. Kenneth had said he liked the necklace. He had wanted her to wear it while they were making love. So she had worn the necklace only, nothing else. They'd played around in bed. She'd gone along with his wishes. And he'd gone along with what she wanted. That night of adventures transported them. Afterwards, she'd unhooked the necklace and fallen asleep in his arms with a smile on her lips.

She hadn't used the necklace since that night. She must have forgotten it at Kenneth's place. It didn't surprise her that he hadn't mentioned a lost necklace. Boys didn't tidy their bedrooms daily, nor properly either for that matter, if they tidied up at all. Kenneth was thinking of fictitious stories all day long. Housekeeping was one of the last things on the boy's mind. The necklace could have slipped down between the mattress and the bedframe, or between the bed and the wall. She wanted to call his mobile and mention the necklace. At the same time, she was annoyed that he had shied away from their planned dinner at the last minute and then disappeared without saying where he was going. You didn't treat a girlfriend with such nonchalance.

She no longer wanted to make the phone call. Instead, she would drive to his place to look for the necklace herself. If he loved her, if he saw her as a genuine girlfriend, he wouldn't mind her visiting his house on her own.

There was a difference between an SCDX agent on a mission and a girlfriend who only wanted to retrieve her necklace. She would regard her second unbidden visit as a love test. His reaction when she mentioned what she had done would reveal how much he loved her.

He hadn't given her a house key but she had her electric lock-pick gun and he knew she had this gadget. Nothing strange at all. A boyfriend and a girlfriend should have no secrets from each other. The SCDX lock-pick device was no longer a secret.

She stepped into her car and drove off towards his house. They lived in different neighbourhoods on opposite sides of the River Claxton. The driving time from her home to his was twenty-five minutes in heavy traffic.

Just as she turned into the avenue she saw a man and a woman leaving Kenneth's residence. An elderly couple with southern European appearance. The couple disappeared into a house straight across the avenue. Neighbours, Jeanne guessed. Retired neighbours who looked after Linda while the owner was away.

How long would he be gone?

Where had he travelled to?

What was his purpose?

Since she was the girlfriend today, not the spy, she parked her car in front of the house and in plain sight. Curtains moved in a kitchen window on the opposite side of the avenue. Nosy neighbours! She walked up to his front door without sneaking. The curious neighbours could stare at her as much as they wanted. She took out the lock-pick gun, entered the house, circumvented the burglar alarm and shut the front door behind her. Maximum five seconds.

"Hi, Linda. How's it going?" She lifted the cat, embraced her, kissed her on the nose and put her down again. Linda miaowed, rubbed her body against Jeanne's leg, miaowed again then went into the kitchen.

Jeanne continued upstairs to the bedroom and flicked on the light. The bedroom was similar to the workroom. The difference was that there was a bed among the bookshelves and stacks of printouts and cardboard boxes. The cosy double bed was made. Her fingers groped along the edge of the mattress. No necklace. She lifted the mattress. No necklace. She peered under the bed and saw several plastic boxes filled with books. She crawled up onto the bed and peered down through a narrow gap between the bedframe and the wall. Only a fraction of the light from the ceiling lamp reached the part of the floor which was under the bed and next to the wall. She could make out the object anyway. Thin as a worm with circular formations. Right there, on the floor next to the wall. She pushed the book boxes out of the way and crept in under the bed. Yes, there it was. The necklace with ivory-white and burgundy-red pearls. She grabbed it and started to back out of the gloom.

She stopped, right under the centre of the bed. There was something else there. The corner of her eye had caught it. In the corner of the floor, under the head end of the bed. A rectangular object. She reached out a hand, swept the object towards her, snatched it up and backed out of the dimness.

She stood in the middle of the room, shook the dust off the necklace then put it on.

The rectangular object was lemon-yellow with cat pictures on the covers. No text on the cover or spine. A diary. Jeanne opened it. Her heart was slamming. A handwritten marking on the front free endpaper said: Rebecka Månsson's diary.

78

They ordered dessert. As he had guessed, the professor doubled his own order. The old man had both crêpes Suzette and the lemon pie of the house. Kenneth, who now felt that he didn't need to eat anymore until next week, was more than satisfied with a small chocolate parfait.

"Who mentioned something about dual nature a while ago?" Kenneth said, smiling.

"Uh?" Osbeck sipped a calvados.

"Double nature. Duality. Dichotomy. We agreed that I have some sort of double nature in me but it wasn't I who ordered double starters, double main courses and double desserts."

Osbeck chuckled. "Okay, I understand. My big appetite for food, I've always had it. Especially in a brilliant brasserie like this." The old man paused, his expression turning serious. "But now I want you to explain what you meant when you said that Leighton didn't kill those girls."

"The puzzle mystery as a whole is greater than the sum of its parts. Please bear with me."

"The long list of devastating evidence?"

"I said that Fenwick isn't the prime-number killer. I didn't say he didn't kill the ninth victim. Thus, we have two killers. Not two companions, but two individualists with different agendas: Leighton Fenwick—and the prime-number killer. Fenwick murdered Elizabeth Peckerton but not the others."

"Can you prove what you're saying?"

"I'm confident I'm right about the outcome. We must remember that the ninth murder is the only murder which Fenwick is connected to beyond a reasonable doubt. The conviction that Fenwick also committed the other eight murders is based on the evidence found at the man's residence, a plethora of evidence demonstrating his controversial activities with female research subjects. Circumstances were interpreted in such a way that they fitted expectations. An excellent chain of evidence in combination with a total lack of alibi was interpreted as proof that Fenwick was the serial killer. His attempt to escape didn't weaken this opinion, of course."

Osbeck couldn't hide the impatience in his voice when he said, "If Leighton didn't kill the first eight ladies then *who* did?"

The phone rang in Kenneth's jacket pocket. He checked the phone's display, identifying the caller. "Please excuse me, Professor. I must take this call."

"No problem, young man. Phone calls can be important, sometimes a matter of life and death."

Kenneth rose from the dinner table and moved towards the bar. He took the call.

79

Jeanne's eyes scanned his bedroom. Nothing had changed. Books everywhere. All the windows with drawn blinds. Next to one window was a chest of drawers. On top of the chest of drawers lay a lonely sheet of paper. Too alone? She thought the sheet of paper seemed out of place, as if he had written and printed something in a hurry. She took a closer look at the sheet. It turned out to be a list of book titles, printed on a laser printer. There was no info on who the authors were.

Books to check:

Zodiac Parameters in the Brain

The Human Body from the Perspective of Astrology

The Trip through Juxtapositions of Stars

Spiritual Astrology and Cosmic Science

■

She called him on his mobile phone.

"Hi, Jeanne."

"I found the diary, Kenneth."

"Diary? What diary?"

"Rebecka Månsson's diary. Please don't pretend you don't know what diary I'm talking about."

"Aha. I've missed it. Where did you find it?"

"Listen to what you're saying, Kenneth!"

"You sound upset."

"I am upset! It doesn't matter where I found the diary! The question is how come you have Rebecka Månsson's diary? Do you understand?!"

"Calm down, Jeanne. I can explain."

"Explain?! How?! You mean explain *away*, as if there never were a problem to begin with."

"Firstly, it isn't Miss Månsson's diary. The one you found belongs to me. The lemon-yellow diary with colourful cat pictures is printed in a limited edition, a few hundred copies every year. When I identified myself with Ronis Nethken—that is, got into his mindset without actually believing I *was* him—I bought a copy of this particular diary in a stationery shop in rural Sweden."

"That's your explanation? I thought that writers were better liars than that."

"It's the truth."

"Guys like you make up crap for a living."

"You still think I'm Mr. Maniac?"

"The diary contains handwritten text in both pencil and ink. The style is Rebecka's.

The signature on the front free endpaper is Rebecka's."

"The style is very similar to Rebecka's but it isn't her writing. A forensic document examiner would prove that I'm right. Ronis Nethken imitated Miss Månsson's handwriting when he made notes in his own copy of the diary. The contents of Dr. Nethken's diary are only to some degree consistent with the contents of the girl's diary."

"There is no Ronis Nethken. You are Kenneth Sorin. And how could a fictional character know the contents of Miss Månsson's diary?"

"As I told you earlier, I met Rebecka by chance in connection with my visit to the Swedish town of Kungsör. The girl stood hitchhiking on the roadside outside the town. I picked her up in the rental car. We started to talk about institutions of higher education and I think I persuaded her to apply to our prestigious Blackfield University. I drove her to her street address in this creepy town. She stepped out of the car and I continued on to my hotel. I discovered the diary on the passenger-side car mat."

"Rebecka dropped it and you stole it?"

"She dropped it. I didn't steal it. I didn't read it. After unsuccessful attempts to return the diary in person, I mailed it from the airport before my return flight."

"If you didn't read Rebecka's original, how

can your copy be filled with text that looks like hers?"

"I read the front free endpaper to identify the owner, a natural act to perform if you find a lost book. And I admit that I had a look at a few pages on the relevant dates in the then current month of June, but I did it only to try to find clues as to how I could get hold of the girl and return her diary. From the signature on the front endpaper, Ronis Nethken discovered the girl's handwriting. Nethken filled his own diary with fiction, written in Rebecka's style. Though not all of his diary entries were fiction. A few exceptions did exist. My memory had registered the girl's plans for the June dates I had glanced at. Ronis Nethken stole from my memory. Dr. Nethken entered the Månsson residence through Rebecka's bedroom window to return the diary. It wasn't me. We've already established that I am me and that Nethken is Nethken. I didn't visit the Månsson house and I didn't break into the girl's bedroom. In my new horror suspense thriller, *Mr. Maniac*, there's a chapter where Dr. Nethken sneaks into a sleeping Rebecka's bedroom in the dead of night."

Jeanne was silent.

"Rebecka's fingerprints can't be found on, or in, the diary you found," Kenneth said. "The diary is really mine."

Silence.

"Jeanne?"

"Yes?"

"Not long ago you said I was innocent. You said that top secret camera equipment had confirmed my alibis at the times of several murders. Doesn't that apply any longer?"

She sighed. "It applies now. But it didn't when I first mentioned it. Back then, I tested your reaction. Mr. Frank's order. But then I got worried about you. The discovery of the diary in your bedroom scared the living hell out of me."

"Wasn't *I* supposed to be the good liar? I'm the guy who makes up crap for a living."

"Sorry."

"You have been in my house uninvited again."

"I needed to find a necklace, Kenneth. The one with ivory-white and burgundy-red pearls."

"It's lovely. Did you find it?"

"Yes."

"Good."

"Are you angry with me?"

"Why?"

"Because I visited your home uninvited again."

"You're my girlfriend. You wanted to find your necklace. Anyway, we spend as much time at my place as at yours. It's about time I gave you your own copy of my house key. Linda will certainly agree. A boyfriend and a girlfriend should be able to share as much as possible, shouldn't they?"

"I love you, Kenneth."

"I love you too, Jeanne. I will marry you."

"What did you say? Could you say that again?"

"I will marry you, Jeanne Russell."

"Hurry home. Wherever you are, please hurry home. I miss you."

"I'll hurry. I promise."

80

"Professor Osbeck, I know who the prime-number killer is. And now I need your help to make clear the circumstances that resulted in those horrific deaths."

"I'll do my best, young man."

"Let's consider the tone of Christine's words. Assuming that the key to the mystery was in my own person, I tried to get to know myself better. I studied, for example, my horoscope. I had never before cared much about horoscopes, only glanced at the temporary prophecies expressed by countless newspaper astrologists, week in, week out. Even if I could be fascinated, attracted, by the sophistication of advanced horoscopes, including the influences of astronomical objects and their positions in the sky, I would always question their credibility. There we see again, Professor, a flash of my double nature."

Osbeck emptied his calvados glass. A gold tooth gleamed in his upper jaw. "Or duality. You will find that astrology is also dual in some respects. Think about it for a moment. Is astrology a science? The simple answer is yes—and no. Like, for instance, medicine, astrology is an art form based on science. The word 'medicine' derives from the Latin phrase *ars medicina*, which means 'the art of healing'. Astrology requires many aspects of science, mainly from astronomy and psychology, just like medicine is dependent on other sciences, a myriad of sub-disciplines of biology, chemistry and physics."

Kenneth nodded. "I told myself I could live with my introspective analysis as long as it didn't dawn on me that I was the serial killer myself. It wasn't long before a shadow of schizophrenia jumped into my head. My horoscope—not the short-term and temporary one that changes from week to week, but the fundamental and permanent—says that I'm driven by fantasy. It's true, of course. I live for the fantastic and the unreal. I'm a fiction writer, after all.

"My horoscope also says I idealise my partner and allow imagined emotions to blur my opinions in terms of erotic attraction. Imagined emotions? This made me wonder: Could a novelist's imagination backfire? Could the imagination be absorbed by the body, mixing with or corrupting the author's authentic feelings? I wondered if I only imagined that I loved Alison, my ex-girlfriend, as much as I then believed. Later, when Jeanne—my present girlfriend and my future wife—stepped into my life, I asked myself the same analogical questions. My inability to find good answers to the issues surrounding these two girls suggests that something blurs my opinions in terms of erotic attraction.

"In addition, I'm supposed to be superstitious. Before this strange serial-killer case, I had never seen myself as superstitious. On the contrary, I had always seen my habits as natural and spontaneous. I didn't analyse them, didn't even think about them. And now I think the most superstitious person I've ever known is myself, to the extent that one can know oneself. The number thirteen has followed me, not least during all this time that I've occupied myself with the prime-number murder case. Before this case, I didn't try to understand why the number thirteen gave me discomfort because, to me, those feelings were natural. Black hellebore, or Christmas rose, the pink and white flowers that my nightmares transported to my bedroom and bathroom on two separate occasions, derive from superstition. The plants are said to expel evil spirits, witches, goblins, phantoms and monsters."

"If you haven't previously regarded yourself as a superstitious person, how could you then dream up those plants?"

"Good question, Professor. I think the answer is that I must have been told about black hellebore many years ago when I was a schoolboy. There was this girl, we were close, went to the same school, same class. The funny thing, was that she learned the facts about flowers and I let her read my short stories. Alison was my very first reader. She must have mentioned black hellebore in passing at some point when we were little. It remained as latent information to which my subconscious had access. I called her a few weeks ago and asked about the plants in my dreams. She gave me the answers I needed."

Kenneth ate the remainder of his melting chocolate parfait. "When I work on a novel, I write the first draft on an electric typewriter, not on a PC. I see no rational argument for that type of action. I work that way because of an event in the past that is associated with my electric typewriter. Call it superstition, if you like.

"Furthermore, my intuitive nature may be useful in solving other people's problems. True again. I use my intuition and my analytical skills to help solve my uncle's and Mr. Frank's problems.

"The final point is about a change in character, back and forth between a lighter and a darker personality, a sort of reversible equilibrium between creativity and depression; progress and frustration; optimism and pessimism; hope and doubt. Too true. It's me again. My double nature."

"Fascinating."

"And yet it's only the beginning."

▪

With a deadpan facial expression, the professor bit into the lemon pie. "Though you have talked about your horoscope, you haven't mentioned your zodiac sign. But I can guess. May I?"

"Be my guest, Professor."

"Pisces."

"Correct. Let's now focus on the murders. A: My zodiac sign is Pisces. The Pisces' lucky day is Thursday. Each of the first eight killings took place on a Thursday. B: The alternating two- or three-week interval between the first eight murders—exactly two different intervals—becomes in this case a metaphor and one of several details which reflect the double nature of Pisces. Double nature is one of the strongest traits of Pisces. C: A superstitious murderer would avoid killing someone on a Friday the thirteenth. The ninth victim met her death on Friday, February the thirteenth. D: Only a cool and calculating killer would sneak into a house which belonged to one of the investigators—my house, in this case. What a risk to take, unless the perpetrator was very confident at carrying out that systematic job and at the same time had the situation under control. Pisces are believed to be endowed with broad visionary forces and they are considered capable of designing large-scale schemes. E: Miss Peckerton never risked being incorporated in Fenwick's perverse universe, of course. P is the sixteenth letter of the alphabet. 16 is a composite number. Fenwick didn't expose Miss Peckerton to his sexual fantasies but he killed the girl, for reasons I'll discuss shortly."

"Stunning," Osbeck said.

"It struck me that Christine's words meant that I share a personality profile with the serial killer. The key to the mystery puzzle was to find someone who, like me, is fantasy-driven. To find someone who, like me, idealises their partner and allows imaginative feelings to blur their vision in terms of erotic attraction. To find someone who, like me, is superstitious in the extreme. To find someone whose nature, just like my own nature, is intuitive and a help in solving other people's problems. To find someone who, like me, has a duality trait, including the dynamic switch in character, back and forth between lighter and darker emotions.

"The person I had to find had unauthorised access to Fenwick's computers to track all sorts of info about the girls. The person I had to find had the motives, the means and the opportunities to commit these eight murders. Who, Professor?"

"I don't know. Say it, young man."

"Rachel Fenwick. Dr. Fenwick's daughter."

81

Professor Osbeck coughed. "Oh my God…"

"Rachel Amelia Fenwick is the only person on earth who meets all the criteria."

"Oh my God…"

"I was born at one thirty a.m. on the sixth

of March," Kenneth said; "that's practically at the very middle of the Pisces phase. Thus the influences of the previous sign, Aquarius, and the subsequent sign, Aries, are minimised or absent altogether. Rachel Fenwick was born at midnight on the sixth of March. The sight of a certain caption in a photo album steered the puzzle pieces into their correct positions. I realised at once that Leighton Fenwick had been charged with eight murders he hadn't committed. Given the media coverage, and considering what was supposed to be a wrapped-up case with an impending trial expected to result in an easy victory for the prosecution, I felt horrified in the light of my new discovery." He paused, his thoughts darting back to Friday, December the fifth the previous year.

"Is there anything at all that you have never suspected?"

"I suspect that there may be something."

Jeanne Russell sighed with force. "Age?"

"Twenty-eight. At least, the last time I checked."

"Birthday?"

"Still March the sixth. I was born at one thirty a.m…"

"There's more to say, Professor. The first time I met Miss Fenwick, she operated a cigarette lighter with her right hand. The second time I met her, she spun a pen with the fingers on her left hand. The conclusion I drew from those two observations is evident. Rachel Fenwick is ambidextrous."

"And so are you."

"How did you know?"

"I'm not bad at reading body language. We have just spent a good dinner together and conversed for hours." The professor paused. "Is there anything at all that proves your arguments?"

From his shirt pocket, Kenneth plucked a digital audio-video mini recorder, a multifunctional pen and USB flash drive with 10 GB of storage capacity, equipped with HD camera and voice recording. It looked like an ordinary whiteboard pen. "Listen to this, Professor."

Kenneth started the playback function.

▪

Karen McNamara's voice: *"Hmm, by all means, Rachel has positive qualities or Liz wouldn't have been with her. It's just that Rachel and I are on different wavelengths, so to speak. She's terribly intuitive and often eager to try to help solve other people's problems, both private concerns and study-related trouble—*

"There're these peculiar little things about Rachel, such as her fear of walking under a ladder or opening an umbrella in the house—

"Sometimes, on the university campus, Liz liked to talk about Rachel. I wasn't interested in

listening, I just pretended to be, to preserve harmony with Liz. According to Liz, Rachel's sexuality was fantasy-driven when supplied with the right mix of fulfilled desires, emotional stimulation and appropriate environment—

"Rachel idealises her lover and allows her fanciful emotions to cloud her judgement when it comes to erotic attraction. You think I'm crazy to talk about this, don't you, Inspector?—

"Anyway, Liz found that Rachel was intuitive and sympathetic while she risked being deceived by the people who fitted her imagination. Well, Liz *fitted her imagination and if the deception which Liz was talking about had to do with me and Liz in bed—*

"Now, one side of Rachel's person is amorous, creative, sensitive, optimistic, sexually satisfied, responsive, imaginative and innovative, while her other side is depressed, guilt-ridden and dispirited. She can flip back and forth between her two sides with alarming ease—"

He turned off the device. "Miss McNamara's words are astounding, Professor. She could have been talking about my own personality traits."

"Extraordinary."

"And no deception. My introspective study and Miss McNamara's characterisation of Miss Fenwick were independent of one another and separated in both time and space."

"Was it legal, what you did?"

"My uncle isn't aware of my multifunctional audio-video mini recorder," Kenneth said, as if it were an adequate response to Osbeck's question.

"Oh," the professor said, "I see."

"I know that by referring to astrology, I have jumped into a domain which many people call superstition or irrationality, but—and the following is extremely important, Professor—public opinion is irrelevant. The essential thing is Miss Fenwick's own opinion. The significant thing is what Miss Fenwick believes. The crucial thing is how Miss Fenwick interprets the fact that she was born at midnight on the sixth of March, the very middle of the Pisces phase. Miss Fenwick's perception of how her life unfolds stems from her powerful belief in the influence of her zodiac sign."

Osbeck nodded.

"Guess Rachel Fenwick's eye colour, Professor."

"Her eyes are sea-green, aren't they?"

"Spot on."

"Pisces' favourite colour. At least one of Pisces' favourite colours. How extraordinary, young man."

"And I haven't finished yet."

"And you thought I thought you had?"

"I think Rachel is more than just the daughter of Leighton Fenwick. I think she's his mistress."

"A disturbing idea, young man. I cannot believe that about Leighton."

"You're entitled to believe whatever you

want, Professor, but I hope you will listen to the rest."

"You have travelled a long way today. It would be a shame if you didn't get to finish what you want to communicate." He waved to a waiter. "Another crêpe Suzette, please."

"Of course, Professor."

"Okay," Kenneth said. "I think Miss Fenwick's sexual relationship with her father is just as serious as the relationship she had with Miss Peckerton. I have visited the Fenwick residence. There's some strange attraction between father and daughter in that house. I could sense it. Peculiar vibrations.

"Then there's the collection of portrait photos which hang on the walls in Fenwick's living room—several dozen portraits of the daughter Rachel and the long since deceased wife and mother Amelia. In their respective photographs, mother and daughter have the same young age, about twenty-one. They are inseparable as identical twins. Rachel's middle name is Amelia. I'm convinced that, to Dr. Fenwick, Rachel *is* Amelia, and in more than one way. Then, the wig collection. Every single wig has a look that is identical to Amelia's and Rachel's inseparable haircuts in the portrait collection."

"Rachel *is* Amelia, and in more than one way," the professor said, like some fragmented echo of Kenneth's words. The old man seemed absorbed in an inner monologue.

The professor's second plate with crêpes Suzette landed in front of him. He thanked the waiter then looked back across the table. "There's something important you haven't said yet, young man."

Kenneth considered Osbeck's words. "What are you referring to?"

"Why did Leighton kill Miss Peckerton? Even if you have two murderers, two individualists with different agendas, something tells me that the ninth murder is linked to the first eight."

A splinter of Kenneth's conversation with Miss Fenwick in the art gallery café ricocheted against the surface of his consciousness:

"When she arrived at the house on the Tuesday, she was happy and talkative and we had the most wonderful evening. However, on the Wednesday morning, she was almost like a different person."

"How?"

"Worried, I would say. Introverted. Maybe a little scared too."

"You're right, Professor. There is a certain link between the ninth killing and the first eight. I shall return to that in a moment. Let me now summarise and tell me what you think about the following.

"Leighton Fenwick is a research psychologist with an enigmatic interest in mathematics and who applies an array of prime-number systems to his computers. Rachel, his daughter and mistress, is known as very superstitious among her friends and acquaintances. As an enthusiastic history student, Rachel has developed a passion for mythology and related subjects, such as astrology and Egyptology. Since she was born under the zodiac sign of Pisces, her favourite day is Thursday. She commits each of her eight murders on a Thursday, since such a plan strengthens her confidence.

"Elizabeth Peckerton's murder is the odd one. Miss P falls outside the mathematical framework. Dr. Fenwick has two reasons to kill Miss Peckerton: the girl's sexual relationship with his daughter, not because the relationship is lesbian, but because Miss Peckerton is his competitor, an obstacle to his relentless ambition to gain exclusive rights to his daughter's heart; and his second reason to kill has to do with the events on February the eleventh. The origin is the text message Miss Peckerton sent to Fenwick's phone. Something had troubled the girl sometime during the previous twenty-four hours. Miss Fenwick herself suggested something of the sort later during our conversation in a cafeteria. But why would Miss Peckerton, all of a sudden, be worried or scared?"

"Something happened at the Fenwick residence on the Tuesday night," Osbeck murmured. "Miss Peckerton detected something in the house or she experienced something that didn't feel right."

"I share your guess. Suspicion grew in Miss Peckerton's mind, suspicion associated with her amorous girlfriend. However, her conscience fought back. She refused to be deceived by sudden mood swings or premature conclusions. After all, the matter concerned her lovely girlfriend and therefore she should have suppressed her ugly ideas. It worried her to be worried. It frightened her to be frightened. She turned to someone she knew and trusted. In the text message to Fenwick, she said she needed to see him. Miss Peckerton had to talk about her anxiety but not in the open. The topic was sensitive. But Fenwick is a master at reading between the lines. He missed no undertones. He realised that it had begun to dawn on Elizabeth that Rachel could be the serial killer. Fenwick murdered Miss Peckerton to protect his daughter. That was his second reason to kill."

"You mean that Leighton knew it was his own daughter Rachel who had murdered his mistresses and research subjects for his project Qz81H?"

"Nothing passed unnoticed to this man, neither truths nor lies."

"The daughter's motive?"

"The subject is complex, double-sided. One side of Rachel loves her father, and she loves him in two different ways, as a daughter and as a mistress. She killed the other eight girls because of jealousy. In other words, she took the lives of her competitors. The father's baroque design of his love life, an erotic state which functioned as his own psychotherapy as well as a substitute for his dead spouse, was part of the motive that drove the daughter to commit these murders. By killing the women against a backdrop of the perverted computer files, the wig collection, the chocolate boxes and the ladies' underwear, the shadow of guilt would be thrown on the father.

"The other side of Rachel despised her father, in part because he used her sexually, in part because he wanted to control her. Knowing that her father manipulated and spent time with several young women with whom he got in contact through his part-time faculty position at a local university, she killed those women in revenge. I'm convinced that Fenwick loves his daughter as intensely as he still loves his long since deceased wife. The man used his professional skills and exceptional experience in experimental psychology and psychiatry to realise a love life with his own daughter. Manipulation and obedience to authority are two significant factors in Leighton Fenwick's arrangement of the incestuous relationship. And although he loves the daughter he cannot forget the wife. Rachel 'is' Amelia."

"According to Leighton's perception," Professor Osbeck said, "all his research subjects for project Qz81H are Amelia."

"I see no other explanation which takes into account the wig collection." Kenneth paused. "Now I need to know how symbolism influenced the lives of the ancient Egyptians. Dr. Fenwick is a world authority in his multidisciplinary field. It looks as if the daughter inherited her father's talent as well as his intelligence. I think the student Rachel explored the mathematical point of view within her own area of interest, which is Egyptology."

"I know why you think so, young man."

"You do?"

The professor pointed to his left eye.

82

"The cut-out eye in the puzzle mystery," Kenneth said, his thoughts darting thousands of years. "There's a mythological link, isn't there?"

The professor lifted a fully-laden dessert fork. His mouth was as wide as a horseshoe. "Sure there is. And I'm more than happy to summarise the basics for you but it is you, and you only, who must decide how you want to categorise the information."

"I don't care about categorisation. The essential thing to me is how Fenwick's colourful daughter interprets symbolism."

Professor Osbeck made an attempt, in this busy, buzzing restaurant, to provide an oral summary of one of the oldest known civilisations, the more than three-thousand-year-old history of ancient Egypt. He did it with an emphasis on symbolism and numerology. He spoke of dynasties and important gods. Mummies, tombs and treasures. The Valley of the Kings. The Book of the Dead. And much, much more. Osbeck spoke for two and a half hours. A marathon lecture. All around them, customers left and new customers arrived. Kenneth and the old man remained seated. Time flew.

"There's a strong symbol of protection and royal power called the Eye of Horus," Osbeck said at some point. "The symbol was used in jewellery to ensure the owner's health and safety and to bring happiness and wisdom. A legend describes a battle between the gods Horus and Seth, a fight in which Set tore out Horus's eye. The god Thoth restored the eye through magic and it got the name Wadjet, meaning healthy or good. According to this myth, it was Horus's left eye that was torn out, which relates to the phases of the moon, when the moon appears to have been torn out of the sky before gradually being restored. Ancient people believed that this symbol of indestructibility, the magic eye, would assist in rebirth."

"Eye torn out and restored," Kenneth mumbled. "Indestructibility. Rebirth." *To Dr. Fenwick, when Rachel was born, Amelia was reborn.*

"The magic eye takes our discussion to mathematics and arithmetic," Osbeck said. "In ancient Egypt's measurement system, the different parts of the Horus Eye represented the number 1 divided by a certain set of powers of two: 1/2, 1/4, 1/8, 1/16, 1/32 and 1/64, respectively. 1/2 was one side of the eye, 1/4 was the pupil, 1/8 was the eyebrow, 1/16 was the opposite side of the eye, 1/32 was a mark below the eye in the form of a curved tail, and 1/64 was a mark in the form of a teardrop."

"Like father, like daughter." Kenneth nodded. "Number series. Primes in one case and ancient Egyptian series of rational numbers in the other."

"If Leighton knew his own daughter was a serial killer and he wanted to protect her by eliminating anyone who had discovered the truth, why would he kill in the style of the daughter? Why did he cut out Miss Peckerton's eye?"

"He didn't want his own murder to stand out among the rest. He needed, wanted, to protect his daughter by deleting the anxious girlfriend from the equation, while avoiding his own killing attracting particular attention. The investigators would then look for a single killer, he estimated, and nowhere near his own family."

"Are you certain that Leighton's ambition was to protect his daughter?"

"Yes, indeed. He made an effort to ensure that Rachel had an alibi for the time of the murder of the girlfriend. The plan was that the ninth murder would look like just another one in the series. The letter P wouldn't fit into the prime-number system but he assumed, quite rightly, that the investigators would take into account the possibility that the serial killer had now begun to alter his habits."

"I'm still shocked about the sexual

relationship between Leighton and his daughter. There's mutual affection in their relationship, you mean?"

"We recall that Rachel is Amelia in Fenwick's world. Amelia died in childbirth. Amelia died when Rachel was born. The daughter has blamed herself ever since she was old enough to understand the circumstances surrounding her mother's death. The father is an expert manipulator. Leighton Fenwick steered his daughter's sexual affection."

They had sat at La Coupole since three o'clock. The time was now almost half past eight. After a brief silence, Kenneth met the old man's gleaming platinum eyes.

"Professor Osbeck?"

"Yes?"

"It's been a privilege talking to you today."

"Ditto."

Kenneth gathered his thoughts. "Please excuse me. I have to make an important phone call."

"I know that, young man."

He discovered that his mobile phone's battery was drained. "I need to find a payphone."

83

"Uncle Ash, it's me. Listen—"

"Ken? Where the devil are you? And what the hell are you doing?"

"I'm in Paris. With Professor Klemens Osbeck."

"Paris?! Why did you disappear like that without telling anyone, huh?"

"Listen. Fenwick's forthcoming trial must be cancelled." The handset crackled. The Paris traffic was booming in the background. "Did you hear me? The upcoming trial must be called off."

"Yeah, sure. And the Lord Mayor must play for Blackfield United next season. The loud-mouthed thug will be a cool central defender."

"Leighton Fenwick is innocent of the prime-number murders."

"Innocent?!"

"Rachel Fenwick is the serial killer."

"*Rachel* Fenwick? Are you out of your mind?!"

"I can explain everything but right now we have no time to lose. Move your team and arrest the daughter." He looked at his watch. Eight thirty-two local time. He had missed the eight thirteen Eurostar departure, the one his return ticket was for. Only one departure remained today. "Uncle Ash, I'm on my way to Gare du Nord to try to catch today's last return Eurostar service to St. Pancras. I won't make it home tonight. I'll spend the night at a hotel in London."

"Have you finished?"

He detected a strange undertone in his uncle's voice. "I've finished, Uncle. For the moment."

"Now, when you've had your say, please be good enough to listen to what *I* have to say."

"You have my full attention."

"Leighton and Rachel Fenwick are dead."

Kenneth was certain he had misheard. "What did you say?"

"I said Leighton and Rachel Fenwick are dead. Dead is the opposite of living."

"Dead? Why…? How…? What have I missed? What happened?"

"Double suicide."

"How in the world could that happen? Isn't… Wasn't Fenwick still held in custody?"

"Fenwick mentioned the murder weapon, Ken. A letter opener. A weapon used in the killing of all the girls. He considered revealing its hiding place. It wasn't possible to describe the hiding place, he claimed, because it was super-secret and impossible to find via a description or map."

"He knew where his daughter had hidden the murder weapon," Kenneth said. "The weapon was hers, not his."

"Listen. He was prepared to personally show us the hiding place. The letter opener was supposed to be in a place that was indescribably difficult to find. In the basement, or even beneath the basement, in his house. Four officers, including the musclemen Hammerman and Jefferson, escorted Fenwick to his own residence. I didn't get there myself. When the detectives and Fenwick arrived, Rachel and her visiting grandmother Elise were there, which they shouldn't have been. Nobody should have been in the house at that time. The grandmother was sleeping upstairs. The daughter put an end to everything. And she did it in her own way. The collection of the murder weapon went down the drain. Hammerman swears that Fenwick and the girl were never alone. Still, they managed to kill themselves."

"How? How on earth could it happen, Uncle?"

"Hammerman said that Fenwick's and the girl's eyes revealed that everything would end right there, right then. And Jefferson said that the unanimous decision that the two members of the family made in silence gave the air a bitter taste. In no time, the daughter had already loosened her earrings and slipped one of them into her father's hand, says Jefferson. The other earring she kept in her own fist. They were emerald earrings with silver spikes. And before anyone could imagine what was about to happen, Fenwick and his daughter cut their carotid arteries. Fenwick died in the ambulance on the way to Crow City Hospital. Rachel died on the operating table."

Kenneth said nothing. He didn't know what to say. He scanned his brain for something to say and found nothing.

"You still there, my boy?"

Silence.

"Ken?"

"I'm going to say goodbye to Professor Osbeck… Then I'm coming home… I miss you all back home… I… I've never been so mentally exhausted… I must… must…"

"Ken? Are you okay?"

"No, I'm not okay… I'm not okay at all."

"Don't be so hard on yourself, Ken."

"I'm going to say goodbye to Professor Osbeck… and then I'm coming home…"

EPILOGUE

The May sun cast its warming light on the two men where they sat at the picnic table in the older man's garden, eating spicy hotdogs with mustard. Spring in Blackfield was a mere passage of time in the calendar, a swing door between winter and summer. After six months of cold rain, it now began to seem as if a warmer season had arrived.

Kenneth's gaze floated through the garden. He allowed himself to be captivated by the variety of expressions—lights, colours, contrasts, smells. He enjoyed it here, in this season of the year. The light reached even the darkest corridors of his soul. The sparrows sang in the greenery. Linda hunted insects across the lawn.

"Another hotdog, Ken?"

"Thank you, Uncle, but I've had three."

"Good things come in threes, uh?"

"As the saying goes."

"I have enough tinned hotdogs for three dinners a week until next Halloween," Uncle Ash said. "You know what, I want to organise a hotdog party in my garden this summer. What do you think?"

"A brilliant idea."

"Not many guests, only a few. And lots of grilled hotdogs with mustard. I'll invite the

Franks and the Morrisons. And Tina Tanner."

Kenneth smiled. "Something special happening between you and Detective Tanner?"

His uncle ignored the question. "Do you think that Jeanne would like to come?"

"Of course. She wouldn't want to miss a party in your garden. Speaking of Jeanne, I have something to tell you."

"Now I'm curious."

"Jeanne and I are getting married."

"Fantastic news, Ken! A super gorgeous, super nice girl like Jeanne. To score with a girl like that… Congratulations!"

Kenneth chuckled. "Her mum and dad put it in a somewhat different way."

"When are you getting married?"

"In August."

"Honeymoon?"

"On the Swedish west coast."

"Aha? Sounds exotic."

They sat in silence for a while. A time that appeared to mark the beginning of a new, brighter future. A breeze caressed the apple trees. A bunch of blackbirds sailed into the garden and landed in the lilacs. Uncle Ash broke the silence.

"I also have something to say, Ken."

"Tell me."

"I've quit smoking. I've quit altogether. Feel free to believe whatever you want about my decision."

"Brilliant news. Good luck with your ambition."

"Thank you very much. But now I want you to say what's bothering you. What's on your mind?"

Kenneth cleared his throat. "Uncle, have you ever thought that evil people are never completely evil? That even the most feared psychopath or killer has a pinch of goodness within?"

"Whenever you get philosophical, Ken, I know you think you have a valid point. Plain English?"

"I mean that even if Leighton Fenwick was a perverted madman and a one-time murderer, we mustn't forget the other side of him, the successful psychologist who helped innumerable patients during his career. He still deserves recognition as a brilliant scientist and research experimentalist. In another world, in another time, he could have been a respected individual, integrated in society."

"I understand what you mean. As a psychologist, he worked for a good cause."

"Then we can look at me."

"What do you mean, Ken?"

"I obey the law, I tend to believe, while Rachel Fenwick was the most spectacular serial killer in this country's modern history. Imagine how similar we still were, Rachel and I. Before I discovered we shared a zodiac sign, I felt that Rachel knew me better than I knew myself. I was right."

Rachel knew me better than I knew myself.

"I found parallels between two personalities," Kenneth continued, "the serial killer's and my own. Then the headaches, the memory losses and the creepy sensation that reality had slipped into my latest novel. I was afraid I was the killer myself."

Uncle Ash took out an envelope from his briefcase. He opened the envelope and pulled out a folded sheet of paper. The fold of the sheet was bulging, as if something was kept, hidden, inside. "May I ask you a question, Ken?"

"I wouldn't be able to stop you, would I?"

"Your first book signing. How long ago?"

"Five years ago."

"Many book buyers who wanted signed copies?"

"A few. Why?"

"Do you remember any of them?"

"You haven't yet said what this is about."

"Do readers and book buyers have to attend the signing events to get signed copies?"

"No. For each of my novels, a limited number of signed copies are sold through online bookshops. But if you want a personalised inscription, you have to attend one of the signing events."

Uncle Ash pushed the folded sheet of yellowish paper across the picnic table. In that very moment, the beauty of the spring day went out. Tar-black clouds passed in front of the sun. The temperature dropped. It looked as if it would rain.

Kenneth picked up the sheet. When he unfolded it, a plant slid out. Its flowers were white. The bracteoles had a reddish shade and a surface layer of silvery hairs on their undersides. The stem had been cut down to about two inches.

"We found it like that," his uncle said, "tucked into the fold."

"Black hellebore," Kenneth said. The idea was impossible to repress. "Christmas rose… to keep away evil spirits, witches and lightning… A cure for madness." His eyes wandered from the Christmas rose to the sheet. An uneven edge hinted that the sheet was actually a page that had been torn out of a book. It turned out to be true. It was a page that had been torn out of a novel. "She lied to me."

"Even if we had found this earlier, Ken—"

"We could have prevented the double suicide," Kenneth snapped. "We could have prevented the double suicide if we had found this earlier."

"We've already checked the jagged edges. This is the very title page that was missing in the copy of your novel that we found in Fenwick's bookcase."

"She lied to me when she said…" He couldn't finish the sentence.

"Yes, my boy. She lied to you when she said she wasn't familiar with your fiction. Only a hardcore fan would break into your house and thereto have special knowledge of your cat's favourite foods. She might have been aware that she should have got rid of the title page but, as a massive fan, she couldn't bring herself to do it. Torn between love and hatred for her father, she put the novel on her father's bookshelf at a time when the darker side of her personality dictated her actions."

Kenneth stared at the title page that lay on the table. It must have fallen out of his hands. Tears pricked his eyes. The inscription, in black ink:

For Rachel

BLUE MOON PSYCHO
Stay scared!

Kenneth Sorin
/– Kenneth Sorin

AFTERWORD

I want to thank Michael Mackenzie and Jago Turner for criticism of an early version of this book.

The details surrounding the Swedish sixteenth-century king Gustav Vasa in chapter 56 are taken from the Kungsör municipality tourist brochure, *Kingdom Kungsör*. Source: Knut Barr, Kungsör. And I want to thank Knut Barr for taking the time to see me.

My meeting with horror film director George A. Romero at the London Frightfest film festival influenced my fictitious character Kenneth Sorin's dedication of a particular copy of a certain novel. 'Stay scared!' is George A. Romero's handwritten phrase in connection with his signings of DVD/BD covers and movie posters, a phrase I borrowed for the closing page of *Mr. Maniac*.

J. F.,

Sheffield, South Yorkshire

APPENDIX

CHESS COORDINATE SYSTEM.

R a8	N b8	B c8	Q d8	K e8	B f8	N g8	R h8
P a7	P b7	P c7	P d7	P e7	P f7	P g7	P h7
a6	b6	c6	d6	e6	f6	g6	h6
a5	b5	c5	d5	e5	f5	g5	h5
a4	b4	c4	d4	e4	f4	g4	h4
a3	b3	c3	d3	e3	f3	g3	h3
P a2	P b2	P c2	P d2	P e2	P f2	P g2	P h2
R a1	N b1	B c1	Q d1	K e1	B f1	N g1	R h1

CHESS TERMINOLOGY.

K: king
Q: queen
B: bishop
N: knight
R: rook
P: pawn
files a–d: queenside
files e–h: kingside
ranks 1–2: start positions, White
ranks 7–8: start positions, Black

ABOUT THE AUTHOR

Johan Fundin grew up in Kungsör, Sweden. He has a Ph.D. in physical chemistry from Uppsala University and a background as a research scientist in the dynamic field of condensed matter physics, the most active subfield of modern physics. He has published a variety of articles in world-renowned scientific journals. Today he lives in Sheffield and is always at work on the next novel.

fantastikthrillerspace.blogspot.com
goodreads.com/jfundinbooks
facebook.com/jfundinbooks
@jfundinbooks